The Life of Hope

The Life of Hope

Paul Quarrington

1985
Doubleday Canada Limited, Toronto, Ontario
Doubleday and Company, Inc., Garden City, New York

ISBN 0-385-25004-5
Library of Congress Catalog Card Number: 85-16001

Interior design by Irene Carefoot
Typesetting by Compeer Typographic Services Limited
Printed and bound in Canada by D.W. Friesen

Canadian Cataloguing in Publication Data

Quarrington, Paul.
 The life of Hope

ISBN 0-385-25004-5

I. Title.

PS8583.U334L54 1985   C813′.54   C85-099250-8
PR9199.3.Q37L54 1985

Library of Congress Cataloging-in-Publication Data

Quarrington, Paul.
 The life of Hope.

 I. Title.

PR9199.3.Q34L54 1985   813′.54   85-16001
ISBN 0-385-25004-5 (U.S.)

for Peggotty

For man also knoweth not his time: as the fishes that are taken in an evil net, and as the birds that are caught in the snare, so are the sons of man snared in an evil time, when it falleth suddenly upon them.

Ecclesiastes, 9:12

Come now, and let us reason together, saith the Lord: though your sins be as scarlet, they shall be white as snow; though they be red like crimson, they shall be as wool.

Isaiah, 1:18

Part One

Hope

Hope, Ontario, 1983
Wherein our Young Biographer flees
the Great City.

I first came to Hope early in the evening of my thirtieth birthday, which is July 22nd. I arrived half-stewed and given my druthers would have been completely stewed. The train from Toronto, however, only took a little over two hours. In that time I'd managed to consume several bottles of beer and three shots of whiskey, the whiskey being supplied by Brian, a nice man who did something with computers and was eager that I have fun on my birthday. "Especially your thirtieth birthday," Brian had said. "It's the big one."

"All grown-up now," I'd mumbled without conviction.

At the same time as I was celebrating aboard the train, my friends back in Toronto were arriving at my apartment heavily armed with food and alcohol. They'd planned a surprise party for me, one I'd known about for weeks. Elspeth, I imagine, met them at the door grimly. She likely said nothing, just glared at them, or maybe she said two quick words, "Not here," or "Fucked off." Elspeth has an economy with words and communicates mostly with facial expressions. I'm sure the expression she assumed for my friends was a doozy, guaranteed to shrivel.

But I'd had big fun on the train with Brian and the Lorne Baxters. Lorne Baxter was a large man who, having introduced his wife and himself as The Lorne Baxters, immediately demanded that I call him Bosco. Mrs. Lorne Baxter, Bosco advised, I could call whatever I wanted.

It saddened me when I found out that Brian and the Lorne Baxters were traveling all the way to Ottawa. I was the only one who disembarked at Hope, and not really there either, but rather at the only town of any size near it. From there I'd taken a taxicab fifteen miles to the east, to Hope.

I studied the back of the cabdriver's neck for a few minutes and then informed him, "It's my thirtieth birthday!" Maybe he had a bottle of champagne in the glove compartment. Maybe he'd say, "That's the big one," and stand me to drinks in some roadside tavern. He hadn't done any of that. The driver mumbled a strangely accented version of "Congratulations" and whistled the first few bars of "Happy Birthday to You."

The countryside was gentle and rolling, cut quite often by small rivers. The farmers all seemed to cultivate the same crop, a plant I didn't recognize, being a city boy. "What do they grow out here?" I asked the driver.

The cabbie had just finished a cigarette, tossing the butt through the no-draft. He pointed to where it was bouncing along the highway behind us, and I was made to understand that the big crop out Hope way was tobacco.

We passed a small church (Established 1889, a sign told me), and I was immediately filled with shame. After a few moments I felt better.

My destination lay two miles outside of the Hope limits, but the road went straight through town. Hope seemed a nice enough place—although the large green entry marker placed the population at a meager 1,000, I spied no less than three bars. My kind of town.

"Do you live in Hope?" I asked the driver.

The driver shrugged, perhaps misunderstanding.

Suddenly, and surprisingly, we passed a huge factory, a colossal thing surrounded by barbed-wire fences. A sign on its lawn announced UPDIKE INTERNATIONAL. The U had been fashioned to resemble a fishhook.

Then I was at my new home, or at least what was to be my home for the next little while.

I found myself (having paid the driver, tipping him extravagantly — sometimes I suspect that God invented alcohol to ensure that waitresses, bartenders and cabbies make a decent living) in a small valley, a basin surrounded on all sides by tall trees. In the middle of this green bowl was a pond, a small lake really, about the size of two football fields placed end to end. It was the gloaming, and the only sound in the air was that of fish flipping above the still surface for their dinner.

I turned around to look at my dwelling. The house was built up a piece from the pond, where there was enough flat land to accommodate not only it but a monstrous and ancient barn. I'd seen the house before, in one of those glass paperweights, the kind you flip over and it looks as if snow is falling inside. It was the same house, except it was now the middle of the summer and the house was nestled among trees, fat weeping willows and tall spruce.

Outside the front door was a wonderful flagstone patio, ideal for the consumption of mint juleps and gin and tonics. I studied it briefly, trying to figure out the best place to put my chaise lounge, to maximize sunlight and minimize the journey to and from the house. As I was doing this I noticed that years before someone had taken a stick to the wet cement and painstakingly dug out "GEORGE."

This wonderful place was on loan to me by Professor Harvey Benson, who teaches English Language and Literature at Chiliast University. It is Harv's belief that I am a young writer of great promise, and it's good he has tenure if he's inclined to believe such things.

"But in Toronto" — this is Harv's standard speech — "there are too many distractions. There're all the *bars*, and all the *girls*, and there's that bitch you're married to!"

"Harvey," I say sternly at this point, but that's as far as I go.

"But I have this place out in the country, and I hardly ever use it, and if you want to finish your second novel, you should move out there and goddam write!"

So when the shit hit the fan late the night before (I'd just officially turned thirty, although you'd never have known it from the way I behaved) I phoned Harv and said, "I'm going to Hope."

Now, someone had been taking wonderful care of the place, and you can bet it wasn't Harvey. His place in Toronto is squalid to say the least, a one-bedroom apartment filled with books, term papers and filthy magazines. This country home consisted basically of four rooms: a large kitchen/dining room area, a living room (with a huge stone fireplace) and two bedrooms on the second level, the second level being achieved via a set of stairs leading up from the kitchen. The bathroom was built under this staircase, and contained a wonderful old tub that had legs and feet like a dog's. Everything about the place was so clean and neat that I suspected that the house had been used in some competition for prissy ladies — it looked like a horde of old biddies had rampaged through, gathering up particles of dust for bonus points. I remembered that Harvey had given me some sort of note concerning the upkeep of the place, and I removed it from my shirt pocket and read:

MARTIN GOM COMES BY EVERY NOW AND AGAIN TO CHECK ON THINGS. IF ANYTHING GOES WRONG (PUMP FAILURE, ELECTRICAL DYSFUNCTIONS) CALL HIM AT 555-4587. IF LOUIS DROPS AROUND, DON'T BE ALARMED. ENJOY YOURSELF, BUT GODDAM WRITE YOUR NOVEL!

Thereupon followed a list of more precise instructions — how to prime the pump, how to check the generator, how to start any number of machines out in the barn (a lawnmower, a chainsaw, a weedwhacker, a tiny tractor), what mixtures of gas and oil I needed to fuel them (how did Harv know all this stuff?), and how to operate the moped, the wonderful little vehicle that was to spirit me in and out of Hope. Nowhere on the list did Harv tell me anything crucial, such as where he kept his liquor. However, a quick check through the kitchen informed me that the booze supply was kept in a cupboard immediately to the left of the big white fridge. There was a healthy collection there, and I selected, as a special treat on my thirtieth birthday (the big one), a bottle of Glenfiddich. I poured some into a tumbler and went back outside.

The sun was setting, burning the tips of the trees. A few frogs had started to croak, warming up, gingerly testing the equipment before getting down to some angst-ridden, truly horny bellows. The swallows were flitting above the barn, frantically using the last minutes of light to find some food for their peeping broods. And somewhere deep in the woods to the south, some dogs were screaming as they ran down a deer. I recalled Harvey's strange bit of advice: don't be alarmed.

The Stone Boner

Hope, Ontario, 1983
Wherein our Young Biographer makes his
first Acquaintance of Joseph Benton Hope.

The pond on my property was a section of a stream called Round River, and this stream continued past the property, building in size and power, eventually feeding into Lookout Lake. I could get to Lookout Lake quite easily on my moped, it being about two miles away by gravel road. The fishing there, Harv assured me, was magnificent. Harvey seemed to know what he was talking about, and he confused me for almost an hour with a discourse on various techniques and stratagems. The walleye, he said, like minnows and tiny jigs (I nodded sagely, visualizing myself executing a subdued stepdance by the side of the water) and the bass like almost anything, being huge and piggy, but for the really big fish, Harvey concluded, what you need is the Hoper!

"Ah, the Hoper."

So the next afternoon (having spent the morning trying to write despite my rumsick state; I'd managed to complete a single paragraph), I hopped on the moped and roared into Hope. The road to Hope was up and down and full of curves, and although I had to assist the vehicle by pedaling when cresting a hill, on the descent I could really fly, and the noise reverberating inside my motorcycle helmet was deafening. Gophers and rabbits, snoozing in the warm sun, would wake with a start, mumble animalese for "Oh, fuck!" and hurry off to the side of the road. I flushed any number of crows, ravens and red-winged blackbirds from the thickets; the birds would rise to a height of twenty feet and peer down apprehensively. Only a goshawk, alone and high in the sky, seemed indifferent, circling and not caring a tinker's cuss about the asshole on the moped.

Sometime during the night, vandals had been up to no good, although not much of it. Whereas the green WELCOME TO HOPE sign used to record a round POP. 1,000, someone had crossed out the final 0 and added underneath a bent and hasty 1.

In the middle of Hope, Ontario, is a tree-lined oval of green grass, perhaps one hundred feet long, that the townspeople perversely insist on calling The Square. I leaned the moped up against a tree, chained and locked it securely. There were benches and pigeons in the Square, garbage cans and a water fountain. I had a sip of water and spat it out on the grass. The water was warm, almost hot, and bitter.

At one end of the Square was a cannon, the barrel filled with candywrappers and condoms. At the other was a tall granite obelisk that announced TO OUR GLORIOUS DEAD. In the middle of the Square was a statue. I wandered over.

The statue was green and mouldy, especially around the base, and I suspected that dogs and drunks made frequent use of it as a leaking post. The man who was the statue had one arm raised, tiny fingers pointed at the clouds, and in the other hand he held a large book. He was dressed in a way that looked vaguely clerical, a stiff collar and a coat with long, mournful tails. The statue-man's face was rather odd — one eye was made much larger than the other, and both were set well back, hidden by shadow underneath the forehead. The man sported a beard and long hair, giving him a stern, almost biblical aspect.

Then something about the statue caught my eye. It had a stone boner. At first I was sure that this was some trick of the sunlight and shadow, but a closer inspection proved me wrong. The statue was clearly possessed of an erect penis. It lurked underneath the marble trousers, cocked slightly to the right to avoid meeting the waistband. It was a huge thing, this stone boner, perhaps ten inches long and thick as a baby's forearm. I giggled, reached out and touched the thing gingerly. "Poor guy," I laughed out loud. I bent down to read the tarnished plaque, eager to find out the identity of this man with the eternal hard-on. It was:

JOSEPH BENTON HOPE
1824–1889
OUR FOUNDER

Special Boots

Lowell, Massachusetts, 1858

Regarding the life of Hope, we know the
following: that he was born on January 14,
1824, in the town of Hadley; that he abided
the state of Massachusetts until September of
1858; that at such time he journeyed
northward into Upper Canada.
*   The reason for this emigration is*
obfuscated.

Even in the weak candlelight, the girl's face was a startling red. She looked as if she might explode suddenly, like a shotgun shell that had been tossed into a campfire.

Joseph Benton Hope studied her, pleased though slightly alarmed. He imagined the Spirit of the Lord moving through her, flowing in her veins and mixing gloriously with the humors, activating the corpuscles to produce this brilliant hematic display. Joseph Benton Hope shifted slightly in his seat.

The girl's chest was heaving, the shape of her bosom defined regularly and almost perfectly against the white fabric of her smock. J. B. Hope rose to his feet suddenly, leaping up as though his chair was aflame. The red girl merely raised her eyes to follow, obedient and calm.

The other young woman, dark and dour, reared back in fright and then giggled. Hope silenced her with a quick and jagged look, knowing how frightening his eyes could be. His right was large and blue and motionless (it was glass), the other small, dark and quick.

"And they brought unto him also infants," J. Benton Hope intoned in his queer, croaky voice, "that he would touch them. But when his disciples saw it, they rebuked them . . ." Hope forgot his place. The red girl had taken to rocking back and forth in rhythm with his words, or perhaps he had taken to gasping them out in strict time to her rocking. Joseph Benton Hope remained silent for many moments before speaking again.

"But Jesus called unto them, and said, 'Suffer naked children to come unto me, and forbid them not, for of such is the Kingdom of Heaven.' "

Some small portion of Hope's mind registered a complaint over the substitution of the word "naked." *The Lord Himself placed it on my tongue*, countered Hope silently and with faith, for which he was rewarded by a Vision of the red girl naked. She was no older than seventeen, this girl, and the fat that rounded her belly and behind was still fresh and icily pink. Her breasts were swollen (Hope had a theory about the female bosom, that the right breast was the home of the amative soul, while the left housed the propagative — it was a complicated theory, and what it boiled down to was that in moments of excitement the breasts would become swollen) and her sex was silky. The Vision was gone in an instant, and left behind in Joseph Hope a strange, choking sensation. Wishing to dispel it, Hope clenched his tiny hand and stabbed it upwards toward Heaven.

The thunder alarmed even Hope, coming as it did at the instant his fist was thrust to the limit of his reach. It was a loud peal, as if the cloud that produced it sat on the roof of his own house. Hope shook his fist then, and the thunder seemed to boil and bubble at his command. Sensing it would die soon, Hope let his hand drop slowly. By the time it was once more at his side, the clangor had been replaced by another sound, the soft sound of rain falling to the earth.

Remarkably, it was the other girl, the dour and dark one, who seemed most affected. Her eyes were closed, and she seemed to be having some difficulty breathing. This girl parted her lips (the bottom lip, Hope noticed, was twisted in the middle by a thin, white scar) and whispered the single word, "Yes."

"Yes," Joseph Hope repeated, letting the word fall as softly as the rain.

And now the red girl did explode. She shouted "Yes!" with such vigor that two of the buttons on her tight bodice flew away. (J. B. Hope's theory about the female bosom seemed beyond doubt at this point.) The red girl ran to the window and pressed her face against the glass. "It's raining!"

Hope had to stifle a desire to snap, *Of course it's raining, we knew it was raining.* Instead he beamed magnificently and watched the pitchings of the girl's chest.

The dour and dark girl said, so quietly that it was almost inaudible, "To wash away the sins of this wicked, wicked place." J. B. Hope thought initially that she was referring to his own house, number forty-two Dutton Street, but then realized she was being more general and meant the world, or at least the entire state of Massachusetts.

Meanwhile the red girl seemed to be losing more and more buttons, and the fabric had torn around one of her armpits. Joseph could see the crisp white of an undergarment and a thin slice of red flesh. The entire area around her armpit was damp (a huge area, Hope noted, a wet ring larger than he'd seen on anyone before), and large beads of perspiration sat on the girl's forehead and upper lip.

The other girl stood up. She was tall, much taller than Joseph B. Hope, and slender. "I'm going to arise and be baptized, and have my sins washed away," she announced, much as she might have announced her intention of going to the market. She made for the door, and Hope was reminded of her clumsy gait. Her left foot was in a special boot, one with a three-inch sole. Hope pursed his mouth, as if to spit out some slight bitterness.

The red girl was now clothed only in her undergarments, although Joseph hadn't noticed her taking off her dress. It was possible, Hope thought, that the garment had simply blown away from her swelling body. "Yes!" shouted the red girl, and she bolted for the door as though it was somehow important that she precede the crippled girl through it. "Suffer naked children to come unto me!" sang the red girl, and Joseph Benton Hope said, "Actually . . ." and then fell silent. This was, after all, a Bible study, and he'd had half a mind to explain that the word "naked" was used in a metaphorical sense—maybe even half a mind to admit that the word wasn't there in the first place, that it should be "little." But the girls were already outside.

J. B. Hope moved to his window and looked out upon the streets of Lowell. Across from his house, beside the dark Merrimack, was a boot factory, and Joseph wondered whether it had manufactured the special boot for the crippled girl. (The crippled girl was soaking wet and still fully dressed, although she was struggling frantically to remove her clothes.)

Was it indeed possible, wondered Joseph Benton Hope, that the factory opposite made nothing save boots for crippled feet? (The red girl was now naked, her undergarments slipping to her ankles with the first touch of rain. The rain had mixed with her sweat, and the red girl was glistening.) J. B. Hope pondered, almost idly, how much of this he had wanted to happen. He'd certainly wanted to see the red girl denuded, but hadn't the Lord already granted him that Vision? (Although, gazing at the red girl through the window, Joseph noted certain discrepancies. Her breasts, for example, were more ponderous, dragged toward her belly by gravity. Perhaps the Vision was of the girl in Heaven, where all is free of earthbound forces.) Hope felt no true desire to have amorous congress with the red girl, although he did have an erection. Hope touched it, shifted it to a more comfortable position. It was J. B. Hope's theory that his penis was not engorged with blood, as so many thought, but rather with the Spirit of the Lord. Therefore, should he have amorous congress with the red girl, he would merely be placing the Spirit of the Lord directly inside her. (The crippled girl had finally torn off her dress, and she now stood sternly corseted despite her slender frame. The red girl was smiling toward the sky, and it hadn't occurred to her that the crippled girl might require assistance.)

A church bell began to chime in the distance, and Joseph Hope absentmindedly counted along. When it reached nine he scowled, and with the tenth toll Hope rapped his tiny knuckles against the pane with annoyance. At any moment the crippled girl's father would arrive in his buggy. (The red girl had helped the other after all, and now the crippled girl was bare-chested. For some reason the crippled girl turned away in order to pull down her bloomers, and Joseph saw a shallow and shadowed posterior emerge. She was naked now, except for her boots. The crippled girl spread her arms toward Heaven, the elbow joints bending awkwardly backward. The red girl pointed at the cripple's boots and laughed.)

"Silly," muttered Joseph, in reference to any number of things, not just the red girl's adolescent scorn. Suddenly Joseph had desire so strong that it hurt, made him spit out air and fog the window. Joseph Benton Hope realized that his erection had vanished, the Spirit gone uselessly elsewhere. He also realized that he could hear the sound of horses' hooves. Joseph Benton Hope wanted to go fishing.

Joseph spoke aloud, saying, "Even unto this present hour we both hunger, and thirst, and are buffeted, and have no common dwellingplace . . ."

Joseph Benton Hope decided to leave Lowell, Massachusetts.

The Hoper

Hope, Ontario, 1983
Wherein our Biographer acquires the Tool
whereby he might practice the Art of the
Angle.

Across from the Square were the shops of Hope. There was, among other things, Delanoy's IGA, which would supply my grocery needs, not that I have many; a liquor store (where I hoped to open a charge account); two of the three taverns spotted the night before; a butcher's shop, a bank, a bakery, and something called Edgar's Bait, Tackle and Taxidermy.

Edgar's display window was a strange thing to behold. A handwritten sign taped to the glass proclaimed LIVE WORMS, CRAWLERS, MINNOWS. The tackle portion of his trade was represented by an assortment of hooks and lures that appeared to have been flung in angrily. There were any number of stuffed fish, a stuffed skunk, and then, as if to show that he didn't merely stuff trifles, there was a stuffed bear's foot. Give me a bigger window, Edgar seemed to be saying, and boy you'd really see something! Edgar's display window also inexplicably contained a violin, a dressmaker's dummy and a Ouija board.

Inside the shop there was comparatively little. Almost all of

Edgar's stock seemed to be in the window. There were a few rods lined up along a wall, and there was a long counter with some books on it, scuzzy mimeographed things with cardboard covers, obviously written by and for the locals— *What to Look Out For at Lookout Lake*, by Lt. Col. Alan Skinner (ret'd), *Hunting & Killing Grizzlies*, by S. and L. McDiarmid and *Fishing for Ol' Mossback*, by Gregory Opdycke.

Behind this counter stood Edgar.

Upon seeing Edgar I wondered why the shop wasn't called Edgar's Bait, Tackle, Taxidermy and Axe-murder. He was as evil-looking a man as I've ever seen, his head bald, his face covered by a prickly black beard. Edgar was also immense, a good half foot above six feet, muscled like a mountain. I guessed he was somewhere around forty-five years old, but the T-shirt he had on, several sizes too small for his chest and arms, bore the name of a popular heavy metal band. Edgar stared at me as if he meant to damn me to Hell. He removed something from his mouth, maybe the butt of a cigar, probably the leg of some cute forest-dwelling animal, and barked, "Yeah?"

I wanted to flee, but somehow I found the courage to tell him, "I need a Hoper."

Edgar stared at me for several long moments. He appeared to process the information slowly, reflecting on each of my words. Then he reached down below the counter and produced the item in question.

A Hoper is about the size of a small finger, and a finger is what it looks like, to a certain degree. It's carved out of wood and jointed twice where the knuckles would be. At the tip there is a large treble hook. This Hoper was painted a fleshy pink, spotted by big drops of red. It seemed as unlikely a lure as I could imagine, but Harv swore by the thing, so I asked, "How much?"

Edgar thought about that for a while and then said, somewhat arbitrarily, "Four bucks."

"Oh," I mumbled, "that's a little dear."

Edgar stared at me.

If I had my life to live over, I thought, I would say "expensive." Never mind about screwing up my marriage to Elspeth, never mind about all the rotten things I've done to my friends and loved ones, just let me live my life over, and all I'll change is I won't say to Edgar, "That's a little dear."

Edgar said, finally, "The wife says that."

"I beg your pardon?"

"The wife says things are 'a little dear.' " Edgar crossed his arms and placed his elbows on the counter. "So get this," he said. "Last summer, we go visit her brother, 's got a cottage up north near Sudbury. So we stop at one of those places along the highway, y'know, a restaurant like, to get something to eat. And the place is full of all sorts of *gift* shit. I swear, I don't know what those people are thinking. I mean, after driving a couple of hours, I want a burger and a coffee. I do not want to buy a Ookpik, or a piece of wood with the Lord's Prayer burned into it, or a placemat with a fucking Mountie on it, or nothing. I want a burger and a coffee. Anyways, see, they got these china animals in this place, little bunnies and stuff. And they got this china Bambi, right? Yea big." Edgar spaced off three or four inches between his massive thumb and forefinger. "Frigging thing costs eight bucks. So I take this thing, this Bambi, over to the wife. Okay? And I says, 'Hey, hon, you want to buy this Bambi? It costs eight bucks.' "

Edgar started to chuckle.

"Ha!" I realized what the point was and started chuckling myself.

Edgar looked suddenly crestfallen. "The dumb twat bought it." He shook his head, world weary. "Didn't say a word." Edgar tried to forget about it. He dangled the odd lure in the air and demanded, "You want to buy the Hoper?"

"Does it work?"

Edgar answered, "So the story goes."

The Willing Mind

Hope, Ontario, 1983
Wherein our Biographer, after suffering
sundry Inconveniences, discovers an
Establishment that is to his liking.

Not only did I purchase a Hoper, I also picked up a copy of
Gregory Opdycke's tome, *Fishing for Ol' Mossback*. Edgar had
told me all about this legendary Mossback in the half-hour or
so I'd spent chatting (axe-murderers are people, too). Ol' Mossback, according to local myth, is the premier denizen of Lookout Lake. Edgar told me that there are various schools of thought
concerning Ol' Mossback's species. The most popular has it that
he is a muskellunge, and this seems probable given his length,
conservatively estimated at five and a half feet. Others think
he is a mutant pike, and this notion appeals for its supernatural
aspects, supernatural in the most literal sense, Ol' Mossback
having arrogantly overstepped Mother Nature's bounds. There's
a few, Edgar confided, who think Ol' Mossback is some sort of
walleye pickerel. These are usually people who claim to have
seen the beast, for they report that he has the strange metallic
eyes of that breed, large and round, with a luminous aspect
like those of a blind Buddhist monk.

Whatever he is, Ol' Mossback is reported to be a monster,
his body covered with scars, a record of his battles with mankind. He is adorned with fishhooks like jewelry. If anyone ever
managed to land Ol' Mossback (no one ever has, Edgar was
quick to point out) the collection of terminal tackle stuck to the
fish would supply one with the history of sport angling in North
America; Ol' Mossback is at least two hundred years old.

At this point in the tale I advised Edgar, "Get real."

Edgar shrugged, but I could tell he was wounded in some
small way.

"You don't gotta believe me if you don't wanna," he muttered,
and then Edgar went to an antique cash register and methodically rang in my purchases.

So there I stood on Joseph Avenue in downtown Hope, on a

very hot summer's day. I decided that what I needed to do was find a place to sit down and look at my new stuff. A bar, I thought, would do nicely.

The closest bar was called Duffy's. It was also the nicest looking of the three town taverns. It appeared to occupy the bottom level of an old hotel, and the hotel was whitewashed and ornate with pillars, cornices and curlicues. The windows to Duffy's were thick and stippled, but signs with fat, cartoony letters spelled out what you would find inside. BEER, one announced, and a drawing underneath showed how the beer came in big, frothy pitchers, and jagged lines all around it showed how it was icy cold. A larger sign read PINBALL, odd in this age of video. By far the largest sign read EXOTIC DANCERS. I decided I'd try Duffy's. I was so taken with the notion of exotic dancers that I failed to notice the number of motorcycles that were lined up out front.

Before I go any further, I should make some mention of my appearance. I spent my childhood and adolescence as a fat and bespectacled lad, but during my twenties I'd started running and lifting weights in a frantic attempt to reverse the ravages of my life-style, so my thirtieth year found me with something vaguely resembling an athletic build. Sheer vanity had convinced me to abandon my spectacles for contact lenses, although they cost me a fortune because I lose them all the time. I now sport a beard, because I hate shaving, and I have long hair, because I can never be bothered to get it cut.

I was wearing jeans, a T-shirt and cowboy boots, which seemed somehow suitable attire, also a get-up of which Elspeth would never approve. ("Who are *you* supposed to be?" Elspeth would ask.) I was, furthermore, covered in dust from my moped journey, and my protective helmet was nestled in the crook of my arm.

So when I entered Duffy's and found myself in the midst of a sizable collection of bikers, no one paid any particular attention to me. Still, I wasn't so big a fool as to hang around. I turned, took a step, but someone grabbed my arm. A voice said, "Hiya, bud!"

The fellow who owned this voice, and was also grabbing my arm, sat at a tiny, round table. He was a fairly handsome young man, except that the skin around his eyes was prematurely wrinkled, and his teeth were bad, horrible in fact, two rows of misshapen, yellow stumps. "Have a sit-down, bud, and I'll buy you some beers!"

Another thing you have to know about me is I'm usually near broke. The rest of the time I'm broke. "Oh. Thanks." I tossed my helmet on the table (his was there already, one with a black visor, licks of flame painted on it) and sat down.

This fellow's T-shirt read *Fuck You*. I tried to determine if I was missing something (these T-shirts usually make some attempt to be clever), but all it said was *Fuck You*.

The man reached forward and grabbed my knee, squeezing it hard. Then he lifted his other hand as if to slap me, but he kept it suspended in mid-air. After a long moment I realized that he wanted to give me a "high five," so I lifted my hand and we slapped palms. Then he grabbed my hand, and we shook in that reversed manner. The guy said, "Geez, it's good to see ya, bud."

The waitress came over. The waitress was a plump, blonde girl with a red rose tattooed on her shoulder. She said "Hi," in a friendly fashion and then pointed a finger at me. "Three draft, a salt shaker and a pickled egg, right?"

I said, "Sounds reasonable" (even though the pickled egg didn't, particularly), and they both laughed.

As soon as the waitress left, my companion grabbed my knee again. His knuckles read L-O-V-E in fading purple ink. "So what you doin', bud? I thought you lived in T.O."

I know I'm going to seem a bit conceited here, but my first thought was that this guy knew who I was. My novel had been reviewed in most Canadian newspapers, usually accompanied by my photograph. I'd also done a number of television interviews and been on a game show. (Really, I was. It was a low-budget thing called "That's A Sport," and I'd distinguished myself by knowing absolutely nothing.) So I answered this fellow by saying, "Thought I'd do a little fishing," and showed him my Hoper and Mossback manual.

"Just keep your dick in your pants," the guy advised.

"I, um, intend to."

My companion laughed, and I wondered why I apparently kept making jokes.

"What," asked this guy, "did the old lady shoot you the boots?"

This lucky guess I attributed to my generally looking hard done by. "You got it," I nodded.

"Oh, bud," this fellow said, smiling and shaking his head. "Still fucking around, eh?"

It was only then that I noticed the capital B. Bud was my name.

Confirming this, the waitress set down three glasses of draft beer, a salt shaker and a pickled egg with a cheerful, "Here you go, Bud."

I reached for some money, but the guy waved his hand at me. (The other hand, the knuckles reading H-A-T-E.) "I got it, Bud. I just want to see you do it."

Oh-oh, I thought. I drained some beer into my mouth rapidly.

The waitress lingered by the table. She wanted to see me do it, too.

"Do it, do it," urged my companion.

"First thing in the afternoon?" I bluffed.

"That's *why* you do it," the guy said. "First thing, so that all your daily nutritional needs are taken care of."

"Eat the pickled egg, you mean?"

This was another of my big jokes. The guy exploded with mirth. " 'Eat the pickled egg' the guy says. Did you hear him, Rose? 'Eat the pickled egg!' " Then he turned slightly more serious. "Quit fucking around, Bud. Do it."

"It's been a while," I said. "Remind me."

"What, have you been doing heavy-duty dope or what?" He was getting annoyed with me. "Fucking put salt on the egg, fucking drop it into the brew, and fucking chug the whole fucking thing!"

"Oh, that!" Bud was some strange goomba. Still, it hardly seemed like an impossible feat. I picked up the salt-shaker with flourish and gave the egg a dosing. I could tell when I'd salted it enough by looking at my companion's face. When the egg was liberally covered he gave a little nod. I plopped the egg into the beer. There was a fair amount of fizzing. Then I raised the draft glass, said "Cheers," and knocked it back.

The actual beer went down easily enough while the egg bounced against my teeth. When it was gone I opened my mouth wide and the pickled egg tumbled in. After a few seconds it joined the beer in my belly.

I thought I'd done wonderfully well, but my friend looked outraged. "You chewed," he muttered, deeply betrayed.

"Bud doesn't chew?"

He cocked his head, bewildered.

"Bud doesn't *chew*," I repeated evenly. "I was just shifting it around in my mouth so I could swallow it better."

After a few moments the guy nodded, but he looked far from convinced. The waitress left with a quiet tsking of her tongue. I threw back the remaining beer and stood up. "See you around."

The fellow nodded, unwilling to look me in the eye. "Sure, Bud. Anything you say."

I got the hell out of there.

The next establishment was two or three storefronts down the street. It was called Moe's Steakhouse and Tavern. Not my favorite sort of place, just your basic restaurant that happens to serve booze as well. The tables, seen through the large front windows, were made from plastic and lined out in a neat, orderly fashion. Moe's place was nearly empty, the clientele being an old man seated at the formica counter drinking coffee, and two young girls at a table near the back smoking cigarettes and eating home-fries. Still, I decided to try Moe's. For one thing, "Moe" is a name you can do business with, especially business of an alcoholic nature. I could imagine myself wandering in on a daily basis and saying, "Hey, Moe, what do you know?" "The regular, Moe!" "How about them Blue Jays, eh, Moe?" The other thing was, a stenciled sign informed me that a bottle of beer would cost ninety cents. A buck a beer ("Keep the dime, Moe!"), I could easily accommodate, even within my rather limited budget. So into Moe's I went.

The place seemed to be run by an enormous woman, a woman that could easily have been Edgar the axe-murderer's twin. She was standing behind the counter reading a paperback that had something to do with nurses. She glanced up and watched as I seated myself a couple of stools down from the old man, then she fished out a ballpoint pen that she'd held trapped in her cleavage. This monstrous woman (not Moe, I saw, because "Sophie" was stitched on to her white uniform) snatched up an order pad and poised the pen above it. "Yo?"

"A beer, please. An Export."

The young girls giggled over their potatoes.

I took out my Hoper for further inspection. I chuckled in a bemused way, for no reason, other than it seemed like the sort of thing Red Fisher might do while looking at a Hoper. Meanwhile the enormous woman walked to a glass cabinet that contained a few bottles of beer beside pies and dishes of rice pudding. She slid the door along and took out a beer, opening it with a churchkey she'd also taken out of her bosom. I began to wonder what-all she had down there.

She brought the beer to me and then once more made ready to write on her order pad. "How do you want it done?" she asked.

"Beg your pardon?"

"How do you want it done?" she enunciated more clearly.

I asked, "How do I want what done?" thinking that if it came to that I wanted to be on top.

"Your steak," she responded.

"I don't want my steak done at all," I told her, and then, hearing how it sounded, I said, "I didn't ask for a steak."

"You gotta have a steak," she said. "It's a steakhouse and tavern."

I started to laugh, but this was obviously a no-nonsense breed of enormous woman. "I don't want a steak."

She snatched up my bottle. "No steak, no beer."

I pointed towards the old man. "He's not eating a steak. And those girls aren't eating a steak."

"They're not drinking beer, either," she argued.

The young girls giggled furiously, and I detected the old man's shoulders bouncing with senile mirth.

I decided to try a moral stance. "Do you know," I said, "that if everyone in the west didn't eat red meat, no one in the world would be starving?"

"If everyone ate steak, no one would be starving, either," the enormous woman countered.

"Is this a joke?"

"It is a policy," she informed me.

"Right. A policy."

"You got to have policies," she said with near-religious fervor.

"If I have two beer, do I have to have two steaks?"

She glared. "Don't be radickallus."

"Well, I don't know. I don't want a steak. I sure want that

beer, though. Listen, couldn't you check with my old buddy
Moe?"

"It's Moe's policy. If it was up to me, I would give you the
beer. I am not unreasonable."

"I suppose a further policy would be that, despite the fact
you're not going to let me have that beer, you still want me to
pay for it."

The enormous woman nodded. "That's the policy."

"Even if I were a very strange goomba named Bud who was
likely to trash the joint with the rest of his biker cronies? The
type of guy who swallows pickled eggs whole, no less?"

"Right," she nodded.

"Okay," I said. "Lucky for you I'm not." I rose out of my seat
and presented the woman with a dollar bill. She rammed it
down between her breasts and made change from the same
place, handing me a cold dime.

"Well, so long. It's been a pleasure." I proceeded to leave.

"Hey, young feller!" This was the old fart at the counter. He'd
spun around on his stool and was grinning at me. Despite the
heat of the day he was dressed in a thick hunting jacket and a
woollen toque pulled down over his ears. He was approximately one hundred years old, his face toothless and wrinkled.
"You forgot your Hoper!" he cackled.

"Oh, yeah."

"Goin' after Ol' Mossback?" The name of the mythical fish
burbled in his throat, jiggling the ancient folds of skin.

"Right."

He held out the Hoper in a twisted claw that shook with palsy.
The lure had buckled at its joints and was pointed limply earthward. With a tiny flick of his wrist (although this was a fairly
strenuous act for the geezer) he snapped it so that it was standing rigidly erect.

The old man began to laugh, great wheezy gulps of backward air, as if this was the funniest thing imaginable. "Keep
your dick in your pants!" he managed to snort.

I snatched back my Hoper and left Moe's.

I had one remaining option, The Willing Mind. I'd been afraid
it might come to this.

The Willing Mind lay beyond the line of shops and businesses, isolated from them like a leper. Beyond it rolling fields sprang up with determination, as if this single piece of civilization was the final straw, too much for Mother Nature to handle.

Many years ago, I suppose, the building that held The Willing Mind might have been nice enough, but now it looked deformed and humpbacked. Its angles and joinings were cockeyed, its oak-shingled roof rolling like waves on the ocean. The house had last seen fresh paint, I guessed, around the turn of the century, and that paint had been a garish crimson. Time had stolen all but a few stray peelings, tiny slivers that looked like blood.

The Willing Mind was curiously windowed. The upper storey had a line of what looked like portholes, tiny, round and imperfectly spaced. The lower floor had three oddly shaped windows, glassed in dissimilar fashion. One pane was thick and smoky, and, seen through it, the inhabitants and furnishings appeared to be melting, engulfed in some great blast of heat. The second window, a small elliptical one, was a mirror, and yielded my own reflection, distorted and distant. For the third window, the largest and most prominent, the builders had pilfered a stained-glass window, one that pictured Christ's crucifixion. It had been inserted upside down.

By far the oddest thing was the sign that swung above the front door. Ornate gold-leaf letters named the place, THE WILLING MIND, and a painting underneath showed a stylized heart beating within a mass of gray tissue. It was crude and off-putting, and left to my own devices I would never have passed beneath it. But, circumstances being what they were, I didn't see that I had any choice.

The inside of The Willing Mind was full of more strangeness. For one thing, although outside lingered a hot summer's day, as the heavy door slammed shut behind me, I had the immediate impression of having escaped foul weather.

Much of the tavern's interior was dominated by a stand-up bar, something stolen from the set of a B Western; it snaked around the walls, following all of the improbable dents and bumps. This left room for three or four tables, lonely and unused. It was obvious that all of the bar's business was conducted over the antique wooden counter.

The interior decoration, I suspected, had been done by my

friend Edgar the axe-murderer. Stuffed animals lurked everywhere, a bear raging mutely in a corner, a lynx crouched and
snarling near a window, any number of squirrels, skunks and
birds frozen above the cabinets that held the tavern's liquor
supply. Another Edgartonian touch were the items suspended
on The Willing Mind's walls: the front grill from a Ford pick-up
truck, a poster advertising a circus that had toured Oregon in
1927, and a purplish photograph of a chubby woman testing
her bathwater with a big toe.

As I took all this in, the inhabitants of The Willing Mind turned
and stared at me.

The most singular of these was a tall, gaunt man with skin
the color of autumn leaves. His hair was midnight black, speck-
led with bits of white, like starlight. It was long, combed back
from his high forehead, and tumbling on to his shoulders.

Of all the eyes that rested on me, this man's, the Indian's,
were the most unsettling. For one thing, they were buried deeply
into the leather of his face. For another, his eyes didn't look to
be functional. What should have been white was distinctly silver, and what should have been black shone pearly white. But
this was all some trick of the light, because the man nodded at
me and smiled politely. He held a cigarette between the tips of
his fingers, and with this he gestured aristocratically at the emptiness beside him.

I obediently went to stand next to the man, taking note of
the other people as I did so.

There were three more standing at The Willing Mind's bar,
two of them isolated and obviously a couple. The man, or boy,
was perhaps nineteen or twenty, ginger-haired and smiling. He
would have been handsome except that acne had invaded his
face savagely, leaving it scabbed and scarred. His mate was a
small girl, a year or two younger, whose body had run to fat
but stopped just before it got there. She had been burned golden
by the sun.

The last occupant was a jerk. Everything about this guy announced JERK so loudly that a Venutian would understand.
He wore striped bellbottoms and a green and orange checked
sports coat with bulging pockets, the pockets obviously packed
with palm-buzzers and chewing gum that turned your mouth

black. Underneath this he wore a satin shirt with none of the buttons fastened, either for reasons of fashion or because he possessed an incredibly large belly. Around his neck he wore about a dozen medallions and mandalas, and each of his fingers was ringed, each ring so enormous that he had to hold his hands spread open like fat little bird's feet. The jerk's face was basically pleasant, but he'd covered it with sunglasses, and topped it with a curly hairpiece. The guy had likely paid hundreds for the rug; I judged it to be worth four dollars.

The jerk broke the silence in The Willing Mind by bellowing, "Mona!!"

From somewhere beneath us a voice responded, "What?"

"We got a live one!" the jerk bellowed.

"No fuckin' around?" came the voice from below.

"Abso-loota nyet!" shouted back the jerk.

"Hold on, I'll be right up."

I stood beside the Indian and looked where he was looking, that being an opened trapdoor in the floor on the other side of the bar. After a few moments a head appeared there. "Hello!" said this head. Then the head continued upward, followed by a woman's body.

I said, "Hello," right back.

I'd found my bar.

Mona

Hope, Ontario, 1983
Wherein our Biographer meets a Diverse
Crowd, including one of an exciting
Physicality, and is Found Out.

Mona reminded me at once of Elspeth, and no one, not even one of Elspeth's detractors, has ever claimed that she is less than stunning. Elspeth and this woman shared a particularly Irish look, eyes of a light green and a pale complexion framed with raven-black hair. Both women had upturned noses, although this woman's was more pixie-ish than Ellie's. On the other hand, while both had prominent chins, Elspeth's was the more jutting — this may be more a matter of mental attitude than physiology. The greatest difference was in the length of their hair. Elspeth's was fabulously long, falling well past her derriere. (We had a running joke: every Christmas we'd pretend to be the young lovers from that O. Henry story, "The Gift of the Magi." I'd come in on Christmas Eve with a beautiful ivory comb, doing my best to give the impression of a young man who'd just pawned his gold pocket watch — God knows, I'd usually had to pawn *something* — and Elspeth would receive me, as gloriously maned as ever. "You bitch!" I'd rave. "Where's my frigging watch fob?") Mona wore her hair cut very short, like she'd just come out of boot camp. Her hair was disheveled to say the least, little tufts and clumps springing out in random directions; you couldn't even call these things cowlicks, because if a cow had been licking the lady's head it would have been much neater. Her one imperfection (peculiar hairdo notwithstanding), so tiny it was many moments before one even noticed it, was that her left eye was slightly askew.

Both women had general issue female bodies if you accept as standard something near perfect. But Elspeth had a tendency to overdress in a severe fashion, usually wearing baggy tweed trousers, a bra, a blouse and a thick sweater, completely hiding the curve of her breasts. Mona wore shorts and a man's undershirt, the armless singlet style; the undershirt was too big for her, and her every movement afforded me a peek at her tits. When she bent over to shut the trapdoor the view was unobstructed. I saw that her breasts were slightly larger than my wife's, the nipples many shades darker. Mona's shorts had a military look to them, khaki in color and multipocketed; they also were too big and rode dangerously low on her hips. On her feet Mona wore sandals. I thought they too were oversized, until I noticed that her feet were crammed into them. Mona's feet were the biggest I've ever seen on a woman, and that's going some considering how many times I've been given the boot.

"How do," said Mona. She'd obviously been up to something fairly strenuous in the basement. Mona wiped sweat off her

face and then fanned air with her hands. (Her hands were enormous, too, much bigger than mine.) "What can I do you for?"

"Draft. Please. Thank you."

"Draft." It looked as if Mona spent a moment trying to recall
just exactly what draft was, a moment during which she reached
down the neckhole of her undershirt and absentmindedly wiped
the perspiration from her breasts. "You want a pint of draft?"

"Yes. I do. Please. Thank you."

" 'Kay." Mona picked up a heavy pewter tankard and wandered away to the other end of the bar. She went to an antique
draft pump and began to draw my ale.

The man beside me, the Indian, touched his fingertips to my
shoulder. When I turned he said, "Hello. My name is Jonathon."
He proffered his hand, holding it high, near his shoulder, so
that I had to reach out and up in order to shake it. "Hello,
Jonathon," I returned. "My name is Paul."

"Oh yes." Jonathon smiled and took a puff of his cigarette.

"My name is Big Bernie!" shouted the jerk, although he stood
about five foot nine and (apart from his enormous tummy) was
almost slight. "And this," he said, patting his belly affectionately, "this is Little Bernie!"

"Hi, guys," said I.

"Hi! Say hi, Little Bernie!"

Big Bernie's stomach said, "Hi, Paul!" — or that's how it
seemed to me. The crease at the belly-button opened and closed
like a mouth, and a strange, high voice issued forth.

I guess I looked a little dumbfounded, because the young
couple laughed lightly. "Don't worry," said the boy. "You get
used to it."

Big Bernie now spoke to his stomach. "What do you say, Li'l
Bern? How's about one more martoony?"

"How's about some food?" Bernie's stomach responded testily.

"I'll get the Moaner to put an olive in it," said Big Bernie.

"An olive, big fucking deal. I mean, like maybe I should put
the whole system down here on red fucking alert, huh?" Little
Bernie was a sarcastic son-of-a-gun. Incidentally, during the potbelly's little tirade I could see Big Bernie's lips moving.

At least, I was pretty sure I could.

Mona came back with a pint of ale. "How much is it?" I asked,
reaching for my pockets.

Mona looked momentarily confused. "Don'ya wanna run a tab?"

"You're going to let me?"

"Sure. Why not?" Mona shrugged. "Anyways, it's a buck-fifty if you wanna know."

"That's very reasonable," I said, taking a sip.

Well, the price may have been reasonable, but the beer sure wasn't. I'd once made a plastic container full of beer from a kit called Homebrew and was almost hospitalized for my efforts. This stuff was a notch or two below Homebrew quality-wise. I involuntarily made a face.

Mona scowled. "I don't know what it is," she said.

"You told me it was beer."

Mona laughed, a pretty sound, though slightly rough, like the lightest grade of sandpaper. "I mean, I don't know why it tastes like that. That's what I was doin' in the cellar, checking the keg and the pipes and all. They seem okay. It's not very good, is it?"

Mona seemed so saddened by this that I lied. "Well, it's not going to take the Gold Medal from an International Jury of Beer-Tasters, but I mean, it's drinkable."

"Bullshit!" shouted Little Bernie. "The jerk sent a bunch of that swill down here and I said, 'Like, no fucking way!' Right back up the spout with that horse-piss!"

"Maybe my stomach's not as sensitive as you," I said, adding, "As yours."

"Sensitive!" shouted Little Bernie. "I haven't been sensitive since the jerk was weaned!"

Big Bernie nodded. "He's not a sensitive guy. But he's my buddaroony!" Big Bernie gave his gut a little pat.

"You stayin' in town?" asked Mona.

"Just outside town. You know Harvey Benson?"

Mona thought about it briefly. "Nope."

"Anyway, I'm staying at his place. Couple of miles that way." Even though I'd said "that way" I hadn't pointed, because I'd lost my sense of direction. "Down the road."

"Uh, yeah." Mona nodded and scratched her stomach. Her hand had doubled back through the arm-hole in order to do this, pulling the material out and leaving an entire breast exposed. It bounced up and down as she scratched.

"I know Harvey Benson," said the Indian, Jonathon. "He lives in the old Quinton place."

"Oh!" said Mona, surprised. She leveled a look at me. "You stayin' out there?"

"For a couple of months. While I work on my second novel."

"Are you a writer?" This was the response I'd wanted, but the source was Little Bernie.

"I try," I answered anyway.

"I'm thinking about writing a book," Little Bernie announced. "Sort of a book about food, written from the stomach's point of view. You figure something like that would sell?"

"I don't know."

"I'd have a chapter called 'Steak: Cook It or Lose It.' Like the jerk is always ordering his steak rare! What does he think I'm doing, building a fucking cow down here?"

"Well ..."

"Hey, jerk, what was that stuff you had one time?"

"You mean steak tartare?" Big Bernie supplied.

"Yeah! Now this was a pleasant fucking surprise! Raw fucking meat! Up the spout with that doo-doo!"

"Give it a rest, Little Bern," said Mona. She turned back to me. "So how long you been out there?"

"Just got in last night."

Mona nodded and reached into her shorts pockets for a pack of cigarettes. She smoked a brand popularly believed to be a favorite among truckdrivers and shipyard workers, although I suspect that even they won't touch them. Once she had the cigarette going she nodded again, vaguely this time, and said, "That must be pretty inneresting."

"Living at Harvey's?"

"Bein' a writer. What do you write? Articles for magazines or sumpin'?"

"Novels."

"Biographies," said Mona. "That's what I read. And I don't much care who they're about, neither, could be Harry S. Truman or Marilyn Monroe or some bugger in ancient Rome, Nero or somebody."

"Why do you like biographies so much?"

Mona shrugged. "How should I know? Why do I like anna-thin'? I dint ever think about it."

"Mona?" This was from the girl of the young couple. She and her mate hadn't been listening to us. They'd kept their foreheads touching while they conversed in warm, lush whispers. "Can we have a couple more?"

"Sure." Mona went to prepare their drinks.

Now the boy spoke to me. "We're Kim."

"Come again?"

The girl came again. "We're Kim. We're both named Kim. Pretty funny, eh?"

"It's a fucking laff riot," muttered Little Bernie.

"Nice to meet you, Kim," I said, and they nodded and went back to their private world.

Jonathon began to act strangely. He put his long fingers to his temples and pressed very firmly, as if he was afraid that his head might blow apart. Jonathon said, "Oh-oh," and everyone else in the bar said "Oh-oh" too. And then he collapsed to the floor with a loud "boom."

I was pretty sure he was having an epileptic fit, so I frantically began to search through my pockets for something to ram in his mouth. The other people, Mona, the Kims and the Bernies, remained calm. Mona leaned across the bar so that she could peer at Jonathon; then, satisfied that he'd done himself no injury with the tumble, she went about her business. Mona remarked to Bernie, "Looks like a pretty big one."

Bernie nodded and said, "Encore ein martoony, Moaner."

"Shouldn't we put something in his mouth so that he doesn't bite his tongue off?" I almost shouted. My pockets had yielded nothing but a few crumpled dollar bills. I picked up an ashtray from the bar, but it was full of butts and anyway seemed much too large for Jonathon's mouth.

"He'll be all right," said Little Bernie.

Big Bernie agreed. "Sure. But it looks like a pretty big one."

"Big what?" I demanded, but then Jonathon's lids popped open and his eyes, strangely colored and moist, began to roll around in his head. "Sheesh," said Jonathon, and he struggled to his feet.

Mona had poured a shotglass full of whiskey, and Jonathon's

first act was to shoot it back. During the brief "attack" Jonathon had perspired heavily, and I saw with alarm that tears were streaming down his wrinkled face. "That was a big one," he confirmed. Jonathon lit a cigarette with trembling hands, and after a few drags he was calmer. He wiped tears from his face and gestured for another drink. Then Jonathon turned and looked at me in a way that I've never been looked at before. His cats' eyes seemed like knots in wood, dead and full of circles. "You, sir," said Jonathon, "are an asshole."

"Well, I'm sorry!" I said indignantly. I had to admit that my search for something to place in the Indian's mouth was a little foolish, but accusing me of being an asshole was, I thought, a bit much. "I was afraid you'd bite your tongue off."

"What?" said Jonathon, puzzled.

"I wasn't going to stick the ashtray in your mouth," I added.

Jonathon turned to Mona. "What's he talking about?"

Mona explained, after which Jonathon said to me, "I'm touched by your concern."

"Well then, what did you call me an asshole for?"

"Because that is what you are," explained Jonathon. "Please don't take it personally."

"How else am I supposed to take it?"

Jonathon shrugged, tapped a long ash off his cigarette artfully. "There are worse things than being an asshole."

"Like what?"

Jonathon shrugged once more, not in a manner to suggest he didn't know, more that he was unwilling to say.

"Well," said Little Bernie, "Big Bernie's a jerk."

"Yeah!" said Big Bernie. "I'm a jerko! That's at least just as bad."

"And me," said Mona. "I'm sort of a, you know, slut."

"There!" said Jonathon. "Everyone is something. Bernard's a jerk, Mona's a slut, and me, I'm a drunken fool. Not to mention old and ugly and gay as all get-out."

"How about you guys, Kim?" I asked, saying their shared name rather snidely.

They answered, almost in unison, "We're in love."

"Then you guys are in the worst shape of anybody," I commented.

Jonathon tapped my shoulder. "You see? That was the sort of thing an asshole would say."

Jonathon's remark calmed me, somehow. I took a long sip of the rancid beer and looked around The Willing Mind. "Hope," I said, more to myself than anybody else, "is one crazy fucking place."

"Feeling better now?" asked Jonathon, gingerly laying his long brown fingers (stained yellow here and there with nicotine) on my arm.

"Just once," I said, staring into my ale, "just *once* I wish people would let me in on some of the shit going on around here."

"Like what, for instance?" asked Jonathon.

"Well, for starters, I haven't been to a lot of bars where the guy next to me goes 'Oh-oh,' keels over, then climbs back up and calls me an asshole."

"Oh, well, that's easy enough to explain," said Jonathon. "I had a Vision."

"Sure, why not."

"He has a lot of them," Mona put in. "He doesn't always drop, though, only when it's a big one."

"Sometimes," said Big Bernie, "Jon-Jon just goes like, '*Whoa!*' and has to have a couple more scootches."

"But one time," recounted Little Bernie, "the Mystic One threw himself right out that window over there."

"That was, I presume, a big Vision?"

Jonathon nodded. "The biggest."

"So let me get this straight," I said to the Indian. "You have these Visions. And in the Vision you just had, you saw that I was an asshole. Is that about right?"

Jonathon nodded. "It was very strange. I saw this face, painted to look happy, painted with a big red smile and big eyes like a child's. But the only thing happy about the face was the paint, because the real mouth was sad, and the real eyes were crying. And I saw you. It was because of you the face was crying. You could have stopped the crying, but you didn't. Then you were gone, and a voice said, 'Asshole.' And mind you, the voice sounded like it knew what it was talking about. Then I was awake."

I looked at the inhabitants of The Willing Mind. "Doesn't that sound like one dumb Vision?"

Everyone shrugged, even Little Bernie, the enormous belly jerking up and down.

"Nice meeting all of you," I said. "Now I'm going after Ol' Mossback." I threw two dollars at Mona and left the bar. And as I walked out the door, someone said (probably one of the Bernies), "Keep your dick in your pants!"

Visions

Hope, Ontario, 1983
Wherein our Young Biographer pursues the Art of the Angle, and later has a disturbing Vision of his Own.

Gregory Opdycke's book *Fishing for Ol' Mossback* has this to say:

It behooves me at this time to dispel the spurious "myths" concerning Mossback and his "predilication" for leaping out of the Lake in order to bite various "body parts" from unwitting anglers. Although this "myth" may well have its origins in some bit of "history", the local admonition of "Keep your trouser stays fastened!" is little more than good-natured "frippery".

Rest assured, however, that Mossback is most "acrobatic". I recall once fishing from a "dinghy" in the Lookout, enjoining the company of three "stirpicults", among them Ashley Hope. Ashley (using as "bait" a live "fieldmouse") took a colossal "pickerelle".

It was a glorious struggle (the species' reputation for "lethargy" notwithstanding) but after many a long moment, Ashley managed to lift the fish from the water. The "pickerelle" was levitated to a height of three or four "feet", prepatory to dropping it into the vessel, at which moment Mossback struck, emerging from the lake, rising fully into the air, and tearing the fish from the "line". All that young Ashley had to show for his "day's work" was a largish head, the body bitten off cleanly below the operculum.

I was reading this out at Lookout Lake. The book *Fishing for Ol' Mossback* was first published, at the author's own expense, in the year 1902. (Mine was a reprinting done in 1966, although I didn't see why anyone bothered. Surprisingly, my edition was published by a reputable, and scholarly, house.) I suppose the book's antiquity accounts for the rather free-style use of inverted commas and the stilted syntactical constructions. Certain things struck me as more idiosyncratic, such as the use of that word "stirpicult," which I had never encountered before, and seemed a most unlikely synonym for "fisherman." Mostly I wondered about using a live mouse for bait. (Actually, mostly I brooded over the Indian's Vision.)

Lookout Lake, by the way, was hardly what I'd expected. I'd expected, and longed for, an awesome God-wrought spectacle, alive and colorful and magnificent, something that would make whole my heart, dry the tears that I hadn't the courage to shed. Instead I found a tiny, mucky thing, surrounded by desolate terrain of outcroppings. I realized that the lake wasn't called "Lookout" because of any splendiferous view, it was called "Look out!" because rocks kept dropping out of the sky. The only thing I found soothing about it was the loneliness. No one lived beside Lookout Lake as far as I could tell; there was one cabin by the water's edge, but it was long-abandoned and ravaged by the wilderness.

Beside me I had my fishing gear and a bottle of Harvey Benson's whiskey. I sat on a rock, drinking and leafing through my little book. Soon, I thought, I'll do me some serious fishing.

The most amusing of the "myths" concerning Mossback is the one profferred by the aboriginal community whereby the Fish is granted through some "Power" the faculty of human "speech". Jonathon Whitecrow, for example, despite his impressive talents and "intelligence" (all the more impressive for his being an "Indian") is constantly claiming to have engaged Mossback in "conversation". We have often baited the old man, and I recorded one such encounter. This took place some years ago. Present are the author, Lemuel and Samuel McDiarmid, and Isaiah Hope. We met Whitecrow at The Willing Mind, where we four had gone after a luckless "expedition". It behooves me to state that the McDiarmid twins and myself were slightly "intoxicated", while Isaiah Hope, as was his wont, was well into his "cups". Jonathon Whitecrow seemed sober enough, although this seems unlikely in retrospect, given his "heritage".

Lem McDiarmid: How, Whitecrow.
Jonathon Whitecrow: How?
Sam McDiarmid: How!
Isaiah Hope: I believe they mean "hullo", Jonathon.
Whitecrow: Oh! Hullo, boys.
Lem: Talked to Ol' Mossback lately, Whitecrow?
Whitecrow: Why, um, yes. Just the other day as a matter of fact.
Sam: What did he say?
Whitecrow: He said that he doesn't like fieldmice, and that they are especially unappetizing when someone has stuck a hook through them.
Lem: Oh, yeah? What would he have us use for bait then?
Whitecrow: He would prefer it if you used guile, respect and a fullness of heart.
Isaiah: Far simpler just to stick a hook in some poor mouse, Jonathon.
Gregory Opdycke: I take it, then, that Mossback intends not to be taken?
Whitecrow: This is true. But he doesn't want you boys to stop trying. He thinks life would become rather boring.
Lem: What else do you talk about —
Sam: When you and Mossback talk?
Whitecrow: Just everyday things. How his children are.
Opdycke: He has children?
Whitecrow: Oh, yes. Many.
Isaiah: Does he ever mention my father?
Whitecrow: Often.

Lem & Sam: Does he say that Joe Hope was a man of good taste?

(At this point Isaiah and the McDiarmid twins exchanged verbal insults too "ribald" to recount. They went outside The Willing Mind and had blows. Isaiah, small and besotten, came out "the worse for it". I remained behind and chatted with Whitecrow.)

Opdycke: Does it not strike you as odd, Whitecrow, that a fish should be able to talk?
Whitecrow: Why, yes! Very odd.
Opdycke: Is Mossback, in your opinion, wise?
Whitecrow: Yes, very wise. Mind you, he is a fish. He has a rather limited perspective on things. He likes to tell me, for example, what the water's like. Too hot or too cold. He tells me how much he hates it when people piss into the lake.
Opdycke: Next time you talk to him, tell him that Opdycke means to see him stuffed and mounted!
Whitecrow: I will. Shouldn't you go carry Isaiah home?
Opdycke: I suppose.

Soon I had finished all the whiskey and was so drunk that I thought I was sober. "Time to go fishing," I announced. It took me many long moments to affix my Hoper to the line. Then I stood up and wobbled up to the water. I actually stood up twice, having fallen on to my butt on the first attempt. "Hey, Mossback!!" I screamed. "Here come sumpin' good! Dig your toothies into this, boy!"

I raised the rod and cast. It was a fine cast, and I watched with delight as the Hoper sailed high over the water, flying out far and softly disturbing the stillness of Lookout Lake. I began to reel in, and noticed a certain lack of resistance. Then I saw the end of my line lying a few feet in front of me, the knot unravelled.

"Fuggit," said I.

I decided to go home and telephone Elspeth. It's a good thing I'm sober, I told myself, or else she would never talk to me. I threw my stuff into the moped's carrying bags and climbed aboard. For a few feet I managed a peculiar serpentine motion, and then the moped and I keeled over sideways on to the gravel road. It's a good thing I'm blasted, I told myself, or else that would really hurt! I tried again, and soon I was on my way. The sun was setting, and night had covered the earth by the time I reached the homestead.

The big problem here was to keep my speech clear, evenly modulated and well-elocuted. Elspeth had an uncanny knack for picking out even the tiniest drunken irregularities. What I needed was a crisp, earnest conversational style. I spent about half an hour practicing. "Elspeth? How are you? I'm fine. Listen, I've been doing some thinking and soul-searching out here ..." I was drinking a bottle of beer as I practiced and noticed that this was making the inside of my mouth feel a bit fuzzy. So just before I dialed the telephone, I had a short pull on a bottle of tequila.

The phone rang endlessly, but I knew that she was home. I had a deeply disturbing vision of Elspeth in the sack with some clod, nakedly listening to the phone ring. "Don't worry about it," she was saying, massaging this jerk's chest. "It's just my goddam husb ..."

She picked up the phone, said, "Hello?"

"Elspeth," I said.

"You're drunk."

"All I said was 'Elspeth'!"

"I can always tell."

"I'm not drunk. I been fishing. Fishing for Ol' Mossback, that's what. Mythical fish of the golden tongue!"

"Listen, I don't want to talk to you now."

"Why the fuck not?"

"Because you're drunk."

"What difference does that make? You don't want to talk to me when I'm sober!"

"And when is this that you're sober?"

"I'm sober a lot of the time!"

"I guess I never noticed because I've got a class from nine to ten o'clock in the morning."

"Hardy-har-har."

"I'm hanging up now."

"Don't."

"There's someone here."

A definite low blow. "Who you got?"

"June."

For various reasons, this was sickening news. I gave Elspeth my phone number, told her to call me when I was sober. I hung up the telephone.

It was about ten o'clock in the evening. I was pleased that I'd already done all my important stuff for the day, because now I could fart around for a couple of hours.

Harvey Benson was, among other things, a music lover. One corner of the living-dining area was occupied by a strange futuristic turntable, surrounded on either side by stacks of albums. Taking the bottle of tequila along for company, I went and searched through these records. I could find nothing to suit my mood. (A record called "Tunes for Shriveling Hearts and Souls" would sell well, I reflected.) Still, I wanted music, so I finally elected to play the album already on the turntable, whatever it was. I put on the needle and went to gaze at the night through the picture window.

I can report to you now that the piece of music that filled the room was the "Vocalise" by Rachmaninoff. I didn't know that at the time, having never heard it before. All I knew was that never had music messed around with my innards so violently. I felt like an instrument (an old and out-of-tune one, like a cigar-box banjo) and I was plucked. All the world became beautiful and miserable. Through the window I could see almost nothing but the sky, ink-black, studded with stars. I imagined that I could discern the constellations, that the night was filled with hunters and heavenly creatures. The music seemed to say that there was room in the sky for Elspeth and I, that we could remain forever up there, naked and lonely and tragic in our own small way. I was soon weeping in a very general manner.

I pulled back from the window, having wept, and was caught by my own reflection.

Through the old glass of the window, through my tears, my face looked monstrous. Everything about it was misshapen, the eyes oddly matched and randomly set, the nose squashed and inches away from where a nose should be, the mouth long, twisted and drooling. I wiped some tears away, but nothing changed about my other face.

It came to me suddenly that my reflection hadn't bothered to wipe any tears away. I stepped back quickly then, but it remained glued to the other side of the window. I saw that this being was stark naked, which I was not, and fabulously obese. It had bent down in order that our faces should be level, and now that I had broken contact, the creature decided to stand up. It did so, rising to a height of seven or eight feet. And then this monster began to dance, or at least it began to do a lurid and alien burlesque of dancing, touching fingertips to the crown of its head and sashaying back and forth. This man (a term I apply only in the loosest sense, although he was assuredly male, if only by virtue of a tiny pink penis) was absolutely hairless, even to the extent of lacking eyebrows and lashes.

His dance became more energetic, and the fat began to bounce obscenely — he had fat everywhere, even on the tops of his feet. His arms and legs were clearly segmented by rings of lard, his elbows and knees padded with the stuff, places where only a baby should have it. The music ended, and after a few moments of silence (the creature continued to dance throughout this silence, a silence so profound that I guessed the frogs and crickets were likewise struck dumb by the performance) another piece of music issued forth. This one was quick, almost violent. The monster stopped his dance immediately, cocked his head sideways to listen, and then abruptly turned away. He waddled off into the darkness then, his gait splayfooted and plodding. He had to lift his arms high for balance, his hands bouncing merrily in the air. Soon he was gone.

I decided it was time for bed.

A Beautiful Clown

Hope, Ontario, 1983
Wherein our young Biographer reveals much
about His Self to Everyone, except Himself.

The next morning I managed to complete another paragraph
of my novel-in-progress. I was very pleased with this paragraph,
so pleased that I became profoundly dissatisfied with the previous day's paragraph and deleted it from my thin manuscript.
Then, having done my work for the day, I jumped on the moped
and took me into Hope.

As I rode by Updike International a loud horn blew, and the
workers drifted out on to the front lawn to eat their brown-
bagged lunches. There were hundreds of them, it seemed, and
I found myself wondering what Updike International manufactured.

My first stop in town was Edgar's Bait, Tackle and Taxidermy,
where I purchased another Hoper. This one was slightly bigger
and cost thirty-five cents less. Edgar was in a very good mood
and insisted on telling me some filthy jokes. I laughed heartily
at them all, trying to hurt Elspeth in some cosmic way. These
jokes all had to do with the way certain parts of the female
body smelled, and Ellie would have gone berserk if she'd heard
them. After a while, Edgar's repertoire was exhausted.

I asked, "So anyway, what gives with this 'Keep your dick in
your pants' business, Eddie?"

Edgar shrugged, lifting his mountainous shoulders up and
down quickly. "They say that around here," he informed me
needlessly.

"There must be some story behind it. Like, a guy was taking
a whiz by the side of the water and all of a sudden Ol' Mossback jumped up and bit his pecker off."

Edgar chuckled a bit, nothing even resembling the guffaws
he'd awarded to his own jokes, and then asked, "How'd you
lose your first Hoper?"

"Something bit it off," I lied dramatically. "I was reeling in
and then—bang!—just like that, something bit it off clean as a
whistle."

Edgar nodded. "So, you want me to show you how to tie an improved double clinch-knot or what?"

"Yes, please."

This kept us occupied for half an hour or so. Edgar's hands were so enormous that I actually had to move around, peeking through the occasional gap between his fingers to see what he was doing. Then I practiced while Edgar retold some of his filthy jokes. In time I became proficient at tying an improved double clinch-knot (actually I didn't, I became bored with it) so I stopped and wondered aloud what to do next. "Maybe," I said, "I'll go get a beer."

"Go quaff a frosty," Edgar agreed. "That's a good thing to do."

"Wherever should I go?" I mused.

"You got three choices." Edgar lifted the appropriate number of fingers and counted them off. "One, Duffy's. Two, Moe's. Three, The Willing Mind."

"Which one do you prefer?" I asked.

"You go on over to The Willing Mind," Edgar responded, more an order than anything else. "That's a good place to quaff a frosty."

"Yeah, okay." I decided to confide in Edgar. "But, I'll tell you, Ed. There's this guy there, Jonathon his name is, who kind of gives me the creeps."

"Whitecrow?" asked Edgar. "He's a good guy. A little strange, maybe, but a good guy."

"His name's Jonathon Whitecrow?"

"Indian?"

"Yeah."

"Yeah, his name's Jonathon Whitecrow."

I only knew that the name was somehow familiar. Anything I'd learned from *Fishing for Ol' Mossback* was state-induced, so I had to be drunk again to recall it.

"You want to go quaff a frosty with me?" I asked. Edgar would be wonderful protection against Jonathon Whitecrow and his crazy "Visions."

Edgar shook his head. "Sorry. I can't go quaff a frosty with you." He stabbed his chest with his thumb. "A.A."

"Oh." This news saddened me deeply.

"I'm an alcoholic," he elaborated.

"Yeah, right," I almost snapped, hoping to silence him. "Hey, Edgar," I asked, "what's the difference between an alcoholic and a drunkard?"

Edgar actually thought about this, rubbing his jaw for half a minute before throwing up his arms in wonderment. "I dunno. What is?"

"Us drunkards don't have to go to all those damn meetings."

Edgar didn't seem to realize that this was a joke.

Maybe it wasn't.

"See you later," I said to Edgar.

"Bye-bye, Big Guy."

The day was a scorcher. The Willing Mind lay down the road, shimmering and distorted in the haze. I didn't want to go there, but my alternatives were swallowing a pickled egg whole and eating (not to mention paying for) a steak. "I'll just go quaff a frosty," I announced to the world at large. The taste of Mona's beer came back, reminding me of bogs in medieval England. "Or a little Scotch," I decided. "A little Irish whiskey." This clarity of purpose gave me the wherewithal to begin walking toward the humpbacked tavern. "Pop back a whiskey, that's all I'm gonna do." Maybe the Indian wouldn't even be there, I reasoned, although I knew he would. He'd be standing in exactly the same place, smoking a cigarette, his long fingers touching a half-full shot glass. Jonathon would nod at me as if he'd been waiting.

I was right.

The Bernies and the Kims were there as well, and Mona was behind the bar. They all smiled, but only Li'l Bernie seemed happy to see me.

"Hey, hey!" the stomach shouted. "It's the Hemingway of Hope! Hey, listen, kiddo, I been thinking. Maybe we should collaborate on this book of mine. I even thought of a title: *Straight From the Gut*. What do you think?"

I was in no mood to talk to tummies, so I ignored him.

Mona was dressed in exactly the same clothes, although they were now wrinkled and close to filthy. "Beer?" she asked, very businesslike.

"No, thanks. Maybe some Jameson." I nodded in the direction of the bottle of Irish whiskey.

Jonathon was infuriating in his gentleness. "Hello, Paul."

"Hi."

Then he was silent. I turned away.

The boy Kim had his hand firmly fastened on to his girlfriend Kim's breast, caressing it through her T-shirt. Her nipples were boldly erect.

Mona presented me with my shot glass. "Run a tab?"

I nodded and sipped at my drink.

Big Bernie muttered, "Somebody's cranky."

"The thing about it is," I said suddenly, "my wife is a clown."

"Mine, too," said Big Bernie.

Of course, if I had a nickel for every time that exchange had taken place I'd be a rich man. "No, I mean she's a *clown*. A professional clown."

Jonathon Whitecrow was enlightened. "Aha! That's why there was a painted face! I should have figured it out myself."

"That's pretty inneresting," said Mona genuinely. "With a circus like?"

"She's not with a circus now, but she was. Now she teaches clowning and puts on a few shows at fairs and things." I gestured for another drink. "She's a very good clown," I added. "A beautiful clown."

"It had me worried," Jonathon mentioned. "I thought I was losing it."

"Does she live out there, too?" asked Mona. "At the old Quinton place, I mean."

"No. She lives in Toronto."

"Oh."

Big Bernie asked, "Know any good jokes?" I deemed this a pretty jerky thing to say, given my obvious heaviness of heart. But I think, in retrospect, that Big Bernie was trying to be kind. A chilly silence had entered The Willing Mind, trailing along behind me, and Big Bernie only meant to chase it away. At any rate, no one knew any jokes, good or bad.

The curious thing about Elspeth is that, despite being a clown, she's not a particularly humorous person. She can make people laugh, certainly, can make children hysterical, but in her own heart of hearts she doesn't seem to find anything at all funny. The state of the world alarms her, and in a certain mood I can see that it should alarm everyone, what with the threat of nuclear war and all that shittiness hanging over our heads.

"The way I figure it," said Big Bernie, "there's nothing you can do. If they drop it, they drop it."

"You just bend over and kiss me goodbye," mumbled Little Bernie.

For a while Elspeth fought back, marching in anti-nuke demonstrations, writing letters to the government, that sort of thing, but in the past couple of years she'd abandoned all of it and assumed a position of resolute hopelessness.

"Can't say as I blame her," commented Mona. "It's a no-win kind of thing."

I missed her — not, so much, the grim Elspeth who ejected me into Hope (although I did miss that Elspeth, too) but the one who, when we were younger, made silly, grotesque faces and generally thumbed her nose at the world. The one who used to announce, for no real reason, "Peoples is good folks!" The one who ...

Jonathon laid his hand on my shoulder. I was on my fourth Irish whiskey, rendering me intoxicated enough to make the connection. "Hey! Jonathon Whitecrow!" I said happily, brushing away tears. "How does it feel to be a hundred and seventy years old?"

"I beg your pardon?"

"Talked to Ol' Mossback lately?" I demanded, waving my hand in the air to indicate to Mona that I required yet another shot of booze.

"Why, um, yes. Just the other day as a matter of fact."

"Oh, really? What did he have to say?"

"Well, not much. The water's been hot as soup lately. And, of course, people keep peeing into it."

"I see."

"Sounds pretty fishy to me," chortled Big Bernie.

Little Bernie said, "Geez, what a jerk."

Jonathon Whitecrow lit one of his cigarettes reflectively. "Now that I think about it, he did say something interesting. As you know, Mossback and I share an interest in the human heart. His interest is purely scholastic, of course, mine being more, shall we say, professional. And I was saying that I often long for a purity of heart."

"Me too, me too," I put in eagerly.

"Well, Ol' Mossback had this to say." Jonathon Whitecrow

changed the timbre of his voice, as if imitating the fish. It was a completely foreign sound. "Take this lake. It's got weeds in it, and rocks in it, and dead fish in it, and live fish shitting in it, and kingfishers and herons diving into it to kill fish, and people pissing in it, and everybody in it is either eating each other or screwing each other, right? It's just a normal lake. A good old-fashioned lake. But it ain't pure. The only pure lakes I ever heard about are the ones that have been killed by that acid rain." Whitecrow returned to his normal voice. "Pretty smart, for a fish."

Somehow I'd managed to cheer up. It was, I believe, the combination of a) Irish whiskey in quantity, b) Jonathon's fish impersonation and c) Mona's leaning on the bar to listen to b), affording me an excellent view of her breasts. At the end of the story they jiggled merrily.

"Whitecrow," Mona said, "sometimes I think you are full of shit."

"Too true," said Jonathon Whitecrow.

"Speaking of that," I asked, "where's the john?"

Mona pointed toward one of the room's many dark corners. "Over there, Paulie."

"I'll be back in a minute," I told all of them — they nodded back, except for the Kims who were locked in a soul-kiss. Then I stumbled off for the head.

The bathroom of The Willing Mind was ancient, made from green wood and yellow porcelain. It contained two sit-down toilets, side by side with no partition between them, and a huge stand-up urinal. It was this latter convenience that I used (perhaps I'd originally had other business to conduct, but one look at the loo convinced me against it — spiders, ants and other crawlers roamed about the enamel in hordes) and as I pissed I read the words carved into the rotting wood. Some of the inscriptions were new, a year or two old: "S.M. from the Soo was here," one said; another, "Hope sucks." Far more interesting were the older ones, faded to near-illegibility:

ISAIAH IS A FAIRY
THE McDIARMIDS SUCK DEAD BEARS
DRINKWATER NEVER DOES
TO A QUINTON, EVERYTHING IS RELATIVE

Owing to my usual drunkenness, and to my even more usual dullheadedness, it was only then, standing at the pisser, that I noticed the frequency with which certain names cropped up in the town of Hope, Ontario.

Then I turned around.

The Willing Mind's interior decorator had decided against putting a real mirror in the washroom, probably because glass and drunkards don't get along too well together, and instead had mounted a piece of sheet metal above the sink. The metal was scratched and bent, and when I turned around I saw my own distorted reflection, floating in a silver cloud. I began to tremble. The image of the naked monster in the night came back full force, an image that my mind had managed to lock away for the day. Even though the memory was vivid (so vivid that I could almost hear the music that accompanied it, the heart-twisting "Vocalise") I was uncertain as to whether it had actually happened or whether it was some fabrication of the booze. "Oh, fuck," I moaned aloud. Our little blue world was flying through space, and I felt as if I'd found the cockpit, there in The Willing Mind's john.

I began to search for the radio, muttering over and over again, "Mayday. Mayday."

Part Two

The Veiled Lady

Cambridge, Massachusetts, 1846
Regarding the career of Hope, we know the
following: that he received his Licence to
Preach when he was twenty-two years of age;
that at least one of his Instructors had been
reluctant to award it; that his thinking was
generally thought to be A Tad Maverick.

Joseph Benton Hope had a way of scurrying about — furtive, hunched-over and almost panicky — as if a giant rock had been lifted, and a beetle disturbed. One autumn's day in 1843 he scurried down Brattle Street, took a corner (keeping his frail body very close to the stonework) and entered a small private auditorium. This was the eighth occasion in the past two weeks that Benton Hope had entered this establishment, shoved some coins at the old woman in the booth, and taken a seat in the twenty-fifth, and last, row.

Joseph Benton Hope was very early, forty-five minutes, and all alone in the theater. He opened up his gilt-edged Bible (a huge thing with four generations of Hopes listed inside the cover) and read a line. Truth to be told, he only read two or three words. Then he tilted his head backward, shooting his Adam's apple outward and shutting his tiny eyes (he still had two at the age of nineteen), and allowed the passage to sound somewhere within.

Joseph Benton Hope was the prize student at the Harvard Theological Seminary — at least, he had been up until a year or so back. Scholastically speaking, he was still, excelling in such disciplines as eschatology and hermeneutics, possessing an unprecedented knowledge of the Bible, but his thoughts had lately taken a turn that most of his instructors found unsettling. When Benton Hope had first entered the school at age fifteen, he had been heralded as a prodigy, a young boy perhaps blessed with the gift of prophecy. He had lectured to his fellow students passionately and convincingly — convincingly, for in those days his thoughts were of an immediate Second Coming. "Look about," Joseph Benton Hope had screamed, his voice hoarse, his blond hair slick and matted, "and know that His time is nigh!" His listeners, students and instructors alike, had nodded.

But the Second Coming had failed to materialize, and Hope seemed suddenly to tire of waiting on it. Joseph began to dream of Perfection.

Joseph Benton Hope realized that Perfection — "If by Perfection we mean a purity of heart, an absolute communion with our Heavenly Father, and a complete inexistence of sin" — was simply, even easily, attainable.

Joseph came up with the following regimen, designed to help purge sin from the spirit: repeated fasting for two days (only grains and nutmeats allowed on the third); continuous self-denial (three and one half hours of sleep nightly); exercise (a four-mile walk in the forenoon, six miles in the evening); prayer (five times daily, no small or petty entreaties); three hours of spiritual activity (Bible study and the reading of works of acknowledged theological merit) and contemplation. Joseph Benton Hope found this very effective; emptied of sin, his soul was purged of everything earthbound and sullied.

His teachers and peers wanted none of this. They wanted Beelzebubs and Lucifers. They wanted Hellfire so hot that they burned to hear of it.

The auditorium was perhaps half full now, some twenty minutes before the exhibition began. Benton Hope looked at the people with disdain. Most of them were Harvard men, young louts with rich fathers and small intelligences. Some were townsmen, laborers and farmers, and they found it for some reason incumbent to attend in their Sabbath finery. Joseph snorted haughtily, propelling a thin line of mucus on to his upper lip. He wiped it away and shifted in his seat. Hope realized, with dismay, that he was possessed of an erection.

Joseph Benton Hope was boyish in appearance, looking in all respects to be no older than fourteen. His face didn't need shaving, and his voice was adolescently temperamental. His manly endowment was therefore anomalous. It was long and thick, ribbed with veins, and perpetually insistent on growing even larger. Joseph had been forced to adjust his tailoring, making sure that all his trousers were loose-fitting and roomy. Now, in the theater, Joseph shifted and dug a fist into his groin covertly. He rifled the pages of his Bible and read. When next he looked up, the auditorium was all but full. Two weeks ago, when Benton Hope had first attended, he had been one of perhaps two dozen. Now there were close to four hundred, including many of the faculty. Benton Hope watched as Henry Wadsworth Longfellow dashed through the door. Longfellow stopped, dusted himself and ran his fingers through his sideburns. Longfellow then proceeded into the auditorium, quickly and hurriedly, and Hope was reminded of the familiar Harvard doggerel — "With his hat on one whisker and an air that says 'Go it,' you have the great American poet.'" Joseph Benton Hope attended Longfellow's special lectures on Goethe's *Faust* (which was viewed as a trifle rebellious of him).

Then Dr. Charles X. Poyen walked out on to the stage. He was a small, silver-haired man, gracefully into his middle age, one of the university's most distinguished lecturers. Poyen looked at the assembled (nodding briefly to Longfellow, who was having trouble choosing a place), and then Poyen said, "Good evening." His accent was continental French.

Joseph Benton Hope had, of course, heard Poyen's lecture before. It had to do with Franz Anton Mesmer and his discovery of the fluids (and the empathic balancing thereof) that are inherent in the human body. Not only had Hope heard it before, he had most of the speech written down on the endpapers of various textbooks. After some minutes, the lecture was concluded, and Hope refocused his attention.

Dr. Poyen asked for a volunteer. A young freshman with a peculiar, froglike face virtually bolted on to the stage. Poyen took the fellow by the elbow and stationed him so that his back faced the north. Poyen induced in the lad "human hibernation," the state in which the subject's magnetic fluids are most susceptible to the influence of another's animal magnetism. The young man's mouth dropped stupidly open, and his tongue pressed flatly against his lower lip. "Now," said Poyen, "I would like to demonstrate the powers of the science of Phreno-Mesmerism." The words rang in J. B. Hope's ears, cloaked exotically in Poyen's French accent — "ze poors of ze seance of Phreno-Mezmereezem." Poyen touched his hand to the fresh-

man's head and excited several phrenological sites. When Dr.
Poyen touched the Organ of Veneration the young man folded
his hands together as if in prayer. When Poyen excited the
Antagonistical Site the subject snarled and brandished his fists.

At this point someone in the audience yelled, "You're a
croakus!" For the past several nights, such protests were made
with increasing frequency. Dr. Poyen merely smiled, a trifle
embarrassed, and quoted the great *philosophe* Voltaire: "Those
who believe in occult causes are subjected to ridicule, but we
ought rather to ridicule those who do not."

Joseph Benton Hope was momentarily distracted by the bulge
in his lap. He scowled at it, then looked again to the stage. The
Veiled Lady had been introduced and stood in Joseph's sight.

She was covered with silver drapery, all of her, from the
crown of her head to the tips of her toes. Poyen explained that
this was to separate her from the material world. Benton Hope
was reminded of a cocoon he'd found as a boy, and some part
of his mind envisioned a glorious springtime emergence, even
though the cocoon from his childhood had dried up and turned
to dust. The Veiled Lady moved then, at least her mantle danced
as if touched by a breeze. Joseph sat forward in his seat. He
was certain that light was cutting through the veil, illuminat-
ing the woman within. He had the distinct impression of nakedness. The head of his penis pressed painfully against his
trouser stays.

The Veiled Lady's voice was soft, often unable to break free
of the silver hood, forcing Poyen to repeat her words. "Ze Veiled
Lady," he announced, "needs an assistawnt!"

A young woman was propelled (by a crude type, Joseph
thought, a well-dressed puttyhead with a braying laugh) toward
the stage. The young woman was plump and golden-haired.
Hope's body was wracked with a strange sort of pain, one that
emanated from his groin and tied his stomach in complicated
knots.

The Veiled Lady raised an arm (Hope thought he spied breasts
through the draperies) and touched the volunteer upon the forehead, immediately inducing human hibernation. Then she announced her intention of demonstrating the empathic relationship now established between the two sensibilities. This inten-

tion was repeated by Dr. Poyen, although Benton Hope didn't know why. (Benton Hope likewise didn't know that his hearing had become preternaturally sensitive.)

The Veiled Lady drifted down to one end of the stage, and the young woman was placed at the opposite. Dr. Poyen, standing between them, produced the following objects: a glass ball, a pin and a piece of tree bark. He held them aloft, in the view of everyone (everyone except the young woman, who slumbered in peaceful human hibernation). The esteemed professor (of mathematics, by the way—J. B. Hope therefore assumed that this new world made some sort of arithmetical sense) explained that the volunteer was to enunciate any sensations she might have. Poyen handed the Veiled Lady the glass ball.

Her hand, emerging from within the shroud, was enough to start Hope's poor netherparts screaming. The hand was so pale that it seemed to glow. The other hand appeared, and Joseph doubled over.

The Veiled Lady caressed the sphere gently. After a few moments the volunteer, her eyes closed, her words soft and dreamy, said, "Smooth. Round." There was a smattering of applause. The Veiled Lady was next handed the pin. She pricked her finger with it, producing a small crimson dewbead. The volunteer and Joseph said "Ouch" simultaneously. Then the treebark was touched. The young woman whispered, "Rough. Hard."

Then the Veiled Lady reached within her own silver cocoon and touched something. The subject said, "Soft. Warm."

Joseph Benton Hope's crotch exploded with pyrotechnical fury. His lower half was immediately soaking wet, so wet that he imagined rivers of jism flowing down his legs and collecting in his boots. This ebullition was so intense that it drained the whole of Hope's body.

Having worked at being pure in all things, Joseph had never before consciously experienced orgasm. He avoided his nagging erections with a deep-seated fear that they were not good things — being, as they were, wildly uncontrollable. Yet when he came, for the first time wide awake and aware, *more* aware, it seemed, than he'd ever been before, the feeling was an old one, recognizable. It seemed to recall times and lives he had no present awareness of. It linked him strongly to something he could only understand as human, but felt must be divine. His erections had to be from God. He even checked his Bible, but it seemed obscure. There were references only to "his staff" and "his rod" which shall lead them.

This liquid from his loins, Hope thought, there was something to this.

Liquid

Boston, Massachusetts, 1846
Regarding the Fortunes of Hope, we know the following: that they reached a nadir in his so-called "Black Days"; that he was frequently Intemperate.

Joseph Benton Hope devised the following theory: the word wasn't made "flesh" at all, this being somehow a mistranslation. (The etymology Hope would work out later.) The word was rather made "liquid." Liquid is the basis of the Lord's creation, after all. Did not the Spirit of God move upon the face of the waters? And — this was all preached in a sermon, one of the last that J. B. Hope delivered — when the men of Ai smote them thirty-six men, did not the hearts of the people melt, and become as water? And hearken to the words of the twenty-second psalm: "I am poured out like water, and all my bones are out of joint. My heart is like wax, it is melted in the midst of my bowels." Liquid is the basis of human life, Hope contended. And thus, ye should drink deeply.

Joe Hope became the town drunk, no mean feat considering he had recently moved to the city of Boston. His face was known in every tavern within a twenty-mile radius; known, laughed at, resented and often feared. Joe Hope took to wearing black clothes, and these in turn made his pallor so white as to seem lifeless. Joe Hope would lunge into an establishment with his

Bible held high, and as he drank Hope would quote from the
Good Book endlessly. "Mine heart within me is broken because
of the prophets!" Joe Hope would shout. "All my bones shake!
I am like a drunken man, and like a man whom wine hath over-
come, because of the Lord, and because of the words of his
holiness!" Joe Hope shouted so loudly and for so long that his
voice broke in the most literal sense; it collapsed into his throat,
froglike and inhuman.

Alcohol seemed to be the only thing that could heighten his
awareness and expand him the way his first orgasm had. He
seemed to learn new things and be open to the voice of God.
He thought things he had never thought before. He did things
he would never have done before. He also bumped into things,
broke things and generally found himself wrestling more often with the reality of the physical world. It took its toll. During
one drunken rampage Joe Hope lost his right eye. Various rumors circulated as to how this had happened. One story had it
that he'd been hexing a milk-maiden beneath the moon, forcing her through Phreno-Mesmerism to dance naked and to copu-
late with bulls—according to this tale, the girl's father still had
Joe Hope's eyeball impaled on one prong of his pitchfork. Another story was that a discomfuddled Hope had become over-
exuberant during one of his barroom sermons. "And if thine
eye offend thee, pluck it out! It is better to enter the king ...
dom ... oh-oh." Most likely Joe Hope had stumbled into something, for he had no resistance to alcohol; one or two sips and
he began weaving, and by his fourth or fifth drink he was spas-
tic. So, although his Christmas Eve tumble off the ropewalk
and into the icy Boston Harbor was widely regarded as an
attempt to commit suicide, it seems equally probable that Joseph Benton Hope had but tripped over his own two feet.

Nothing So Petty As Dreams

Boston, Massachusetts, 1847
*Regarding the followers of Hope, we know the
following: that his two most loyal disciples,
George and Martha Quinton, discovered his
seemingly lifeless body in the waters of Boston
Harbor; that George could affect no
resuscitation; that Martha, after her fashion,
beat upon Joseph Benton Hope's body; that it
was revived.*

Joseph Benton Hope was having a strange dream (although from around that point in his life forward, he would acknowledge nothing so petty as "dreams") wherein his body was stripped naked and began to float. Joseph realized that he was entering Paradise, although the journey was bumpier than he'd expected, accompanied by little grunts. The Gates to Heaven also screeched like a door with hinges long deprived of grease. And instead of being blinded by a glorious radiance, Joseph Hope found it increasingly difficult to see, things getting dimmer and dimmer. Hope discovered that he could turn his head to the side, and having done so, saw that his fellow Angels were old men, old gray men from whom Time had stolen body parts; teeth, eyes, even arms and legs. These old men lay on little cots, motionless, and Joseph would have thought them devoid of life except that their collective breathing sent out a great, wheezy wail.

Joseph began to suspect that he wasn't in Heaven, if only because he couldn't imagine that it was necessary to breathe in Paradise. Experimentally, Hope held his breath. For many a long moment Hope was satisfied that he had no need of air. Then his lungs shuddered and forced his mouth open, and Hope pulled in great drafts, more smoke than anything else. Smoke? thought Joseph Hope. Quickly he turned his head the other way, and there in the darkness roared a great red fire. J. B. Hope hadn't truly expected eternal damnation, but he accepted his judgment immediately. He was lowered on to a cot, one just beside the fire, and covered with a sheet.

"Theah," said a voice, "that should keep him all toasty."

At one point Hope opened his eye (this was the ultimate irony of Hell, apparently, that you still had to endure corporeal tediums, your eyes opening and closing, your heart and lungs thudding along without desire or end) and suspended above him was a face. Oddly, this was a kindly face. The man's eyes were huge and slightly crossed, and made the face look a little addled, perhaps even stupid. But the smile he wore seemed genuine and heartfelt, framed on either side by healthy red cheeks. The face moved closer, more of the body coming into view. Hope got the impression of outlandish largeness, for the man's head (which had in itself seemed big) looked dwarfed upon his massive shoulders. Hope closed his eye again, and didn't open it for a good long while. When he did, the face was still there, but now it had transformed itself into a hideous parody of femininity, a wig of girlish blond curls attached to the skull. The eyes, still slightly crossed, had been ludicrously adorned with long lashes, which were being batted rapidly. The face loomed closer, and Hope saw that the mountainous body had been stuffed into female attire, although the musculature threatened to rend the garments to tatters. Hope shuddered, rammed his eye shut and refused to open it again, afraid of any further transmogrifications.

" 'Ey!" came a voice. "This 'ere is Joe Hope!"

"Joe Hope?" came another. "What's he doing here?"

"Not bloody much!" the first voice returned with a phlegmy cackle. "Looks like he's got the ork-orks."

Joseph's body had begun to twitch convulsively, his limbs lashing out, his toes and fingers trembling. Hope had stoically accepted this as some brand of punishment, but this diagnosis of "ork-orks" made sudden sense. Someone gave a second opinion. "That's the whoops and jingles if ever I saw it!" J. B. Hope became almost deliriously happy. He had the whoops and jingles, the blue horrors, alcohol dementia. Joseph Hope opened his eye and announced, "Then I'm alive!"

An old man stood next to his bed, a man whose right arm had been reduced to a tiny stump. "Oh, you be alive, all right, Hope. But once you've had a bowl of Miss Martha's chowder, you'll wish you warn't!"

The old men explained it all to Joe Hope. They were ensconced in the Harbor Light Mission, an establishment operated by George and Martha Quinton. All of them, the old men admitted sheepishly, had been fished out of Boston Harbor by the Quinton siblings. The Quintons (twins, the old men pointed out, although Joseph had deduced that) were fervently religious and, moreover, literalists. They accepted everything in the Good Book at face value, and so, being instructed to become "fishers of men" they'd bought a dinghy and a huge seining net and begun to search the water for unfortunates. These were always nocturnal searches ("That's where they are now," an old man pointed out, "looking for poor buggers who's stumbled in.") and catches were brought to the Mission with amazing frequency. "It's strange," commented one ancient, "t' think that so many are clumsy and wrong-footed," for none would admit to having jumped.

George, they went on, was all right, a large-hearted though somewhat simple man. Miss Martha, on the other hand, was terrifying. The old men recounted beatings they'd suffered at her hands. Joseph listened to each tale patiently, without much real interest; without interest because he knew what the story would be as soon as an old, wrinkled mouth opened. The one instant he'd spent staring into Martha's face had told him much. Joe Hope lay on his cot and waited patiently.

It was around six o'clock in the morning. The men were in a huge room without windows, so that time was suspended like the firesmoke, but J. B. Hope, with his sensitive ears, could hear a bell, somewhere, tolling hourly. The door opened, and the Quinton twins entered. George came first, and Joseph saw that his impression of largeness had been well-founded, although not at all adequate; Quinton was some seven feet tall, massively built. The full-grown man George held cradled in his arms appeared almost baby-sized. George rocked the man slightly, occasionally cooing, "Theah, theah," into his ear, because the man was blubbering incoherently, drowning in emotion. George looked at the room's occupants. "Do you know what it is?" he asked gently. "It's when it wains. Then the docks get all slippy, and no one can keep a toe to them. Now, Mr. Opdycke was just out foh his constitutional—isn't that so, Mr. Opdycke?—and all of a sudden found himself in the wateh! But it's all betteh now."

Joseph Hope found himself wondering why the waning of the sunlight should affect the surface texture of the docks when he realized that George Quinton had a speech impediment and could not enunciate an R. George went to a cot and gently set Mr. Opdycke down on it.

Opdycke was a man in his early years, Hope guessed, although he looked to be the veteran of many deaths, wrinkled on the outside, wasted from within. He was a shocking scarlet color, all brandy-faced, his nose redder than blood and severely grog-blossomed. He wore ludicrously large mutton chops, which gave him the appearance of a baboon.

Martha followed behind, a presence of furious energy. Hope tried not to be alarmed. George wore his grotesque size well, seeming at least natural if monstrous, like a whale or an elephant. Martha was distinctly freakish, every bit as big as her brother, even bigger for her breasts and derriere.

"Don't coddle him!" Martha barked. Her voice sat in a lower register than her twin's. Martha cleared her throat. "Proverbs. Chapter ten. Verse eight. 'He that walketh uprightly walketh surely: but he that perverteth his ways shall be known.' " Martha crossed to Mr. Opdycke, whereupon she roughly and methodically tore off all of his clothes. Despite his blubbering state, some vestige of modesty forced Opdycke to cover his parts frantically. Martha pulled away his hand and glared at the open sores. "And Mr. Opdycke has patently perverted his ways!"

George covered Mr. Opdycke with a sheet; Opdycke pulled it up over his head and whimpered in a tiny way.

Hope swung his legs over the side of the cot, sitting up. He fixed Martha Quinton with his eye and said, "Verse nine."

Putting her massive hands on her hips Martha demanded, "I beg your pardon?"

"The scripture you quoted. It is not verse eight. It is verse nine."

"Is that so?"

"You shall find that verse eight reads: 'The wise in heart will receive commandments, but a prating fool shall fall.' "

Martha and Joseph Hope stared at each other for almost a full minute. Finally, Martha averted her gaze.

"It seems odd," said she, "that one in your sorry state should be so well acquainted with the Holy Word."

Inwardly, Joseph Benton Hope had to agree with the woman. He'd certainly been in a sorry state, drunk continually, tearing off great jagged pieces of his heart and soul.

Joseph Hope rose to his feet. "I, like our Lord Jesus, was made a little lower than the angels for the suffering of death." Hope had no real idea of what he was going to do. He only knew that he had to do something, and he'd known that since the old men had first mentioned the names of George and Martha Quinton. His biggest consideration was this: he had risen with his sheet drooped over his shoulders, for beneath it he was naked. Yet, for whatever he was going to do, he needed his hands, and whatever effect he was going to create would certainly be diminished if he had to waddle around clutching a sheet. This was not a problem of simple modesty, for everyone had been made naked by Martha Quinton, probably in the same ruthless manner she'd disrobed poor Opdycke. (Mr. Opdycke, Hope noticed, was still blubbering beneath the bedsheets.) The problem was that Hope's root was erect.

Joseph wondered at this logically, puzzled by it. He didn't have the time to wait, stalling until his shaft withered away. Furthermore, he realized that his erection was driving him in some small but urgent way. "For verily," Joseph Hope spoke— he'd spoken fast upon the heels of his last words, all of his cogitations done in a thrice — "He took not on Him the nature of angels, but He took on Him the seed of Abraham!" Joseph Benton Hope thrust his arms toward the skies, allowing the sheet to fall. Then, quickly, Hope spun to face George Quinton, who alone (and only for that short moment) had the physical power to stop him.

"Now see heah!" said George, and he advanced on Hope.

Joseph drove the gaze of his eyeball as a carpenter drives a nail. George Quinton stopped so suddenly that his momentum threatened to topple him over. Joseph Benton Hope began to quote from Isaiah, rounding out the edges of his croaky voice. "Is it not to deal thy bread to the hungry that thou bring the poor that are cast out to thy house? When thou seest the naked, that thou cover him, and that thou hide not thyself from thine own flesh?" George Quinton, Hope saw, was motionless, pinned like a butterfly in a collection.

Hope had achieved chilling effects with his readings of the words "naked" and "flesh;" several of the old men were now propped up on aged elbows, one or two were even sitting upright. Hope began to turn, addressing them all. "Then shall thy light break forth as the morning, and thine health shall spring forth speedily! And thy righteousness shall go before thee, and the glory of the Lord shall be thy reward!"

Something was bothering Hope, and he relegated some small portion of his sensibilities to find out what it was. Hope's mind was operating on several different levels at once; searching through Scripture, selecting body movements, regulating inflections in his froglike voice. A very large part of his senses was taken up with keeping himself removed from Martha Quinton. So long as he kept a certain distance (vague, but very real) Hope was all right. As soon as he crossed that invisible line, Martha would beat him to a pulp. And at the highest level, Joseph Benton Hope was merely watching all this, aloof and removed like a general; and, like a general, he was relayed the following message—Mr. Opdycke was still blubbering beneath the bedsheets. This is what had been bothering him, of course; the effect was undermined by this man's pitiful simpers. Hope lowered his voice until it was almost a whisper, only a notch or two louder than Opdycke's sobs. "Then shalt thou call, and the Lord shall answer! Thou shalt cry, and He shall say ..." Hope moved to Opdycke's cot and pulled the sheet away. "Here I am!"

Hope touched his fingers to Mr. Opdycke's head, quickly finding and gingerly exciting the Site of Tranquility. Nothing happened. Opdycke's brain had no doubt been so scrambled by alcohol and disease that nothing was where it should have been. Hope moved his fingertips elsewhere, trying to locate the Organ of Veneration. Still nothing happened. Desperately (although without any visible sign of desperation) Hope simply massaged Mr. Opdycke's lousy skull, hoping to achieve some change in the man's behavior. After a moment, Opdycke stopped sobbing, and even dared to open his eyes. Once Mr. Opdycke's eyes were open, Hope dropped to his knees, his own eye descending as a hawk descends on a rabbit. "And if thou draw out thy soul to the hungry, and satisfy the afflicted soul, then shall thy light rise in obscurity, and thy darkness be as the noon day."

"I couldn't help killing her," Mr. Opdycke said to him, almost conversationally.

"And the *Lord*," Hope howled quietly, "shall guide thee continually, and satisfy thy soul in droughts." Hope sprang to his feet, drawing the old men upward with him so that they were all sitting, withered and wrinkled. Hope looked at the most emaciated of them. "And make fat thy bones!" he cried. "And thou ..." Hope spread his arms, including them all. "Thou shalt be like a watered garden, and like a spring of water, whose waters fail not." Hope gestured lightly toward the skies, and all of the men stood up, even Mr. Opdycke, all of them naked as newborns. Now it was time for the dangerous part. Joseph Benton Hope turned around and began to advance on Martha Quinton. "And they that shall be of thee shall build the old waste places," he hissed. Martha's eyes were fastened on Hope's staff, which he knew was huge; it throbbed and ached and longed to burst. "Thou shalt raise up the foundations of many generations." Joseph was crossing the threshold. Martha Quinton's eyes leapt up to meet his, terrified but defiant. "And thou shalt be called," Hope whispered, "the repairer of the breach, the restorer of paths to dwell in."

Joseph Hope now stood a few inches from Martha, almost touching her with his root.

Martha dropped to her knees.

Perfectionists

Boston, Massachusetts, 1847
*Regarding the teachings of Hope, we know the
following: that his concept of a sinless
perfection was greeted by some small
enthusiasm by the lay community, though the
Church viewed it with a measure of
skepticism.*

"Perfection," Joseph Benton Hope said, "must be available for
all men and women, and salvation must be a continuous process, not a fixed achievement."

The faces were all flushed and smiling blissfully. Joseph let a
silence hang in the air, then he gathered it up into his small
hands and lowered his head in prayer.

They did likewise.

It was a small assembly, but they more than made up for it in
enthusiasm, proudly labeling themselves Perfectionists and ex-
tolling the thoughts and virtues of their spiritual leader, Joseph
Benton Hope.

The most loyal were the Quinton twins.

George took care of the more practical things, replacing the
cots in the windowless room with rows of chairs, building for
Hope a lectern, and outfitting the exterior of the edifice with a
new sign. George took down the one reading:

Harbor Light Mission — Geo. & Mtha. Quinton, Props.
"In Whom the Lord put Wisdom & Understanding To
Know how to Work All Manner of Work for the
Service of the Sanctuary."

and put up a sign that announced:

The Harbor Free Church, est'd. 1847
Dedicated to the Attainment of Earthly Perfection
The Most Reverend J. B. Hope
"With the Pure Thou Wilt Show Thyself Pure," Ps. 18:26

Martha had done the actual recruiting, first persuading friends and acquaintances to attend, then starting to work on the general populace. Martha had many and varied recruiting techniques, ranging from thoughtful arguing to insistent badgering to physical overpowering. Hope himself had seen Martha literally drag a gentleman in off the street, his ear locked and twisted between her mighty fingers.

Mr. Opdycke, poxy and consumptive, had remained with them since the "Meeting in the Mission," as they all referred to it. Mr. Opdycke had proven himself a valuable asset. For one thing, Opdycke was very demonstrative in his faith, forever dropping to his knees with great, gleeful cries of "Hallelujah!" For another, his love for Hope was boundless. Mr. Opdycke's open sores had started to vanish the instant Hope had touched him, or so it seemed, and his heart had been filled with a wonderful warmth.

When J. B. Hope had first declared that all people could be perfect, Mr. Opdycke was sure that he alone would be the exception. He was so far from perfect it was almost humorous. His horrendous conduct aside, Mr. Opdycke's physical being was imperfect to the extent that his stomach refused to hold down food, his pecnoster pissed red and at all other times discharged a smelly yellow stuff, his eyes colored everything various hues, and his brain jumbled memory and delirium until they formed a nightmare that Opdycke suffered through every minute of the day. But, miraculously, Hope had then pointed at Mr. Opdycke, there at the "Meeting in the Mission," selecting him as an example. "This man *can*," Hope intoned, "*must* be, and *shall* be perfect!" This was when the warmth came, a flood in his ravaged body. Mr. Opdycke sank to his knees, and suddenly he had a memory from his boyhood, and he with clarity recalled the words to a hymn. Mr. Opdycke began to sing. "I was heavy laden once with guilty sin, but it's all gone now ... "

"Stop!" commanded Joseph Hope, and Opdycke did so, instantly. "Singing," said Hope slowly, "serves no earthly purpose. It is a crude imitation of our angelic life-to-be. As such, by its nature, singing is imperfect. Therefore, refrain from song."

This was considered by some to be the oddest thing about

the Free Church, the fact that no singing was allowed there. The local clergy had other concerns. It was an odd and unsettled time for established religion, perhaps because the nation had only recently been born out of revolution, and a sense of idealism and adventure still hung about the countryside like fog.

In the church's view, Joseph Benton Hope was a small, but nagging, problem. His Perfectionist doctrine flew in the face of prevailing theological thought: that thought being, "If all of you lowly debased sinners don't pull up your socks, God is going to fry you eternally." The popular religion those days was terrifying, even demonic, its ministers blackclad and given to pitching fits. Joseph Hope was idiosyncratic in his thinking, certainly, but he was cut from the same cloth. He preached in the orthodox sense, he quoted from Scripture and taught the life of Christ, and he was charismatic, that is, fired up with the Spirit. There were others far worse; lunatics who claimed that nakedness was man's natural state and therefore preached in the nude to an assemblage of nudists.

There was a sect that had concluded that the faculty of speech was an aberration not intended by our Creator, and these people never spoke words, never even wrote words down, living a life of total silence and, presumably, extreme poverty and hunger. One man had counted up all the letters in the Bible and found that the astronomical total was divisible by thirteen, from which he concluded that the Good Book was in truth some cunning forgery of the Devil's. Fortunately, some other man had totaled the letters himself and discovered that the original tally was off by 1, but the clergy still had to wonder at all the energy being poured into these peculiar pursuits.

The most troublesome of all was Theophilius Drinkwater. At least the others found their individual peculiarity and held on to it fervently; Drinkwater's mind was a fertile garden of weirdness, and it seemed as if his theories and beliefs changed daily, attacking the church from different angles and positions so that it was impossible to find a suitable defense. Theophilius put out a weekly periodical called *The Battle-Axe & Weapons of War* (Drinkwater was well aware of the violent aspects of his struggle with the church) and in that small tabloid he made his very odd ideas known.

His specific heresies changed all the time, but Drinkwater harped on certain themes. For instance, Theophilius was no great lover of clothing, although, being a Bostonian, he acknowledged its occasional convenience. It was another of his beliefs that too much was made of the idea of "Hell," that it was a threat sneaked into the Bible by purposefully mistranslating the Hebrew for "grave." Where Theophilius acquired his linguistic erudition was something of a mystery; what was most alarming about this last theory was that the man presented a very strong case.

Drinkwater's other constant theme had to do with marriage. Although seemingly happily espoused, Theophilius didn't care for the institution, writing and publishing in *The Battle-Axe & Weapons of War*:

> Men and women had better change their partners twenty times over, under the best regulations they can make with each other, so as at length to have one with whom they can live in harmony and be then in the order of God, than to live in any kind of strife and disagreement and live in the order of the devil.

Compared to this, J. B. Hope's occasional writings (likewise published in *The Battle-Axe*: those interested should read "Malevolent Benefactor: the Influence of Theophilius Drinkwater on Joseph Benton Hope," *The Journal of American Antebellum History*, vol. 4, no. 15) seemed to the church almost sweet in their innocence. Hope wrote, in a calm, eloquent way, of the "perfection" possible to mankind. The notion was laughable, certainly, but contained no virulent threat. If Hope and his people chose to ignore their very natures (for we are all sinners in the hands of an angry God) and wake up one morning to find Mephistopheles stoking the furnace, so be it. In fact, the church would have been perfectly willing to ignore J. Benton Hope, except for one small, worrisome thing. His congregation included an inordinate number of girls. Fully half of his followers were young, marriageable women. Something, the clergy felt in their bones, was amiss.

Most of the young women were there because Polly Drinkwater had told them about Hope and his preachings with such passion and excitement that it would have been impossible to stay away. Having seen J. B. Hope once, the girls kept coming back.

It was not his teachings that drew them, for although Perfectionism was a sweet song, it was the only one Hope sang, and it soon became tiresome. What drew them was Joseph himself. He was a boyish-looking man, even angelic, his head topped with long flaxen curls. The eyepatch sat on his face deeply black, an exhilarating discord, speaking great mysteries. (It would be two years before kind-hearted George Quinton would make a gift to Joseph of an oversized, pale blue glass eyeball.) Hope's mouth was perpetually fashioned into a crooked sneer, even when he talked gently of paradise. Hope's voice was in itself arresting, a queer croaking thing, jagged as broken glass. His stint of debauchery had done little to change his lithe, muscular body.

The only thing demonstrative about Hope was this small body, a fact of which Joseph was ignorant. While he preached, Hope moved constantly, prowling about the room, making large circles, bouncing up and down on the balls of his feet, shaking his fists in the air as if offering to do battle with invisible demons. And finally, although not one of the girls would admit it even to herself, it was often readily apparent that Hope's manly endowment was incongruous with his small frame.

Polly Drinkwater, seventeen years of age, slim and golden-haired, was madly in love with Joseph Hope. (Mind you, Polly Drinkwater was madly in love with a number of older men.) For his own part, Joseph thought Polly overwhelmingly beautiful. Her one imperfection, so slight that it was hardly noticeable, was that her left eye was askew. Beyond the fact that she was beautiful, Joseph knew nothing about her. So, when one Sunday Polly invited him to dinner, Hope accepted without knowing that he was about to make the acquaintance of the mad old heretic, Theophilius himself.

If All Flying Wants Is Wings

Boston, Massachusetts, 1847
*Regarding the contemporaries of Hope, we
know the following: that he made the
acquaintance of Theophilius Drinkwater; that
they argued over points of theology; and that
some measure of enmity was established.*

Theophilius Drinkwater lived in a tiny, tiny house because he
was a tiny, tiny man. He escaped actual dwarfdom by an inch
or two—inches never granted by nature, Joseph thought. Drinkwater's boots appeared to have inordinately thick soles, but
even given these Theophilius only managed to achieve the brink
of normalcy. Drinkwater made up the difference by perpetually jumping up and down, lightly and rapidly. That's what Drinkwater was doing when he met Joseph Hope at the door of his
tiny, tiny house. "Ah, Mr. Hope!" shouted Theophilius. His voice
was an operatic baritone, cultivated to further the illusion of
height. "So pleased you could come!" Suddenly Theophilius
bounced heavily on the balls of his feet, propelling himself upward so that he could grab hold of Hope's shoulders. Thus suspended, Drinkwater planted a large, wet kiss directly on to
Joseph's lips. Then he dropped back to the earth.

Joseph drew the back of his sleeve across his lips.

Theophilius watched, bemused. "Hope!" he barked. "Don't
tell me that you put credence in those madmen who say that
disease is caused by minuscule animals invisible to the naked
eye?" Drinkwater laughed scornfully.

Joseph didn't, in point of fact, but he shrugged as if the notion merited some thought.

"Disease," shouted Drinkwater, even though his sole listener
was inches away, "is an outward manifestation of inward dis-
cordance! If the soul is not complete and harmonious, the body
will inflame with sores and pustules!" Theophilius Drinkwater
nodded, agreeing with himself enthusiastically. "We must talk
about that sometime," he said to Hope.

Drinkwater was wearing a dress, or such had been Joseph's

first impression, although upon closer examination the garment would be better described as a "robe," long and white, held together loosely with a length of hemp, as if Drinkwater had stepped out of a color plate in the old Testament. Theophilius's beard was long, white and angry, falling almost to his knees. If Drinkwater was, say, sixty years old, then he would have had to have been growing his whiskers since age five. The top of his head, however, was hairless and pink; it reflected no perversity on Hope's part that he was reminded of a female behind.

"Might I call you 'Joseph?' " asked Theophilius.

Hope, staring blankly at Drinkwater's face, nodded.

The odd thing about the face, even odder given Drinkwater's near-midget stature, was that all of his features were grotesquely oversized. His nose was a huge vegetable-like thing, warted and twisted, his ears distinctly elephantine. And Drinkwater's eyes looked bigger still, immense and perfectly round, like those of a nocturnal animal.

"Come in, Joe," said Theophilius, bouncing up and down and waving his arms toward the interior of the house. "Come in and meet the family!"

Joseph took a hesitant step forward.

He had learned, prior to coming, who Polly was, who her father was. Martha Quinton had informed him, bluntly and petulantly, as if something angered her about Joseph's dining elsewhere. "I've made your favorite dinner," Martha had muttered. Joseph shrugged, trying to be apologetic, although he reflected that he had no favorite dinner, and even if he had it would be rendered nauseating, at best tasteless, by Martha Quinton. "Go have dinner with the great Theophilius," she'd said. "You'll be sorry."

Joseph had dismissed all this as a manifestation of some obscure jealousy. In fact, Hope had a measure of respect for Drinkwater, if only because *The Battle-Axe & Weapons of War* published his articles. But as he stepped into the Drinkwater household, Joseph suspected that Martha may have been right.

Hope had expected to be greeted by Mr. and Mrs. Drinkwater, Polly and perhaps a brother or sister. Instead, Theophilius introduced Joseph to a mob. "Polly you are acquainted with. 'Polly' is the familiar for 'Polyphilia,' denoting an all-encompassing love. This young fellow is Jakeh, this is Caleb, this is Sarah, this is Manasseh — stop that Manasseh! — this is Ephraim ..."

The young man indicated made some objection.

"Oh! *This* is Ephraim, *that* is Hebron, and this is the fair Jezreel ..."

On and on Drinkwater went, pointing at the huge crowd that was his family.

The younger children were all naked, and the others wore Biblical robes like their father. The line of delineation seemed to be around the age of thirteen, and one of the daughters, Manasseh, was absolutely nude despite swelling breasts and a light sprinkling of pubic hair. It hardly mattered, as the robes were all of a light cotton material and very loose. Polly's robe, for example, had opened in the front, and her bosom was spilling out, pink-nippled and bursting with dainty blue veins. Polly was either ignorant of this or simply didn't care. She nodded shyly at Hope and bit at her thumbnail.

"And here is the fair matriarch, Rose!" shouted Theophilius.

Mrs. Drinkwater waddled forward, a fat and kindly woman. Her robe was likewise opened, the better to nurse a small newborn she held cradled in her arms. "Good of you to come, Reverend," she said. "I've enjoyed your correspondence in *The Battle-Axe.*"

Hope bowed graciously.

"Yes," nodded Theophilius, "you write very well. And it's not *absolute* hogwash, that much I'll grant you!" Hope realized that this was meant as a compliment, but he still bristled. He looked over at Polly and their eyes met. Joseph Benton Hope smiled, a quick smile that vanished from his lips in an instant.

"I have a spare robe," said Theophilius, "if you'd be more comfortable."

Hope was indeed uncomfortable. His clothes, black and heavy, had been tailored for him by Martha Quinton, who was no better a seamstress than she was a cook. They were uniformly too tight, always squeezing air from his body. Still, he declined the offer.

Joseph turned to look at his surroundings. Despite the size of the house, the great horde of Drinkwater offspring were all of normal stature and seemed crammed and cramped inside.

The interior of the house had no partitions, and all of the household activities took place in the one room. The walls were lined solidly with books, stacked up until they met the ceiling. At the back of the room Hope saw a line of pallets on the floor, actually one very long pallet, and he imagined that at nightfall the family lay down all together and in no prescribed order. Also toward the back was a pot-bellied stove and a large tin bathtub (and, Joseph noted with small alarm, after the introductions had been made, one of the older Drinkwater daughters, Jezreel, had climbed into it and was soaping herself vigorously). The most prominent piece of furniture was a dining table that sat in the middle of the floor; in fact, other than the complementary chairs, this table was the only piece of furniture. Theophilius Drinkwater waved J. B. Hope toward it. "Come, Joseph," he said, "let's argue!"

The children disappeared on this cue, Joseph had no idea where. Polly went to aid her bathing sister, taking the soap and applying it to Jezreel's back. They shared some soft laughter and Joseph felt himself turning red.

Theophilius jumped on to a chair and pointed at another for Joseph. From where he sat Joseph could view the bathtub. Polly was scrubbing her sister with such energy that she'd shaken the robe from her shoulders.

"Um," said Theophilius, putting a long-stemmed pipe into his mouth, "here's what I think. Um ..." Drinkwater lit a match, crushing the white tube between his fingers so that it fizzled and exploded into flame. His arm was so short that he had to extend it to its length to suspend the fire over the pipebowl. "I think that man is intended to live in the water." Drinkwater grinned craftily.

"Pardon me?" asked Joseph.

"Man," said Theophilius. "In the water. Like a fish."

At this point Polly stood up, letting the robe fall to her ankles. She got into the tin tub with Jezreel.

"Dumbfounded, eh?" shrieked Theophilius. "A bit nonplussed, are we?"

"Why," asked Joseph quietly, "do you think that?"

"Because, was not man given dominion of the fish of the sea?"

Polly, her hands full of lather, began to soap herself.

"Man was likewise granted dominion over the fowl of the air," muttered Joseph. "Do you therefore feel that he should be able to fly?"

Joseph didn't pay attention to the old man's answer. As she soaped the back of her neck, Polly was looking at Hope and smiling.

"What do you say, Hope?" shouted Drinkwater.

"I beg your pardon?"

"Man! Flight! Like a bird!"

Joseph shrugged indifferently. "I deem it a physical impossibility."

"Then, sir," Theophilius screamed, "you're no better than the rest of them!"

"Do you sincerely believe that a man could fly?" asked Joseph, his eyes fastened on Polyphilia. She was lathering something below water level, her eyes still fastened to his.

"Yes indeedy-deedy-do!" returned Theophilius. "I'd be a damned fool if I didn't! And stop staring at my daughter, man! She's got nothing but bubs and a pranny like any other gal!"

Hope sheepishly turned his eyes downward.

"Now, Joseph," said Theophilius, firing another match-tube because he'd yet to get the tobacco properly burning, "tell me why, in your opinion, flight is forever denied to mankind."

Joseph stared at the patently insane old man. Drinkwater was fuming, smoke curling around his monstrous nose and ears, more smoke than could have been produced in the small pipe-bowl. "Well," said Joseph, "a bird has certain physical attributes that make flight possible. Wings, for example, and tail-feathers."

Theophilius Drinkwater jumped down from his chair and began to bounce up and down. "A man could fashion himself wings!" he hollered. "Wings and tailfeathers!"

Jezreel and Polyphilia splashed each other with water, rinsing the suds from their naked bodies. As they did, the two young girls screwed their eyes shut and turned their faces up, laughing.

Joseph muttered, "I suppose."

"Here's what I think," said Theophilius Drinkwater. "There are no limitations placed upon man. He was granted dominion over the earth, sea and sky, and I believe that the Lord meant us to take our rightful place in all of those realms. We need air to breathe, surely, and cannot subsist on water like the fishes. But what is preventing us from taking air into the water with us, carrying it below the surface in bottles and Mason jars? And if, as you state, the Lord did not give us wings, did He not give us birds aplenty, thereby handing us detailed instructions of how such wings could be constructed?"

Joseph Hope realized that Theophilius was saying, or shrieking, all this off the top of his head. Hope was impressed, possibly even a bit exhilarated by the extempore creation of lunatic theory. Jezreel and Polyphilia, now rinsed and glistening, rose to their feet. Polly had a rump like a gazelle's, thickly muscled and taut.

"If all flying wants is wings," Theophilius said, the amplitude of his bounce increasing steadily, "then we are fools to have been so long earthbound. Man should be in the sky, in the clouds, near the stars! There is no heavenly body beyond our reach. We could live on the moon!"

Drinkwater giggled as if even he himself found this notion ludicrous. Possibly for that very reason, Theophilius began to defend it passionately. "We could do it, Hope! Start a new world, a new civilization, on the moon! A world dedicated to harmony, harmonious intercourse with our fellow men and women, and harmonious intercourse with our Lord! You and I, Joe!" Drinkwater was bouncing high into the air at this point. Hope half expected the old man to crash through the ceiling soon, to bounce up into the heavens. Jezreel and Polly were toweling themselves, bending this way and that, affording Joseph new and unique angles to view.

"We make ourselves wings," Theophilius bellowed, "and, because I've heard there's little air beyond the clouds, we get the missus to bottle us some air in Mason jars!"

Joseph realized, with a start, that Drinkwater was suggesting all this as a feasible and practical course of action.

"Then we go to the moon, you and I, and Polly and Jezreel, all of us, and we recreate the garden of Eden!"

Mrs. Drinkwater, who was seasoning some food over in the corner, laboring over the black pot-bellied stove, reminded her husband, "You've a meeting a week Thursday."

"Quite right," nodded Theophilius, "we must go a week Friday. Hope! What are you doing a week Friday?"

Jezreel and Polyphilia were putting their robes on again. Joseph answered, a bit stupidly, "Nothing in particular."

"Let's go to the moon!"

Joseph Hope answered, "I think not."

Drinkwater's bounces began to diminish in height, and in some moments he had stopped altogether. "I thought you were a man of vision," he snarled. "All your talk of 'perfection.' Now I see you just wanted to make things simple, more easy to understand. You can't see past the end of your own nose, unless it's to stare at my daughters. What you need, boy, is a good shagging, make you realize that the world doesn't spin because of twammies and justums!"

Theophilius spat, the stuff getting caught in the hairs of his mustache and beard. "J. B. Hope, the great religious innovator," he muttered sarcastically, "sitting here and glowing like firewood because two young gals are taking a bath, which is a common daily occurrence, as well it should be." Theophilius Drinkwater sternly crossed his arms. "You won't do, Hope," he decided. "You won't do at all."

Joseph rose to his feet. He enjoyed the sensation of towering over Drinkwater. "And you, sir," he said, his voice almost inhuman when he spoke quietly, "you are quite mad."

"I am the greatest religious thinker of our age," responded Theophilius matter-of-factly. "I am a prophet, and have been chosen to write the next installment of the Bible. You, on the other hand, are a small, insignificant speck of dust, a little tiny ant with a great big thingummy!" Drinkwater gestured toward Joseph's crotch.

Mrs. Drinkwater came over with a huge pot of soup. "Boys, boys," she admonished them gently. "Let's be friends."

"I've no intention of being friends with this young, small-minded puppy!" barked Theophilius.

"And I," countered Joseph, "have no intention of being friends with this old, crack-minded ... dwarf!"

Theophilius launched himself at Joseph with tiny fingers fashioned into claws. Drinkwater raked his nails over Joseph's face, tearing off the black eye-patch, raising long red welts on Hope's pale skin. Joseph made no move to defend himself. Instead he began to search frantically for the covering to his empty eye socket. He ignored the weak little blows that Theophilius was administering.

"*Dwarf*!!?" screamed Drinkwater. "I'll pummel you to a pound of horsemeat, then we'll see who's a dwarf!" Joseph found the patch and affixed it on his face even as his face was being slapped by Theophilius. Then Joseph simply shrugged, and Drinkwater flew away, crashing into the chairs and table.

"Get out!" screamed Theophilius Drinkwater.

Joseph decided that it was a bad time to ask for Polyphilia's hand in marriage.

The Modern Novel: What Purpose Does It Serve?

Hope, Ontario, 1983
Wherein our Young Biographer takes part in a
Conversation of Literary Interest, and his
Friend Benson is Delighted.

You know you've progressed beyond the rudimentary, abecedarian levels of fucking-up when, at thirty years of age, you're caught sitting on your bed, hunched over your own meat, grinning like Mr. Monkey, consumed by lust.

This is what happened to me.

Harvey Benson appeared in the bedroom doorway and exclaimed, "Aha! Having a tug at Wee Willie, are we?"

I had awoken with the sort of rock-hard erection that only multiple hours of drunken half-sleep can bestow. So I recalled making love to Elspeth and tried to deal with the thing as best I could, using said memories as accompaniment.

Our love-making, by the way, was of a very satisfying nature. After ten years of practice, Ellie and I were very good at getting each other off. "How's that?" one or the other of us

would ask constantly. "That's, um, fine." "Okay?" "Sure, okay."
There was very little in the way of passionate grunting and
gasping when Elspeth and I made love. There was instead a lot
of conversation.

"Does that hurt?"

"Nope."

"Okay."

"Hold on. I think there's some air trapped up there."

"Right-oh."

"Okay, go."

"Is this good?"

"Not really."

"How about more like this here?"

"Sure, okay."

"Is that good?"

"Yeah, this is nice."

"Okay. Then I'll just get up on my knees."

"Sure. Fine."

"Here we are."

"I can't breathe."

"Sorry."

"Don't mention it."

"Okay?"

"Okay, go."

Anyway, Harvey's entrance into my bedroom had the effect
of shriveling my boner to near nothingness, despite his ad-
monitions of, "Don't mind me. Just pretend I'm not here." It
struck me that this was a new attitude on the part of my dick,
this throwing in the sponge and knuckling under at the slightest
pressure. My dick, formerly a "Never Say Die" kind of guy, had
become a quitter.

I'd noticed it the week before with Elspeth, when we were
still happily married. I was making love to her. We'd maneuvered ourselves into the doggy position and I was on my knees
and knuckles, merrily, obliviously, thrusting in and out of Ellie.
Elspeth had begun a low humming, which meant that she was
on the brink of orgasm, as was I. Suddenly, I was filled with this
quick and awful foreboding. This had also been happening more
frequently, this sudden dread invading my being, so much

so that I'd considered getting one of those Medic Alert wrist bracelets that would clearly explain "Suffers acute fits of depressing epiphany and realizes that everything is overwhelmingly fucked: administer booze and any/all other available drugs." My sweat turned clammy, and my knees gave out. My dick all but disappeared. "Return to Mothercraft!" I bellowed, and Elspeth and I collapsed, fortunately at the moment of her climax. I pretended to have come, too; I ran my fingers through Ellie's hair. Elspeth, shuddering beneath me, asked, "Return to Mothercraft?" Ellie's hair was everywhere, all over the bed, raven-black and smelling somehow of leaves in autumn. I wiped my tears away with her hair. "Sometimes you're weird," Elspeth noted with characteristic clarity.

"No, it's a natural thing," Harvey went on. "I don't masturbate myself, but that's only because I get laid so much."

Harvey lies through his teeth.

My wimpy dick now wanted to go to the bathroom. I couldn't see going through life with that mamby-pamby attached to me. I jumped off the bed and plodded toward the staircase. Harvey Benson trailed along behind me. "Wow," said he, "is your ass ever flabby."

The staircase led down to the kitchen. I emerged there to find three young girls seated at the table drinking tea.

"Here's the great Canadian novelist!" roared Harvey, blocking my only avenue of escape. I covered my private parts and made a valiant attempt to smile. "Paul," Harvey went on, "I'd like you to meet some students of mine ..."

"Harv, could I just pop off to the washroom first?"

"It won't take a second. This is Sheila."

Sheila was a rather obese girl with a great bubble of curly black hair. She said "Hi" and I nodded.

"And this is Lee ..."

Lee was tall and blondish. She wore spectacles with extremely thick lenses that distorted her eyes, making them appear huge and fishlike. Lee waved, and I waved back.

"And this is Sara."

Sara was a small, dark girl with gray eyes. I'd rarely seen a sadder looking face, and her attempt to fashion that face into an attitude of friendly greeting almost broke my heart. "Want some tea?" asked Sara. Her voice was thick and sultry and seemed to come from deep in her throat.

"Um, maybe in a minute. I'm going to the john now."

"We're having a seminar," explained Harvey. " 'The Modern Novel: What Purpose Does It Serve?' We thought you might have some insight, even if you are a baseball novelist and a tad on the trivial side."

"I'm going to the john," I snarled at Harvey.

"Oh, right. Sure."

I headed off for the can, wondering if my ass was really as flabby as all that. I spent a long time in the washroom before emerging, modestly wrapped in a huge towel.

Harvey was saying, "Fine, fine, we can decide that the novel should be a political tool. But, and this is the thing, the danger is of the medium becoming a vehicle for propaganda! What do you think, Paulie?"

"Well ..."

"Paul is apolitical," explained Harvey to the young women. "A moral coward through and through."

I wouldn't say that, Harv," I protested. "I mean, I'm concerned about the state of the world."

"You're concerned about the state of your own sweet ass!" Harvey laughed. Harvey has one of the ugliest laughs imaginable, desperate and rhythmic, too loud by a hundred decibels.

"I think I'll go throw some clothes on," I muttered.

"Hey, you don't have to because of us," said Harvey quickly. "I was just telling the girls."

"Huh?"

Lee said, "Yeah. If you're a nudist, that's cool." The two others nodded gracious agreement.

"Sure," said Harvey. "I mean, hey, it's no big thing."

"Harvey, might I just have a word with you?"

"By all means, Paulie." Harvey followed me up the stairs and into my bedroom. I shut the door behind us and whispered, "What the fuck are you doing?"

"We can get those chickies naked, no sweat!" said Harvey urgently. "Did you check out the snoobies on that Sheila? Fucking out to here! And they all got young skin, not a wrinkle between them."

"I thought you were conducting a seminar."

"I can conduct it with them in the nude! It'll be great. I think we can get an orgy happening."

"I don't want to get an orgy happening."

"I want to get an orgy happening."

Harvey's trouble was, he was fairly ugly. Not very or profoundly, just fairly and obviously. He was short, bald and paunchy and looked years older than his actual age of thirty-seven. Harv sported a long beard and wire-rimmed granny glasses, relics from his hippie days. Harvey was also chock-a-block full of hormones. "All you got to do is go back downstairs naked," Harvey continued, "and I'll say like, 'Look how comfy Paul is,' and then I'll suggest we all take off our clothes." Harvey grinned evilly, and looked like one of Santa's helpers on dangerous drugs. "Think of all those twenty-year-old asses," he whispered, "all puckered and perfect!" Harvey Benson smacked his lips.

"I'd like to help," I said, "but I ain't gonna walk around naked. I'll just stay up here and read, and you can tell them I don't have any clothes on."

"You gotta help with the seminar. You're the only novelist in the house."

"Anyway, I thought you told me you never use this place."

"I said I hardly ever use it. Sometimes I conduct seminars here, on weekends."

I'd lost track of the days. "Today's Saturday?"

"Right."

"Harvey ..."

"Please!!" Harvey folded his hands together imploringly.

"No." To show Harvey how adamant I was about the whole thing, I began to pull on clothes.

"Stop!" he bellowed quietly.

I put on my jeans and pulled a T-shirt over my head. "There," I said.

Harvey Benson looked close to tears.

"Look," I said, my heart softening toward the little man, "conduct the seminar outside, in the sun. Then, when they get hot, suggest a refreshing swim in the pond. They'll get naked, just like that." I snapped my fingers, or at least I tried to, producing only a fatty, almost inaudible sound.

"They will?"

"Sure."

"Okay, okay!" Harvey was almost beside himself with excitement. He ran down the stairs and burst into the kitchen slightly sweaty and out of breath. "Outside!" he roared. "Let's go outside and conduct the seminar in the sun!"

"Sure," the girls said.

I entered the kitchen behind Benson.

Sad-looking Sara asked, "Are you coming, too?"

"Yeah," I answered, and the girl turned her thick lips upward in a brief and pitiful smile.

The day was gorgeous. I turned my head upward and examined the sky. There wasn't a cloud to be seen, only a bright blue stretched from one end of the world to the other. High in the sky was a hawk, turning lonely, savage circles.

The five of us sat down on the grass near the pond.

"God, it's hot," said Harvey, and he undid two or three buttons on his shirt.

Down at the other end of the pond was a great blue heron. The bird crept toward the water on stilty legs, his head moving back and forth slowly. When the heron reached the edge it remained motionless for a long moment, frozen as if struck by a sudden thought or memory, and then it lashed forward. Its head was briefly in the water and resurfaced with a fish writhing in its bill.

"Who do you like?" asked Sara. She seemed suddenly embarrassed by the quality of her question. "I mean, who do you like to read? What novelists do you admire?"

"I like a lot of writers," I started.

Harvey added, "Goddamn, it's hot."

"I like, for instance, John Gardner a lot."

There was a general shaking of heads and tsking of tongues.

"You guys don't like John Gardner?"

Lee answered, "He sucks. All that 'moral' shit." Lee said "moral" as if it were a dirty word, and she said "shit" like it floated in the air. "Let's face it," she went on, "the world is going to hell in a handcart, and who needs books about people in Vermont who are totally oblivious?"

Sheila nodded. "*Grendel*," she pronounced, "was not a bad little book. Cute, I would call it."

"And where," Lee pondered aloud, "does Gardner get off

writing that *On Moral Fiction*?" Lee proceeded to make her point in a non-academic fashion. She rammed her long forefinger down her throat and gagged.

"I thought he made some valid points," I said.

"Bullshit! He writes all this dumbo crappola, *Mickelsson's Ghosts* and *The Sunlight Dialogues*, both of which are totally laughable, and then he goes and says nasty things about the few writers who are making valid points!"

"Like whom, pray tell?" I demanded.

Lee named someone whose work I had never read. I had, however, gone out drinking with him on one occasion. I was aghast. "The man's a psychopath! He weighs four hundred pounds and carries a gun! He's an ..." I stopped myself.

"Irrelevant," snapped Lee. Something in her eyes dared me to add "alcoholic" to the list. "His work is socially meaningful. He deals with what this warped society has come to, *ultima ratio regum*. Not like your boy Gardner. Gardner is stuck in Vermont and places, writing about these, these *people!*"

"Gardner's dead, you know," I told them. "The man got wiped out on his motorcycle."

"Irrelevant," was Lee's assessment of this information.

"Christ, Harvey," I said, half laughing, "what the hell are you teaching these people?"

Harvey pulled off his shirt. Harvey had an incredibly hairy body; tight little curls covered his chest, shoulders and back like a two-inch pile rug. "Whew," he puffed, "it surely is hot."

"Who else do you like?" asked Sara.

"Well, let me see." I decided to proceed in a cavalier, devil-may-care manner. "I like Charles Dickens."

The answer received a good many titters.

"You guys don't like Charles Dickens?"

"I guess there's nothing wrong with him," said Sheila, "if you happen to like comic books."

"Or," I proceeded bravely, "James. Henry James."

"Sorry," said Lee.

"What the hell do you mean, 'sorry?' "

"Why don't you read someone who has some inkling of what's going on?"

"And what the hell is going on?" I almost shouted. "I don't

know what the hell is going on."

"That's because," Sheila said calmly, "you don't read the right people."

"How about Graham Greene? John Fowles? They might have some slight conception, some vague glimmer in the back of their minds ..."

Lee interrupted. "Let's please keep this serious."

"Hey!" I shouted. "I'll tell you who I like. I like old farts. I like Hermie Melville and Tony Trollope."

There was giggling and even a couple of guffaws.

"Get this!" I screamed. "I like Nathaniel fucking Hawthorne!"

Lee and Sheila laughed with derisive delight. Sara stared at me sorrowfully.

"I got an idea," said Professor Benson. "Let's go swimming."

"Good idea," said Lee. She climbed to her feet and pulled off her shorts. Her underwear was red and very tiny. Lee reached behind her and yanked at the string that fastened her halter-top. It fell away to reveal small, elegantly fashioned breasts. She began to walk toward the water, taking off her underwear en route, a deftly executed maneuver that involved some nimble footwork. Finally, at the water's edge, she removed her thick spectacles. The glasses were the one item Lee seemed reluctant to shed.

Sheila pulled off her shorts and removed her top. A mosquito immediately landed on the right breast, probably crazed by the sight of the white, fleshy mountain. Sheila squashed it, her tit bouncing back and forth. She brushed at her breast vigorously and gave me an impish look. "Hawthorne," she snickered, and ran off for the water.

Sara pulled off her shorts slowly. They were too tight, and her white underwear was dragged downward with them. For some reason Sara tugged her panties back up, took off her shorts, and then pulled down her underwear. "Coming in?" she asked me.

"Sure." I began to pull off my clothes.

Sara waited for me, idly scratching her backside.

"Coming, Harv?"

Harvey's eyes were glazed like an opium eater's. He seemed incapable of speech. Sara and I left him sitting there.

The Thing Contained in the Night

Hope, Ontario, 1983
Wherein our Biographer presses his Friend
Benson for information and is Set Upon by
Hobgoblins, both tiny and large.

"What a great fucking seminar!" said Professor Harvey Benson.

Harv and I were sharing drinks out on the flagstone patio. From where we sat on our chaise lounges we could see the pond. It was feeding time for the little fish, and therefore for some big birds as well, the heron down at the far end, two kingfishers closer to us, and the scene was one of subtle, muted massacre. I concentrated on the kamikaze kingfishers. They soared at an altitude of twenty or thirty feet and then suddenly plummeted as if shot, diving into the water. I knew, from watching "Mutual of Omaha's Wild Kingdom," that in the world of nature the odds are four to one in favor of the prey, against the predator. As I watched the spearing and skewering that was going on in the little pond, it occurred to me that I wouldn't take those odds.

"Yup," nodded Harvey. "Just a great fucking seminar."

The seminar had resumed after the girls and I had our little swim. Sara, Sheila and Lee hadn't put their clothes back on. Instead they'd assumed various naked sunbathing positions around Harvey, directing him to start afresh the discussion of the modern novel and its purpose in a world that was about to get nuked into nothingness. Harvey Benson had done so, although it required for him a superhuman act of will. The girls flipped over like meat on a barbecue spit. After almost three hours of discussion the three young women rose and put on their clothes, announcing their intention of hiking through the woods. I pointed out the pathway, warned them against poison ivy, and they set off for the hills. Harvey watched them leave, smiling like a man who'd lived a long, good life and was now prepared to throw off the mortal coil. "What a great fucking seminar," marvelled Dr. Benson.

He and I had made drinks, and now we were drinking them in the great outdoors.

"So, Harvard," I said.

"So, Paulie."

The mysteries of Hope seemed too many, too jumbled in my own mind with sadness and drink. "How long," I asked, "does a fish live?"

Harvey was oblivious to the quiet carnage taking place at pond level. He shrugged and sucked on a cigar. "Maybe three, four years," he told me. "I don't know. Maybe longer."

"So then, I take it that you personally don't believe in Ol' Mossback?"

"Believe in him?" said Harv, his voice rising. "Man, I fucking seen him!"

"Oh yeah?"

"I was fishing over there at Lookout Lake," he remembered, "and I saw some bird come flying across, real low over the water, and all of a sudden ... kerpow! ... Ol' Mossback comes up, grabs said birdie by the throat, and then they were both gone. Christ, that motherfucking fish has got to be like six feet long!"

"No shit?"

"I wouldn't shit you about something like that," said Benson with great sincerity.

"I bought a book about him," I told Harvey. "*Fishing for ...*"

Harvey completed the title, "*Ol' Mossback*, sure," and even knew the name of the author, "by Gregory Opdycke. It's a classic."

"It is?"

"Sort of." Harvey reconsidered and changed his opinion slightly. "It's a well-known book."

"Hmm!" I decided I'd have to finish reading the thing. "So, anyway, I been spending some time down at The Willing Mind."

"I figured you would," nodded Harvey. I had the impression he was still viewing the girls' nude bodies somewhere in his bald and twisted head.

"There's a guy there who's in the book," I mentioned quietly.

Harvey said, "No way. The book was written eighty, ninety years ago."

"I know. But it's the same guy. Jonathon Whitecrow, the guy who talks to Ol' Mossback."

Harvey pulled himself forward in the chaise lounge and began to look around, searching for something or someone.

"What are you doing?" I asked him.

"Looking for Rod Serling," Harvey answered.

"Come on," I snapped, a little annoyed.

"Did it ever occur to you," asked Harvey, "that some guys have fathers and even grandfathers, and that sometimes they have the same fucking name?"

"Oh." I had to admit, it hadn't.

"I know Jonathon Whitecrow," said Harvey. "He's that old, gay Indian, right?"

"Right," I nodded. "The guy who has 'Visions.' "

"Yeah, yeah! He had a Vision about me once. Told me I was going to meet a very extremely beautiful young chickie-poo."

Well, I thought, it was good to know Whitecrow didn't bat a thousand.

"He had a Vision about me, too," I said. "He saw Ellie crying."

Harvey took a puff on his stogie emphatically. "Don't you worry about that!"

"Huh?"

"Don't worry about it, that's all." Benson finished his drink and waved the empty glass at me. "Want another?"

"What did you mean, don't worry about that?"

"Just don't worry! Why worry? Relax and work on your novel!"

"Harvard," I said sternly, "what did you mean?"

"Okay. All I know is, I saw Ellie on the street last night, just by accident, and you don't have to worry about her crying, that's all I'm saying. You were worried about it, I'm here to tell you not to be. Drink?"

"Why shouldn't I worry about it?"

"Why? Because she was happy. Okay? Don't worry."

"Why happy, how do you mean happy?"

"Gay, carefree! Waltzing down the street with friends!"

"How many friends?"

"How should I remember? Friends!"

"How many, Harvard?"

"One."

"Male or female?"

"Do you want another drink or what?"

"Aaah!" A horde of invisible hobgoblins began to beat on me. One pummeled my stomach, another kicked me a series of stern ones to the groin, and three or four took turns boxing me about the ears. The most awful of them, the Bruce Lee of the hobgoblin set, poked his fingers through my ribcage kung-fu style and ripped out my heart.

Harvey went to fix me another drink.

By the time Harvey returned I'd somehow driven the manky little gits away. My system was on standby, waiting for a deluge of alcohol. I sipped at my beverage (Harvey had thoughtfully made my favorite, a concoction we called "The Top Shelf in a Pail") and once more attempted to make conversation. "In town," I said, "they call this the old Quinton place."

"That's because" — Harv sang some thriller-type music, bumba-bum-ba — "it is. A man named Quinton used to live here."

I thought of the naked monster in the night. "Harv ..." I began.

The three girls came back, all wearing queer and disgusted faces. Sad Sara looked sadder still.

"Do you know what's up there?" demanded Lee. "Up there on that path?"

"It's gross," said Sheila, as if she were giving us hints.

"A deer," said Lee, "with its goddam throat ripped out!" Lee buckled her hands on her hips, making this clearly my fault.

"What would do something like that?" asked Sara.

"Dogs," answered Harvey. "Probably just a couple of dogs. And I'll tell you what else. After they killed that deer, those dogs trotted on home and hunkered down in the family room to play with the kiddies, and they have names like Fido and Rover and Prince." Harvey puffed on the cigar. "That's the way it is, baby."

Lee sat down on Harvey's lap. "What's for sups?"

"Tonight," said Harvey, *"linguine à la Bensoni."*

I caught Sara looking at me. Sheila and Lee might have been living in expectation of a nuclear holocaust; Sara was clearly waiting for fallout.

After dinner, Harvey produced the dope. Harvey was always in possession of dope, although that night the holdings didn't amount to all that much, three or four joints, a nugget of hash and a little white pill.

"What's the pill?" the girls and I demanded in unison.

Harvey examined it, raising his granny glasses on to his forehead and squinting like a jeweler. "I think it's acid," he decided, bouncing it on an open palm as if he could learn something from its weight. "I think."

I lost interest. I had a head full of naked monsters, giant fish and Elspeth screwing others with gleeful abandon. Sara, Sheila and Lee remained in the running. Sheila, whose curls had become an even bigger bubble, dropped out graciously. "Me, I think I'll get tanked on booze tonight."

"Good idea, good idea," seconded Harvey.

Lee likewise declined, although not so graciously. "Acid sucks," she said. "It's as bad as Nathaniel fucking Hawthorne."

That left Sara. Sara was the most sober of us, having spent the evening slowly sucking on a bottle of beer. Harvey handed her the pill. "Go ahead, take it," he told her gently. "You'll hardly notice it. Today's stuff is nothing like it was in the old days." Harvey turned nostalgic. "Hey, did I ever tell you girls that I was at Woodstock?"

"Where?" asked Sheila.

Sara popped the pill willingly.

It dawned on me that everyone was planning to spend the night. I did some arduous mental arithmetic, adding up the number of people present and dividing by the number of bedrooms available.

Harvey put a record on the turntable, some piece of new wave shit to show the girls that he was hip. Professor Benson began to bounce up and down, explaining that this was how one danced to such music. Sheila joined him, jumping with such vigor that her halter-top exploded away from her breasts. Sheila giggled and didn't bother to reattach it. Lee found a book on the shelves, some novel translated from Swedish, written by a man whose name was surmounted by a row of double periods and full of slashes through the "o"s. The cover notes seemed to say that the author was so depressed that he committed suicide several months before the novel was even begun. Lee sat down in the easy chair and began to read. I located a bottle of booze and wandered outside.

Sad Sara followed me, carrying a lit joint. We walked down to the side of the pond and didn't say a word.

When we went back to the house, Harvey and the two girls were no longer in the living room. I could detect a furious giggling coming from the second bedroom upstairs, and it was Harvey's, his asinine laugh excited into tiny little yelps. I went over to the stack of records and located the one I'd played the night before. Only then did I read the title of the piece, out of the corner of my eye, so that I could name it for Sara in an offhand way. I set it on the turntable. Perhaps I'd done this to impress the girl with my alleged sensitivity, but as soon as the "Vocalise" filled the air my knees weakened and I had to sit down in the big chair. The composer, Rachmaninoff, seemed to have insight into my tiny life and problems, every note and chord corresponding to some ragged piece of my spirit's tale. Here's Elspeth in bed with someone else, sang the lovely melody, here's a sky full of moon and stars, here's the last pull from a bottle of whiskey, here's sad Sara sitting down on your lap. I kissed Sara and rudely yanked off her top. Sara arched her back as she kissed, feeding her breasts toward me.

The chair we shared faced the picture window, and in the middle of the kiss (Sara's tongue was like a friendly neighbor on moving day, popping in and saying, "Hi! How're ya doin'? Need any help? My name's Phil!") I opened my eyes.

The monster was there.

Again the thing was dancing, huge and naked. When first seen the monster's back was toward me, one hand reaching awkwardly toward the moon, and as he revolved I saw that the other hand was at his groin, two enormous fingers tugging at his penis, jerking off in the style of a seven-year-old. The monster's dick was as tiny as it had been the night before, but it had achieved the horizontal. One of the monster's crooked eyes was aimed at Sara and I, the other was closed in transports of rapture.

"Ouch," mumbled Sara, without removing her mouth from mine, and I realized that I had been squeezing her breast overly hard.

"Let's go," I mumbled back, "upstairs."

Sara was eager, and set off for the staircase, and thankfully she never saw the thing contained in the night.

Being Foolish

Boston, Massachusetts, 1848
Regarding the character of Hope, we know the following: that, with the exception of a few hours on an autumn's day, he was never in his lifetime foolish.

Joseph Benton Hope, some months after his meeting with Theophilius Drinkwater, entered the kitchen of his residence (he and the Quinton twins lived in rooms above the Free Church proper) to find George drinking tea and eating bread and butter. George immediately looked sheepish, because it was late in the afternoon and Martha would disapprove, claiming that George was spoiling his appetite. The truth of the matter was, George Quinton had so healthy an appetite that nothing short of a complete turkey dinner could come close to ruining it. Still, George didn't like to annoy his twin. He was relieved to see that his discoverer was Joseph Hope, although George still felt guilty in a vague but profound way.

"Bread and butter?" said Joseph. "Whatever would Martha think?"

"I'm sowwy," mumbled George.

Oddly, Hope laughed, or at least the short birdlike noise that he produced sounded more like a laugh than it sounded like anything else.

"George," said Joseph Hope, "I was ..." Hope searched about for the right word. "I was teasing."

"Oh!" George was puzzled. "Teasing me?"

"Yes. Go on, eat. I won't breathe a word of it."

George Quinton tore off a chunk of bread and buttered it lavishly. He put the whole thing in his mouth and began to chew.

"George," said J. B. Hope, "I've been foolish."

George began to make protestations, but his mouth was full of bread and butter. He swallowed desperately and said, "Neveh, Wevewend Hope! Not you."

"Yes, I have." Joseph pointed his bony backside to the fire

inside the belly of the stove. "I meant to be."

George must have looked very alarmed, because Hope produced the queer birdlike sound again. "I was with Polyphilia," Joseph started to explain, but then something occurred to him. "Isn't that a lovely name? Polyphilia," he murmured softly.

"It's vewy nice," agreed George. "But ..."

"We were out for a constitutional, over in the park. And all the leaves were on the ground, you see, and some children had gathered together an enormous pile right in the middle of the walkway. Might I have some bread and butter, please?"

George frantically began to prepare a piece. He was clumsy by nature, even more so because of his agitated state. George got more butter on his finger than on the bread. He handed it to Hope, who said, "Thank you, George."

"Vewy welcome, Wevewend."

Joseph Benton Hope looked surprised. "Is that how you call me? Wevewend—that is, Reverend?"

George nodded hesitantly, trying to think of options. "Your holiness" came to mind as a possibility.

"Call me Joseph," said Hope. "Why, call me Joe!" he decided suddenly.

George didn't think he was capable of calling Hope "Joe."

"At any rate," said Joe, "as I approached the leaves, I turned toward Polyphilia and said something. I disremember what. I always disremember what I've said to Polyphilia, although I seem to have perfect and total recollection of what she says to me." Joseph took a moment to marvel at this truth.

"You tuhned to Miss Polly and said something," George prompted him.

"Indeed. You see, I pretended to be oblivious to the existence of the pile of leaves. So when we walked into it, I made to be very startled. I shouted 'Egad!' and I fell into the leaves." Once again Joseph produced the short birdlike noise. "Don't you see, George? I was being foolish."

George nodded, considering Hope's story carefully. "I don't know that it was foolish," George said slowly. "It seems to me that you wuh making mewwy."

"That's it," agreed Hope with enthusiasm. "I was making merry. Although one has to admit I was being foolish as well."

Hope sat down at the table with George. "I must say," he confided quietly, "I enjoyed it. I've never been foolish before."

"No! Not even as a boy, Joe?" George had used the familiar without thinking. He reared back, alarmed by the ease with which it had tumbled out of his mouth. Hope seemed to think nothing of it. Joseph sat across the table, shaking his head in a thoughtful manner. "Not even as a boy."

George reached for more bread and butter. "I have been foolish many times," said George Quinton. He licked a gob of butter off his hammerlike thumb. "Martha never has."

"Martha? No. Heavens, no, I should think not!" Hope's face was twisted oddly. George, staring into it, realized that Joseph was grinning.

Suddenly, George Quinton was filled with a vast sadness. For a moment he was not sure why, and then his thoughts caught up with his emotions. Joe was in love with Polyphilia Drinkwater, George understood with a quick pain. George understood further that the love was a tragic one, for various reasons. One reason was, Polyphilia was a trollop. Every month or so George Quinton would sneak out of the house and take his monstrous body over to The Sailor's Wife, a groghouse down by the docks. George would drink ale and whiskey, buckets of it, but he wouldn't get drunk. Drinking made most men dullheaded, but not George. Alcohol seemed to give his thoughts clarity and precision; often it seemed to give George insight and even scraps of knowledge he hadn't had before.

George Quinton would actually converse at The Sailor's Wife, talking with men about politics, religion, whatever subject wanted discussing, which more often than not was the subject of 'Woman.' George Quinton therefore knew that Polly Drinkwater had lain with many men. He'd learnt about it at The Sailor's Wife, drinking and talking. George didn't understand all of what the men said — a fellow once told him, for instance, that Polyphilia enjoyed it "in the back door," which George found a baffling statement; another man said that Polly's favorite food was "the living sausage, covered in cream." When the men said things like this they winked and chortled hellishly. If half of them — even three-quarters — were lying about it, Polyphilia Drinkwater would still have had, at her eighteen years of age, scores of lovers.

Now, even if Polyphilia were pure and virginal (and, George reflected, it was very unchristian to think the worse of her for not being) Hope's love would still be tragic because her father hated him. In all of Boston only one man seemed ignorant of Theophilius's immense dislike for J. B. Hope, and that one man was Joe himself. The other thing that Joseph didn't know was how vicious and underhanded Drinkwater could be and, sadly, how powerful.

The reason Hope was ignorant of all this is that on a superficial level nothing in his relationship with Drinkwater had changed. If anything, it had improved. Joseph still sent his small articles to be published in *The Battle-Axe & Weapons of War* and Theophilius still published them. In the past few months, Drinkwater had given Hope's articles front-page prominence, often summarizing their contents in bold type at the head. J. B. HOPE SAYS THAT HE LIVES WITHOUT SIN or HOPE PROCLAIMS HIMSELF PERFECT. Joseph interpreted this as some indication of professional respect; even George could see that Theophilius only meant to get Hope into deeper trouble with the established church.

George realized that Joseph Hope, while sitting at the kitchen table eating bread, had been recollecting his boyhood. George felt a burning shame, because he had not been listening. He'd been thinking of these other things, and now knowledge that might have enriched and enlightened him was lost to George forever. Quinton shook his massive head and concentrated on listening.

"Apparently," Hope was saying, buttering bread in a quick, efficient manner, dividing the pieces between George and himself, "I spoke not at all until I was three and a half years of age. And when finally I did speak, it was to quote Scripture. Do you know, George, I'd memorized the Bible, cover to cover, by the time I was nine? I was made quite an exhibition of. My father would have me at his side as he preached, and when he came to quoting, he'd tap me on the head, tell book, chapter and verse, and I would speak them. Go ahead, George."

"Pahdon?"

"Try one. Book, chapter and verse."

For a long while George could think of nothing, not even one of the books. Then he remembered—slowly the story came back, Jesus and his apostles—"St. Peter," George said happily.

"The first or second Epistle?"

"Fust," George decided arbitrarily. And then he selected some numbers. "Chaptuh thwee. Vuss fowah."

" 'But let it be the hidden man of the heart, in that which is not corruptible, even the ornament of a meek and quiet spirit, which is, in the sight of God, of great price.' "

"Vewy well done, Joe." George clapped his hands together enthusiastically, producing cannonworks in the small kitchen. "Vewy impwessive."

"I suppose," agreed Hope. "At any rate, it impressed at the revival meetings."

George Quinton experienced another shock of understanding. He saw that Joseph Hope's Christianity, a stately refined thing, was a direct attack against the brand of religion that was currently all the rage. George Quinton had gone to revival meetings, he knew what went on there. First of all there was singing, at the outset calm and harmonious, and then a demonic, black-clothed man would appear in front of the crowd. This man's first word was always *you* and it was always shouted, and it was always accompanied by an accusatory, all-inclusive sweep of the forefinger. "*You*"—and then the voice would fall away to a mere whisper—"sorry, sinful people." The man would next begin to catalog their sins, speaking as if it were common and public knowledge what they'd all been up to. "There is *lust* in your hearts, there is *anger* in your bones, there is *pride* in your haughty spirits!"

Everyone would nod, secretly hoping to sneak one by the nightclad preacher, though no one ever did. "Gluttony! Sloth! Lechery! Drunkenness!" The people would turn red, try to take their eyes away from the preacher. By this time the man's voice had risen again, and the list of sins was accompanied by a fine mist of spit.

This wasn't even the worst part. Once he'd gotten through all that, the preacher would tell them what they could expect in the Hereafter due to this astounding amount of wickedness. Eternal damnation, and the preacher seemed to have firsthand experience of Hell and could describe it very graphically. "Have you ever put your finger into candleflame? Well, recollect that pain — but do not confine it — oh, no! — do not confine it to a fingertip, because it will consume the whole of your body, from the hair on your head to the ends of your toes!! And it shall be the flame of a thousand *thousand* candles!! And it shall be everlasting."

This was something George Quinton had never done, stuck his finger into candleflame, until he'd heard a preacher suggest the analogy. Then George had gone home and tried it. "There will be weeping and gnashing of teeth!" Gnashing of teeth, upon first hearing, didn't seem too bad to George, until he'd spent a few minutes gnashing his own late one night. The sensation made his skin crawl, made him feel as if serpents, snakes and eels shared his bed. He couldn't sleep after that.

Once the people were all profoundly terrified, the preacher would announce the existence of "Good news and glad tidings!" If he'd done his job well he'd have to spend several minutes harping on the announcement before the people were inwardly settled enough to listen. The good news was, of course, that you could accept Jesus as your Savior, something all of them had been doing on a weekly basis for years. The preacher would read to them from the Bible, words repeated countless times. Then it was singing again, only this time the singing was frenzied, all hand-clapping and thigh-slapping, full of desperate jubilation. The people would sing until they were exhausted, and then they'd fall back into their seats to wonder how many days, hours or minutes it would be until they sinned again.

Again, George was guilty of not listening to Joseph Hope. George shook his head, dug a finger into his ear as if some plug of wax had been hampering him.

"So," Hope said, "by the time I was fifteen and attending Harvard, my boyhood was spent, and I'd never been foolish. I had done nothing even vaguely boyish, with the possible exception of fishing. But fishing always seemed to me a very serious pursuit."

George Quinton nodded for a long time, much longer than he wanted to in case Joseph suspected that he hadn't been listening. "Joe," said George finally, "do you want to be foolish now?"

"Here in the kitchen?"

"Yes. Wight heah." George himself had a profound wish to be foolish and, moreover, knew that tonight he'd make one of his secret nocturnal expeditions to The Sailor's Wife.

"Shall I pretend to lose my balance?" asked Hope.

"No, Joe." Later that night George would marvel at how many times he'd addressed Hope as "Joe." "Let's dance, Joe. That would be vewy foolish indeed."

"Dance?"

George Quinton nodded.

Joseph Hope thought about it, then sprang to his feet energetically. "Let's do, George! It's very foolish. Very, very foolish!"

George Quinton rose and folded Joseph into his arms. Hope's face met George's belly, his hands wrapped around the giant at waist-level. George began to hum a waltz. The two turned about the kitchen, George bumping the table, knocking over chairs, Joseph lightly hopping from one foot to the other. They danced until an all-too-familiar voice demanded, "What are you doing?"

George gently pushed Joseph away. "Sowwy," George said.

Martha stood in the kitchen doorway, her shoulders hunched so that her bonnet wouldn't be knocked askew. She looked red and windy; leaves clung to her enormous boots. Martha carried bags and parcels, minuscule in her arms. She asked once more, "What are you doing?"

"Sowwy!" said George, louder and more miserably.

"We are dancing," answered Hope. "Executing a small terpsichore. We are," he proclaimed grandly, "being foolish."

Martha set down her parcels on the table. "You've never danced with me," she mentioned, and then her eyes lit on the heel of bread, the many crumbs and patches of butter. "George," she said sternly, "you've been eating before supper."

George was disconsolate. "Sowwy," he moaned.

"You'll have ruined your appetite," Martha snarled.

"George is a grown man," said Joseph Hope. "If anything, he is overly grown. I hardly think a little bread and butter takes up much room."

Martha clenched her fist, even raised it into the air a little. Then she stuck it into one of her bags and came up with the mail delivery. "Here we are, Reverend Hope." She spoke quietly. "We must do the Lord's work."

The mail was two pieces, one a letter, the other the latest edition of *The Battle-Axe & Weapons of War*. Joseph had little interest in the periodical, because he had contributed nothing to it himself. Lately his mind had been too full of Polyphilia to think of other things. Joseph was about to toss the magazine aside with a show of disdain when something caught his eye. T. D. ANNOUNCES WEDDING PLANS said a banner on the front page. "T. D." was how Theophilius Drinkwater referred to himself within the pages of *The Battle-Axe*. Joseph held the newsprint close to his eye and read:

For many a year, T. D. has had his own private misgivings concerning the institution of matrimony. But age perhaps grants wisdom, and T. D. has seen that his philosophical musements must not (can not!) offer a deterrent to the Godwrought workings of the *coeur humaine*. Therefore, it is with pleasure that T. D. bestows his blessing upon the proposed nuptial union of the fairest flower in his primogenitive bouquet, POLYPHILIA ROSANNA, and a fellow worker for His Greater Glory, BUFORD SCROPE DAVIES, most Rev. T.D., however, refuses to abandon his complaint re: the sectarian nature of Modern Worship, and insists that the ceremony be held Out of Doors, under His everwatchful Eye.

All are welcome.

The date of the wedding was two weeks away.

"What's the mattuh?" asked George gently.

Buford Scrope Davies was a man who, although he had all the mental propensities for insanity, lacked the moral courage to be outrageously insane like his mentor Theophilius. Hope seemed to recall that Davies was clubfooted and fat, some thirty years Polyphilia's senior. Hope noticed that his little hands were shaking, badly in need of something to do. Joseph reached quickly for the letter, tearing it open. His eye devoured the message angrily. J. B. Hope (Joe no more) crumpled the letter and flung it away.

"What?" asked George.

Martha retrieved the letter, opened it out, and read. She then summarized the contents for her twin brother. "It's from the Association of the Eastern District of Massachusetts," she said. "They have taken away the Reverend's licence to preach."

"By what wight?" screamed George. "On what gwounds?"

The grounds, as stated in the letter, were, "Intoxication. Consorting with prostitutes. Heretical thought." The first charges stemmed from Hope's period as a drunkard—although he hadn't consorted with prostitutes in the physical sense, he had been guilty of talking to them, preaching at them. The heretical-thought charge, of course, was leveled against the concept of Perfectionism.

George Quinton found himself in tears.

"It doesn't matter," croaked Joseph. He was staring at *The Battle-Axe & Weapons of War.* "I have taken away their licence to sin, and yet they keep sinning. They have taken away my licence to preach. I will keep preaching."

George Quinton understood that Joseph Benton Hope would never be foolish again.

Upped

Boston, Massachusetts, 1849
Regarding the disciples of Hope, we know the following: that there were few of them; that they were very loyal.

Joseph Benton Hope did indeed continue to preach; what's more, he upped the intensity of his message considerably. This drove away many of his followers, but others came to replace them.

Cairine McDiarmid was a small woman with coal-black hair and green eyes. Cairine always dressed in mourning, complete with a veil the color of midnight, a veil she lifted only when watching J. B. Hope. Cairine was thirty-one years old, and for the first while everyone felt a vast pity for the very young widow, until it was discovered that she had never been married. The mourning clothes, Cairine McDiarmid explained with an accent more musical than music, were for the world in general. Cairine was a great one for prophecies of doom, and once started she would sing them endlessly. "*Wahr* larks abaht the carner," Cairine would say, "an' brooder shall roise against brooder!" Cairine had seen it all in her native land, and often told tales of unbelievable horror. She'd lost her entire family through murder, war and accident (any accident being, of course, a punishment from God) and she knew it was just a matter of time before this moral horror invaded the United States of America. And if by some miracle the country managed to avoid epidemic bloodshed, it would still suffer at His great hands because of the monumental spiritual decay.

Cairine McDiarmid cataloged many examples of insidious evil; huge factories where children worked from dawn until dusk, parties and dances where adolescents lost themselves in frenzied tribal ritual, plantations and farms where human beings were accorded less respect than dogs and horses because they happened to be black, elderly people cast out from society once they'd outlived their economic usefulness, aberrations a-plenty and lunatics everywhere, people who arrogantly meddled with God's beautiful plan. Cairine had studied these people with scholarly thoroughness, and could quote them word for word.

Most of them dealt with the subject of sexual intercourse, which Cairine thought so simple a thing that only a fool would muck about with it. Still, there were any number of fools, fools like Robert Dale Owen, who in his book *Moral Physiology* advocated a practice he dubbed "coitus interruptus," an unnatural and useless expenditure of seed, or fools like Charles Knowlton, who in his *Fruits and Philosophy* described various "douching" techniques designed to purge the seed as if it were some bit of slime, even fools who argued for abortion or *celibacy*.

Cairine McDiarmid couldn't fully understand why God was allowing this all to happen, why He didn't simply blast the planet from the sky and start over again somewhere else in the universe. The only answer she could come up with was that He meant to send His son Christ once more into the world, and Cairine had a hunch (she was born with a widow's cowl, and therefore second-sight) that He had already done so, and that Christ was Joseph Benton Hope.

Cairine had first attended the Perfectionist Free Church after reading in *The Battle-Axe & Weapons of War* that J. B. Hope's licence to preach had been removed. The man must be doing something right, she told herself, and she donned her heavy mourning clothes and went to a service. At first she hadn't been impressed — Hope was no more than a boy, really, at any rate far too young to possess any true knowledge. But as Hope spoke she found herself drawn into the words, and the words were wise and gracious. To say they made sense hardly did them justice, except if one took the phrase literally, that is, they constructed sense where once there was only chaos. Cairine was a bright woman, quick to spot hidden inconsistencies and contradictions, but Hope's words flowed like a symphony, as unified and complementary as a work of Beethoven's. If Hope's thoughts sometimes struggled (as a melody might struggle with its counterpoint) it was only to attain a glorious resolution. Cairine felt her bosom swelling, a bosom that was already, by Cairine's own reckoning, too large.

Then Hope began to move among the people, bouncing, thrashing with his arms. Cairine had attended more churches than she could recall, but the only time she'd seen anybody expend so much energy was at a Shaker service, and there the people had twitched convulsively, almost inhumanly. Hope was lithe and graceful, and Cairine discovered that she could tap her tiny toe in meter with his movements. That was when the notion of Christ and a Second Coming had first entered her mind, even though Hope looked nothing like the gaunt, golden-haired and bearded man that she'd been taught to worship. And she could no more imagine Christ dancing (that was what Hope was doing, plain and simple) than she could imagine Him, say, drinking a pint of dark ale and throwing darts. And, Cairine chuckled inwardly, if Hope was Christ and destined for a Cross, he wasn't going without a fight.

By the time Hope had finished the service (Cairine had felt a brief pang of disappointment when she realized there would be no singing, for she had a lovely voice), Cairine McDiarmid was an avowed Perfectionist.

A collection was taken, two monstrously immense people, a man and a woman who looked exactly like the man, passing through the assembled. Cairine was sitting still, sweating slightly and basking in a reverie, a reverie that was snapped short when the giant man trod on her toe.

"Sowwy," he mumbled.

Beside Cairine, Abram Skinner hid a small smile.

Abram Skinner was a man who had never doubted the existence of God. If a reason or proof had been demanded of him, Abram would have lit his pipe reflectively, spent many minutes laboriously thinking out the answer, and said, "Plant a seed. Watch it grow." Abram Skinner had been performing this experiment for years, planting many seeds in long, neat rows, and marveling at their struggle Heavenward. Manifestations of Our Creator were everywhere, as far as Abram's eyes could see; in the cycle of the seasons, in the sun and moon, even in the teats of his cows. Abram was still held in childlike awe by the teats of his cows; a few quick yanks, and milk issued forth. Furthermore, the milk could be easily rendered into butter and cheese. (Although his wife Abigal might argue with how easily the rendering could be done, she agreed with Abram in principle.)

What Abram wondered at was man's place in this grand scheme of things. Man should be as glorious as a sunset, as magnificent as the moon. Instead, most men were small things with incoherent emotions, petty lusts and dreams. And, moreover, although Abram Skinner had seen a seed as tiny as a speck of dust become a tall, hearty plant, he had also seen Abigal give birth to four shriveled, lifeless husks. This was the mystery of life as far as Abram was concerned, why mankind should be so dysfunctional in a world of order and beauty.

So Abram had turned to religion, only to discover that religion dismissed things as they are, promising instead a better life in the hereafter. Abram wondered why. A man is given three score and ten years upon the earth, what purpose does it serve that they be miserable? The stock answer was, so that Heaven could serve as a reward. Abram's rebuttal was that if the world served as some sort of testing ground, it was a contest in which Skinner had never asked to compete. God creates flowers and asks nothing of them, He creates birds and yet never demands that they fly only as He wishes, and all the beasts of the world behave as they will, not according to a set of rules and regulations designed to earn them happiness after death. No, Abram simply wasn't having it. The world was a beautiful thing, and Abram Skinner was determined to take his place there.

Abigal Skinner felt much the same way, although she hadn't given it as much thought as her perpetually brooding husband. All Abigal knew was, at twenty-nine she had delivered still-born babies four times and miscarried twice. Something was very, very wrong.

How the Skinners came to Hope was as follows: Abigal's mother, a somewhat elderly widow woman, was a "Theo-philian," this being the term that had lately been applied to adherents of T. Drinkwater's various philosophies. According to Abram, the old woman had become Theophilian only to keep herself occupied, for staying up to date with Drinkwater's various theories and ideas was a fulltime occupation. Abram Skinner, at this point in his life disdainful of any religion, would have nothing to do with his mother-in-law. Abigal, being more sentimental, made a weekly trip to Boston for a visit. On one such visit, Abigal discovered her mother engaged in a very singular activity, that is, racing throughout the house with empty Mason jars held aloft, sealing them tightly and neatly stacking them in a corner. Abigal's mother had a collection of thirty to forty empty and sealed Mason jars. Abigal was not alarmed by the fact that her mother was naked as she did this; the old woman had given up clothes months ago, as per Theophilius's instructions. Abigal was alarmed, though, by the fact that the task was both apparently useless and obviously strenuous. Abigal's mother was sweating profusely, it being somehow of great necessity that her charges be made full-tilt, the Mason jar held as high as her arms would allow.

"Mother," asked Abigal, "what are you doing?"

Abigal's mother was too out of breath to answer, and at any rate didn't seem willing to stop what she was doing, so she thrust a copy of *The Battle-Axe & Weapons of War* at her daughter and launched off once more.

On the front page T. D. announced, much as he might have announced a picnic or a raffle, that he wanted all of his Spiritual Brethren to collect air in Mason jars (Theophilius stressed the importance of gathering the air from as high a level as possible, the air near the ground being more used and often malodorous) as he was planning an expedition to the moon.

Abigal was a sensible person and understood that the notion of bottled air was ill-conceived. Remarkably, the planned expedition to the moon struck Abigal as an exhilarating prospect, and some small part of her wondered if she'd be allowed to go along. She briefly imagined herself and Abram living on the moon, and it seemed right, the bleak terrain (Abigal pictured a world of mountains, silver seas and wispy gray clouds) somehow suiting her husband's poetical moods. Abigal wondered what crops would do well on the moon, and she imagined that hearty grains might, might in fact do fabulously well; she envisioned a field of wheat that had grown to a height of thirty feet. Their children would do well there, too. Abigal had no knowledge of gravity or atmosphere, but she intuited that growth on the moon would be somehow unhindered, that their sons and daughters would be glorious giants.

Abigal Skinner realized with a start that her thinking was addled, and quickly she looked elsewhere in the newsprint for distraction. This passage caught her eye, mostly because a printer's devil had blemished it, covering the lines with a mark that looked for all the world like a cross. Abigal managed to read:

> Perfection must be, not merely a dream of the future, but a guide here and now on earth. Man must become altogether ... [this word was covered completely by the printer's devil] ... and happy.

Abigal's first thought was that her husband had written this, because it was what Abram was always saying, or at least it was what Abram was always trying to say. Abram, though, would become tongue-tied, and he'd rub his temples and look at the world gloomily and remain silent. Abigal searched for a name at the bottom of the column and she found: "J. B. Hope."

The next Sunday she and Abram went to the Free Church.

During the service Abram nodded at practically everything Joseph Hope said, and he dug his elbow into Abigal's side constantly, excited with discovery. Abigal herself was frightened by Hope — at one point Joseph pointed at her, fixed her with his tiny hawklike eye, and Abigal's heart literally skipped a beat. As she watched Hope, Abigal discovered that her bowels were burning, that she might at any time faint. If she'd had any true choice in the matter, Abigal Skinner would have walked away right then and there — but, being a dutiful and loving wife, she did not. Abram and Abigal Skinner became Perfectionists.

Abigal Skinner did find one thing about the Free Church comforting, that — the freakish Quinton twins notwithstanding — the congregation was comprised of rather attractive people, most of them their own age. Abram and Abigal had no real friends, isolated as they were on the farm, and Abigal thought it would be nice to make the acquaintance of some of the other Perfectionists. Abigal and Cairine McDiarmid were on speaking terms immediately, and Abram soon found a companion (at least someone he could talk with, which he did every week after Hope's service) in Adam De-la-Noy. This pleased Abigal immensely.

One of the things that gave the Perfectionist Free Church some prominence was the attendance of Adam De-la-Noy, for he was one of the most celebrated young actors in Boston, or, for that matter, in the United States. Most of his success was based upon his looks; Adam was a stunningly beautiful young man. He was tall, an inch above six feet, and his body was broad-shouldered and thin-hipped. Adam had blond hair, wavy in a very disciplined manner, and blue eyes, a light blue like a robin's egg. These stood out in sharp contrast to his general complexion, which was so deep and mellow a brown that Bostonians suspected either that it was stage make-up or that there was the proverbial nigger in the De-la-Noy woodpile.

Adam's one physical imperfection was that his ears were too big and stood at right angles to his head. Adam was quite often able to hide his ears upon the stage, either with a wig or hat, but sometimes a role called for him to be bare-headed and his entrance would be greeted with a quiet round of snickers. He

had, early in his career, played Hamlet, and for most of the
play his Prince had gone about wearing a foppish hat that Adam
thought looked vaguely Danish. When it came time for the famous soliloquy, De-la-Noy pulled off the hat reflectively. "To
be or not to be," he began, at which point someone in the front
row burst out with a loud farting sound and succumbed to laughter. It wasn't that Adam's ears were ridiculous, that they de-
tracted that much from his overwhelming handsomeness, it
was just that they made it difficult for people to take him
seriously.

And so Adam had been forced to make his living playing in
melodramas. He was always the heroic romantic lead, and the
audience loved him, even when they could see his ears. Adam's
great success came when he portrayed the swashbuckling Mor-
gan le Francis in a play entitled *The Beauty and the Buccaneer.* This role was perfect for De-la-Noy, allowing him to
display all of his acrobatic prowess, leaping nimbly about the
stage and engaging in thrilling sword duels, and although the
emotional range was rather limited, when Adam/Morgan (mis-
takenly) assumed that the Beauty had been tortured to death,
his rendition of the line "Oh, the torture I feel now, even hers
could not compare with" left not a dry eye in the house. More
importantly, Adam discovered the perfect remedy for the problem of his ears — he tied them down with a red polka-dotted
bandana. Adam De-la-Noy knew that no true buccaneer would
ever do such a thing — it would be somewhat akin, in our day
and age, to a Marine choosing to wear high heels. Still, the
audience accepted it without question, and in time it became a
stock part of stage piracy, even extending into the twentieth
century, when Errol Flynn took a red polka-dotted bandana
and tied it around his head in *Captain Blood.*

Adam De-la-Noy was not the only reason *The Beauty and
the Buccaneer* was such a huge success. The Beauty was played
by one Mary Carter and although, as several critics noted, the
role consisted mostly of exaggerated pitchings of the bosom,
no one could pitch a bosom like Mary. Quite often Mary came
close to actually pitching her bosom out of her costume. The
most famous scene in the play was the so-called "Torture Scene,"
wherein the Beauty is tied across a rum barrel and given a

lashing with the cat-o'-nine-tails. The cutthroats who did this rudely tore the dress off her back, and through some clever bit of stage business the flesh soon became cross-hatched with cruel red welts. Throughout the scene, Mary Carter's bosom pitching was astounding, elevated to a fine art. The "Torture Scene," the last before intermission, always brought the crowd to their feet.

The other reason that *The Beauty and the Buccaneer* did so well was that its two stars, Adam De-la-Noy and Mary Carter, married two weeks after it opened. Since then they had always acted together, either reviving *The Beauty and the Buccaneer* or doing some variation of it. Adam was always a bandanaed pirate, Mary was always tortured, and there was always much sword play and bosom pitching.

This made them very rich and famous, although for many years Adam considered himself spiritually impoverished. This changed when he attended the Free Church, which he did on a whim. Adam was impressed with Hope, thought he made good sense. Mary was the more passionate convert of the couple, and in her declaration of Perfection she gave the assembled an impromptu demonstration of bosom pitching.

Joseph Benton Hope was very pleased.

Ghosting the Glass

Hope, Ontario, 1983
*Wherein Sara opens a box, and our Young
Biographer confronts the Darker Side; after
which he and his Friend Benson go off to
pursue the Art of the Angle.*

"Listen!" Sara cocked her head sideways toward the night. "Listen."

I was lying on the bed, wanting to go to sleep, half reading some magazine. I turned it over and listened. The world seemed quiet enough. In time, though, I realized that the northern wind carried with it the sound of a freight train. "Choo-choo," said I.

"Of course it's a train, pea-brain," said Sara (I found that many of her statements contained these internal rhymes), "but listen, it's playing a sixth chord." Sara stuck a finger into the air like a grade two music teacher. "Bum-bum-bum-baaaa!" Sara sang along with the train's distant whistle. "Sixth chord," chimed Sara. "All aboard the sixth chord!"

Sara was puttering around the bedroom, had been for about an hour. Sara was apparently a post-coital putterer. She went through my books, six or seven ragged paperbacks that I'd tossed into my suitcase as I was leaving Toronto. Sara read the titles aloud, and I grunted. "What do we have here?" Sara demanded. "A copy of *King Lear!*"

I grunted. I was tired and weary, and grunting seemed as good a response as any, a lot better than the ones I felt like giving. "Ugh."

"Don't this beat all? *Legends of the Fall!*"

"Ugh-ugh."

"Here's a story! *The Power and the Glory!*"

"Ugh."

"What a cornucopia! A book called *Failed Utopias!*"

"Ugh?"

"*Failed Utopias: A Study of the Utopian Impulse in Four North American Communities.*"

"That one's not mine."

Sara carried the book over to the bed. It was an immense, leatherbound volume, the spine ornately gold-leafed with the whole of the scholarly title. Sara kicked out her legs and landed on the bed bouncing. Sara was still naked, so I began to maul her. Sara opened the tome and read further from the title page. " 'An Inquiry Into the Settlements at Oneida, Powf-keep-sie, Balforton and' "

"Poe-kip-see," I suggested.

" 'Hope.' "

"Come again?"

" 'Oneida, Poe-kip-see, Balforton and Hope.' "

"Lemme see that."

"I'm cold!" Sara announced suddenly. She grabbed one of

her breasts and examined it closely. "*Les bumps de goose,*" she diagnosed. "*Regardez!*" Sara pointed at the puckered nipple. "Fucking thing's about to disappear!" Sara stood up and presented her backside to my face. "Goose-bumples, right?"

"Right."

"It won't do, it won't do," muttered Sara. "I need clothes, dammit! Vestments! Garb!" The acid had taken over in a silly but determined way. Sara began to stalk. She stared at a pile of my dirty laundry for a long time and then shook her head decisively. "I need women's clothes," she said, "for I have a need to be feminine." Sara marched over to a far corner and exclaimed, "Here we are!"

There was an ancient cedar chest there. I'd never really noticed it, mostly because it was buried beneath a mountain of folded blankets, towels and washcloths. Sara threw all that stuff over to one side and pulled at the top of the chest. Nothing happened.

"Lockèd," Sara announced.

"Probably nothing in it," I said, picking up the large book and glancing through for references to Hope.

"There are lots in it," Sara said. She folded her arms across her breasts, both to warm them up and to facilitate thought. "What am I to do?" Sara wondered aloud. Then, with a giggle, she reached up to her dark hair and removed a bobby pin. "Master criminal at work!" Sara hunkered down and began to pick the lock with the bobby pin. Just as I was about to mutter, "Give it up," I heard a loud clunking sound. Sara lifted the top of the antique cedar chest. "Hey, Joe," she muttered, "what do you know?"

"What's in there?" I asked.

"Well . . ." Sara bent over and pulled out a dress, a white one, lacy and ladylike. "What did I tell you?"

"Huh!"

"Close your eyes, I'm going to put it on."

"What, close my eyes," I mumbled.

"Close them! It's not right to watch a lady dressing!"

I obediently closed my eyes—if I fell asleep, it would be her fault. Just as I was about to drift away, Sara began to laugh hysterically.

I opened my eyes, and I began to laugh, too.

The dress was too big. The only way to do justice to how overly sized the dress was is to state it that simply — "too big." Sara's knuckles ended up near the elbow of the sleeve, and the excess dress around her feet reached a length of a dozen inches. The neckhole of the garment was so large that it barely sat on the edges of Sara's shoulders, and the neckline swooped well underneath Sara's breasts. The most outlandish of the dress's measurements was shoulder to shoulder, which seemed to be in excess of three feet.

All Sara had to do was give a little shrug and she was no longer technically "wearing" the dress, although the dress still surrounded her and likely offered some warmth. She wrapped it around herself loosely and sat down, turning once more to the ancient cedar chest.

Sara then pulled out two more articles of clothing, masculine apparel this time, a pair of cloth trousers and a workshirt. Having seen the dress, we were prepared for how hilariously outsized these would be, and Sara and I again fell into fits of laughter. Sara stepped out of the mountain of lady's dress and put on the workshirt. The tails dangled almost to the ground. After endlessly turning up the sleeves Sara managed to clear her wrists. "There we go," announced Sara. She looked down at her body's new covering. "Hey," she said, "this thing's got rust or something all over it."

The shirt was basically gray, unfinished material, but much of it was spotted brown. Sara picked at one of these brown parts and found that it came away in her hand, leaving a hole in the fabric. "Hmm!" piped Sara. "Wonder what it is?"

Sara was talking to a boy who'd read more mysteries than was good for him. I knew what turned rust-brown with age, but I wasn't about to tell her. "Probably just oxidization," I lied. "That shirt looks like it's about a hundred years old."

"How's about that?" Sara was as awestruck as a three-year-old. She turned back to the cedar chest. "Newspapers," she told me, and she pulled out a small yellow thing about a foot square. "Not really a *newspaper*," Sara judged, pointing at the spine where the pages were tied and glued. "But it's not a book, really. It's a ..."

"It's an old magazine," I told her.

Sara read the title page. "*The Theocratic Watchman*. What does 'theocratic' mean?"

"Search me. It probably has something to do with religion. God, see. Theo."

"God's name is Theo?" Sara joked. She crossed her legs beneath her and began to look through the contents. "Whoa!" she exclaimed. "This was published in 1859." Sara turned some pages — the outer ones came away in her hand, a few crumpling into nothingness, but as she got further they were more substantial. Sara began to read.

Whatever Sara read was engrossing. She read in silence for some minutes, until I asked, "What's it about?"

"Fucking," Sara summarized. "Fucking without getting into it. You ought to read it when I'm through."

Without stopping to wonder what she'd meant by that crack, I said, "Come off it. Your basic hundred and twenty-odd year old spiritual periodical doesn't often talk about fucking."

"Without getting into it."

"Even without getting into it."

"This one does."

I suspected that this was some clever trick of the LSD. "Some of these old religious guys tended to sublimate sexual urges," I said in a grandiose, bullshitty way, "and often the language is couched in pseudosexual terminology."

Sara began to read aloud. " 'Here follow the three stages of amorous congress. One, the simple presence of the male organ in the female reciprocator, followed by 2) a series of mutual motions followed by 3) a nervous reflex action or ejaculatory crisis which expels the seed.' "

"Exactly as I was saying. One might well think this person was actually talking about sex!"

"And making it sound like gobs of fun, too." Sara read further. " 'The process of physical communion must be divided into two phases; amative and propagative. In order to raise the process to the level of spiritual perfection, the "amative" must be accentuated. Consider the analogous bodily act of ingestion. The food is chewed, subsequently swallowed. The first act is pleasurable, the second necessary to prolong existence. It affords no pleasure, however, to swallow. The only manner of garnering more pleasure from the function of eating is to chew longer. This elevates the exercise to one of spirituality, for we are indulging in one of the Lord's great boons. So be it with amorous congress. The sweetest and noblest period of intercourse is the moment of penetration and spiritual effusion, before the tedious muscular exercises begin. Therefore, this should be prolonged, the muscular exercises dispensed with. The method employed is one of concentration, what I shall call "wilful countenance." Via this method I personally have been able to maintain an erection for hours, and to postpone ejaculation indefinitely! The communion with my sisters ...' "

"Say again," I put in.

" 'The communion with my sisters has become a thing of great spirituality, and not what intercourse so often is, a momentary affair terminating in exhaustion and disgust.' "

At that moment all hell broke loose in the room across from us. Three voices came all at once—Harvey screaming "Bitch!" over and over again, Lee countering every "Bitch!" with a "Bastard!" of equal venom, and Sheila sadly wailing.

"Oh-oh," said sad Sara and I. I hopped into some pants, and we dashed over.

The three froze as soon as we opened the door, caught in the following tableau. Sheila was cowering on the ground, her arms folded to protect her head. Sheila's body was red, violently red. Above her stood Harvey, a belt held swinging at his side. Harvey, I could see immediately, was crazed with alcohol and pharmaceuticals. (I noticed with a quick glance that the dresser's mirror had been removed from the dresser and was lying in a corner, traces of white dust ghosting the glass.) Lee had Harvey's arm in her mouth, and had bitten deeply enough that blood trickled slowly through the thick hair. All three were naked.

"Hi, Paulie," said Harvey.

I moaned, "For fuck's sake ..."

"It's this bitch!" Harvey pointed at Sheila and instantly became drugaddled and angry. "She sucked the life juices from me, and I couldn't pork the other one!"

Lee let go of his arm. "That's not her fault! You're impotent!"

Harvey began to weep. "They're all the frigging same. Women! They want your juices, they collect them, I don't know what for, but they do!"

"I'm sorry," whimpered Sheila.

"Bitch!" Harvey raised the belt again, Sheila tightened into a cowering ball and Lee reset her teeth. I caught Harvey's wrist before the belt could come down.

Sara and Lee helped Sheila from the ground. It looked like Harvey had done some minor damage to her, nothing horrendously serious.

"I'm wise to you guys!" Harvey called menacingly as the three girls left the room. "You're a, what-do-you-call-it, coven, right, of witch-bitches, and you suck out my very substance like I was a Tootsie-Pop or something! Just because you got tits and twats and stuff, you think you can get away with that shit!"

The girls slammed the door behind them.

"Come on, Harvard, cool it."

"Did you pork that little bitch, Paulie?"

"I didn't pork her ..."

"Good for you. You've got to keep all your juices. They want them. I-I-I was gonna pork that Lee, right, but then that fat cunt Sheila sucked me off and I couldn't! Bitch!"

I'd known Harvey for years, knew that the only way to get him off a train of thought was to seriously derail it. "Hey, Harv," I asked, "what does 'theocratic' mean?"

Harvey Benson let the belt fall to the ground. "Want to do some cocaine, Paulie?"

"Okay."

Harvey plodded over to the dresser, opened a drawer and got out the cocaine. Harvey had hidden the stuff in a rolled-up pair of dirty socks. Doing cocaine was the perfect activity for Harvey right then, because he loved the ceremony and ritual of dope-doing, and applied all of his concentration to it. Harvey took the little packet of cocaine over to the mirror and knelt down. He spilled some out on to the glass and then picked up a razor blade. Harvey began to chop at the crystals in a rapid and decisive way, forming it into lines, then shaving some off one, adding it to another, until the four runs of cocaine were perfectly equal.

This pleased Harvey immensely. He sat back on his pudgy, naked haunches with a lopsided grin. "Have some Lady C," he instructed, picking up a ten-dollar bill and forming it into a straw. Harvey handed it to me.

I spent a long time looking at the lines, making sure they all were equal, because if one was heavy, even by a grain, I wanted it. Cocaine can turn bishops and cardinals into pig-fucking cutthroats, so imagine the effect on the likes of Benson and me. Satisfied that all the lines were the same, I stuck the bill in my nose and lowered my head, sucking half the line up my right nostril, half up the left, and then I spent several seconds racing over the surface of the mirror, vacuuming up the ghostly traces. I took the bill out of my nose and unrolled it, finding a few specks of white dust. I rubbed them off with my forefinger and then used this digit to massage my gums. Having done all that, I reluctantly rerolled the ten-spot and returned it to Harvey.

The doing of cocaine kept us in a state of near-silent activity for half an hour or so. Then I went to the kitchen and brought back up a bottle of whiskey and a case of beer, because I wanted to talk. I felt as if my Fairy Godmother had informed me, "Talk. I guarantee that you'll say something beautiful and true." As soon as I opened my mouth, I knew there was a catch. "But," my Fairy Godmother had gone on, "mostly it's gonna be ca-ca."

"Harvard," I began, feeling in my bones some stellar connection between fish, lunar cycles and beating women with a belt, "ummm..." It was hard to formulate a statement based on those three components. I selected one as the most important. "Fish!" I shouted, taking a sip of beer.

"Hey," said Harvey, "what did God say when Eve went swimming?"

Harvey didn't want to speak beautiful truisms, he wanted to tell jokes. I was deeply saddened. "Heard it," I mumbled, which was the truth. Edgar the axe-murderer had told it to me.

"Of a theocracy, obviously," Harvey piped up. "A government or state in which God is the sovereign and religion the law."

I scowled. "I don't get it. 'Snot funny."

" 'Snot a joke, asswipe. Didn't you just ask what theocratic meant?"

"Right. What does it mean?"

"What I just fucking said."

"God as the sovereign and religion the law," I repeated. "Do they have a theocracy anywhere?" If they did, I thought, it might be a nice place to visit, maybe even settle down.

"A succubus, that's what she is. Sucking the life right out of me."

"Oh, shut up, Harvard. All it was was a blow job. Most guys would be glad to get a blow job, but not you." This reminded me of something. "Hey! There's a guy in town who's got a stone boner!"

"Say what?"

"He's a stone guy, that's why he's got a stone boner. The town founder, J. B. Hope. Maybe he can find a stone lady to give him a blow job." I opened another beer. I now had five nearly full beer bottles in a strange configuration around me. The stone lady image made me think of Elspeth. I considered commissioning a marble statue, one that would lock Ellie and I together forever in carnal embrace.

"Rub it," commanded Harvey Benson.

"Rub what?"

"Rub the stone boner. It's good luck."

"It is?"

"Sure. Ask anybody around here. Why, every year after a farmer plants his tobaccy, he drives into town to rub Joseph's dick."

"Who's Joseph?"

"Joseph Benton Hope. J. B. Hope."

"Oh, right, yeah, got you."

"Or, on the night before her wedding, a girl always goes to the Square to give Joseph's dick a little rub."

"Hey," I remembered happily, "I did rub it."

Harvey dealt me a strange, cruel look. "You didn't even know it was good luck and you rubbed it anyway? That's pretty weird!"

"I just wanted to make sure it was really there."

"It's really there."

"He's the town founder, right? Sara found a book in my room, and it had about Hope in it. Hope the town."

Harvey leaned forward and grinned. "You mean you don't

know about this place yet? How Joe Benton Hope and his so-called Perfectionists settled here? How they practiced complex marriage, wilful countenance and stirpiculture?"

"Fishing, you mean?"

I had unsuspectingly hit a bull's-eye, tapped into some motherlode of drug-induced lunacy. Benson jumped on to his feet and let loose with a horrible cry, simultaneously jubilant and inhuman. "Fishing!" bellowed Harvey. "Let's go the fuck fishing!!"

I considered it and began to chortle. "Ol' Mossback," I whispered lowly. "Let's go get Ol' Mossback."

And singing the theme music from *Jaws* all the way (bum-*bum*bum*bum*) Harv and I mopedaled to Lookout Lake.

Leaving the Pale Blue Sky to the Moon

Hope, Ontario, 1983
Wherein our Biographer (Drunk as a Boiled Owl!) Entertains a rather Fanciful Muse & makes a New Acquaintance, One of a Piscatorial Nature.

I was considerably more taken with Lookout Lake on this, my second visit. God seemed to be hard at work, although I suspected Him of drunkenness. The sun had risen, reluctantly and sleepy-eyed, and seemed to be on the verge of saying, "Fuggit," leaving the pale blue sky to the moon. The moon, by the way, was still floating about the world, looking like a photograph scotch-taped to a bedroom wall. Still, the lake gave the impression of industriousness, infested with hobgoblins and elves making hay while the humans slept, while the humans dreamed their tiny dreams.

Cocaine is an impish drug, in that while your nose is full of it, your body and sensibilities acquire a magical resistance to alcohol. "Another beer and a shot of Scotch? Sure, send it down, no problem, we won't even notice!" Then, of course, the co-caine pulls out with a sardonic chuckle, rendering you instanta-neously plastered. This is what happened to me out at Lookout Lake, and I sat down on one of the lunar rocks grinning, telling myself that I'd found a fine rock and that there was no earthly reason for me to vacate the rock until sometime around the next Ice Age.

Harvey Benson was more active. "Paulie!" he said, assem-bling his tackle with great expertise, "we got to take off all of our clothes!"

"Why for?"

"Because Ol' Mossback, he's a cagey bastard, he can hear the rustle of material, and then he knows that people is after his ass." Harvey was already butt-naked, I noticed, and it oc-curred to me that if Ol' Mossback could hear clothes rustling he could also certainly hear the breeze whistling through Benson's body hair. Still, I'm a good sport, ask anybody. I slipped out of my clohes and thought of Elspeth.

I remembered Ellie and me skinny-dipping in some northern lake, remembered the way the silver water ran between her breasts. Actually, though, this was complete fabrication, be-cause Elspeth would never do it. "Swim in a *lake*?" Elspeth would shriek. "It's all full of things!"

Elspeth has an unnatural fear of "things." She can always account for specific fears, citing past experiences, all of which have the quality of nightmares suffered by a three-year-old. For example, she wouldn't go skinny-dipping in a lake because, "Once I got a leech on my leg that was about a foot long!" or, "A cousin of mine had all of his toes bitten off by a huge snap-ping turtle!"

"Hey, don't laugh. Some of those snappers are very nasty!"

"Say what?"

Harvey was busy executing the butt-naked overhand cast. He planted the Hoper far out in the middle of the lake and let it sink a bit. Then, retrieving it slowly, he asked, "Huh?"

"You just say sumpin'?"

"Nope."

"Oh."

Neither would Elspeth engage in the skinny aspects of the

dipping. Even if I convinced her to enter a lake full of "things," she would dash off into the woods and come back wearing a severe one-piece suit, goggles and a flowered bathing-cap, looking as if she intended to conquer the English Channel.

I looked down upon my own nakedness and giggled. Something struck me as humorous.

Harvey walked up to me and demanded the bottle of Scotch. "Haven't you had enough?" I asked, something I say to my friends when I'm convinced, against all logic and odds, that I haven't.

"The thing about it is," said Harvey, grabbing the bottle out of my hands, "Ol' Mossback is very sensitive to the presence of human beings."

"Unlike some people I know," Harvey seemed to add under his breath. Benson took a long pull at the whisky. "See," he continued, "when you drink alcohol quickly, it lowers the body temperature. So this way, Ol' Mossback won't even know we're here!"

"I'll bet Red Fisher don't know about that one," I said, getting back the bottle. I had a healthy measure of whisky, hoping to lower my body temperature.

Well, I don't know about body temperature, but it sure hammered down my IQ. I lay back on my rock and fell into a sort of sleep.

So, ah, you married?

Yes. But she gave me the boot.

How come?

Well, she's got this friend, June. And—hold on, hold on. What am I telling you for?

I'm interested, that's all.

But who the hell are you?

Bum*bum*bum*bum* ...

Ol' Mossback?

Right first time out of the box.

A likely story.

You think perhaps I am but a figment of your pickled imagination?

Wouldn't put it past you.

So, am I right in assuming that you and this girl June engaged in sex, thereby occasioning said action on the part of your wife?

Pretty smart, for a fish.

Why'd you do it?

I was drunk.

Hey, buck, come off it! I wasn't born yesterday.

I don't know why I did it. June's got great tits.

And your wife doesn't?

Sure she does.

As you may know, fish don't have tits. But I'm doing my best to understand. I've seen a few in my time. Those lumps of fat that women have on their chests, right?

Right.

And you're saying that some are better than others?

I suppose.

Well, gosh, it's hard for me to relate to this. The tits I've seen looked by and large the same. I mean, all my wives have dorsal fins, but I don't go around saying one's got a great set of dorsals and another's are only so-so.

Well, aren't some of your wives prettier than the others?

Hell, no. They're all fish! Excuse me.

Where'd you go?

Just popped off to chomp a fingerling.

Ah.

Are June's tits prettier than your wife's?

They're different.

How so?

Mostly because they're on June's chest.

Now we're getting somewhere. Look out! What the hell is *that*?

What?

What's that gizmo your buddy is fishing with?

It's called the Hoper.

Mostly because you got to hope that I'm either crazy or blind if you think I'm going to go for it.

Well, Gregory Opdycke says it works.

That putz! Him and those crazy stirpicults.

Speaking of that ...

Hey! I'm going to give your buddy the thrill of his lifetime.

What are you gonna do?

"Whoa!"

Harvey's cry made me sit up on my rock, just in time to watch him execute what looked like a triple half-gainer before he disappeared into Lookout Lake.

The Boston Letter

Boston, Massachusetts, 1849
Regarding the popular image of Hope, we know the following: that it was tarnished early on.

The trouble all began this way. Joseph Benton Hope had seen Polyphilia Drinkwater Davies on the street one day, in the company of her new, fat husband, Buford Scrope Davies. If Davies had simply been fat, Hope reflected, he would have been grotesque enough — but Davies added to this quality those of shortness (like his father-in-law, he approached dwarfdom) and facial unsightliness. Then Hope saw the painful catch to Buford Scrope Davies's gait. Davies had a clubbed foot — it met the ground sideways and was pulled behind rather than propelled forward in any sort of perambulatory manner. The sight of Polyphilia had turned Hope's root to stone; the sight of Scrope Davies had the same effect on his heart.

That night, alone and by candlelight, Joseph wrote a letter. He addressed it to Adam De-la-Noy, for no particular reason, other than the fact that Adam was a worldly man and not likely to be shocked by what Joseph had to say.

Hope spent the first three pages reviewing the doctrine of Perfectionism.

And now [Joseph wrote], I am going to speak my heart to you on a certain subject. I trust you to hold this in the most sacred of confidences.

When the will of God is done on earth, the marriage

supper of the Lamb is a feast at which every dish is free to every guest. Exclusiveness, jealousy and quarreling have no place there, for the same reason as that which forbids the guests at a Thanksgiving dinner to claim each his separate dish and quarrel with the rest for his rights. In a holy community, there is no more reason why sexual intercourse should be restrained by law than why eating and drinking should be — and there is as little occasion for shame in the one as in the other.

Adam De-la-Noy read this in his bedroom, by candlelight. He had just finished making love to Mary.

Mary lay on the rumpled bedsheets, naked and dead to the world. Adam spent a long time staring at his wife's body. Even in slumber her bosom was pitching, a subtle heave with each whispered breath. Mary's legs were spread-eagled, her cunnicle glistening. Adam realized what J. B. Hope was getting at. It did not anger him in any real way. Adam refolded the letter and replaced it in its envelope. Then he crossed over to the bed and woke up Mary. They made love once more, consecutive sex for the first time in their marriage.

The following day George Quinton showed up at the De-la-Noy household to fix a door. George wasn't much good at these household repairs, but somehow he always ended up doing them, even for handy, practical men like Abram Skinner. George didn't manage to truly fix the door at the De-la-Noys', which refused to shut tightly, but after hours of beating on it George convinced the door to remain shut, at least as long as he was around. As George was leaving, Adam met him at the door, and handed him an opened letter.

"Take this back to Reverend Hope," Adam instructed quietly.

George stared at the envelope, recognized his master's handwriting. "What is it?"

"It is the philosophy of Perfectionism," said De-la-Noy. "He sent it to me because I was unsure on a few accounts. But now I am satisfied and I'm sending it back to him to illustrate that fact."

George grinned heartily. This made him very happy.

George headed for the harbor and the Free Church, but he

absentmindedly crossed two streets over to the west before descending to the docks. There he found The Sailor's Wife.

"Ho!" George was startled, even astounded, to have stumbled across the tavern. "Heah's the gwoghouse," he commented aloud. "I think I'll just pop inside."

In Boston, that season, the favorite topics of barroom conversation were the uppity South, the alleged liaison between Senator Archibald Guy Tollery and a twice-divorced woman, and Theophilius Drinkwater's attempted expedition to the moon.

George entered The Sailor's Wife, taking the cap off his head and crumpling it humbly in his massive hands. He nodded to the men in a very general way, for quite a few were staring at him. George took two steps over to the bar; the clutch of men beside him laughed, and George found himself grinning from ear to ear.

"Yes, George?" asked the barkeep.

George was astonished to hear his own name. For a long moment he forgot what he'd intended to drink. Then it came to him. "Ale, please." George Quinton held a coin up, and as the publican drew the draft, George polished the piece on his shirtfront.

The men beside him laughed again.

"And they're all at St. Mary's!" one roared.

"All of them?"

"All except Theophilius, 'cause he never jumped!"

George knew what they were discussing. Theophilius Drinkwater and seven of his most devoted followers (Abigal Skinner's mother among them) had tried to go to the moon. They'd all donned huge wings, wooden frames covered with chicken and goose feathers, and they'd jumped from the roof of Drinkwater's tiny house.

"They was naked as the day they was born!" one man added, evoking another great howl of laughter.

It didn't seem funny to George that the people would be naked, if only because he couldn't think of what attire would be most suitable. George briefly imagined that Polyphilia and Jezreel were among the moon-voyagers. (They weren't — Polyphilia was pregnant and Jezreel thought the whole thing stupid.) George had no clear concept of the naked female form, but he knew basically where and what the lumps should be, knew there should be a triangular patch of hair where a man would have a peter. George had, of course, seen Martha naked, because she had no concept, or need, of modesty. When she bathed, Martha often ordered George to scrub her back, and while he did that Martha would methodically scrub away at various protuberances and orifices. But George had no way of extrapolating Martha's huge, muscular nudity to Polyphilia and Jezreel. So he made do with a little knowledge, and memories of a William Blake illustration he'd once seen and of a statue in a museum.

"Mostly they have cuts and bruises," another man went on, "but the old lady broke both her legs."

George's ale came in a pewter tankard. He picked it up, placed it to his lips and in a few seconds the mug was empty. George scowled, then politely asked for another. He hadn't been concentrating; he'd been distracted by the talk of Drinkwater's moon voyage.

Fortunately for the lunar travelers, Drinkwater's roof was only seven feet from the ground, because by and large, a neighbor reported, they plummeted earthward like great sacks of rocks. The exception was old Mrs. Chandler (Abigal's mother), who managed, perhaps because of her aged frailty, to sail some twenty feet away from the house. According to some observers, Mrs. Chandler even managed to execute an aerial maneuver, the Loop-de-loop — although they didn't describe it that way because no one had ever done a Loop-de-loop before (or, for that matter, any aerial maneuver). Then Mrs. Chandler had fallen from the sky, mostly because of the weight of the Mason jars she had harnessed to her back. The air-filled Mason jars, Theophilius Drinkwater acknowledged, had been a mistake. He recorded in *The Battle-Axe* that his error had been one of scientific oversight, in that, "air, although lacking material substance, still has weight. Although I had made the appropriate arithmetical allowances for the jars *per se*, the added poundage of the air prevented our escape from the atmosphere." Theophilius Drinkwater was in no way discouraged. His new thought was to transport the air in balloons, which would even assist the actual flying process. Theophilius optimistically set a date for the new expedition, some two months hence. Abigal's mother, unfortunately, would not be able to participate. She died of pneumonia a few weeks after the accident.

As one of the tavern-dwellers had commented (George's second ale came — he took a small sip and rolled it around in his mouth, savoring the cool foam, then he became distracted and drained the tankard dry), Theophilius had not himself jumped. The reason, Drinkwater claimed, was that he had to orchestrate the launching, which he did by counting backward from ten and then screaming, "Off we go!" He then fully intended to bung himself heavenward, except that he saw with sudden clarity his scientific boner. According to Theophilius, he'd even warned the moongoers, shouting after them, "Come back!", but they were too intent on their mission to heed him. Theophilius was forced to watch them all fall, cracking like eggs upon the cobblestones.

"One moah beah," said George. He produced another coin and brandished it for the barkeep. When his ale came, George drank it, smacked his lips appreciatively and announced to no one in particular, "I am a pehfectionist!"

Most of the men sidled away from George, having heard it all before, always immediately following George's third beer, but the man beside him at the long wooden counter looked up quizzically. George Quinton assumed that the man needed and desired clarification. "I adheah to the philosophies of Joseph Benton Hope! It is his belief that a sinless perfection is attainable ..."

George stopped to watch the man. The man wore a pair of tiny round spectacles; upon hearing the name "Joseph Benton Hope" the man had torn them from his face, fished out a soiled handkerchief, and was now cleaning the glass furiously.

"... in owah lifetime," George concluded.

"Yes," agreed the man. He was tiny and fat, although his features, his chin, nose and ears, seemed to be fashioned for a very tall and slender type. Even George was startled by the unpleasantness of this fellow's aspect. Quinton smiled briefly and returned to his (empty) mug.

"Do you, do you," stammered the little fat man, "know him?"

"Wevewend Hope?"

"Yes."

"Yes," answered George simply, hoping to end the conversation. Then pride overcame him. "I live with him. It is my gweat fohtune to be counted among his intimates."

"I see. May I buy you a drink?"

The thing was (and even George remarked inwardly at the strangeness of this), Quinton didn't like this man. Still, George assumed that this was some failing on his part, and that with familiarity a kinship could be established. "Yes, thank you," he answered the man, and surrendered his empty tankard to the publican.

The fat man was still cleaning his spectacles. He was very drunk, and spectacle-cleaning seemed to be a measure taken toward sobriety. "Yes, yes, yes," the man said. "A sinless perfection. Attainable. Yes."

George Quinton said, "Theah cannot be two pehfections, one foah the wookaday wohld, the otheh some spuwious pehfection attainable only by pwiests and clewics!" George was delighted at the ease with which J. B. Hope's words tumbled out of his mouth.

"What does he do?" asked the fat man quickly, his nose twitching.

"Beg yoh pahdon?"

"With all the young girls? All the pretty ones?"

"Oh. He teaches them about pehfection."

"And then? Then does he stable his naggie?" The man put his spectacles on and blinked. "Then does he poke his piggie?"

George was puzzled by these references to livestock. He drank some beer, searching for understanding.

"Does he plant his oats in all the little rows?" persisted the strange fat man.

"No, he doesn't," said George firmly. "He is not a fahmah."

"No, but does he put old Nobby out to grass?"

George Quinton was exasperated. Suddenly, however, he had an inspiration. "Heah," said George, pulling the envelope out of his pocket. "Witten heah — in the hand of the Wevewend himself — is the philosophy of pehfectionism. Take it. And when you ah feeling betteh, weed it."

"I feel bully," snarled the tiny man, and he ripped open the letter and savaged it with his eyes. "Aha!" he ejaculated. The man pocketed the paper and then placed an enormous three-cornered hat on his head. "Must dash," he told George.

George watched the strange little fat man leave, and saw that "dashing" was something he could not, in fact, accomplish. His right foot was saddled with a pronounced infirmity, meeting the ground almost sideways.

George Quinton shrugged and placed his tankard to his lips. It was, needless to say, empty.

Two weeks later, the now-famous "Boston Letter" appeared in *The Battle-Axe & Weapons of War*. "When the will of God is done on earth," it began; the column ended with the name Joseph Benton Hope.

Across From the Dark Merrimack

Lowell, Massachusetts, 1850
Regarding the peregrinations of Hope, we know the following: that he went to Lowell; that it was a new "industrial" city; that a river ran adjacent to his home; that the river was dark.

Joseph Benton Hope was a pragmatic man, and following the publication of "The Boston Letter" in *The Battle-Axe & Weapons of War* he made a number of decisions. The first was to publish his own magazine, as there was obviously much power there. Theophilius Drinkwater had managed, through that seemingly innocuous medium, to render the name of Hope synonymous in the minds of Bostonians with moral decrepitude and depravity. The city of Boston quickly fabricated legend and rumor concerning the Free Church, all of it nastily lewd. Hope's services, they whispered, were nothing other than mass orgies, Joseph impassively directing all the couplings, treblings and *quadruplings*, only indulging himself with the cream of the crop, by which Bostonians meant Mary Carter De-la-Noy, she of the wonderfully pitching bosom. They also accused J. B. Hope of sodomy, which surprised Hope a good deal. Still, Joseph made no move to dispel any of these rumors, and walking the city streets he met every passerby's eyes with his own sharp, hawk-like orb. He did decide, however, to leave Boston.

Martha Quinton told him that she and George had a cousin in Lowell, a cousin sympathetic to their philosophy, and more-over, a cousin with a huge house that he would rent to them at a very reasonable cost. There was only one catch ...

Joseph Hope decided to marry Martha Quinton. They went to live in Lowell.

George followed behind, carrying all of the luggage.

Mr. Opdycke went with them, for now that his world was free of disease and delirium, or almost so, it held only J. B. Hope. Mr. Opdycke would never abandon Hope until the bitter end.

Cairine McDiarmid likewise saw no reason to remain in Boston, her family all dead in the old country, the globe on the brink of devastation, its only hope Hope himself, so she went to live in Lowell.

As for the Skinners, all they owned was their farm, and it was impossible to justify selling it, so they remained behind. But Abram became even more brooding, more sad-eyed and poetical, and finally Abigal decided it was better to be impover-ished but spiritually happy. They moved to Lowell.

Adam De-la-Noy pointed out to his wife, Mary, that they'd first achieved fame in Boston and that the city had ever since supported them splendidly. What's more, Lowell was a grimy little "industry" town with no major stage. But Mary's bosom pitched at a furious clip.

They all lived at Number 42 Dutton Street, across from the dark Merrimack.

Part Three

Mutual of Omaha's Wild Kingdom

Hope, Ontario, 1983
*Wherein our Biographer discovers his Subject,
and his Obsession.*

" 'By the time Hope and his followers settled in Lower Canada
(at a point situated approximately 100 kilometers west of
Kingston, where today exists the eponymously named town of
Hope) they had been practicing "complex marriage" for some
months. The practice of "wilful countenance" was introduced
by Hope thereafter, in an attempt to stem the production of
progeny.' "

I was propped up in bed, reading *Failed Utopias* aloud to
myself. It was six o'clock in the afternoon, and I was all alone
in the house. At some point earlier in the day, I presumed,
while I slept, Prof. Harvey Benson had loaded Sheila, Sara and
Lee into his tiny red Fiat and headed back to the great city.
The silence they left behind was jagged and, if you'll pardon
me, disquieting, so I accompanied my reading with a great deal
of whistling and finger-drumming, beating out rhythms on the
thick leather cover of the volume I was holding.

I was also somewhat excited, buzzing in my bone marrow.
My failure to write a second novel (and thereby replicate even
the dubious success of my first) was based on several factors,
not the least of them being drinking too much and screwing up
on the home front. But also, and perhaps most importantly, I
had nothing to write about. The novel I was hacking out paragraph by paragraph was of a vaguely autobiographical nature,
by which I mean that I had contrived a little story that enabled
me to attack Elspeth in a thinly disguised way. And I suppose
my heart wasn't in it, because I knew that the book was paltry
and glib, that I was giving novelists the world over a bad name.

I was, in a very real sense, ashamed of myself. All of my
heroes, everyone from Charlie Dickens to Graham Greene, were
standing around tsking their tongues. But as I leafed through
Failed Utopias, I began to sense that I was being granted a
reprieve, that I might yet avoid the fate of becoming a TV sitcom

writer or, worse yet, a book reviewer. I had found an interesting story, one that contained at least this single revelation: a man named Joseph Benton Hope had made marriage complex. Move over, boys, I thought, the kid has a little yarn to spin.

None of this thinking was concrete in any way; it was still at the level of bone-marrow buzzing, the same feeling one gets when one is about to fall in love. Whatever level the thinking was at, it was interrupted by a horrible sound, a loud wail like banshees hurling their guts out. I leapt out of bed and rushed to the window as the sound repeated. There in my laneway was a beat-up black pick-up truck; the vomiting banshee noise was produced by the truck's freon-fueled horn; the horn was being sounded, over and over again, by Mona.

Mona looked up and caught sight of me in the window. She grinned crookedly and hollered, "What, are you in bed?" Mona had overestimated her distance from the house; her bellow was overpowering, actually causing me to take a step backward from the window.

"Just napping!" I returned.

"You all alone in there or what?" Mona screamed impishly.

"All alone!" I called down. "I'll be right out!"

" 'Kay!"

As I pulled on my jeans and T-shirt I continued to look at Mona. She turned away from the house, toward the pond, and jumped up onto the hood of her pick-up truck, placing her lovely butt on to it. Mona was differently dressed that day, or at least her top was different. Instead of the undershirt, she had on a bright red nylon baseball jersey. On the back was a large white "7" and a name was spelled out above this, a long name that stretched from shoulder-blade to shoulder-blade, DRINKWATER. The material of the jersey was thick, I figured, too thick given the warmth of the late afternoon, because I saw Mona lift the front and flap it idly, fanning air on to her breasts. Then, hiking it up even further, Mona wiped the sweat from her eyes and forehead. Needless to say, Mona wore nothing underneath, and I was enthralled and delighted to see the soft sides of her breasts. I raced down the stairs and out to the truck.

"Hi!" I said.

Mona jumped down from the hood and grinned. "It's nice

out here," she commented, seeming a little bewildered. "I ain't never been here before." Mona cocked her head toward the pond and asked, "Got any fish in there?"

"Little guys."

"Uh yeah."

"You want to come in and see the house?" I offered.

Mona reached into her pockets for a cigarette, lighting it and blowing smoke from the corner of her mouth before answering, "Nope, I don't, thanks."

"Okay."

Mona made a perfectly formed smoke ring and said, "We missed ya yesterday."

"Huh?"

"We thought maybe you'd come in yesterday, but ya dint."

"I had unexpected company," I told her. "People from Toronto."

"Your wife, the clown?"

"No, just my friend Harvey and some of his students. We conducted a seminar."

"La-dee-dah," said Mona. She flicked away her cigarette even though it was far from finished. "Lookee." Mona pointed to her left breast.

"Nice," I commented.

"Not the tit, stupit," giggled Mona. "The frigging 'C'."

Over Mona's nice tit, someone had sewn on a big C. The rest of the jersey's front was occupied by the profile of a large, evil bird's head. Letters underneath spelled out HOPE HAWKS.

"It's the women's softball team," Mona explained. "I'm the Cap."

"Great."

"The thing of it is, is," Mona went on, "tonight we're playing the Falconbridge Falcons. What a bunch of bimbos they are! And I thought that, if you dint have annathin' else to do, you might wanna come an' watch."

"Great."

"Hey, maybe you can even get a idea for another book or sumpin'."

"Maybe," I agreed.

"So, like, let's hop in ol' Esmerelda here!"

Esmerelda was, apparently, the name of Mona's pick-up truck. I ran over to the passenger side and threw open the door.

"Don't mind Joe," said Mona as a mastiff of overwhelming size and viciousness lunged at me. I managed to throw the door shut. There was a loud crunch as the dog's head collided with the metal. "His bark is worst than his bite," said Mona as she climbed in behind the steering wheel. The hound pressed its face up against the window, all bloodshot eyes and drooling maw. The dog seemed to grin evilly at Mona's comment, resolving not to bark at all, thereby granting me no clue as to how truly horrific its bite could be.

"Nice Joe!" said I.

Joe laughed, lather forming in great quantities at both sides of his mouth. Joe jerked his huge head backward — Get in, I dare ya.

"You're not a'scared of dogs, are ya?" asked Mona.

"No," I answered, "although I have a little thing about the Hounds of Hell."

Mona giggled and wrapped her arms around Joe, pulling him away from the window. "Come on, Joe-Joe," she cooed. "It's just Paulie. He's my new friend."

Joe studied me with interest. Oh goodie, thought the dog, a nice fat one.

"Get in," urged Mona.

My courage was spawned by Mona's comment that I was her "new friend." I opened the door to the cab and jumped in, holding my breath all the while. I stared straight ahead and listened to Joe's maniacal breathing.

Mona fired up her truck and backed down the laneway at about forty kilometers per hour.

Having decided not to bite me, at least for a little while, Joe elected to demonstrate just how bad that bark of his could be. I had rolled down my window a few inches, because it was as hot as a furnace inside the cab, but only a few inches because Mona was driving like a madman along the dirt roads, engulfing the truck in a great cloud of dust and pebbles. Ahead of us, rolling along the side of the road in a quiet, dignified way, was an old man on a bicycle. Joe waited silently until we pulled up behind the geezer, and then he leaned across me and stuck his muzzle through the window's opening. At the instant we were alongside the old man, Joe barked. It was a truly awe-inspiring bark, short in duration, but enormous in volume and speaking unspeakable atrocities. Then we passed the old man. I watched through the side rear-view mirror as he suffered a massive coronary and tumbled into the ditch, bicycle and all.

Joe looked at me, grinning and demanding comment.

"Good, Joe," I mumbled.

Joe laid his head on my lap, covering my jeans with foul-smelling drool.

"You like Hope?" asked Mona, oblivious to her pet's sadistic antics.

"Yeah," I nodded. "As a matter of fact, I'm thinking about doing some research on it."

"What's that mean?"

"You know, researching about how it was founded and all that."

"What for?"

"It might be interesting."

Mona worked the gearshift as we rounded a corner. "Yup," she nodded. "I s'pose it might be."

"You know anything about that?"

Mona nodded but remained silent.

Suddenly Mona threw on the brakes. Both Joe and I were shot forward, Joe crumpling against the dashboard and then slipping with a startled yelp to the floor of the cab. Mona jumped out of the truck and took a few quick steps away, her hands dug into her back pockets, her face turned to the sky. I watched her through the windshield (the glass spider-webbed with cracks), and it occurred to me that Mona was very, very pretty.

"There he is, eh?" Mona nodded toward the clouds.

Joe and I joined Mona on the dusty road.

High above us sailed the hawk.

"I love that fuckin' birdie," Mona went on. "Sometimes I think I love him more than practically annathin' else."

It would be hard, I thought, to love something so distant; but then I remembered about Elspeth.

"What do you call him?" I asked.

"I don't call him nothin'," muttered Mona. "He don't need a

name, on account of he's all alone. Just him and the sky."

"Do you know," I told her, thankful that I'd wasted hundreds of half-hours watching "Mutual of Omaha's Wild Kingdom," "that hawks never drink water?"

"No shit?" Mona placed her enormous hand above her eyes for shade, because the bird was flying into the sun.

"No. They get all the liquid they need from their victims' blood."

"Hey-hey!" Mona gave the hawk a fisted salute. "Way to go, Birdy-baby!"

"And did you know," I went on, "that hawks can't stand to be looked directly in the eye?"

"Neither can I," responded Mona.

"I'll remember."

"You do that," said Mona.

The hawk disappeared, floating behind the tops of some trees. The bird made a strange sound, the sky squeaking as if the Pearly Gates had rusty hinges.

"I love him," repeated Mona, looking sadly earthward. Mona noticed her beast Joe hanging his head in splendid hang-dog fashion, so she dropped to her knees and pressed the hound's head against her bosom. "Hey, Joe-Joe. I love you too! You're my wittle Joe!"

I lowered my eyes in a poetic, woebegone way, but Mona didn't seem to notice. She rose to her feet, hiked up the back of her shorts and said, "The thing of it is, is: Falconbridge has got some pretty fair ballplayers." Mona returned to the truck. Joe and I followed behind. "That's on account of they're all a bunch of bull-dykes, and, if you ask me, we should have a pussy inspection before the game to make sure they aren't bringing in no ringers. Maybe that could be your job, eh, Paulie?" Mona teased.

"Maybe."

The Falconbridge Falcons were demolished, nine to two, at the hands of the Hope Hawks. DRINKWATER (catcher) went three for four, including a double that scored two runs. She was also a very aggressive base-runner, sliding with kamikaze intensity, scraping her knees and tugging down her shorts. The Hope pitcher (SKINNER) was the enormous woman from Moe's Steak-house and Tavern. She was awesome. Skinner had a quick, windmilling wind-up followed by a wrist release that was so violent it produced an audible crack.

Even after my brief perusal of *Failed Utopias*, the names sewn across the backs of the jerseys were jarringly familiar: SKINNER, McDIARMID (short stop), GOM (outfield), CUMBRIDGE (first base) and DELANOY (third).

I sat there on the bleachers, nestled in among old men wearing cotton shirts, overalls and furry Elmer Fudd hats, and cheered for all I was worth. We were an excitable crew, us boys, and we filled the air with whistles, hoots and catcalls. The guy immediately to my left could imitate a coyote, a talent he demonstrated every time the Hope Hawks did anything. The fellow to my right performed a sort of old geezer's strip-tease. With the first questionable call by the umpire, he threw away his Elmer Fudd hat. Next he pulled off his hunting jacket and fired it behind the bleachers. When the third iffy call came, the old man unfastened the bifocals from behind his ears and tossed them disdainfully toward home plate. Then he crossed his arms and sat in silence, presumably with no idea of what was going on.

Someone among us chose to honor the play with a loud, animal-like bellow. This was a frightening sound, a call devoid of meaning or emotion. The bellow began to get louder and louder, and the source seemed to change constantly. I searched through the crowd, which was close to a hundred people all together, but I couldn't see who might be emitting this horrible noise. Yet sometimes the sound seemed to be coming from right around me. Once, when Skinner made a pitch of such enormous velocity that the air trembled, the bellow came from underneath me. I realized, with a sickly concoction of fear and adrenalin spreading in my stomach, that he (for I knew it was the creature, and I heard once more Rachmaninoff's "Vocalise") was beneath the stands, prowling back and forth, peeking out at the action from between our legs.

I forced my head downward (a move that I told myself at the time took courage, although it truly required nothing like it) so that I was peering into the darkness underneath the bleachers.

He was staring back at me, or at least one of his eyes was, while the other cocked dreamily elsewhere. With some strain, the monster rearranged his features, features that looked like a blind person had been playing with a Mr. Potato-Head, shifting some upward, moving others off to the sides. I intuited that this was meant to be a smile, so I smiled back. Coyly, the creature flapped his arms and waddled some feet away. He was wearing a large Hope Hawks jersey, but as large as it was, the thing was larger, and the shirt couldn't come close to covering the mammoth belly. This belly, ghostly pale and looking as soft as water, bounced hideously whenever the creature took a step. He often took steps, or turned himself around in lopsided circles, and I got the impression that, should he stop, he would tumble over from his eight feet in the air. Waddling over to an opening, the thing watched as a Falconbridge Falcon struck out. Then he hollered, lifting his hands over his head and making them flutter like dying birds. The creature spun around once more, and I read the name stitched on to the back of his jersey: HOPE.

A Desperate, Animal Act

Hope, Ontario, 1983
Wherein our Young Biographer dances the Goat's Jig.

After the victory, and a few quick beers at Moe's Steakhouse and Tavern (the "no-steak, no-beer" policy was temporarily relaxed) Mona seemed in a mood to celebrate. She took to stroking my thigh and wedging her enormous hand into my back pocket, and I realized giddily that I might benefit by her high spirits. Mona looked at me and said, "Let's pop this blow stand." We left for Mona's place.

Mona lived, I was not really surprised to discover, in The Willing Mind itself. We entered that establishment through a back door. The tavern was housed in a much bigger building than I'd originally thought, a veritable mansion. Mona led me upstairs and into a hallway that contained about thirty doors. (Joe, by the way, we left tethered outside, where he immediately began a baleful song to the moon. Joe was a horrible singer, even by canine standards.) The only light in the hallway was from the moon, spilling on to the carpet through a round window at the corridor's end. Mona took me by the hand and led me to one of the doors. "This one," she whispered. The doorknob was ancient and wooden. Mona softly touched it and the mechanisms clunked and chunked eagerly. The door swung backward; Mona pulled me into the room.

The only light was from the moon, but the moon that night was full and radiant, peeking through the window and painting everything silver.

The first thing I saw was the bed, because other than a chair and an endtable that supported a flowered enamel washbasin, the bed was all that was in the room. It was a truly magnificent bed, a mammoth brass and mahogany four-poster. Little angels and demons were carved into the head- and foot-boards, and the thick legs of the bed had been given feet, or at least cloven hooves. I imagined that as soon as I got onto the bed (which, given its height, might require a running start and a high jump) the thing would gallop away.

Mona pulled off her HOPE HAWKS jersey. She did this with as much technical "grace" as a seven-year-old boy about to go skinny-dipping, but the effect was pretty stunning. The odd peek I'd had of Mona's breasts hadn't really prepared me for their full beauty, and blood charged into my netherparts so quickly that I felt faint. Mona's body was also tightly muscled, knots of flesh swelling over her ribcage, her stomach a small, perfect oval. Mona smiled at me, then removed her shorts. This she did by unhooking a fastener and lowering the zipper. The shorts tumbled down to her ankles, and then Mona kicked them away, propelling them off one foot with such force that they whistled by my ear and connected with the wall behind me loudly. Mona was now dressed in crimson bikini briefs (pubic hair mischievously escaping over the top) and an enormous pair of black Keds running sneakers.

In that getup, Mona moved forward to kiss me. Mona's mouth tasted of cigarettes and ale. Her breasts were delightful to touch.

Mona wrapped herself around me, and one of her hands immediately worked itself down the front of my jeans. Initially, this caused my penis some distress, even caused it to shrivel a little, because my penis was no match for Mona's gargantuan paw. But Mona's paw was friendly, knew exactly where the little fellow liked to be rubbed and tickled, and before long all was well and good. For my own part, I had placed a hand down the back of Mona's underwear, and she seemed to be demonstrating how it was possible for her to crush my fingers between her buttocks. My other hand I kept fastened to one or the other of her breasts.

Mona tore off my T-shirt (she actually yanked it over my head, but in the morning I did discover a large rent in the front) and then she took a step backward and tugged down my jeans and underwear in one swoop. This hurt. My dick got caught in the elastic waistband of my gotchies, so that for a moment it ended up pointing at my feet (this is what hurt) and then, freed of my underwear, it came rebounding back with a boing. Mona dropped to her knees and took it into her mouth. More of my blood rushed to the scene. Even important blood, blood in the brain that was supposed to be keeping an eye on things, said "Fuck this noise" and headed for my dick.

Meanwhile, Mona's hands sneaked around back and began to explore that opening. Given the length of her fingers, this soon became uncomfortable. I opened my mouth to tell Mona that I was about to come when she released me and headed for the monstrous bed. En route, Mona grabbed her underwear and pulled sideways. The thin material ripped apart, and she tossed the remnants off into a corner. Mona's bottom was, if not perfect, as close as God could get without making it lethal. Mona jumped on to the bed, scurrying under the covers, still wearing her huge, great Keds. I stepped out of my gotchies, jeans and shoes, took a running start, and soon I was beside Mona.

Elspeth is very particular about positions, rating them on a five-star system (the rating goes up for gratification, down for perceived depravity) and refusing to participate in any that rate less than three-and-a-half stars, and I think it's fair to assume she would not have coupled with me in the same manner in which Mona and I ended up coupling. In fairness to Ellie, though,

I should point out that a) she would never have heard of this position, which must be a three-digit number in the Kama Sutra and b) she wouldn't have been capable of it. Mona twisted herself around like a pretzel (I still can't figure out exactly how) and ended up sitting on me and clutching my foot to her breasts as she moaned. Mona did all the work, bouncing up and down on my shaft with joyful vigor. Mona made a lot of noise, too. Her first little grunt was louder than anything Elspeth ever uttered even in the throes of orgasm. Before long Mona was howling with more volume than the baleful Joe. Sometimes she would call out my name, and this pleased me and made me want to prolong things as long as possible, although how I even lasted as long as I did is one of the great mysteries of life. At one point Mona raised an arm into the air, a desperate, animal act, and she reached as far as she could and spread her enormous fingers as if trying to touch the moon. She moaned, then cried out something unintelligible. At least, I pretended to myself that it was unintelligible; in fact, it was not. Mona had said (naked and moonlit silver, her juices flowing out of her and on to me), "Joseph."

World of Flesh

Lowell, Massachusetts, 1851
Regarding the Followers of Hope, we know the following: that, by and large, they were not as they appeared to be; that they were conscientious about personal cleanliness.

Mr. Opdycke sneaked into the kitchen. His first act was to cross over to a cupboard and remove a large bottle of liquor. Joseph Benton Hope did not forbid the consumption of alcohol, but he did claim that it could serve no earthly purpose to the true Perfectionist. The bottle in the kitchen was for guests — lately the House had been receiving a great number of guests. Ministers, city councilmen, any number of dowagers, all had paid visits to the big brick house on Dutton Street. Mr. Opdycke took a sip of the whiskey and was suddenly filled with a radiant rage. The ministers, he thought, he would beat senseless with a large stick, and then Opdycke imagined bending over any one of the dowagers, pounding into the suetty backside. Mr. Opdycke recognized such thoughts as lingering symptoms of his illness, and he was not alarmed by them. The thoughts occurred with such regularity that Opdycke was accustomed to them, sometimes even anticipated them eagerly, as they made for a pleasant break in his otherwise dreary day.

Mr. Opdycke heard the giggling. That would be Abigal Skinner and Mary De-la-Noy. Martha Q. Hope never laughed at all, and Cairine McDiarmid possessed a lusty cackle, rough as treebark. Opdycke had another sip of whiskey. He imagined, briefly, that the kitchen was full of beasts, crouching and waiting to spring. Mr. Opdycke sank to his knees, his hands trembling. Opdycke's hands were trembling because of fear, because of the tremens, but mostly because of what lay behind the door to the scuttle.

Thursday was the day the women bathed.

Opdycke crawled toward the door.

Mr. Opdycke screwed his eye around the keyhole, and first of all saw nothing but white. Then the white vanished, and Opdycke realized that one of the women (Cairine, he reasoned, because he could see the other three) had been standing just in front of the door. Martha Q. Hope was squashed into the tin tub. Mary Carter De-la-Noy was scrubbing her back while Abigal Skinner raced to the potbelly stove and back, getting potfuls of steaming water. The women were all wearing cotton frocks, all except for Martha, of course. Martha sat in the tub, quite naked, so huge that the water barely covered her haunches. Mr. Opdycke had little interest in Martha's body. It was muscled and brawned into sexlessness, her breasts massive and rocklike, her belly and arms like a farmer's, swollen, toughened by hard work and bitterness.

Cairine McDiarmid, next in line for the tub (the women had a definite bathing order, although Opdycke had no idea why or how it was arrived at) removed her frock. Cairine's body was the opposite of Martha's. (Martha stood up now, her hips amazingly wide, wider even than her amazingly wide shoulders. Abigal Skinner began to towel her.) Cairine's body was petite and freckled. (Mr. Opdycke reflected that part of Martha's ugliness, her gargantuan size notwithstanding, was due to the fact that her skin was unnaturally clear, unblemished by a solitary mole or freckle.) Cairine, on the other hand, was covered with wens, spots and maculations. Her body reminded Opdycke of the night sky, as if wonders and mysteries could be found by grouping the marks into constellations. Cairine McDiarmid was also more hirsute than the other women, hairier on the arms and legs, her downshire a thick little bush. Cairine had one or two hairs springing from the edges of her dark nipples. The most impressive thing about Cairine's body (Mr. Opdycke had watched the women many times, and had thought over his judgments carefully) was her bust. Cairine was a tiny woman, but her breasts were large and full. Not so big, of course, as to droop lazily and bend her small back, just big enough to take Mr. Opdycke's rancid breath away.

Cairine had a manner of walking, more a march than anything else, that caused her bubs to pump up and down like a drum beat. Cairine marched over to the tin tub and climbed in. Her backside was tiny, two little pear-shaped mounds, and right at the top of the cleft was a large birthmark, thick and black and looking like a leech. Cairine McDiarmid always splashed the most as she entered the bathwater. She didn't really enjoy being wet, and she spent the shortest time washing herself. When she got out, even though a fire burned some few feet away, Cairine's body puckered with goosebumps and her teeth began to clatter. Abigal Skinner wrapped Cairine in a large towel, and then the little woman marched over to the stove. Cairine opened the towel and let the heat play upon her body.

Mr. Opdycke felt something growing in his trousers. He was tempted to deal with it straightaway, but decided, as he always did, to wait for his favorite.

Mary Carter De-la-Noy was third. (Opdycke had another sip of whiskey, and everything became tinged with a light blue. This was a mischievous trick the witch-piss often pulled, coloring the world in different ways.) Mary De-la-Noy had the most beautiful body of the women, in fact, Mary probably owned one of the most beautiful female bodies in the world. Michelangelo might have chipped Mary Carter De-la-Noy's body out of marble, that's how perfect it was, that's how alabaster white (blue now, as Mr. Opdycke saw it, but normally white) and smooth it was. Mr. Opdycke didn't much care for it. Opdycke couldn't imagine forming the Beast with Two Backs with Mary De-la-Noy, he couldn't imagine twisting her long legs over her head and trying to split her down the middle. Opdycke couldn't imagine chewing on her nipples (Mary's nipples were just a shade or two darker than her white skin, small soft circles) and he certainly couldn't imagine ramming her up the bunghole.

Mary Carter De-la-Noy enjoyed her bath more than the other three. She lay back and closed her eyes contentedly, and Abigal Skinner slowly soaped the whole of Mary's body. Mary made small noises as this was done, a purring deep in her throat. Once or twice Mary twitched as Abigal's fingers touched some ticklish spot. Mary De-la-Noy soaped her own breasts, lathering them so thoroughly that Opdycke imagined no dugs in the world could be cleaner. Mary's nipples blossomed under the soap-bubbles, appearing almost out of nowhere. Finally Mary stood up, glistening, and Martha Q. Hope poured water on her, hot water that streamed down in violent twists and turns as it followed the curves of Mary's body. Mary Carter De-la-Noy's fleece, even soaking wet, was a golden blond. Cairine McDiarmid came over with a towel. (Cairine was warm again, so warm and comfy that she hadn't bothered to put on her cotton frock. Cairine McDiarmid didn't mind being naked, seemed to think little or nothing of it.) Mary De-la-Noy made haste to cover herself, drawing the towel across her body perfunctorily, and then pulling the frock over her head even though she was still damp. The material clung to her body, her nipples plainly visible, and this effort at modesty struck Mr. Opdycke as oddly exciting, and he slowly undid his trouser stays. His pecker jumped out, a short, pugnacious little brute. Opdycke took another sip of the whoozle-water, and everything in the world colored a dark red. Mr. Opdycke took his penis into his hands, for now it was time for his favorite.

Abigal Skinner was not particularly pretty; indeed, calling her plain was something of a kindness. Her eyes were too small, and placed close together on her face; between them was a crooked nose. Abigal had thick lips and an overbite, the overbite causing her weak chin to be displayed prominently. Abigal's best feature was her hair, which was colored a dull brown but kept long, tumbling down to her waist if she allowed it, which she did on Thursdays, bathing days, alone.

Abigal stepped out of her frock. Mrs. Skinner was slightly obese, her breasts pendulous, her belly round and pushed forward. Abigal's nipples were huge, the dark brown aureole covering almost the whole area of the breast. Abigal's thatch was black, and a heavy line of down marched up, across her stomach, and surrounded her huge, protruding navel. Mr. Opdycke knew that this was not beautiful, knew that in some ways it was unsightly, but he pulled at himself with abandon. Abigal turned around and tested the bathwater. She bent over to do this, and Mr. Opdycke went into a frenzy. Abigal's backside was the true object of Opdycke's lust, a huge world of flesh where a man might live happily ever after. Mr. Opdycke knew Abigal Skinner's behind by memory, knew where it puckered and dimpled, knew how it shook whenever she made the slightest little move. Opdycke was determined to own that globe, to mount the hill and claim it as his own. Abram Skinner's presence was no deterrent. Indeed, if Mr. Opdycke understood correctly the implications of much of what J. B. Hope said, it would speak worse of Abram if he made any objection. No one spoke much of these implications but (and Mr. Opdycke came into his own hand, hot and thick) Opdycke was going to do something about that.

Roadwork

Hope, Ontario, 1983
*Wherein our young Biographer decides to
Take some Air and Exercise.*

I woke up and knew it was time for some roadwork.

Beside me snored Mona. She lay on her stomach, awkwardly spread-eagled, her face crushed against the mattress. There were no sheets on the bed; Mona, thrashing during an obviously bad dream, had hurled them clear across the room. I studied Mona's backside, and knew that it was time for some roadwork. I said the word aloud, speaking it to the fat yellow sun perched on the windowsill. "Roadwork," said I.

Mona seemed to have little intention of waking up. The sun told me that it was between nine and ten o'clock in the morning, so she had some time before the legal Ontario bar opening of eleven, and at any rate I judged that The Willing Mind and its regulars weren't overly fussy about legal hours.

Mona flipped over on to her back, so suddenly that I had no chance to get out of the way. A set of enormous knuckles clipped me on the bridge of my nose.

Mona's snoring became incredibly loud, each snore serving as a drumroll for the dramatic and regal rise of her breasts.

"Roadwork."

I jumped off the bed and hunted down my clothes. Items of apparel, both Mona's and mine, were strewn everywhere. It looked as if a hurricane had howled within the tiny room. I dressed and then tiptoed through the door, perfectly aware that there was no need for quiet. Mona, I imagined, could sleep through almost anything. But such is how I chose to vacate the room, furtively, holding my boots in my hand until the heavy door was shut behind me.

The staircase to the rear parking lot lay at the opposite end of the hall; halfway down the hall was another staircase, wider and more substantially constructed. I guessed that it led down to The Willing Mind tavern itself, and decided to take it. I certainly didn't want to face Joe, still tied up outside, howling occasionally at the waking world. It wasn't the hound's bite or even his bark I was afraid of, it was his bloodshot, leery eyes.

By the time I arrived at the bottom of the staircase, I was in pitch blackness. The dark surprised me, coming all at once and with no real warning. I pushed at the walls around me, at first methodically and soon with something like panic, and finally one gave way and took me through to The Willing Mind.

"Hey-hey-hey!!" Big Bernie sat in his usual place, a nicely chilled martoony in front of him. But Big Bernie was not wearing his four-dollar hairpiece, and I was startled to discover that he wasn't simply mostly bald, he was totally and absolutely bald. Neither did Big Bernie have his tinted glasses on, and his eyes, which I always imagined to be as fat and languid as the rest of him, were like those of a cornered wildcat. "It's Paulie!" Big Bernie announced to the assembled.

They were all there, Jonathon Whitecrow and the two Kims, who were locked together as usual. The boy Kim was wearing only a pair of underwear, white BVDs, while the other Kim was wearing a negligee. She was quite obviously naked underneath it, a happy assortment of fattish bulges. It was definitely time for some roadwork.

All this was somewhat alarming, but nothing more so than the appearance of Jonathon Whitecrow, who would have needed considerable cosmetic improvement to look dead. Jonathon Whitecrow was quivering. Sitting in front of him was a shotglass full of whiskey, but every time Jonathon reached for it his hand began to shake so violently that picking it up became impossible, and he would pull his hand back and rest it on his lap, where it twitched like a wounded animal.

"What's the matter?" I asked him.

"Nothing," answered Jonathon, forcing a smile. Sweat ran off his high forehead, made his hair hang in thick, tattered clumps. "I'm just a wee bit hanged over."

"Yeah," Big Bernie put in. "*Moi aussi.*"

"I get fairly bad hangovers," Whitecrow explained. "Gruesome." He made another attempt to pick up the shotglass, even managed to touch his fingers to its side. Then his hand jerked away suddenly, knocking the drink but fortunately not upsetting it.

"Fucking piss!" he snarled. "Fucking goddam whiskey."

Kim disengaged herself from Kim and turned toward Jonathon. "You want some help, Mr. Whitecrow?"

"Yes." Jonathon stared straight ahead as he said this, stared into the mirror that lurked behind the bottles of liquor.

Kim reached over and picked up the shotglass. She touched it to Whitecrow's lips, and he more or less inhaled the whiskey. After a few moments, his shaking stopped. "Ah." The whiskey bottle sat on the wooden counter, and Jonathon poured himself another measure with a steady hand.

"Hey, Paulie," said Big Bernie, "if you want a little pick-me-up drinky-poo, just go and help yourself."

"No," I answered, although God knows I longed for a little pick-me-up drinky-poo. "No, thanks. I'm gonna go do some roadwork."

"Sometimes," Big Bernie reflected, "I need a little pick-me-up drinky-poo in the morning." It was hard to talk to Big Bernie with his gleaming bald head and panic-stricken eyes. It was likewise hard to talk to Kim in his BVDs, Kim in her negligee and Jonathon Whitecrow in general.

"Good morning!" said a voice. I have to admit, it was even a welcome voice.

"Hiya, Little Bernie!" I responded.

"Every morning I wake up, it's the same friggin' thing," complained the stomach. "Back in this old dump."

"It's better than some places," commented Big Bernie.

"So, Hemingway, what are you doing here? Have you come so that you and me could get together on this book deal? Hey, listen, I had another idea for a title. This is a lot classier than *Straight From the Gut*. Get this: *An Unbounded Stomach*. Is that class or what? It's Shakespeare, no less! You like it?"

"Pretty good," I mumbled.

"Pretty good?!" shouted Little Bernie, outraged. "Hey, Mister F. Shoo Fitzwerrit, I haven't heard you come out with any great ideas!"

"I got to go," I told the assembled. "I got to do some roadwork."

I hitch-hiked home, getting a lift from a thirteen-year-old boy driving a huge red Dodge. The boy sat behind the wheel, steering with one finger, using his other hand to hold a cigarette. The boy and I did not make much conversation. When I told him that I lived at the Quinton place he gave me an odd look. The boy dropped me at the bottom of the laneway and did not turn on to the property.

I hadn't run for some days, not since I lived in Toronto and was happily married to Elspeth. We usually ran together, Elspeth setting a panting pace, her arms and legs turning with cool precision as I clomped along behind. I enjoyed running behind Elspeth and staring at her muscled backside. Elspeth wore nylon running shorts, and with every footfall the material would flip up and the pantie portion could be seen digging into her rump. Needless to say, Elspeth was oblivious to this.

I put on my shorts, shoes and a T-shirt that had a picture of a moose on it. I stretched out of doors, limbering up on the stonework patio. The day was a beautiful one, cloudless and still; after a few stretches I was coated in perspiration, hot and slick. That, after all, is the purpose of roadwork.

Then I lit out for the territories.

My plan was to run to Lookout Lake and back, a distance of some five miles. This, I figured, entitled me to five guilt-free beers. Then I remembered that Canada is a metric country, so I converted the distance to eight-plus kilometers, upping my liquid reward to as many ales.

I knew from the outset that it was going to be a long and odd run. I hadn't gone more than ten yards before a sharp, pointed pain materialized near my heart. "Hi! Mind if I join you?" I did my best to ignore it.

Out there they cover the gravel roads with a layer of black stuff so that passing cars don't raise huge clouds of dust. This stuff (I understand it's crankshaft oil, but I'll call it what everyone out there calls it, goosh) had for me an overwhelmingly nostalgic aroma. Of course, I couldn't identify the scent of goosh with anything specific, but it filled me with my childhood and made the sharp pointed pain jump up and down. I ran harder, so hard that the goosh-related memory almost came to me. It had to do with wargames, clods of dirt fired from slingshots; it had to do with a time when the world seemed to make mathematical sense (and the only mathematics I knew was what four plus three made: six).

At that point I bounced to my left to avoid stepping on a snake. I don't know why I bothered. The snake was dead already, paper-thin, flattened by a car's tire. The sun had dried its skin and bones, and in a few hours there wouldn't be anything left but snake-dust.

I took off my T-shirt and tied it around my head. I was sweating everywhere, even from my elbows and kneecaps, which is, of course, what roadwork is all about.

I remembered naked Mona, and for some reason that made me increase my pace substantially. The sharp, pointed pain attached itself to my heart so that it wouldn't get thrown clear.

Various parts of my body began a debate as to just whose idea this goddam roadwork was. My legs were perhaps the loudest, screaming incoherently about spasms and seizures. My stomach and digestive tract pointed out that there was no real food to work with; they'd salvaged what energy they could from the little reservoirs of alcohol that I'd left scattered about, but it just wasn't enough. Scotty, the Chief Engineer down there, estimated I could last another three-quarters of a mile. Meanwhile, my muscles unionized and complained about the horrid conditions, how they were being viciously bounced along a gravel road in ninety-degree weather; and my shriveled, dehydrated corpuscles began to wail for water.

Whose idea was this? they all demanded.

My tiny heart remained silent, muffled in the sharp, pointed pain. I ran faster.

To take my mind off the pain, I lifted my eyes skyward. One lone fubsy cloud sat in the sky. I prayed that some wind would blow it over the face of the sun. I was sweating from my ears, and in another mile I was sweating from my eyes.

By the time I reached Lookout Lake I was sweated out, so hot I was chilly and goose-pimpled. My body insisted on throwing up, even though I was as dry as snake-dust, empty except for the sharp, pointed pain. After many long minutes of dry heaving I lay down by the water and went to sleep.

I dreamed, for the first time, of Joseph Benton Hope.

The Cold Freedom

Lowell, Massachusetts, 1852
*Regarding the pastimes of Hope, we know the
following: that he was a Fisherman. Indeed, it
is of some scholarly interest that it was a
clergyman and personal acquaintance of J. B.
Hope's who, in 1847, produced the 1st
American edition of Walton's* The Compleat
Angler. *Hope was given an inscribed copy
(which presently resides in the Rare Books
Room of Harvard University). The inscription
reads:*

To Jsph. Hope,
from
Geo. Washington Bethune
Apr. 19, the Yr. of our Lord, 1847
Good fortune, & good fishing!!

The men were fishing.

This was one way they'd found to supplement the House's
pitiful income, pulling fish out of the Merrimack. If not for their
proximity to the dark river, Hope and his Perfectionists would
likely have starved to death. Their periodical, *The Theocratic
Watchman*, was supported by private donation, and after its
weekly publication there were few dollars left over. George
Quinton brought in some money, earned doing odd jobs and
chores throughout the city. The De-la-Noys performed the occasional melodrama, but Lowell, a brand-new city of stonework factories, had no taste for either Adam's heroics or Mary's
bosom-pitching.

Abram Skinner fished the river most frequently, virtually every waking hour. He felt useless in the city and longed for his
rows of grain, the huge steaming mountains of compost. Hope
encouraged Abram to contribute articles to *The Theocratic
Watchman*, and Abram had tried, but he found he always became whatever the stylographic equivalent of tongue-tied was,

producing smudgy pages of sentence fragments that made no real sense. So Abram had started fishing the Merrimack, not only for the meat, but for the comfort he found beside the water.

Abram often had company. Mr. Opdycke enjoyed fishing for the same reason schoolboys enjoy fishing—that is, he was usually supposed to be doing something else. Opdycke had certain house responsibilities, mostly janitorial, but he fobbed them off on George Quinton and always had much time on his hands. Mr. Opdycke was an ingenious, if lazy, angler, a great one for setting out a series of trotlines and then snoozing beneath the sun. The deceit and treachery of the new sport appealed to Opdycke; he delighted in discovering new ways of concealing hooks inside tiny fishes, in discovering the most tantalizing way of dancing them in the water.

George Quinton, those times he was free, was an avid fisherman, although his clumsiness cost him a lot of his potential catch (and, the others felt, their's as well; Quinton was incapable of doing anything quietly, and even his tiptoeing and whispering likely drove the fish miles downstream). George was always welcome, though. The men would give him a dangling seining dish and order him to find bait. George had a knack for catching fingerlings and minnows, supplying the anglers with more than they could ever use, and the odd thing about it (something George kept a secret from them) was that he didn't use the net at all. George knelt by the water, bearlike and patient, and scooped out the fish with his massive hands.

Another of George's responsibilities was pole assembly. The men's rods were cane, two four- to five-foot pieces that had to be tied together. Everyone made George do this for them; Mr. Opdycke out of slothfulness, Abram Skinner because he thought that George enjoyed doing such things, and Adam De-la-Noy because he couldn't master the trick of knotting the sections together for himself.

Before becoming a Perfectionist, Adam De-la-Noy had never fished. He had never considered it. "Angling" was a decidedly ungentlemanly sport to engage in, not to mention malodorous. Adam disliked baiting his lure (usually Mr. Opdycke did it for him anyway, running the hook's shank down the little creatures' gullets) and the few times Adam had caught something he'd become alarmed, even frightened, handing his quivering rod to whoever happened to be standing nearby. Still, Adam seemed to prefer the company of the men to that of the women, and he spent much time with them beside the Merrimack River.

Surprisingly, even amazingly, J. B. Hope was perhaps the most enthusiastic practitioner of the Art of the Angle. Each dawn would find Joseph on the riverbank, his line in the water, his tiny eye glaring at the surface. Hope claimed to be able to see a fish approach his bait, and his performance bore him out. Hope was a "snap-fisherman," pulling the fish out of the water as soon as the bait was touched. The others were "pouchers," waiting until the bait was all but swallowed before hauling the prize upward. And there were never any false-sets or errant jerks when Joseph fished, just one sure, quick lift and the thing was landed. What the others wondered at most was Hope's expertise, the deft way he made his horsehair line, small perfect knots that never broke, the manner in which he grabbed fishes by their gills and plucked out the hook.

Hope alone fished for something other than food. As he waved his line out upon the water, Joseph would cackle, heckle and taunt the prey. "Come now!" J. B. Hope would call. "Let's don't dally! You are peckish, don't deny it!" Hope's boyish teasing alarmed the men somehow, and each was saddened in his heart, for Joseph was more open and friendly with the fish than ever he'd been with them.

Sometimes Joseph Hope would fish for a monster. According to Hope, the water contained a colussus, a veritable leviathan, a mammoth as big as a man. Hope never told them why he thought such a beast existed, but none ever doubted his faith. When fishing for this brute, Hope would turn each successive catch into bait, so that he took progressively bigger fish. He often ended up fishing with a massive sucker on the end of his line, a hulk so big that only a whale would be tempted.

On this particular day, all five men were fishing, and Joseph Hope was being outfished. Hope was not a competitive fisherman, at least not in terms of his fellow human beings (he enjoyed confronting the animals, one on one) but he couldn't help wondering what he was doing wrongly that Mr. Opdycke was doing right. Opdycke (on lip-hooked minnows; a departure for

Opdycke, but Hope's usual manner) had taken seven fish in an hour — Hope had pulled out four. Joseph, though, was too aloof to ask. He simply rebaited his hook and tried again.

Abram Skinner had taken two out of the river, one a fat female, puffy with roe. Abram had killed this fish by beating her against a rock until she was lifeless, and then he'd carved out her egg-sac and fixed it to his hook. As he did this, Abram felt vaguely angry, and somewhere in his mind he remembered Abigal's stillborn babies.

George Quinton hadn't caught anything. The pole felt awkward and fragile in his hands, making him nervous. George wished he could throw it away. He wanted to strip off his clothes and dance into the water, to feel the cold freedom kissing his body. He would catch fish then, gather them up like apples.

Adam De-la-Noy, his rod balanced across a foot, lay on the ground and studied the clouds above. He saw a bird slice through them. It was a goshawk, but Adam poetically took it for a swan, and quoted, " 'So doth the swan her downy cygnets save,/ Keeping them prisoners underneath her wings.' "

George Quinton was baffled.

This was all how a fishing day usually was, all except for Opdycke's unprecedented fortune. Opdycke seemed hardly aware of how well he was doing. Instead, he wanted to discuss certain tenets of Perfectionist theory.

"Exclusiveness," Mr. Opdycke paraphrased the infamous "Boston Letter," "has no place when the will of God is done on earth. Amn't I right, Reverend?"

Hope nodded.

"It just seems to me," said Opdycke, pulling in another fish, "that some of us are being mighty exclusive."

"How can you say that?" demanded Hope testily. (Opdycke's catch was at least three pounds. Mr. Opdycke dispatched it dispassionately, sinking a knife into the small brain.) "What exclusivity exists?"

"The normal exclusivity," said Mr. Opdycke, "vis-à-vis the state of matrimony." Mr. Opdycke realized almost giddily that he was much better educated than he'd previously suspected.

"Nonsense," said Hope. "My wife is in almost every sense your wife."

"Almost," Opdycke echoed, putting another minnow on his hook.

"Ho, there!" said Hope suddenly. "What are you doing?"

Opdycke looked to where Hope was pointing, that is, Mr. Opdycke looked down into his own hands. Opdycke's thick thumbnail was imbedded into the minnow's side, splitting the flesh and cracking the backbone. "Oh." Mr. Opdycke threw the minnow into the water, where it jerked in a desperate, dying way. "I've found that helps. I don't know why."

Eagerly Hope stabbed his own minnow and then returned him to the water. Almost immediately he felt an enormous tug, and he flipped out a large brownie, landing the creature gently behind him.

George Quinton took a minnow and poked his finger at its side. He squashed the little fishy, rendering it to mush.

Abram Skinner didn't bother. He was thinking about what Opdycke had said. His corporal relations with Abigal were decidedly uninspired. For one thing, Abigal's body reminded him of pudding, all puckered and jellied, pale, pale flesh. More than that, though, whenever they had amorous congress Abram felt called upon to perform a duty, to plant a seed above all else. It was a duty, Abram felt, that he'd been performing inadequately; in his mind, Abigal's miscarriages and stillbirths were all his fault, the result of flawed making matter. What Skinner wanted to do was play at pickle-me-tickle-me, Adamize and zig-zag, rut with and otherwise splice a female, and, truth to be told, he wanted to do it to Mary De-la-Noy. Mary had a way of staring vacantly into space, her mouth half-open and her eyes half-shut, that drove Abram Skinner to distraction. That is, if Abram Skinner were the sort of man who could be driven to distraction, and he wasn't, this look of Mary's is what would do it. So Abram Skinner said, "I see what Opdycke is saying, Reverend Hope."

"I see what he's saying, as well," remarked Hope. "And in theory he makes a valid point. But the thing of it is, we are trying to exist within the constructs of a society."

"But," said George Quinton, delighted to be able to make this point, even though he couldn't see what Mr. Opdycke was saying, "we must live accohding to God's law, not accohding to the laws of man." George knew that some fish had stolen his minnow, but he didn't bother rebaiting.

"True, George," said Hope. "At the same time, it is our spiritual life that is of uppermost import. What we are discussing is not a spiritual matter." Indeed, thought Joseph, it was perhaps the hardest work he'd ever done in his life. Making love to Martha (which he'd done exactly once) was like conquering the Matterhorn (Hope meant no irony in this reflection) except that the mountain didn't sweat, tremble or try to swallow one into oddly smelling crooks and crannies.

"Perhaps," said Adam De-la-Noy, "we should examine more closely the word 'exclusivity.' "

No one knew what Adam meant by that; the word was not examined more closely.

"I wonder why this works," muttered Joseph. He was referring to the trick of stabbing the live minnows. He'd just taken another fish, and now had six to Mr. Opdycke's eight. Opdycke was bogging down, chewing on a stalk of grass, staring at Abram Skinner. "Skinner," said Mr. Opdycke, "what do you think?"

Abram shrugged and turned to De-la-Noy. "Adam?"

Adam stared at the water. Then he glanced up at J. B. Hope.

Suddenly the end of Hope's pole bent, and began to point straight down at the surface of the water. The river seemed to boil around the line. "I've got him!" shouted Hope, and it was obvious from his tone that this was the monster. The men all leapt to their feet.

Then the knots slipped where George had tied the two sections of the pole together. In an instant the separate sections were floating on the Merrimack, the horsehair line twisted loosely in the ripples.

"Quinton!" bellowed Hope, enraged. "You great oaf!"

As Joseph Hope stormed away, George Quinton began softly to weep.

That night, while the others slept and dreamed their dreams, George Quinton tore apart most of the plumbing in the house. In the morning, Martha would give him hell for it, would even give him a good old-fashioned roundhouse that blackened George's left eye, but he would be unrepentant. He had found what he was looking for, namely two sections of pipe that differed in size by only a fraction of an inch. George cut an inch-long segment from each (chewing up his mammoth fingers in the process) and then fitted them on to the pieces of Reverend Hope's fishing pole. George found to his great delight that the pole could now be speedily assembled, and that the jointed rod was as strong as a single length of cane.

Swallow Love

Lowell, Massachusetts, 1852
Regarding the female followers of Hope, we know the following: that they were much interested in Nature.

The women had their own ideas.

Cairine McDiarmid fancied herself a naturalist, and every so often she'd decide it was time for one of her expeditions. Cairine would rally the other women, and out they would go. One might imagine that an expedition was little more than a stroll through some gentle greenery, the women all petticoated and parasoled, armed with only pencils and sketchbooks. One would be wrong. The three other women (Abigal Skinner, Mary De-la-Noy and Martha Q. Hope) hated Cairine's expeditions because they were really wilderness safaris, and they'd have to wear men's clothing. Mary De-la-Noy especially hated this. While they did indeed carry sketchbooks, they also toted nets, jars, bottles, knives, spyglasses and one or two firearms. Being a self-styled naturalist was hard work in those days, because nature itself was different — wild and living outside of libraries and encyclopedias. It was still possible, back then, to turn over a rock and find some furry, winged, and grinning lizard.

The women each had different functions. Cairine was the leader, and she'd decide where they should go, whether they should mount hills or descend into valleys, whether they should strike inland or head for the sea. She would also, many times during the course of their trek, halt and silence them with a tiny upright forefinger and an urgent "Ssh!"

If Cairine had stopped them because, for instance, she'd seen a rabbit, Abigal Skinner had seen it long before. Abigal was often amazed at how unobservant the other women were, even Cairine McDiarmid. Abigal knew that, if these expeditions were to amount to anything, if they were to contribute to the scientific knowledge of mankind, it would be better if she led. But Abigal didn't want to make trouble, and she enjoyed the exercise, the company of the other women. So, rather than leading, her function on the naturalist expedition was to climb trees. As a young girl she'd learned to climb trees, could even shinny up old monsters whose lowermost branches were yards away from the ground. When a bird's nest was spotted, Abigal Skinner would spit on her palms and go up after it. Then she'd bring it back to the earth, where Mary Carter De-la-Noy would render its likeness with pen and pencil.

Mary certainly had artistic talent, although she often wasn't as faithful to reality as Cairine might have liked. Once, for example, Abigal Skinner had fetched down a sparrow's nest in which there was a dead bird. The tiny thing was mostly reduced to bone, its skeleton covered with an evil-looking papery hide. Mary De-la-Noy had drawn it with fluff, cute as a chick, the eyes gently closed instead of popped open by death.

And Martha Quinton Hope was there to do whatever everyone else was unwilling or unable to do. If Cairine was interested in some specimen from the middle of a swamp, Martha would be dispatched into the bog. If a creek needed to be forded, Martha would roll up her trouserlegs and ferry the others across. Once, Cairine found some droppings and decided they warranted study. Martha Q. Hope was instructed to pick them up.

One day, on an expedition through a meadow, the women noticed that all around them animals were copulating. Coupled dragonflies buzzed everywhere. The women startled no end of rutting rabbits, skunks and groundhogs. And the air was full of mating cries, lonely and urgent howls, musical hoots, wild and woolly. Cairine McDiarmid shuddered, felt fingers up her backbone. She touched her left breast and then, realizing that she had, she took her hand away and pointed to the sky. Two birds flew, turning circles around each other, drawing near and then soaring apart, two swallows in swallow love.

Cairine McDiarmid said, "It was an aspecially adifying talk that Himself give us lost night."

The other women nodded.

"My husband," said Martha Q. Hope, "is a saint."

Cairine McDiarmid decided that it was time to sit down. She fell on her little backside, taking a blade of grass and putting it into her mouth. Abigal Skinner hunkered down on her haunches whilst Mary Carter De-la-Noy reclined. Martha Quinton Hope remained standing.

"Now," said Cairine, "isn't that the very thing he was after sayin'?"

"That he is a saint?" asked Abigal, confused.

"No," explained Cairine. "That we should be aver watchful of possassiveness."

"He is *my* husband," explained Mrs. Hope.

"We air all wed t'gather," said Cairine. "So says Himself."

"Then," giggled Mary De-la-Noy, "we should all sleep in one big bed."

None of the other women thought the remark especially humorous, although Abigal Skinner pretended to laugh. Her own wedding bed was getting to be an exceedingly uncomfortable place; Abram would sometimes enter it sweating and snorting like some prize stud bull, and before she even knew what was taking place the act would be over. Then Abram would climb out of bed and cross to the window where he would stare at the moon. Abigal knew that his intentions were good, that Abram thought that only in this industrious and coldly efficient way could babies be made, but what Abigal longed for was some tenderness. Abigal often imagined that her nipple was being kissed, the whole of her body explored with childlike curiosity. Surprisingly, when Abigal Skinner opened her eyes (in her imagination) it was the gentle Adam De-la-Noy who was doing all this caressing.

Mary De-la-Noy didn't know herself what to make of the quip she had authored. Although she giggled, she realized it wasn't very funny, and she hadn't really meant it to be. Mary Carter De-la-Noy was one of nine children, and she and her four sisters had all slept together until well into their teens. They'd tangled limbs and scratched each other's backs, and sleep had been swift and soft. Nowadays Mary slept alone more often than not, Adam always inventing excuses to sleep in their adjoining room. And when Adam left their bed, Mary would imagine other people in it, and sometimes she imagined having amorous congress with them, not that she lusted or was in heat, more that after amorous congress people felt obligated to scratch her back.

For some reason she often imagined that Mr. Opdycke was in her bed. Opdycke was an unsightly man, his face lined with life, all of his features crooked and strange from misadventure. But Mary De-la-Noy knew that on Thursdays Mr. Opdycke hid behind the door in the kitchen and watched the women bathe. She hadn't told the others, probably never would. When Mary stepped out of her robe on Thursdays she could feel Mr. Opdycke's eyes upon her body, feeding on its perfect loveliness. Mr. Opdycke, Mary felt, after having been granted admission to her golden patch, would scratch at her back until Doomsday.

Mary Carter De-la-Noy rolled over on to her stomach, unmindful of the dirt; she enjoyed the sensation as her breasts flattened against the earth. Mary was in no way indifferent to the joys of amorous congress, but, if the truth be told, Adam De-la-Noy was. Mary knew why, had known ever since she first met the beautiful young man, although she had sincerely believed that her pink-nippled body would effect a change. She wasn't angry that it hadn't, and she loved Adam very much, but often her body ached for physical communion. And if, as the Reverend Hope said, exclusivity had no place in the Perfectionist scheme of things, why couldn't she have amorous congress with the poetical Abram Skinner, or even with Joseph Benton Hope himself? The simplicity of this logic delighted Mary Carter De-la-Noy.

Caririne McDiarmid was, as ever, pragmatic. The whole issue of amorous congress (getting hulled between wind and water, getting a shove in your blind eye, whatever; Cairine found the term amorous congress distasteful) was blown out of proportion. Simply, Cairine had a natural desire for it; she had bodily mechanisms that functioned monthly, and quite often she felt a need to do the naughty. "And J. B. Hope," she often told herself, "he's the lad far me." Cairine would even acknowledge being in love with Hope, if by love one meant an enormous respect and fraternal concern.

Martha Q. Hope eyed her companions suspiciously. All three were lost in thought. "My husband," she repeated, "is a saint."

The Fish

Hope, Ontario, 1983
Wherein our Biographer hears a "Tale" to End All "Tails."

The Hope Public Library was situated on Skinner Road, Skinner being a fairly major street, perpendicular to Joseph Avenue and containing not only the library but the municipal buildings and the Hope Art Gallery and Boutique. The Library was housed in a tiny white bungalow with a goldfish pond on the lawn. I arrived first thing in the morning, armed with four pencils and a spanking new notebook.

I like libraries. When your heart is twisted there's nothing like going into a library and hunkering down studiously, pretending to be a rabbinical student. In Toronto, Elspeth and I lived practically next door to a library, and in the weeks before my departure the staff had seen a great deal of me. In their eyes, I was a very serious young man, probably verging on holiness. I liked to give the impression of having lived most of my life in a Tibetan monastery.

That was going to be hard in this library. For one thing, there were no desks or carrels. Instead, there was an assortment of sofas, rocking chairs and settees like you'd find in someone's living room. That was because, having walked through the front door, you were in someone's living room. Granted, the walls were lined with books, but that was the only library-like touch. The Head Librarian (at least, the only human being in sight) sat on a chesterfield watching television.

It was a game show. The quizmaster demanded, "Who described television as 'chewing gum for the eyes?' "

The Head Librarian screwed up her face. She emitted a series of small spitting noises and then screamed, "Frank Lloyd Wright!!" at the top of her voice.

This was correct.

The living room/library, I noticed, was full of cats. I didn't see them at first, because they were uniformly huge, fat and furry, about as active as furniture. The cats all deigned to open a single eye in order to stare at me. There were anywhere from fifteen to twenty of the beasts. They all closed the one eye, all of them thinking, *Asshole.*

Meanwhile, the Head Librarian was batting a thousand. "Who founded the Moravian Church?" "Everybody knows that!" bellowed the Head Librarian. "Jan Hus!"

The game show went to a commercial break, and the Head Librarian lit up a cigarette.

She looked about a hundred years old. I realize that I've used that phrase before, in my flip way, but I have to re-employ it, because she looked about a hundred years old, mostly because she was about a hundred years old. She was, I found out subsequently, one hundred and four. The Head Librarian was a tiny, withered thing, seeming to be much smaller than any one of her monstrous cats. She lit her cigarette with a match and then she waved the match in the air in order to kill the flame. The flame didn't go away; she stepped up the amplitude of her waving, but the flame continued to march determinedly toward her gnarly fingers. Frantically, the old woman began to blow at it—once or twice she caused the flame to flicker, but it was not extinguished. Finally the flame touched her hand. "Fizzle!" she said, dropping the match into the thick pile carpet, where it died a natural death. I saw that the rug was covered with burn marks.

"Hello," I said.

She turned around to look at me. Most of her trembled slightly, and her mouth and eyes worked all the time, opening, closing, doing strenuous facial exercise. "My goodness!" she exclaimed. "Who are you?"

I introduced myself.

The Head Librarian seemed relieved, and one palsied hand went to her breast. "Thank Christ," she said.

"This is the Library?" I asked, for it was possible that I'd made a mistake and wandered into someone's home.

"Is it ever!" said the Head Librarian. "Look at all the books."

There were admittedly a lot of books, but even a cursory glance informed me that few had been published since 1930. Moreover, the books were placed randomly on the shelves so that *Walden* sat between *Nana* and *Treasure Island*.

"I am Miss Dierdra Violet Cumbridge," said the Head Librarian. "Call me Deedee." Deedee had polished off her cigarette, even though it was one of those hundred millimeter jobs. Near the sofa was an enormous ceramic ashtray, about the size and shape of a toilet bowl, and Deedee flipped her butt into it.

The quizmaster was back on the TV. "What is the state bird of California?" he demanded.

"Oh, for gosh sakes. The valley quail."

"Who was Sennacherib?"

Deedee sputtered a bit, the answer getting lodged in her dentures. Finally she spit out, "The King of Assyria!"

"What branch of science deals with the study of cells?"

"Oh, come on, now! Cytology, what else!"

"I'm doing some research," I said politely. "I am researching this town and its founder, Joseph Ben ..."

"You are?" Deedee Cumbridge crossed her arms and nodded vigorously. "Good for you, Patrick. I think more people should be doing research on just that very thing! My gracious, it's a fascinating story. There's nothing like a good murder, that's what I always say."

I've no doubt that my eyes lit up like headlamps. "A good what?"

"Murder," repeated Ms. Cumbridge.

"Yippee!" I clapped my hands and gave a thumbs-up to the Fates. "And who, pray tell, was murdered?"

"Well, who the hickory do you think?" demanded Deedee. "Let's go to the special Hope Room and do some research."

"Okay! Let's go."

Deedee reached down beside the sofa and picked up two thick canes. She laboriously raised herself to her feet, taking about four minutes. Then she stared at me. "Peter," she said, "you're a nice big boy. I don't say porky, I say big."

I nodded thanks for this sensitivity.

"Even though we've only known each other ten minutes, I'm not embarrassed to ask. Would you please carry me into the Hope Room?"

"Sure."

I picked up Deedee Cumbridge, cradling her in my arms. She weighed sixty pounds, tops.

"Thank you, Phillip," she said.

The Hope Room was near the back of the house. Books lined the walls, but the room also contained a bed and another television set. Deedee had me turn it on. There was another quizmaster.

"What was the name of the first professional baseball team?" (It was "That's A Sport," my Waterloo.)

As I laid Deedee down on the bed she yelled, "The Cincinnati Red Stockings!"

"Right!" I said adamantly. Then I looked through the books as Deedee screamed out answers to questions on quiz shows. She didn't miss a single one.

To my astonishment, there were a great number of books written about J. B. Hope and his Perfectionist followers. Without going into my process of selection, which was a little fluky, let me simply state my bibliography right here and now.

For the history of the community at Hope, Ontario, I used *The History of the Community at Hope, Ontario*, written by Parker T. Sullivan in fulfillment of his doctoral program in Sociology, published by Johns Hopkins University Press, 1958. The best biography of Hope I found was written by Edgar Muncie, entitled *The Perfectionist*, published by Kinlow-Clark, Ill., 1944. Mind you, Muncie tends to be sympathetic toward Hope, so for a more balanced perspective I found it necessary to dig into the past a bit, coming up with a masterpiece of abusive literature, *The Lecher* (Copp & Sons, N.Y., N.Y., 1883), by the Reverend Doctor Ian John Robert McDougall, Barrister & Solicitor. A much nicer book, invaluable for its portrayal of the other important Perfectionists, is *O, But the Days Were Sweet* (Mester & Beatty, 1894), which are the memoirs of Cairine McDiarmid. Also invaluable in this regard are my old standby,

Fishing for Ol' Mossback, by Gregory Opdycke, and a two-penny pulp novel, *The Fish*, by Isaiah Hope. Two books that I used sparingly, and that are only of a scholastic interest, are: *Sexual Practices of the Hope Community*, a monograph written by Prof. Sterling Mycroft of Chiliast University (I lacked interest in this work only because I couldn't understand any of it) and a scuzzy little paperback, *Hook, Line and Sinker: The Updike Empire*.

The Hope Library Hope Room also contained a great number of old periodicals, journals and newspapers. It had bound editions of *The Battle-Axe & Weapons of War*, *The Theocratic Watchman* and *McDougall's Journal*. The newspapers were all The Kingston *Whig-Standard*, and they chronicled a week in 1889, a week during which one man was murdered, another hanged for the heinous deed.

"There is nothing about Hope that I don't know," Deedee Cumbridge said during a commercial break. (Then again, there was nothing about anything that Deedee didn't know.) She lit a cigarette and waved the lighted match in the air, without any dowsing effect.

Being the sort of fellow I am, I eschewed all of the scholarly, erudite works and went straight for *The Fish*, by Isaiah Hope. (A quick cross-reference with *The Perfectionist* informed me that Isaiah was, indeed, Joseph Benton's own son; but at the same time Deedee started clucking her tongue disapprovingly.) The cover of *The Fish* announced that it was AVAILABLE FOR THE FIRST TIME, COMPLETE AND UNEXPURGATED and a CLASSIC OF SUPERNATURAL HORROR. This pocket version from the Hope Library was published some time in the forties (and was astonishingly well preserved, as if Deedee had dusted and fussed over it daily) but the book was originally written in 1891. It had then been issued in a cheap nickel magazine format (all this information was supplied by Deedee Cumbridge during commercial breaks) and everyone ignored it, so Isaiah used his life savings to publish it in hardcover, and everyone read it and was appropriately disgusted and revolted by it. *The Fish* was banned everywhere, and Isaiah was arrested for obscenity, and while they were at it the authorities threw in a couple of buggery charges and one of corrupting the morals of a minor. Isaiah was thrown into the Kingston Pen., and there he died, still a young man, thirty-seven years of age. According to Deedee Cumbridge, Isaiah Hope died of "an overdeveloped sense of drama."

The cover painting of *The Fish* shows a lake, lit silver by the moon. A naked girl, obviously fearful for her life, stands frozen in a strange and awkward position, branches in the foreground covering her nipples and pubic hairs. From the water rises a fish, a huge thing, mouth full of cruel teeth, round red eyes possessed of the devil. On some level of my being I felt a slight outrage, intuiting that the fish on the cover was a caricature of Ol' Mossback, not that I'd ever acknowledge having chatted with him, but Ol' Mossback struck me as a fairly decent sort, for a fish.

On the first page there was a quotation from Thoreau serving as a proem. It read:

> Whether we live by the seaside, or by the lakes and rivers, or on the prairie, it concerns us to attend to the nature of fishes, since they are not phenomena confined to certain localities only, but forms and phases of the life in nature universally dispersed.
>
> H.D. Thoreau, *A Week on the Concord*
> *and Merrimack Rivers.*

The book featured a 'John Lockhart' of 'Lockhart, Ontario." Subtlety was not Isaiah's strong suit. I sat down on the edge of Deedee's bed and read.

I will relate with utter candor the strange events occurring that summer so very long ago. Only a courageous fidelity to the truth will spare me accusations of mendacity. All I request is anonymity; suffice it to say that I am a townman, that town being Lockhart, Ontario; that I labor at a trade, that being the manufacture of fishing and angling tackle. As to my personal life, know of me what you would know of any other citizen; that I am happily espoused, that the union has resulted in three fine children, and that of a Sunday I take no greater pleasure than in attending the Service and honoring my Maker. I am no better a man than many others, and I devoutly pray no worse.

Our town is named Lockhart because we were founded by one John Lockhart. The history of our founding is too long for inclusion in these pages, too complicated by the vagaries of fate and the *capriccios* of the human nature. When first he settled, John Lockhart was a man whose most readily apparent trait was nobility, a man, as they say, with a Vision. But years had clouded that vision, and nobility was somehow transmitted into depravity, and John Lockhart, that summer so very long ago, had become an evil old man.

It is time to point the finger of shame at the true villain of the tale, Hanging Johnny, also known by the names of Doctor Johnson, Uncle Dick, Jacques, Old Hornington, my man Thomas and Blind Bob, for it was this mischievous fellow who precipitated the horrendous events that are to follow.

Gretel Dekeyser was, the summer of which I speak, a virgin, fourteen years of age. There is no need to proffer evidence of her purity; indeed, one had only but to look upon her, to see the alabaster whiteness of her flesh, the soft swellings of her breasts (not yet blossom'd with the fullness of womanhood), her slender hips, as slim as a boy's, and her pearly feet...

" 'Her pearly feet'?" I read aloud.

Deedee was lighting another cigarette. She certainly smoked a lot for a hundred-and-four-year-old woman. Again she had difficulty snuffing the flame, huffing and puffing at it uselessly, dropping the match on to the floor (with the mild oath, "Fiddlysticks!") when it began to burn her fingers. "Isaiah Hope," Deedee informed me, "liked feet."

...to know that she had never known dark lust. Perhaps it is this very heavenborn virtuousness that drove John Lockhart to distraction, that reared Hanging Johnny's ugly head. The facts are known to us from Gretel Dekeyser's own mouth; although having divested herself of them, Gretel spoke no more and never again. She had been walking by the lake, on a hot summer's day, and decided, as all children will when sweat stickles their youthful bodies and cool water laps at their toes, to throw off her clothes and plunge therein. There was no licentiousness here, her body not "nude" but simply "naked," her breasts too small to joggle provocatively, her bottom as small as a boy's . . .

"Isaiah was weird," I mumbled.

"Was he ever!" agreed Deedee, adding, in answer to a TV quiz show poser, "Benjamin Franklin."

. . . and her pearly feet churning the water, propelling her forward.

John Lockhart was also at the water's edge, for he was by way of being a Nimrod, and he was in pursuit of the Fish. A word of explanation; it had long been said, although hitherto dismissed by many as foolish prattle, that the waters of our environs contained a prodigious being, an aquatic beast of monstrous proportion. John Lockhart was obsessed with this mythical colossus and angled for it daily, to the exclusion of all else, including any intercourse with his family or only son. Under normal circumstances, nothing could dissuade him from his efforts to take the Behemoth, except on this day, when he espied Gretel Dekeyser's boyish bottom moving about in the water.

Then the devil Wagstaff whispered, "We must have her!"

The having of Gretel Dekeyser was no Herculean endeavor, for she was a petite girl. John Lockhart merely waited by her abandoned petticoats. When she quitted the water, droplets flowing over her as-yet unwomanly breasts, through the sparse thicket of her boyish loins, ultimately arriving at her pearly feet, John Lockhart reared up. "Eek!" exclaimed Gretel Dekeyser. And quickly the deed was done, John Lockhart holding her arms and girdling her boyish frame while Rupert Ramrod did the vile business.

"Pretty spicey, eh?" demanded Deedee.

Karl Dekeyser, Gretel's father, was like many of the Dutch who had emigrated to Canada in order to forge a new life. Karl was a simple man, although by this I allude not to a dullheadedness on his part, rather to a way of viewing the world with a childlike artlessness. When Gretel came home, disheveled and flushed with the crimson of shame and humiliation, Karl knew he had to exact a revenge; moreover, Karl saw that justice must be meted out, not to a single villain, rather to a pair of scoundrels.

"Oh-oh," I mumbled, and my rapidly shriveling groin voiced a request that I read no further.

The moon that night was full and radiant, eager to light the darker deeds of men. There were some thirty men in all; good men, most, certainly none devoid of virtue. I will admit to being in their midst, mute and faceless.

We transported John Lockhart to the scene of his transgression, perhaps thinking that our justice would be more certain there. Few of us, I think, knew what justice we would mete, perhaps not even Karl Dekeyser, although an electricity in the air whispered that blood would be let.

John Lockhart did not protest his innocence; indeed, his manner implied that his culpability was none of our concern, that we were all small, petty things with no business in his affairs. He stared at us with his queer eyes, vicious and defiant as a goshawk. Lockhart's eyes were in and of themselves disquieting; he'd lost one, the left, while fighting valiantly in the American Civil War, and it had been replaced by a pale, blue marble. The superstitious of nature, by which I refer to virtually all who inhabited our town, had it that this small glass sphere was capable of demonological entrancement; and if, as Lockhart claimed, Gretel Dekeyser had denuded herself with full knowledge that he lurked nearby, her behavior was due to this thaumaturgy.

"Do you want," Deedee asked politely, "a beer?"

"No, thanks." I was engrossed in the little paperback, and besides, I was in one of my moods whereby I had quit drinking forever. These moods come upon me quite frequently, though they never stick around too long.

"I do," she said.

I realized that Deedee was asking me to fetch her one, so I searched out the kitchen and went to her fridge. Her fridge was full of beer, row upon row of brown buddies standing shoulder to shoulder. That wondrous sight melted my nondrinking resolve instantly, and I pulled out two bottles. They were perfectly chilled, the fridge's thermostat set with an eye to the ale alone. Of course, aside from the beer, the only inhabitants of the fridge were six Mr. Big chocolate bars and a rockhard quarter pound of butter. I opened the beers pouring them into two tall pilsner glasses that I got out of the freezer, beautiful glasses clouded with frost. When I got back to the bedroom Deedee and I toasted each other.

It was decided, when or by whom I can't recall, that John Lockhart should remove his clothing. Lockhart affected the vesture of clergy in a haughty, arrogant manner, no more ordained than a common mongrel, and these garments were torn angrily from him. Lockhart's underclothes were removed so that he might be further humiliated.

His accomplice was rigid, as if standing at attention. Lockhart himself was small in stature; it was enormous, fat and superposed with thick veins. The One-Eyed Snake stared at us, more insolent than its master, swollen with vainglory, bloated with pomposity. I then realized that the relationship was reversed; John Lockhart was subservient to the purple piccolo, a Nubian to his own Nebuchadnezzar.

Suddenly Karl Dekeyser moved forward, and before we knew what had happened, he (incidentally a butcher by profession) was holding the razor-sharp tool of his trade in one hand, and the huge, quivering quimstake of John Lockhart in the other. We looked on in horror as blood poured from John Lockhart, a thick red stream as if he were a fountaining statue. Karl Dekeyser held Long Tom Lovestaff high in the air and walked to the lake's lapping edge. He held the Hairsplitter over the water and gently released it.

It was then that we first saw the Fish. It rose out of the water, revealing itself to be a length of some six feet. The Fish's eyes were large orbs that held the moonlight within. The Fish opened its mouth, huge and full of tiny, needle-sharp teeth, and then closed it around Lockhart's bloody Dingle-Dangle.

I'll give you a synopsis of the rest of the book. The fish spends the next few moments chewing on the "Goose's Neck," a few moments that John Lockhart spends dying, something I would certainly do if I were him. And the thing is, at the exact second that Lockhart dies, the fish swallows the "bald-headed mouse." There is then some magical transference of spirit and John Lockhart and the fish commingle on an astral plane somewhere in the cosmos. THE FISH is created, a monster that swims around waiting for townsmen to come near the lake, waiting for them to — for whatever reason — remove their "pondsnipes," "spindles," "downlegs" or whatever they happen to have, whereupon The Fish, exacting John Lockhart's monomaniacal revenge, leaps out of the water and chomps off their dicks. The town is finally saved by a woman, hitherto a scorned and laughed-at woman by virtue of her physiognomy, which was huge and bearlike. This woman (named Marta in the tale) dresses up in masculine garb and fishes from the water's edge. After a while, she nonchalantly removes what appears to be an enormous "tallywhacker" from her trousers. The Fish naturally emerges from the water and bites it off. Of course, it wasn't a "flappdoodle" at all, it was a sausage laced with arsenic. The Fish dies (for some reason The Fish's death scene is by far the longest passage in the novel, about fifteen pages' worth), and Marta becomes a heroine, and our anonymous narrator learns not to judge by even freakish appearances. This is, of course, a nice lesson to learn, although the anonymous narrator never mentions that it might also be poor form to lop off somebody's penis. (The word penis, by the way, is not employed in *The Fish*.)

At any rate, the book was a smallish thing, 128 pages in all, and being a speedy reader I managed to complete it that afternoon. Deedee Cumbridge and I also managed to make a fair dent in the Frigidaire full of beer. When I was finished reading we watched television together. The game shows were all over but "Mutual of Omaha's Wild Kingdom" was on. Deedee and I drank beer and cheered for the predators: "Come on, lion! You can catch that gazelle." "Go you Golden Eagle, you! It's only a bunny rabbit!" The only reason we rooted for the predators is because, due to the four-to-one betting odds and the fact that the show is for family viewing, they never catch anything on "Mutual of Omaha's Wild Kingdom," and if you watch the show often enough you get the impression that everything in the wild kingdom is slowly starving to death. As Deedee Cumbridge put it during a commercial break (advertisers were sure wasting their money on Dierdra Violet Cumbridge; she had countless ways of occupying herself during commercial pauses, and not one of them was learning about the product in question), "If you don't go for the dogs," (by which she meant "underdogs") "you'll go to the dogs."

After "Mutual of Omaha's Wild Kingdom" came the nightly news, which we both found a bit boring. Deedee had a very emphatic way of demonstrating boredom: she fell fast asleep. Her mouth fell open and she began to snore, although it was barely audible. Deedee had fallen asleep with a cigarette still burning in her wrinkled claw. I removed it and mushed it into the overflowing ashtray. Then I leaned over and kissed Dierdra Violet Cumbridge on the forehead. "Ah, Deedee," I whispered, "if only you were seventy-seven years younger."

Imperterpitude

Somewhere between Montreal and Boston, 1850
Regarding the contemporaries of Hope, we know the following: that some of them were Assholes.

Ironically, given the subsequent life of Hope, Ian John Robert McDougall was born in Fredericksburg, Upper Canada, and educated in law at York. But McDougall soon proved himself to be an indifferent advocate. His true interest was ensuring that sinners were punished, not judiciously, but righteously and Biblically, an eye for an eye, maybe two eyes for an eye if McDougall felt lucky, so he abandoned both law and the Northland and went to study Theology at Amherst, New York. Thus, in the year of Our Lord 1850, when Henry David Thoreau met Ian John Robert McDougall aboard a train traveling from Montreal to Boston, the latter insisted on the appellation "Reverend Doctor McDougall, Barrister and Solicitor." Thoreau nodded, staring out the window, mentioning quietly that he could be called Henry.

"I was visiting relatives," Rev. Dr. McDougall went on, not that Thoreau had asked. McDougall lit a foul-smelling cigar, which immediately rendered Thoreau many different shades of green. "I reside in palatious New York. But business of a great portentious nature leads me to verdurent Massachusetts." Rev. Dr. McDougall tilted his head briefly. "What business am I in?" he demanded rhetorically. McDougall pointed to his white collar. "I consider myself a watch dog. My good man, are you aware of the moral imperterpitude extantile upon the face of this land?"

Thoreau looked up, puzzled. "No. Indeed, I was not aware of any such word as 'imperterpitude.' "

"Sadly, I am. I have made it my life's work. My card." McDougall reached into one of his many pockets and took out a small embossed card. Thoreau read the card, then looked at the man studiously.

The card, in elegant and curlicued letters, announced:

The Most Reverend Doctor I.J.R. McDougall
Barrister & Solicitor
Chaplain of the New York Magdalen Society
President of the Society for the Moral & Religious
Improvement of the Five Points
Publisher/Editor of *McDougall's Journal*

McDougall was an unpleasant-looking individual. The most unsightly thing about him was his complexion, which was a bright red. As a youth, McDougall had suffered horrendously from acne, and even as an adult he sported pimples as large as silver dollars. McDougall's hair was also red, but many shades duller than his face. McDougall's hair was very sparse, a few valiant strands grown to great length and carefully arranged to conceal a bald pate, and McDougall wore no beard, moustache or sideburns. Thoreau suspected that the man's facial hair simply couldn't force its way past the swelling whiteheads. (For his own part, Thoreau's hair tumbled on to his shoulders, and he let his beard grow unhindered.) McDougall was rail-thin, obviously not a man to enjoy food, or anything else for that matter. He had a disconcerting habit of leaning forward and speaking to Thoreau from a distance of three or four inches, pressing his face to the young man, his voice overly loud, his breath hot and fetid.

Henry David Thoreau handed back the card.

"Don't you wish to keep it?" asked McDougall.

"I hadn't realized that I was meant to." Thoreau reaccepted and pocketed the card. He wondered what he would do with it.

"Lust," said McDougall. "Depravousness. Lubriciousness." Much of McDougall's conversation ran along these lines, that is, he gave voice to synonyms, mostly nonexistent, for the moral imperterpitude that was so rampant. Thoreau's interest, if he had any at all, was on a linguistic level.

"I began my illustrated career," said McDougall, "by visiting the seraglios of New York City. I was stunned to discover that the women there were both beautiful and elegantily dressed. I

have since visited sundrous establishments. In fact," McDougall
opened a satchel he had resting on his bony knees, "I have
listed more than two hundred and twenty such zezanas in Man-
hattan alone!" He handed Thoreau a small periodical entitled
McDougall's Journal. "I have gone so far as to make an exact-
ment of the street addresses," said McDougall, "so that these
particular cantonments might be eschewèd."

Thoreau leafed through the magazine idly. One article caught
his eye: "The Maidens of Owahoo; An Investigation into the
Diversions of the Yankee Marine Upon Tropical Shores." The
article began:

> Mimmumi was denutated, but with unabashness, for she
> was as Our Lord did create her, save for a small bit of sack-
> ing that modested her pudiciousness.

The article was unsigned, but Thoreau thought the wording
was a bit of a giveaway.

"Rampacious uncleanness," put in McDougall.

Thoreau had spent two years, all alone, living beside a pond
near Concord, Massachusetts. Even though it had been three
years since he'd left, the young man still had a problem making everyday conversation, especially conversations to which
he could ascribe no purpose or benefit. He therefore flipped
through the periodical and tried to give the preacher across
from him the impression of being engrossed.

Certainly, much of the magazine was interesting in a way. It
did, for example, have many pages listing brothels, suggesting
in an introductory paragraph that anyone interested in "in-
continenciality" and "libertinousness" would be well advised
to visit the establishments, simply to see firsthand how disgusting they were. There was an article about the street gangs of
New York City.

> The "forties" are a group of lads whose mean age is 13.
> Yet, these young boys occupy themselves in what they
> term "gooseberry lags," which are, in fact, plundering
> expeditions, the likes of which for cruelty and violence
> have not been seen since the Viking and the Visigoth.

The article did indeed engross and alarm Thoreau, as he read of the gang wars, the improvised yet terrible weaponry, "black-legs" and "knucklers." He wondered if what so many said was true, that the world would never see the twentieth century, that total and utter annihilation was inevitable. Thoreau silently argued against this. Societies might change, he thought, and certainly governments would change (hadn't Thoreau spent a day in jail for trying to precipitate this?), but the world itself, he reasoned, would always remain, fair and fine. He'd learned that from his pond, and he often wished that everyone might have a pond to learn from.

Henry David Thoreau closed the magazine and read the title page, allowing himself a small, unobtrusive chuckle.

McDougall's Journal
The Purposeness of which is to EXPOSE public Immoralousity and to furthermore DEVISE means of preventing Licentiableness. Contains moreover articles germing to the Public *Good* and also ... Spicy Anecdotes of Unsuspected Depths of Depravious Activities.

Thoreau handed the magazine back.
McDougall demanded, "Don't you want it?"
Thoreau shook his head gently.
"Are you not a Good Christian?"
The young man turned and stared out the window. He watched a river that ran beside the tracks, a river full of sunlight and fishes. "I'm a Transcendentalist," Thoreau said.
McDougall felt a little annoyed. Transcendentalists never did anything; they kept to themselves, smiled a lot, and wrote poetry.
"Just so long as you're not a Perfectionist!" McDougall roared.
"A which?" Thoreau saw something then. He took out and looked at his pocket watch, and saw that the train had been traveling some five hours out of Montreal. They were still in Upper Canada, then, somewhere to the west of Kingston, east of Muddy York. Henry David Thoreau took note of all this, because he meant to make mention of it in his Journal. What he saw was this: a fish, some five and a half feet long, rise fully out

of the water, flip over as if in ecstasy, then drop back into the water with a glorious rainbowed splash. Thoreau was a knowledgable fisherman, yet he couldn't recognize the monster's breed. He had heard that the Northern Maskinonge could attain a great length, but this fish possessed huge eyes, round and silver as the moon.

"The Perfectionists," McDougall was saying, "are more minatating than Fanny Wright or Robert Owen! The cult has sprang like poisonal mushrooms! First it was confounded to those in Boston and subsequently Lowell, but now sects are exant in all the towns of fair Massachusetts, not to mention Vermont, New York and even Maine! Hope is decidedly evil."

Thoreau looked baffled.

McDougall spat out the name, "Joseph Benton Hope." The pimpled man took out a pair of spectacles and fixed them on to his pimpled nose. "I mean to see Hope humiliated," said McDougall, as he took some handwritten pages out of his satchel. "Allow me to read to you from my condemnationary speech. Ahem. 'The masterstroke of his Satanic policy ...' I refer to Hope, although others almost as evil abound, e.g., Bryee, Odell, et al. However, I digest. Ahem. 'The masterstroke of his Satanic policy is to open a floodgate to every species of immoralatious undertaking, and by a refinement of wickedity which puts papacy to the blush, to sanctimonify the very incarnate imperterpitude."

But Henry David Thoreau didn't hear. He was thinking about the magnificent fish.

The "Oh-Oh" Chorus

Hope, Ontario, 1983
*Wherein things begin to go badly for our
Young Biographer ... as if they haven't been
all along.*

I busted into The Willing Mind and started a sort of Humphrey
Bogart/James Cagney impersonation. "All right, youse guys, I
scammed it out good," I told Jonathon, Mona, the Bernies and
the Kims. "Here's what went down. Joseph Benton Hope, practitioner of complex marriage, wilful countenance and stirpiculture, went one step too far. Yeah, that's right. He spied some
little enchilada with a hot chassis and he took her for a little
spin, see? Only her old man didn't like it. So he took Joseph out
to the lake, see? And ..."

"D'you wanna beer ... or what?" demanded Mona. Mona
was glaring at me, undeniably and relentlessly. Her enormous hands were buckled on to her hips, and those hips were
tossed aggressively sideways. Mona was wearing a light, see-
through blouse, and I saw through it. Of course, I didn't drop
the Bogart/Cagney impersonation; I'm the kind of guy who
keeps up bad jokes until someone laughs out of sheer desperation. "Yeah, that's right, sweetheart. A beer."

"You're a nerd," Mona declared, marching off for the draft
pump.

I imagined all this petulance was due to the fact that the last
time I saw Mona we were lovers, even passionate ones, and on
this occasion I had yet to say hello to her. Oh, well. I'd make
amends later.

"You. Whitecrow. You were there, weren't you? Yeah, yeah,
sure you were. Come on, tell me everything you know."

Jonathon stared at me, and his strange silver eyes were crin-
kled with amusement, although I knew he was likewise not
taken with my little act. "Sit down, Paul," he instructed me,
drawing over a barstool. "You've been doing some reading,
have you?"

"That's right. Over at Deedee's place."

"The library," Jonathon said.

Suddenly a mug full of beer was dropped on to the counter in front of me. "So you been hanging aroun' at the lib'ary, huh?" asked Mona.

"Um, yes." I grinned. "Hello, Mona!"

Apparently I'd left it a little too long. Mona tsked her tongue and in the very act of tsking managed to stick it out at me.

The beer tasted good. I don't know if it had actually improved in quality or if I'd realigned my tastebuds out of necessity.

"So what happened?" Big Bernie demanded.

"Huh?"

"They took this Bent Hoop and what?"

"Not 'Bent Hoop,' jerk!" said Little Bernie. "J. Benton Hope, our founding father."

"Oh. Anyways, what did they do?"

For some reason the answer required a poor Long John Silver imitation. "They takes him art t' the warter, and they takes a scabbard, and they cuts arf his ..."

"Yes?" prompted Jonathon Whitecrow.

"They cuts arf his whore-pipe! Har-har-har!"

"Kee-rist," muttered Mona.

"Ooh!" went Big Bernie, and one fat hand flew down to cover his groin. "Ouchie-ouchie-ouchie!"

"But, you must have known that, Bern," I told him.

"Maybe I heard sumpin' about it one time," he recalled.

The Kims, interestingly enough, were not locked in an amorous knot. The boy was staring at me. His acne was getting worse, which is what nonstop dry humping will do to you. "Are you serious?" he asked. "They cut off his cock?"

"That's how it's beginning to look, kiddo."

"Yeah, well, it's a bunch of like horse hooey!" This came from Mona, who was sitting away down at the other end of the bar. She was reading a biography of General Patton.

"I take it, then, that you have read *The Fish*?" asked Jonathon Whitecrow.

"Sure. But there's other clues. Everyone around here says 'Keep your dick in your pants' whenever anyone goes fishing. Right? And a Hoper looks just like a penis." It didn't really, but it certainly looked phallic. I remembered the old fart in Moe's

Steakhouse and Tavern, and the way he'd made the Hoper stand erect, the senile and swinish way he'd guffawed.

"Isaiah Hope," said Jonathon, "was a somewhat disturbed young man."

"I gather that's true enough."

"You should write somethin' about Patton," said Mona. "Now *that's* inneresting. Nobody cares about what happened a hunert years ago."

"Somebody already wrote a book about Patton."

"So? There are other fuckin' generals! Jesus, d'you think Patton was the only American five-star general tank commander in the whole fuckin' continent of Africa?!"

I saw that it was possible to have awesome arguments with Mona.

I brought my fingers up to the bar and began to beat out a very complicated tattoo, which is about all I could think of doing. Then I looked around the bar. It seemed to me that the stuffed animals were somehow different, poised more delicately, hackles raised, ready to pounce. Then I spied a way of starting a new conversation. "Ah," I said, pointing toward one of the walls. "Now, that's a very interesting thing. This window here, the stained glass." The window I referred to portrayed, in a highly grotesque fashion, the crucifixion of Our Lord Jesus. "It has been inserted," I continued scholastically, "topsy-turvy. As you may know, inverted representations of the cross are quite common in ..."

"Oh-oh," said Jonathon Whitecrow.

This was my first time as part of the "Oh-oh" chorus. It came quite naturally. I said, "Oh-oh," and watched the old Indian collapse to the floor.

"Looks like a big one," I said to Mona. She nodded. It looked like a huge one. Jonathon's limbs twitched horribly, inhumanly, his body consumed by random electric impulses. Mona reached across the bar and squeezed my hand, worried and fearful for her friend Jonathon.

Big Bernie muttered, "Geez. I hate it when he does that."

Finally Jonathon stopped twitching. During the attack, the Vision, Whitecrow had wept uncontrollably, so much so that his face was slick with tears. His shirt was soaked through, ei-

ther from sweat or overflow from the crying. Jonathon opened
his eyes. They burned darkly, two little pools of black water.
"Oy," he gasped. I helped him to his feet.

Mona fed Jonathon his whiskey.

Then we all pretended nothing had happened.

"In what, Paulie?" asked Big Bernie.

"Beg your pardon?"

"Inverted representations of the cross are quite common in
what?"

"In, um, witchcraft."

"Deedee Cumbridge," Jonathon Whitecrow said suddenly,
"smokes too much." One or two tears escaped from Whitecrow's
obsidian eyes.

Then came the explosion. I can report to you now that it
was an oil furnace (who else but a one-hundred-and-four-year-
old lady would have her furnace going in the middle of the
summer?) some two blocks away, but the sound inside The Willing Mind was deafening. I was pretty sure the world was ending.

Synchronicities

Lowell, Massachusetts, 1853
*Regarding the trials of Hope, we know the
following: that on October 7 he was brought
forward to stand charges that his religious
tracts and pamphlets violated the
Antiobscenity Postal Statute of the Federal
Government; that the offense was punishable
by imprisonment.*

As historians have pointed out, the number of coincidences
(synchronicities, some of the younger scholars have it) in the
life of Hope is quite astounding. This is nowhere more apparent than during that phase of Hope's life that has been variously
referred to as "The Lowell Trial," "The Hope Trial" or, in some
texts, "The McDougall Trial," McDougall being the Reverend

Doctor Ian John Robert, Barrister and Solicitor, who served as prosecutor. Some of these synchronicities are listed below.

1) October 3, 1853. *The Battle-Axe & Weapons of War.*
Four days before the trial, Theophilius Drinkwater published a special issue, a number devoted to Joseph Benton Hope. The front leaf read IN DEFENSE OF PERFECTIONISM, and thereafter, for sixteen pages, Theophilius Drinkwater did what he could to save Joseph's besmirched reputation. Theophilius was very eloquent and persuasive. The main thrust of his argument seemed to be that it was all right to have carnal relations with hedgehogs if that's what one wanted to do. The Reverend Doctor McDougall used the periodical throughout the trial, quoting from it, alluding to it, even handing out copies to the members of the jury. Of course, Drinkwater, a man known to bear a grudge for a long time, knew exactly what effect his "defense" of Perfectionism would have on Hope's trial. Joseph Benton Hope stated over and over that he could not be held accountable for Drinkwater's philosophizing, but McDougall simply twisted that, implying that Hope felt Theophilius had been too tame.

2) May–June 1853. Medical Synchronicities.
Cairine McDiarmid became pregnant around this time. In a few months, when she attended the trial of Hope, her belly would be swelling magnificently, carrying as she was the twins Lemuel and Samuel. Cairine's marital status would not go unnoticed, and although she claimed under oath that the impregnation was accomplished by a young man she'd met somewhere, a young man whose name she could not recall and had no curiosity to rediscover, McDougall and most people believed that J. B. Hope was the father.

A further medical synchronicity, a rather distasteful one, is that in July of that year the Rev. Dr. I. J. R. McDougall, Barr. & Sol., developed a horrendous case of hemorrhoids. His other end became as red as his face, swelling with pustules. This may well account for his disposition throughout the proceedings, which was cranky to say the least.

3) July 22, 1853. An Extraordinary Demise.
There are seventeen authenticated cases of spontaneous com-
bustion in North America (at least, seventeen cases where no
other satisfactory explanation has been offered), and the death
of Buford Scrope Davies is one of them. The fat, club-footed
clergyman had been preaching in front of his congregation. In
the middle of a sentence (popularly held as referring to the
fires of perdition, in fact an etymological argument concerning the Hebrew word *Nacham*) the Reverend Buford Scrope
Davies made a sound like a five-cent firecracker, a tiny little
pop, and burst into flame. The effect, I take it, was rather
dramatic, and many people accepted this as some sort of divine sign, the Almighty singling out Buford Scrope Davies above
all others. Today, in fact, there are some four thousand Daviesians scattered about North America, a sect that believes that, if
you behave very well, you might go poof and get swallowed
up in black flame.

(An intrusion here from the Biographer, one of a personal
nature. Elspeth's mother, a monumentally crazy old woman, is
a Daviesian. This has had a definite influence upon my wife.
Elspeth has told me that throughout her childhood, fevers oc-
casioned great joy on her mother's part. Once, when Ellie's
temperature pushed 103° F, her mother called in several fellow Daviesians and they laid Elspeth down on some aluminum
foil and waited for fireworks. Today, Elspeth does not get sick.
She refuses to let germs anywhere near her, mortally fearful of
fever. I do not know what will kill Elspeth, but I know it won't
be disease; my money is on a bus, but Ellie would have to be
ninety-four years old and never know that it was coming.)

Polyphilia was somewhat distressed by the loss of her husband, particularly by the bizarre nature of his earthly exit, and
she didn't know where to turn. After a few weeks of moping
about her father's house, she decided to go to Lowell, to be
with her friends at their time of need. This she did, taking her
son, the two-year-old (and already markedly obese) Ephraim.
Polyphilia arrived at the courthouse at the precise moment that
Joseph Benton Hope began to speak in his own defense. Polly
sat down in the front row, squeezing herself in between George
and Martha. She smiled encouragingly at Joseph.

Hope's testimony was eloquent and thoughtful, and might well have swayed many minds, had he not been clearly possessed of an enormous erection. Unconsciously, Joseph repeatedly adjusted his rod, shifting it to more comfortable positions within his trousers.

Polyphilia smiled at him throughout.

4) September 1853. The arrival of the Marquis siblings.

It was at this time that Chester Marquis and his sister Charlotte came to Lowell, turning up at 42 Dutton Street and declaring themselves Perfect. Chester was a slender, buck-toothed lad, obviously dying from consumption; his sister was a squat girl of a somewhat unfortunate aspect. No daguerreotypes exist of Charlotte, but one suspects from various sources that she suffered from a thyroidal imbalance, the ailment causing her eyes to bulge, making Charlotte appear constantly amazed or horrified.

The significance of the Marquis siblings upon the life of Hope is marked, although one gets the impression that Joseph was hardly aware of their existence prior to the trial. Chester Marquis died on September 17, just a few days after his arrival. The following day, Charlotte Marquis emerged from the house in a hysterical state, shrieking incoherencies about Mr. Opdycke. She ran right into the arms of the Reverend Doctor Ian John Robert McDougall.

Through the sort of devious ploy for which he was reknowned, McDougall managed to have all this come out at Hope's trial, some days later, for violating the antiobscenity postal statute. Charlotte's testimony was to the effect that Mr. Opdycke had convinced her to indulge in sexual intercourse, and he'd convinced by means of Perfectionist theory. She reluctantly complied, until it became clear that Mr. Opdycke wished to indulge himself in a depravity. The exact nature of the depravity went undisclosed, although McDougall did rhyme off seventeen possibilities, each more disgusting than the previous. The ugly girl turned red and lowered her bulging eyes in shame.

Mr. Opdycke took the stand and calmly denied it all. Unfortunately, Mr. Opdycke was so calm that he gave the impression of being an old hand at denying things in courtrooms. During the course of his questioning, Rev. Dr. Ian John Robert McDougall seemed to imply that Mr. Opdycke was in reality a Mr. Ogilvy of Vermont and that, furthermore, there was still some question, originally brought forward by a court in that state, as to the manner in which Mrs. Ogilivy had disappeared. Mr. Opdycke denied it all, of course, calmly shaking his head.

5) October 7, 1853. George Quinton's ruckus.

After the first day of the trial, several men had waited outside the courthouse in order to taunt Joseph Benton Hope. George Quinton, walking beside his master, had suggested they be quiet. The men, employing what was then a fairly novel retort, demanded to know who was going to make them. George replied that he would, whereupon ensued a donnybrook. George emerged from the fray bloodied, his face a monstrous configuration of cuts, welts and bruises. He did look better than any of the taunters, several of whom had broken limbs. It is felt by modern scholars that of all the negative influences at Hope's trial (Drinkwater's tract, Cairine's immodest pregnancy, Hope's penile engorgement, Chester Marquis's recent death, Charlotte's testimony and Mr. Opdycke's smug denials) none was so damning as the daily front-row presence of George Quinton, a huge and hideous creature.

Hope was incarcerated for a period of three months. During this time, he studied the Bible constantly and read an astronomical number of books, things like *The Social Destiny of Man* and *A Treatise on Fourieristic Phalansteries*. During this time in jail Hope's main body of ideas was established: that man should live communally; that private ownership was in direct opposition to God's will; that hitherto women as a class had been treated as chattels by man and should be freed from the burden of child rearing; that man (and woman) had a dual nature, amative and propagative; that erections were caused by a direct infusion of the Holy Spirit; and that marriage was a man-wrought construct never intended and wholly unheeded by the Almighty.

Upon his release, Joseph Benton Hope instructed his followers that the time had come to begin experiments in complex marriage. The first step, Hope announced, would be that he would have amorous congress with Polyphilia Drinkwater.

This experiment was a success.

The next step, Hope told them, was that he would have amorous congress with Abigal Skinner, and Abram Skinner would have amorous congress with Polyphilia.

Another success.

Next, Hope had amorous congress with Mary Carter De-la-Noy, Mr. Opdycke had amorous congress with Abigal Skinner and Adam De-la-Noy had amorous congress with Polyphilia Drinkwater.

In time, Cairine McDiarmid gave birth to the twins, Samuel and Lemuel, allowing her to take part in the experiments. This was fortunate, because Abigal Skinner soon became with child.

Over the next four years the experiments continued unabated. Six children were born: Samuel and Lemuel McDiarmid, Theodore De-la-Noy, Anne and Alice Skinner, Gregory Drinkwater Opdycke (Polyphilia's child by Mr. Opdycke, or so she calculated) and, finally, little Isaiah Hope, who popped out premature, gray and wrinkled, from Martha's huge groin.

One night, two young girls ran out of the house at 42 Dutton Street and removed all of their clothing. They were discovered by one of the fathers, who immediately called for the constabulary. Joseph Benton Hope feared that he would not fare well should there be another trial; moreover, he recalled that the citizens of Illinois had recently ripped his contemporary, the Mormon leader Joseph Smith, to bits.

Hope decided to continue his social experiments elsewhere, perhaps in an unsettled place where the Perfectionists would be removed from established communities.

They journeyed northward into Upper Canada.

PART FOUR

"Elspeth?"

"Elspeth?"

"What's the matter?"

"Whaddya mean, what's the matter? You're supposed to say, 'You're drunk'."

"All right. You're drunk. What's the matter?"

"Damn right, I'm drunk."

"We've established this. You're drunk. Now tell me what's the matter."

"Well, things are a little weird out here."

"How so?"

"Lemme ask you this. Did Jonathon just *see* what was gonna happen, or did he have something to do with it? See what I'm getting at?"

"Who's Jonathon?"

"That is what I'd like to know! Fucking guy has been alive for about 170 years, for one thing!"

"Paul ..."

"They got some secret out here. There is a mystery! And I think it's got something to do with Joseph Benton Hope. And they don't want me to find out what it is."

"Who's they?"

"Mona and Jonathon and the Bernies and the Kims and even Edgar the axe-murderer!"

"Edgar the axe-murderer?"

"What they don't know is, I signed them *out*."

"What?"

"I have the books. And the magazines. And the newspapers. Deedee let me sign them out."

"Who's Deedee?"

"You care for a sip of this here scootch? Irish scotch, my fave, yummy-yum-yum."

"We're on the telephone, dickhead."

"Too bad for you. So, are you getting fucked regular or what?"

"Paul, do you want to tell me what's the matter, or do I have to hang up?"

"Sheesh, what a grouch."

"Are you crying?"

"No way, Jose! The whiskey is leaking out my eyes, that's all."

"Who's Deedee?"

"Ellie, I'm fucked up. I can't talk now."

"What did you phone for?"

"I dunno."

"Okay. I'll say goodnight."

"Can you come and tuck me in?"

"Afraid not."

"It'll probably be in the papers. About the library."

"The library out there?"

"Yeah. The Hope Public Library."

"What about it?"

"Exploded. Burned down. Kablooey!"

"Oh."

"The, um, head librarian ..."

"That whiskey's really leaking a lot now."

"Yeah, well, the thing of it is, is, the head librarian ..."

"Deedee?"

"That's right. Deedee. Short for Dierdra. She was in there."

"In the library."

"Yeah."

"Was she a friend of yours?"

"Well, I didn't hardly know her, Elspeth, I just met her, but she was a really sweet old lady, and she knew everything, I mean, she was as smart as God, she could answer every question on every game show. And we had a few brew together. And she called me 'Phillip' and 'Patrick' and 'Peter' and I carried her around."

"It's sad."

"But what's worse is ... maybe it was my fault, because I was snooping around, and they decided they had to get rid of the Hope Room. But what they don't know is ..."

"You signed them out."

"I have them right here!"

"Maybe you should come back to Toronto."

"Back home?"

"I—I don't think we should live together anymore. But maybe you should come back from out there. It sounds like you're deteriorating."

"What kind of fucking word is that? Deteriorating."

"Getting worse."

"I know what it goddam means, Elspeth! What I don't know is why you have to use it! You sound like a fucking nurse or a social worker or a clinical psychologist or some fucking thing."

"All right."

"What do you mean, 'all right'?"

"I just mean, I have nothing further to say. I'm sorry, that's all. Sorry about your friend Deedee. Sorry about everything."

"I didn't phone for sympathy."

"What did you phone for?"

"I am your husband, for Christ's sake. I don't need a reason."

"Okay."

"Anyways, I got work to do out here. Research. On the life of Hope."

"The life of Hope."

"Right."

"When you find out about it, you let me know."

"Okay. Goodbye, Elspeth."

"Goodbye, Paul."

"I love you."

"Goodbye, Paul."

The Fourieristic Phalanstery

Upper Canada, 1862
Regarding the original settlement at Hope, we
know the following: that it owed much
philosophically to Chas. Fourier; that it
received attention in American newspapers
and periodicals; that it attracted many curious
visitors.

"So this, John, is our Phalanstery!" Adam De-la-Noy gesticulated proudly at the building. It was peculiar-looking at best,
humpbacked and deformed. It had been designed by Abram
Skinner, so its plan was simplistic and practical, long rows of
bedchambers surplanting the various dining/work areas. The
actual construction had been carried out almost singlehandedly
by George Quinton, which accounted for the awkwardness of
the angles and joinings.

Adam's friend John seemed troubled by something. "That
window," he pointed out, "is the wrong way 'round."

Adam De-la-Noy chuckled lightly. Mr. Opdycke had provided,
somehow, from somewhere, an ornate stained glass depicting
the crucifixion of our Lord Jesus. George Quinton had inserted
it wrongly, topsy-turvy, recognizing it only as a window.

Samuel and Lemuel, Cairine's twins, suddenly rushed up to
the men. They were, at six-and-a-half years, the oldest of the
Perfectionist children (Ephraim Davies was older, nine, but not
born of their philosophy) and certainly the biggest, an enormous pair, especially given the diminutive stature of the woman
who'd produced them.

"Stammed am delibber!" shrieked Lemuel.

"Your mommy or your libe!" added Samuel.

Both boys held wooden guns, ornately carved with rococo
handles and long, thin barrels.

"Oh!" Adam's hand clutched at his heart melodramatically.
"It is Ben Turpin and his fearsome Henchman!"

The twins grinned evilly. Sam waved his pistol in the air and
hollered, "Stan am belibber!"

Adam's friend John was taken with the boys' toys. "How beautiful they are!" he said to Adam. "So lifelike! They look as real as real can be."

Samuel and Lemuel scowled at this.

"John, do you have a copper or two?" Adam pulled at his pockets. "We have no truck with currency here, but we are, you know, being robbed."

John took a coin out of his waistcoat (John was fashionably dressed, but probably boiling to death, given the heat of the day) and handed it to Lemuel. "May I see your pistol?" he asked.

Sam and Lem communicated through a series of shifting glances; finally, and reluctantly, Lemuel handed over the wooden gun.

John took the toy and fired off a number of imaginary shots, aiming with great care and precision. Lemuel looked disgusted; the man was wasting a lot of valuable ammunition.

At long last John handed the toy pistol back to Lem. The boys darted away.

"If you have no truck with currency," wondered John, "why did the lads want money?"

Adam De-la-Noy laughed. "I don't know," he admitted.

"What wonderful toys."

"Yes, well, that's one of the things we do, you know, wood carving. Each Phalanstery, Fourier said, should concentrate on particular crafts."

"Fourier?" questioned John.

"Charles Fourier. He was a wonderful man, a Frenchman. He himself was aristocratic, but he gave it all up for the sake of communal living. According to Fourier, all of the great nations should be subdivided into little communities, and they should each live and work in separate phalansteries."

"I see."

George Quinton walked out of the Fourieristic Phalanstery carrying a mop and a pail of water. "Hello," he said merrily. "Adam, I've just done the floah in the dining womb, so please don't walk on it foh a while."

"All right, George. George, this is my friend John."

"Pleased to make yoh acquaintance." George more-or-less curtseyed.

"We were on the stage together," continued Adam. "Where was that, John?"

"Washington, I think."

"Ay, yes." Adam turned back to George. "I played Don Juan to his Don Pedro."

George nodded uncertainly. "Don't walk on the floah," he reminded them.

The men continued on their tour of the little community. The community consisted mostly of the Phalanstery, but there were a few smaller buildings nearby. One housed the presses that weekly printed *The Theocratic Watchman*, another was a small nursery for the children where they could play without disturbing the adults. There were stables, workhouses and outbuildings.

"How many people live here, De-la-Noy?"

"We are now ..." Adam had to think "... seventeen adults, and, um, eleven children."

"And is it true?"

"Is what true?"

"What one reads. That you and other men's wives ...?" John let the sentence dangle.

Adam shrugged. "Oh, well, I suppose it's true enough. I imagine it's also greatly exaggerated."

"And other men sleep with your wife?"

They do indeed, thought Adam. "None of that is of any importance," explained De-la-Noy. "What is important is our experiments in societal cohabitation. For instance, the children are raised by all of us, regardless of who the actual parents may be, and child-rearing is as much a man's function as a woman's."

"If I lived here," asked John, "could I sleep with other men's wives? With Mary?"

Adam looked at his old friend with a measure of distaste. John had certainly changed. Years ago, when they had appeared together in Shakespeare's *Much Ado About Nothing*, John had been a witty and articulate young man, a trifle on the introspective side but very pleasant and congenial. He had also been critically praised as one of the finest young Shakespearians in the Americas—but that was to be expected, coming as he did from an illustrious family, his father and brother perhaps the finest actors in the nation.

Cairine McDiarmid passed by them with a smile and an Irish, "Top o' the marning." Cairine had the new-born Louisa at her breast, and to facilitate nursing was wearing only her skirts. Adam watched John's little eyes bulge. Adam was thankful that Cairine had been wearing clothes at all; on hot days most of the Perfectionists went naked. Adam had long grown used to it —even the most beautiful human bodies (his wife's, for example) were after all a fairly standardized collection of muscle and pockets of fat.

Then Ephraim Drinkwater Davies appeared almost out of nowhere, no mean feat considering that at four feet and some inches he weighed almost 210 pounds. Ephraim was naked; Adam involuntarily shuddered at the sight. The little fat boy said, " 'Let them be confounded that persecute me, but let me not be confounded. Let them be dismayed, but let me not be dismayed. Bring upon them the day of evil, and destroy them with double destruction!' "

"Hello, Ehpraim," said Adam wearily.

"Fare well, De-la-Noy!" returned the boy, and then he passed wind in a vicious and arrogant manner. Ephraim D. Davies wandered away.

Adam decided to change the subject. "Do you know how our Phalanstery supports itself?"

"No." John's answer was quick and blunt, as if to suggest that he was not at all interested.

Adam continued anyway. "We make angling equipment. We manufacture two- and three-part poles with brass ferrules. It's very handy for putting them together. They've become quite fashionable, I gather, now that fishing is so popular. And we also make plugs. Imitation minnows, you see. The fish mistakes them for real, and ..."

Polyphilia Drinkwater came up to them, smiling shyly. She was, needless to say, naked as a baby, a state in which she existed almost perpetually. "Hello, Adam," she said, then turned. "And you are John. I'm so pleased to meet you. I've always been a great admirer." Polly had, in fact, clipped out a drawing of the man from a magazine and nailed it to the wall of her room.

John's eyes, little and bulging, were a vivid shade of red, fastened relentlessly to Polyphilia's pale-nippled breasts. After many long moments there his eyes stumbled downward, latching on to her pudenda. Polyphilia was accustomed to having her nakedness devoured lustily, but even she found this a bit much. She turned to Adam so that John would at least not be afforded a full-frontal view. "Have you seen Mr. Opdycke?"

"Probably napping somewhere," said Adam sarcastically, and he felt instantly remorseful. Mr. Opdycke may be a little on the slothful side, Adam reminded himself, but were it not for Opdycke it's unlikely that the Fourieristic Phalanstery would be able to exist at all. It was Opdycke who had invented the ferruled fishing poles and the plugs.

One of the first people they'd met in Upper Canada had been an Indian, a tall, gaunt Bigfoot with raven-black hair and very singular eyes, eyes that somehow shone silver and black. This man spoke to them in the Queen's English, informing them that his name was Jonathon Whitecrow, welcoming them to their new home, and then presenting them all with gifts. He'd given Mary and himself bead necklaces, Adam recalled; he'd given Abram Skinner some seeds and Abigal some flowers. The Indian had presented George and Martha with axes, Joseph Hope with a well-fashioned cane fishing pole, and he'd given Mr. Opdycke a long, razor-sharp carving knife. Opdycke had forthwith taken to whittling almost constantly (especially when there was work to be done, which was all of the time) and evidenced innate skill and talent. Opdycke made toys for the children, he made handles for the gardening tools and then, on a whim, he'd carved a little fish. Something occurred to Opdycke; he'd cunningly tied a hook along the thing's back and tossed his creation into the nearby lake. He'd caught a fish with his first toss. Mr. Opdycke had made more, simplifying the design so that in time all of the other Perfectionists could whittle them as well. They found that these "plugs" worked so well that they could be sold elsewhere — in the stores of Milverton, Fredericksburg and Trenton, their closest neighbors. It was a meager income, but a steady one.

"That was ...?" asked John. The pale, blond nymph had skipped away.

"Polyphilia."

"And if I lived here ...?" John let the sentence hang and waved his long, carefully manicured hands in the air.

"Yes, John. You could have amorous congress with her." Adam sighed.

They continued walking and came upon Abram Skinner in his small field of vegetables. Farming the land in any real way was out of the question, the soil being both fussy and stingy, but Abram had torn two or three acres out of the hills and raised up corn and mixed vegetables.

Adam was happy to see Abram. Abram Skinner, Adam felt, was a deep man, dark and poetic. Abram stood beneath the sun, stripped to the waist; he was crudely muscled, tiny knots and veins buckling across his chest. Skinner settled on to his haunches and lit a pipe — he placed his hand over his eyes for shade and took a long, hard look at the earth.

"Some problem, Abram?" called Adam.

Abram gave a brief half-smile. "Weather," he answered simply, meaning that bad weather was on its way.

Troubled as he was, usually gloomy and brooding, Abram Skinner was of late a happier man. His daughters were healthy and robust creatures, cheerful and strong like their mother, and Abram also had a son, Ambrose, six months of age. (Ambrose Skinner died at age nine months.)

Adam made introductions. Abram nodded and formed in his mind a question. Thinking was more laborious for Skinner than any farm work; it was hard avoiding all the crevices of his psyche. "Hamlet," he stated, as if giving his topic a title or subject heading. "Was he, in your opinion, truly suicidal?"

"Oh, yes!" answered John eagerly. "Life to him was a loathsome burden, a mantle as heavy as the moon."

"And yet, and yet ..." stammered Skinner, and then he took a deep breath to calm himself. "And yet I've seen performances where all of Hamlet's dark musings seem somehow nothing ... nothing other than ... that is, nothing more than ... than ... cunning ... artifice. Cunning artifice." The voicing of that statement had actually caused Abram to perspire. "For instance, in Boston, I saw your brother's Hamlet ..."

John interrupted rudely. "I've no wish to discuss my brother, nor his laughable Hamlet."

Abram turned once more to look at the earth; not out of embarrassment or anger, only because the earth would never interrupt rudely.

Abigal came into the field, Anne and Alice clinging to her apron strings, Ambrose a swaddled bundle in her arms. Both Adam and Abram smiled. John turned away, uninterested. This woman was pudgy, plain and completely clothed.

"Time for dinner," Abigal announced. "Has anyone seen Lem and Sam?"

Adam nodded. "We saw them just a few minutes ago."

"Did they have some spoons?"

"Spoons?"

"Martha says some spoons have gone missing from the kitchen."

Adam and Abram exchanged glances. "Did Martha," asked Adam, "prepare the day's meal?"

"Yes," said Abigal quickly, "and you two had better like it, or so help me ..."

"For you, Sweet Abigal," said Adam, "we would eat mud."

"In fact," added Abram, "I think we'd just as soon eat mud, wouldn't we, Adam?"

The two men nodded. "Mud it is," they informed a chuckling Abigal.

Anne and Alice, four and three years old respectively, were staring at the stranger with curiosity and some degree of malevolence. "Who are you?" demanded Anne.

"I am a Prince," answered John, "from a faraway country. I rule there, and everyone is very happy." John dropped to his knees in front of the little girls. "Would you like to come and live there?"

"No," answered Anne.

"*NO!*" bellowed Alice, as loudly as she could.

"But there is magic there," continued John, "and no one is sad."

"No," answered Anne.

"*NO!*" shrieked Alice.

"Very well." John climbed to his feet. "There's no room for you at any rate."

"By the way, Abigal," asked Adam, "have you seen Mary?"

"She's in her room."

"Ah, yes." Adam didn't bother asking if his wife was alone in her room. "John, will you stay for lunch?"

"I do not eat tomatoes," John cautioned them urgently. "Many people do, and I consider them fools. The tomato has a poison in it that is secreted into the brain, and it causes derangement of the faculties."

"No tomatoes," said Abigal.

Along the way back to the Fourieristic Phalanstery, John said, "It is indeed pleasant here, De-la-Noy. And best of all, no negroes."

"I beg your pardon?"

"No negroes. No black apes walking upright, laying claim to the same rights as human beings."

"See here," started Abram Skinner, but Abigal caught his arm and silenced him. It is unlikely that Abram would have been able to speak at any rate — even "See here" had been a struggle, and after that Abram became hopelessly tongue-tied.

Adam De-la-Noy merely shook his head, and wondered about the sanity of his old friend John.

The Play of Sunlight on the Metal

Upper Canada, 1862
Regarding the Angling Innovations of Hope, et al, *we know the following: that Opdycke was responsible for many of them; that the most popular proved to be the Spoon.*

Mr. Opdycke was bored. That's why he'd taken the spoons.

He sat beside the Lake and worked at one of them with a tiny metal file. He'd broken off the handle, and was now smoothing down the edge. Mr. Opdycke sighed out of boredom. He briefly considered conjuring up a mental picture of Abigal Skinner's backside and having a healthy go at himself, but he was even bored with that, both with Abigal's backside (which had lost much of its magic; now it often appeared to Opdycke as nothing but lumps of lard) and with amorous congress in general. Mr. Opdycke chuckled as he considered the term "amorous congress" — he imagined the heads of state gathered together in the Capitol buildings, all of them naked and possessed of cock-upright jiggling-bones.

A fish jumped, far away. Opdycke glanced up briefly and snarled. "Keep it up, darling. I'll have you soon enough."

Who would have suspected, Mr. Opdycke mused, that swiving could become so tedious? (He'd finished smoothing the spoon's edge. Opdycke held the little dish in the palm of his hand and caught the sunlight in it. The glare hurt his eyes, but Opdycke didn't turn away.) Even rutting with Polyphilia, who did most anything he suggested, was, in the final analysis, dull, bone-breaking work. It was all, Opdycke had concluded, J. B. Hope's fault. And, to make matters worse, Hope had recently come up with a new theory to be put into practice, that of wilful countenance. Opdycke took an awl and began digging at a point near the edge of the metal. "Wilful countenance" was, Hope's fancy terminology notwithstanding, sticking the pud into the pudding dish and leaving it there. Hope justified this with his usual mouthful of "amative"s and "propagative"s, and there was, moreover, a practical consideration, in that the Phalanstery was rapidly filling up with small fry. Still, the practice made scant sense to Mr. Opdycke. Joseph Hope claimed that he had withheld himself from orgasm for over two hours, but Opdycke disbelieved him; or suspected that Hope had accomplished the feat with the grotesque Martha, in which case why hadn't Joe withheld himself from orgasm for two weeks? Mr. Opdycke didn't think that he himself had ever lasted much more than two minutes and didn't think he ever would.

Mr. Opdycke heard something rustling in the bushes behind him, and he was startled. Opdycke found the countryside disquieting somehow and half believed that it was inhabited by ferocious beasts, wildcats and grizzlies. Opdycke gripped the awl tightly and looked over his shoulder, prepared to plunge the tool into some creature's eyeball. He saw, instead, the Indian, Jonathon Whitecrow. Opdycke snorted, half out of relief, half out of disdain for the redskin.

"How!" said Mr. Opdycke.

The Indian tilted his head quizzically. " 'How'?"

Opdycke scowled. "Hullo."

"Oh. Hullo, Mr. Opdycke." The Indian took some steps forward. "Do you mind if I join you?"

In principle, Mr. Opdycke did mind. He hated Indians almost as much as he hated niggers. In the war that was currently being fought in the States, Opdycke's sympathy lay firmly with the Confederacy, even though he himself hailed from Vermont. Opdycke was not so sympathetic as to consider taking up arms for Old Glory, but he certainly wished them well. However, Mr. Opdycke shrugged to show the redskin that he was at least indifferent to the notion of his joining him, so Jonathon Whitecrow gingerly lowered his haunches on to a nearby rock. The two men sat in silence for many moments. Opdycke had succeeded in pushing the awl through the thin metal, and now he was twisting it, enlarging the hole. Jonathon watched him do this with an almost scientific interest. Opdycke found the Indian's gaze irritating; he gestured violently at the water.

"How do you call that lake?" Opdycke demanded.

Whitecrow turned and stared at the water as if seeing it for the first time. "We call it *Loo Kow.*"

"What does that mean?"

Jonathon shrugged. Opdycke reflected that the Indian shrugged an awful lot, an aristocratic gesture suggesting that most things were inconsequential. "It means 'Home of the Big Fish,' " said Whitecrow, "more or less."

Mr. Opdycke nodded, picked up some fine wire and a hook. "Is it? Are there big fish in there?"

Again the Indian shrugged.

Opdycke said, "Well?"

The Indian held up a long forefinger, a finger that was stained yellow because Whitecrow smoked the new "cigarettes", rolling up plug tobacco into thin white tubes of paper. "One big fish," explained the Indian.

"*Loo Kow,*" muttered Opdycke. He twisted the thin wire hard, and now the fishhook and spoonbowl were firmly fastened together. Mr. Opdycke threaded the end of some gut twine through the spoon's hole and tied it off. He dangled his creation in the air and watched the sunlight bounce off of it.

"What makes you think," asked Jonathon Whitecrow, "that such a thing will work?"

"I have my reasons," snarled Mr. Opdycke. "Never mind about that. I have my reasons."

The Indian smiled.

"Why are you smiling?" demanded Mr. Opdycke.

"Because, Mr. Opdycke, you have your reasons."

For a brief and alarming moment, Opdycke thought that the Indian knew what his reasons were. Opdycke found himself perspiring. He peeled off his shirt and wiped the sweat from his bulging paunch. "How big is the fish?" he asked the Indian.

The Indian was constructing one of his cigarettes. (Opdycke frowned once more. Cigarette smoking was vaguely effeminate, definitely sissified, a habit shared by women, young boys and old hobos.) "Bigger than a breadbox," the Indian responded rather musically, "smaller than a house."

"How big?" asked Mr. Opdycke once more.

"How big?" repeated Whitecrow in a strange manner, tilting his head as if addressing some third party. Jonathon nodded, and then answered, "Big enough to eat anything in the water. Too big to be eaten by anything in the water. So the answer to your question is, as big as the water itself."

"How big in feet? Two feet? Three feet?"

"A fish doesn't have feet," responded Whitecrow.

Mr. Opdycke didn't like being teased. Mostly out of boredom he considered murdering the Indian. Opdycke thought that the awl would make the best weapon, sharp enough to pierce the skull. Then Opdycke would fill up the Indian's pockets with rocks, toss him into *Loo Kow*, and no one would ever be the wiser.

Jonathon Whitecrow was smiling at Mr. Opdycke in a gentle way. "I see you have a cranking reel-winch," said the Indian, pointing with his smoking white tube at Opdycke's fishing gear.

"Yeh," grunted Opdycke rudely, but pride of ownership overcame him. He picked up the butt of his pole and cranked the contraption's handle. It produced a horrible sound, loud and jagged like a ratchet's. "I made it," he informed the Indian, "at the Phalanstery." Opdycke set about assembling his stuff. First of all he fed the horse-hair line from the reel through the rod's guides. Opdycke's pole was seven feet long, a fairly short one. Joseph Hope owned rods of nine, ten and even twelve feet, which he used when hiding behind bushes and fishing quiet waters. Then Opdycke attached the two lines together, the horse-hair and the gut leader. He was ready to fish.

Mr. Opdycke methodically placed his feet one in front of the other and cocked his legs. He held the rod with both hands, spaced some two feet apart on the long butt. Mr. Opdycke pulled the rod backward until it pointed at the Indian (Whitecrow was standing behind Opdycke, watching him studiously) and then Mr. Opdycke twisted his trunk around sharply.

His lure, the "Spoon", traveled some twenty-five feet out into the lake and landed with a splash.

Opdycke was obviously pleased with himself. "It beats pouching," he said to the Indian. Opdycke cranked the handle of his reel two or three times and then stumbled forward. The end of his pole bent over double and trembled.

"Aha!" bellowed Mr. Opdycke, delighted. "I knew it would work!"

"How did you know that?" asked the Indian gently.

Opdycke was too busy turning the winch to worry about what the Indian said. Opdycke knew he had to land the fish as quickly as possible, before any of the knots in his line gave way. The fish had other notions. It kept racing away, stripping line off the reel. Opdycke soon grew quite annoyed with the fish's antics.

"Give up!" Opdycke screamed. "You are my supper! It's no good trying to get away!" Opdycke was sweating profusely, the perspiration trickling into his eyes and stinging. Mr. Opdycke finally elected to abandon the reel, because the fish was taking line from it faster than he could crank it back. He handed his rod to a startled Jonathon Whitecrow and then rushed forward, taking the line into his hands. Mr. Opdycke hauled away, and after a minute or two (the fish showed no sign of tiring, even seemed to get stronger near the end of the battle, breaking the surface of the water and trying to throw the hook out of its mouth) Mr. Opdycke landed the animal. Remarkably, it was a rather small fish, not much more than a pound. Opdycke studied it with some curiosity. "It's one of those bass," he said to the Indian. Mr. Opdycke was disappointed with his catch, a nuisance fish that wasn't much good for eating. "But what's it doing away up north here?"

Jonathon Whitecrow bent over the fish and plucked the Spoon out of its mouth. The fish flipped eagerly over the rocks and back into *Loo Kow*. "People bring them," the Indian finally answered Opdycke. "People on trains sometimes have two or three in a bucket, and they throw them from the train when they cross water. They are a strong fish, and strong willed, and they live in whichever waters they are tossed into. Personally," said Whitcrow, "I am quite fond of them."

"They eat the good fishes, like the trout," said Mr. Opdycke, voicing the most frequent complaint against the rogue bass.

"When one is a fish," said Jonathon, "it's a dog-eat-dog world."

"At any rate," said Mr. Opdycke, "the Spoon worked well."

"Yes," agreed Whitecrow. "The fish didn't stand a chance."

Again Opdycke got the impression that he was being teased. There's more than one way to kill an Indian, he reflected. For example, there were any number of suitably murderous rocks lying about. Would anyone miss the redskin? Mr. Opdycke rather doubted it.

Opdycke noticed that whenever he thought of these evil deeds the Indian would begin to smile, almost grin. This was, of course, pure coincidence, but it unnerved Mr. Opdycke somewhat.

Opdycke picked up his gear and retrieved his line. He assumed his stance, brought the pole around behind his back, and with a grunt and a twist tossed the Spoon back into the water. This time the lure attracted nothing, but on the next try Opdycke had a fish. Again Opdycke was irritated by the fish's dogged resistance. By the time the fish was on the shore Mr. Opdycke had exhausted his repertoire of cusswords.

"Oh," said Jonathon Whitecrow, "my ears are burning."

It was a bass. Mr. Opdycke suspected it was the same bass. Opdycke ripped the Spoon out of the thing's mouth and then placed the heel of his boot on its head. Mr. Opdycke pressed down violently. The fish continued to flip about, and seemed no closer to death for the flatness of its skull.

"What did you do that for?" asked the Indian.

"I do as I please," returned the other. "Certainly I amn't accountable to no redskin."

The Indian shrugged, as if explaining to his gods that none of this mattered in any real way. "You aren't accountable to me," Jonathon nodded, "but I think the fish deserves an explanation."

"Oh, you are humorous," snarled Mr. Opdycke.

The fish died eventually. Opdycke tossed it into the bushes. Jonathon Whitecrow disappeared, and Mr. Opdycke, bored, took apart his gear and set off for the Fourieristic Phalanstery.

At least the experiment with the Spoon had been a success. Mr. Opdycke knew that he had stumbled upon something very valuable; the lures were easy to make — even a ham-handed lout like George Quinton could manage it if need be—and they could be sold for a pretty profit. Opdycke chuckled aloud, finding the irony humorous. He was about to make the Perfectionists wealthy, and his inspiration had been ...

Mr. Opdycke stopped chuckling, and wished he had some booze. Without some mare's piss Opdycke had no choice but to remember the rowboat out on Moony Lake. Hepzibah had been nattering on, about this, that and the other thing: "this" being Opdycke's (or was it Osborne then? Oswal?) drinking, "that" being his philandering and "the other thing" being the fact that he had embezzled no less than seventeen thousand dollars from his employer. Hepzibah, a God-fearing woman — a God-feared-shiteless woman, Opdycke (Ottaway?) used to say to his drinking companions — was saying that he would have to make amends if he held any hope for his immortal soul. Then, in an instant, there was a dagger-hilt protruding from Hepzibah's left breast. "That answers that," Opdycke (Olson?) said aloud, adding a childish and whimsical sigh.

It was no trouble getting away with the deed. He weighted her body with stones (even though it was hard to believe it didn't weigh enough already) and was just about to toss it overboard when he thought that, in the unlikely event that Hepzibah's body were discovered, it would be best not to have his personal and monogrammed knife sticking out of her bub. Accordingly, Opdycke (Odell?) extracted it and, bending over the side of the rowboat, dropped the knife into the water. Opdycke (Ogilvy!) watched it descend, the blade catching light and sparkling. He was surprised to see two enormous fish rise to meet the knife, attracted by the play of sunlight on the metal.

Presages of Doom

Upper Canada, 1863
Regarding the downfall of Hope, we know the following: that its origins lie in his being somewhat uninterested in the singular activities of his followers.

It was obvious to everyone (especially to Martha) that Polyphilia Drinkwater Davies enjoyed a unique relationship with Joseph Benton Hope. Certainly no other person, male or female, would dare tiptoe up behind the great Spiritual Leader in order to tickle him. And while Hope insisted that he be familiarly addressed as Joseph, no Perfectionist could do it—Reverend, Sir, and Father were the most common appellations — except for Polyphilia. Polly called him Joseph, shortening it easily to Joe, elongating it affectionately to Joe-Joe and sometimes transforming it playfully to Joe-Joe Bones.

Polyphilia also got away with a lot that the others would have been sternly reprimanded for. Not only did she disdain household chores (no one had really expected the pink-nippled nymph to pick up a broom, at any rate), Polly neglected her child-rearing duties. Considering how many of the tykes she was half-responsible for (Gregory Opdycke, Jameson De-la-Noy, Rebecca and Daris Skinner, and the little Louisa, of uncertain siring) this nonperformance quite rankled the other Perfectionists. Not to mention the very strange behavior of Ephraim D. Davies, who not only constantly bellowed Biblical presages of doom, but had recently begun to devour newts, frogs and toads in abundance—the lad needed strong maternal guidance.

Fortunately, more and more adults were coming to the Phalanstery. The crippled girl, the one with the special boot, had come recently, a woman now, still dour, dark, and flat-chested. Her name was Daisy Cumbridge. From Illinois came Thomas and Elna Cragin, bringing with them their young friend Erastus Hamilton. Other new Perfectionists included Margaret Comstick, Trevor Ward Beecham and Juliana Gom.

Everyone in the Phalanstery was first alarmed and then resentful when Polyphilia Drinkwater Davies announced her intention of going back to Boston to visit her crack-minded father, Theophilius. The general feeling was that this was, if not an out-and-out betrayal, at least an insult to the teachings of Joseph Benton Hope. Blood relationships, Hope had long maintained, were of no interest to the Almighty, blood being but an earthly convenience for the corporeal transportation of the Holy Spirit. In addition, Theophilius's philosophy, or philosophies, had recently undergone a change that was bizarre even by Theophilian standards. Now Theophilius was a Spiritualist (a word he coined himself) and claimed to have communion with invisible and unsubstantial beings. What this communion amounted to — and this was recorded in countless newspaper and magazine articles — was an awful lot of noise and racket. Quite often Theophilius would hold Spirit Concerts where, in a dimly lit room, trumpets would toot themselves, drums would beat themselves and tambourines would jingle as they flew through the air. Several prominent Americans, a Professor of Medicine and a Massachusetts Supreme Court Judge among them, had pronounced these Spirit Concerts genuine.

So Polly, one evening in the huge dining room, announced her intention of going to Boston.

J. B. Hope, peppering a pork chop, shrugged.

"There's work to do!" bellowed Martha, quite alarming Isaiah, who sat on her lap. Isaiah alone was allowed to sit at the adult table, mostly because he would be beaten savagely by Sam and Lem McDiarmid if he tried to eat with the children. "We can't go prancing off every time we feel like it!" Martha continued in a loud fashion, loud enough to start Isaiah bawling. "That's the whole notion of a Fourieristic Phalanstery!"

Polly shot Martha Q. Hope a black look. "I didn't ask you."

Abigal Skinner said, "But it's true. Abram's crops are almost grown ..."

"Well, I wouldn't be much use to you there, would I?" giggled Polyphilia. Every time she said the word "I" her breasts quivered three times. (Polly stayed naked long into the evenings and long into the seasons of the year, clothing herself, it seemed, only for the advent of Upper Canada's cruel winter.)

Mr. Opdycke sat up with interest. "Boston? I've got business I could do in Boston!"

"Business?" repeated Joseph Hope. "What manner of business?"

"Well," Opdycke looked around the table. "We need machines."

Adam De-la-Noy laughed out loud. "Machines?"

"Yes, machines," declared Mr. Opdycke savagely. "A punch, a woodlathe ..."

Abram Skinner folded the skin of his forehead with consternation. "But ..." He took his long, work-worn fingers and pulled at his brow furiously, trying to smooth it out. "That is all work that can be done by hand!"

"*Can* be," said Opdycke. "But with machines it could be done much quicker ..."

"Leaving us more time," finished J. B. Hope, "for our spiritual exercise. But surely we cannot afford machines?"

The other Perfectionists exchanged glances. Eventually Cairine McDiarmid answered. "We cahn, y'know. We're rich."

Polyphilia's pink body had reddened with indignation. "Joe," she snapped, "may I or may I not go to Boston?"

"How do you mean, rich?" asked Hope, ignoring her.

"People buy the fishing equipment," answered Mary De-la-Noy. "The Spoon is all the rage among the local anglers."

Joseph Benton Hope frowned, looked at his immense table of followers cruelly. "It is good to remember," he said, "that the manufacturing of fishing gear is an expedience that serves us. We do not serve it. Our only obligation is to the Almighty."

"Exactly," said Mr. Opdycke. "So let us acquire machines. All the menial, time-consuming labor is done for us."

"Do people really enjoy fishing with those Spoons?" demanded Hope.

"Oh, yes!" replied George Quinton, who thought that his master would be delighted. "They purchase them by the bushel-full!"

"Don't they find them a trifle ... facile? It seems to me that the fish attack out of brute instinct, and that getting them on the Spoon requires no guile or artfulness."

Mr. Opdycke shrugged. "I reckon that's why people like them."

Joseph Hope shook his head wistfully. "Whatever is the world coming to?"

"Joe-Joe Bones," said Polyphilia sternly, setting her breasts gloriously aquiver.

"By all means," acquiesced Hope. "Go to Boston. And give my best to your father when you get there."

"Um," started Opdycke.

Hope was resigned. "Yes, Opdycke. Let us have machines."

Polly came back a Spirit Rapper. That is, Polyphilia discovered an affinity for these disembodied spirits and found that they were drawn to her. Polyphilia would sit in the middle of a room, and invisible beings would begin knocking at the walls—quietly, almost inaudibly, but loudly enough for anyone else in the room to hear.

Mr. Opdycke came back with machines. Also, while he was away, Opdycke applied for patents on the two-part ferruled fishing pole, the crank-winch reel, the spoon and several other of the Perfectionist innovations. He also registered a company name, "OPDYCKE SPORT FISHING GEAR AND TACKLE OF THE AMERICAS."

It seems probable that many years later (possibly even as the axe came down) Joseph Benton Hope regretted his decision to let Polly and Opdycke visit Boston.

Burned With the Beauty of Living

Hope, Ontario, 1983
Wherein our Biographer Pursues an End.

On this particular day I was fishing, teary-eyed and miserable. I was wielding my baitcasting rod with tremendous force, driving the Hoper far out into the middle of Lookout Lake. I was having no luck, even though I'd drastically lowered my body temperature with tequila and was butt-naked. Rachmaninoff's "Vocalise" filled the air, whistled by yours truly, even though that was what was making me teary-eyed and miserable. That's the kind of mood I was in.

I was certainly in no mood to see people, but that didn't stop Professor Harvey Benson from waddling down to the water's edge. He stood beside me and watched the surface of the lake for a long moment. "Any luck?" he asked finally.

"Gregory Opdycke says, and I quote page thirty-seven of *Fishing for Ol' Mossback*, that one must be willing to 'sacrifice' everything if one wishes to 'hunt' the Mighty Fish. That's what I've done, Harvard. I've reduced my life. I'm happy."

"That's good."

With a tremendous grunt I threw the Hoper. I watched it fly, and as it neared the water I gently stopped the line with the tip of my thumb. The Hoper tumbled quietly into the lake. I let it sink, quoting page sixteen for Harvey's benefit. " 'Mossback lives, we must "presume", at the "bottom" of Lookout.' "

"Paulie," said Harv, "I think you'd better put on your pants."

"But don't you remember, Harvey? Ol' Mossback can hear the rustle of material."

"The thing is, you're embarrassing Esther."

"Esther?"

"Up in my car."

Harvey and I both turned around. The red Fiat sat some forty feet away, parked on the shoulder. A woman sitting in the passenger's seat waved at us. Benson waved back. I shrugged and turned around once more.

"Paul," said Professor Benson sternly, "Esther is coming down here. Now, this is the woman I love. I plan to marry this woman, and I don't want her to think that I've got friends who wander around with no clothes on."

"Tell her I'm a nudist." I shot the Hoper badly, and the lure kerplunked not far from the shoreline, landing in a bed of weeds.

"Here she comes, Paulie. Could you please just put on your underwear?"

"Oh, all right." I reluctantly put down my rod and stepped over to where my clothes lay in a pile. The tequila bottle was nestled snugly on top, so I picked it up and had a long snort. Then I put on my jeans and T-shirt. Finally I turned around and allowed Harvey to introduce me to this Esther.

I remembered Harvey telling me that Jonathon Whitecrow had once had a Vision in which Harvey would meet a "very beautiful young chickie-poo."

"Wise-ass old Indian asshole," I snarled when I looked upon Esther.

Esther was a very exotic creature, her features and skin coloring indicating some peculiar mixture of bloods. Her nose was long, her lips were large, the eyes slightly Oriental, all of it crowned with an amazing amount of fire-red hair. Esther was heavily freckled, the little spots merging to form a rich, coppery tone. She was a tall woman, this Esther, taller than me and towering over Harvey. Harvey's head was just about level with her breasts, and I knew that for him it had been love at first sight.

"Hey, I'm sorry if you were embarrassed," I said. "It's a well-known fact that fish can hear the rustle of material, therefore, 'the dedicated Mossback hunter quote, divests, unquote, himself of extraneous apparel'."

"That's cool," said Esther. "On a day like this, I wouldn't mind wandering around naked myself."

"Yeah, only we're not going to stick around," Harvey said, his voice sitting in a panicky upper register.

"I'm gonna catch Mossback's ass." I grabbed my rod and raised it above my head. "Go ahead and take off your clothes, Esther. We'll be here for a while."

"No, we won't!" shouted Harvey. "We have to go back to the place."

"The old Quinton place, you mean?" I demanded.

"Yes. You know. Where you live."

"You guys go if you want," I said. "Me, I must practise the Art of the Angle."

"Paul, I didn't want to tell you this," said Benson seriously, "but I'm here for a reason. I got a phone call from Ellie. She seemed to be a little worried about you."

"I know. She thinks I'm deteriorating."

"She's not," Harvey told me. "Boy, is she ever looking great. She's got a real deep tan because she's been going camping a lot, and she's got her hair cut really short ..."

"Hold on, Harv." I stumbled over to a large rock, somehow managing to dive onto it head-first, hobgoblins in close pursuit. I sat on my rock and broke into a sweat. "Is this *Elspeth* we're discussing?"

"Your wife," he nodded.

"Camping? As in sleeping in tents and not showering and eating beans from a can?"

Harvey nodded hesitantly.

"And she's got a tan and short hair?"

"Fairly short," acknowledged Harvey.

"BITCH!" I screamed. "Where's my frigging watch fob?"

"Not as short as all that."

"She probably goes camping with some German fucker named Rolf or something, doesn't she? She probably even goes swimming, maybe even goes skinny-dipping because she doesn't want any bathing-suit lines ruining her great new tan!" The concept of Elspeth with a tan baffled and enraged me. She'd long been timid about the sun, hesitant to even bare her arms on a hot summer's day, fearful of a burn on her lily-white skin. Now here she was with a tan and a blond fellow named Rolf or something, and they probably spent weekends at a nudist colony playing volleyball.

"Not Rolf," said Harvey.

"Huh?"

"The German guy's name isn't Rolf," explained Benson. "I think it's Helmut."

"Oh, that's nice to know, Harvey. I'm certainly glad that you're keeping me up-to-date with my wife's infidelities."

"Hey!" Something occurred to Harvey. "Sara says to say hello."

"Sara?"

"You remember, Sara. Small girl. With Lee and Sheila."

"Oh. Right, Sara. So anyway, this guy Helmut, what does he do? I bet he's an air-traffic controller or a fireman, isn't he? No! I got it. He's a cop! Right?"

"I don't know," said Harvey.

"Are you and your wife separated?" Esther asked ingenuously.

"Damn betchas," I snarled. "Now I live out here, where I've become a piscavorous Nimrod, and she lives in Toronto and sleeps around with the Hitler Youth Movement."

"Too bad," pronounced Esther.

"I don't mind," I said. "I have reduced my life. I have made simple my heart." I burst into tears furiously. I was through crying in a matter of seconds.

"We brought some stuff," Harvey told me. "We thought we could go back to the homestead and cook you a good meal."

"That's all right, Harvey. When I reduced my life, eating was the first thing to go. No, I think I'll just stay and fish, thanks."

"I got some Irish whiskey."

Irish whiskey was tempting, but I shook my head.

"I've got some doobies."

"Good shit?" I asked.

"Very good shit," he nodded.

"Then I don't want any."

"I've got some, um, cocaine."

"Let's go." I jumped off my rock. Esther smiled at me warmly. She and Harvey linked hands and began to walk toward the car, their hips banging together, Harvey's head nestled on her shoulder. I picked up my fishing gear and took one last look at the lake.

Where you going?

"Gotta go now. Me and my friends are going to cook up a nice meal, but don't you worry, I'll be back. If you thought Greg Opdycke was obsessed, you ain't seen nothing yet. I have reduced my life and made simple my heart ..."

Harvey touched me on the shoulder. "Paulie?"

"I'll be right with you, Harvard."

As soon as Benson turned away, Mossback jumped. He drove upward until his tail fin cleared the water. Mossback danced upon the surface, and for that brief moment I burned with the beauty of living.

Bedlam

Ontario, 1869
Regarding the community founded by Hope,
we know the following: that it grew. And, we
wonder, did Joseph expect it to do otherwise?

Joseph Benton Hope went fishing, and here's the reason: there was bedlam back at the Phalanstery. Actually, the word Phalanstery could no longer serve; the Perfectionists now lived in a proper community, three big buildings and many smaller ones all lined out along the main street. Come to think, Hope reflected, he had authorized no building of a street, but someone had made one, lining the sides with skids and cobblestoning the narrow thoroughfare. Hope sighed and knew the answers he'd be given should he ask. Mr. Opdycke would explain that the road facilitated commerce; certainly horses and wagons came into the community constantly, either bringing raw materials or carting away the finished fishing gear. George Quinton would look miserable and twist his massive hands. "Sowwy," George would moan, meaning that he had actually constructed the damnable road, likely without assistance from any of the other men. Hope estimated that there were perhaps forty able-bodied men (not counting Samuel and Lemuel McDiarmid, boys but massively constructed ones) yet when there was arduous labor to be done, everyone seemed to vanish except for the monstrous George.

Joseph was headed for the lake they called Look Out, walking down a rough and dusty lane. He realized that eleven years ago, when he'd first come to Upper Canada (Ontario, he reminded himself) the route to Look Out had been thick with trees, bushes and shrubbery.

Polyphilia was holding one of her exhibitions, which was
one reason for the bedlam back at the community. Perhaps
seventy people had come to witness it (from where, Joseph
could not fathom) bringing their children with them, making a
picnic of it. (Samuel and Lemuel would have a grand day, bully-
ing all of these strange tykes, systematically beating the boys,
pulling handfuls of hair from the heads of little girls.) The people
were currently, Hope guessed, gathered in the main dining hall
of the Fourieristic Phalanstery. Cairine and Abigal would be
giving out little snacks. Ephraim, dressed in black, would be
bellowing the Bible at the top of his breaking voice: "But there
is a spirit in man: and the inspiration of the Almighty giveth
them understanding!" Soon Polyphilia would be led in, dressed in
a long white robe. Her face would be ashen, her golden hair
matted and dulled by sweat. Polyphilia had lost an enormous
amount of weight in the past while, and when seen nude was
all bone, her ribcage sharply defined beneath paper-thin skin,
her breasts virtually vanished. Polyphilia had taken to hiding
this emaciated body beneath these long robes, robes that were
emblazoned with images of the moon.

Polly would enter the dining hall with tiny, faltering footfalls.
Everyone in the room would gasp and then fall silent, for there
was something terrifying in the sight of Polyphilia, an intima-
tion of demonic power. Martha would rush forward with a chair
just as Polyphilia began to swoon.

Why is it, Hope wondered, that everyone was so caught up
in this theatricality? Mary De-la-Noy, for example, always
claimed a front row seat, and during Polyphilia's exhibition,
Mary's bosom would start to pitch, at first subtly, then monumentally, and by the end of the ordeal Mary De-la-Noy would
be exhausted. And Adam, of course, gave a running commen-
tary on the proceedings. "Look there!" Adam would point
energetically. "That candle was just lighted by one of our spirit
friends! And what's this?" — cocking one of his elephantine ears
— "Do I hear a low wailing? Yes! Yes, indeed I do!"

"Ah, well," said Hope wistfully. The reason he didn't put an
end to Polyphilia's little entertainments was two-fold: 1) Hope
had no reason to suppose that these spirit beings didn't exist —
if one accepts a heaven, one need also accept its inhabitants —

and 2) the exhibitions earned a lot of money. George Quinton circulated throughout the audience with a collection plate, and the people were inexplicably generous. Hope remembered the pennies and halfpennies the populace had given over, reluctantly, when he was a young preacher. Now, after an exhibition of Spirit Rapping, the average donation was fifty cents, often one whole dollar, sometimes even more! Hope acknowledged that there was an economic factor—this "inflation" that he'd read about — but he knew that there was far more to it than that. It had to do with the times. The world was spinning wildly, almost out of control; there were riots in China, upheavals all over Europe, and the United States of America had come within an ace of erasing itself from the face of the earth. So people turned away from all that, and looked for comfort elsewhere.

What really disappointed Hope was this: Polyphilia claimed that she could call out to the Heavenly Kingdom, that she issued an invitation to all in that Holy Realm to journey across the Spectral Divide and commune once more with the living. All well and good, Hope agreed, and the few times he'd gone to a Spirit Rapping he had hoped that, for example, Dr. Ben Franklin might choose to commune, or any of the great poets, philosophers and religious leaders. But none of that ilk ever deigned to traverse the Spectral Divide. Instead, the living were usually set upon by a horde of spiritual hooligans, who seemed to make the return journey from beyond the veil for no better purpose than to knock on walls, bang pots and pans, and light and extinguish candles. So Hope rarely attended these days. He preferred, more often, to go off by himself and pursue the Art of the Angle.

Joseph Benton Hope came to Lake Look Out. It was gentle and pristine, but Hope knew that the water was a touch murkier than it had been at the time of the Perfectionists' arrival. Joseph Hope started assembling his gear. Hope had a ten-foot cane pole, the same kind he'd used as a boy. (Hope was a bit surprised that he remembered fishing as a boy—the recollection was dreamlike, and part of Hope doubted its authenticity. But Joseph seemed to recall standing beside a railroad pond, astounded that such stagnant, stinking water could contain living things — beautiful living things, even the catfish. Hope hadn't recognized much in the world as beautiful — even the sight of Polyphilia's erstwhile body, while engorging his penis, did nothing for Hope in his strange heart of hearts — perhaps had recognized nothing as beautiful except for those stupid, immigrant fish.) Hope tied the end of his line to the tip of his pole and rolled his wrist sharply, gathering the excess around the end like a ball of yarn. Then he tied on his hook and affixed a worm. Joseph Benton Hope gave out the short birdlike cry that served as his laughter, the irony being, of course, that he used none of Opdycke's little niceties, even though they'd made him wealthy. (All of the Perfectionists were wealthy, because they shared all of the profits jointly. Mr. Opdycke received a larger share than did the others, but that was his private and personal knowledge.) Hope, now that his fishing gear was assembled, began his cautious approach toward the water's edge.

Opdycke and his angling inventions were the other reason for bedlam back at the community. Mr. Opdycke had invited a number of prominent wholesalers to the community and was busy trying to convince them of the merit of the Opdycke product. Hope suspected he'd be successful. Opdycke would be dressed in a fine suit, his hair pomaded, his whiskers curled, and he'd offer these men whiskey. The businessmen would drink all afternoon (so would Opdycke, but without any sign of inebriation), and by the end of the day contracts would be signed.

Joseph Benton Hope reached forward and dropped the end of his line into the water. He immediately felt something, and he instinctively went to snap his wrist, but he contained himself. The fish had become wary of late, finnicky and hesitant to commit themselves to the bait. Hope allowed the tugs and nudges to increase in frequency and amplitude, and then he pulled sharply upward. Holding his pole in both hands, Hope threw the tip over his shoulder, high into the air. A fish broke the surface of the water, a small sunfish that flipped frantically, trying to throw the hook. Hope continued the backward motion of his pole so that he could land the fish behind him. Things began to happen too quickly for Hope to note accurately. Perhaps the fish threw itself clear, perhaps not; Hope tumbled backward, either by dint of this sudden release or because of the fury that erupted from the lake. Hope was still concentrating on his little fish — he watched it vanish. Only then did Joseph notice that the bass had disappeared into the maw of an awful and stupendous monster. Hope watched the Fish twist in the air (which the Fish seemed to do endlessly, somehow managing to suspend itself until its image was forever imprinted in J. B. Hope's memory), and then it was gone.

It was little Isaiah, a strangely imaginative lad, given to flights of fancy and poesy, who said that the monster's name was Ol' Mossback. Isaiah was delighted by the story, and badgered his father constantly to retell it. Joseph Hope, of course, told it once or twice and then never again, so the tale had to be told by the boy himself. The other youngsters agreed that Isaiah told the story well, embellishing it with unlikely but frightening details.

"Ol' Mossback," Isaiah improvised one day, "is the same color of silver as the moon, because he's a moonfish. That's how come Father didn't know the sort of fish he was, because Ol' Mossback is a fish from the moon!" Isaiah had to watch himself, because if he terrified the others too much, he'd be beaten upon. Once he casually mentioned the probable contents of Ol' Mossback's stomach, adding to the list such items as cows' tongues and lizards. All was rolling along fine (indeed, the cataloging was one of his most popular inventions to date) until he mentioned kittens. At that point Sam and Lem McDiarmid rose as one, advanced on Isaiah, and boxed him stoutly on the ears (Lem on the left ear, Sam on the right). Isaiah's hearing was never the same after that, and toward the end of his short life he was quite deaf.

Gregory Opdycke was a young boy when he first heard the tales, and although Isaiah soon had a wonderful story worked out (Ol' Mossback was in reality a prince on the moon, but an evil witch had enchanted him, changed him into a fish, and thrown him into a lake on the earth), little Gregory's reaction was, "I'm going to catch dat fish!" With minor variations, those were the only words Gregory Opdycke ever said for the rest of his life.

Magick in Theory and Practice

Hope, Ontario, 1983
*Wherein our Young Biographer Proves himself
to be the Vessel of Strange Theory.*

The homestead was full of books and empty bottles. All the
shutters were drawn, and all the rooms were dark as midnight,
despite the sunshine in the great outdoors. Lopsided candles
set up here and there did the best they could.

Harvey Benson gave me a withering look. "Where are the
other inmates, Paulie?"

I bent over and picked up one of the many volumes on the
floor. It was *The Blithedale Romance* by Nathaniel Hawthorne.
I set it down on top of a huge pile of books (the uppermost
being the Rev. Dr. I. J. R. McDougall's *The Lecher*) to show Harvey that I wasn't totally negligent in my housekeeping duties.

The kitchen table was the worst, a foot deep in smudged
and stained pages, dog-eared books and dirty glasses. Esther
wandered over curiously while Benson proceeded to make
coffee. I stood still and wondered about the whereabouts of
this highly touted Irish whiskey.

"What are you working on?" asked Esther, sitting down at
the table and touching my pages.

"Hope," I answered.

"As in the emotion, or the town?"

I smiled cryptically.

"As in Joseph Benton Hope," explained Harvey while puttering. "He was a religious leader who settled here with his
followers. They were what they called Perfectionists, and they
thought it was all right to sleep with each other's wives."

"Not a German among them," I added.

"They all lived in a big house ..."

"A Fourieristic Phalanstery."

"... that's still standing in town. It's a tavern now. The Willing Mind."

"Wow! Can we go there?" asked Esther.

"Surely," answered Harvey.

"No," I said, "we can't go there."

"Why the hell not?" demanded Professor Benson.

I shrugged. "The draft sucks."

"I lived in a Free Love Commune," announced Esther, "back when I was sixteen or seventeen. Out in B.C. It was okay. We did acid and fucked a lot. But," Esther shrugged, "that got pretty boring after a while."

"I was at Woodstock!" Benson piped up proudly.

"I was in the movie," said Esther. "I'm one of the people skinny-dipping. I was so wasted, though, I don't remember hardly any of it. Freaked me out when I saw the flick, boy. There's my bare-naked ass, fifteen feet across." Esther shook her head wistfully and started sorting through my reference books.

"I went skinny-dipping at Woodstock," Harvey lied, "and I screwed some chick right in the middle of the crowd."

Esther nodded vaguely. "People fucked a lot back then."

The coffee was brewing merrily. I scowled at the chirping little percolator. Benson went to his satchel and took out a bottle of Jameson. "Your fave!" he said to me, holding up the whiskey.

Esther tried to be friendly. "Is that your favorite, Paul?"

I nodded and whispered, "Booze."

"Well?" demanded Benson. "Are you going to stand there all night?"

"Do you understand," I said suddenly to Esther, grabbing another chair and pulling it up to the table, "that Hope and his followers existed in the last half of the nineteenth century?"

"Wow!" exclaimed Esther. "Far out."

"And do you know what else?" Harvey butted in. My trick worked; he was distracted. I pulled the bottle of Irish whiskey out of his hand. "Joseph Hope was murdered by one of his followers," Benson went on eagerly, "and the guy was hanged."

I pulled the bottle away from my lips long enough to add, "Twice."

"Huh?"

I reluctantly stopped nursing. "The rope broke the first time they tried to hang him," I explained, "so he was actually hanged twice."

"Wow!"

"The ironic thing about it is this:" said Harvey, assuming his lecture hall tone and posture, "To support themselves, Hope and his Perfectionists began to make fishing equipment, as sport-angling was just then becoming popular in North America. Actually, they were responsible for a lot of innovations and developments."

"Like what?" asked Esther.

"Lots of things," I answered. The Jameson had returned me to the land of the living—at least, I wanted to talk. "They were the first to put ferrules on poles so that they could be easily taken apart and put back together. They were among the first to manufacture a crank/winch reel. They made lures, primitive ones admittedly, and one of the Perfectionists, Opdycke by name, is credited with inventing the Spoon."

"The Spoon," repeated Esther.

"The Perfectionists also started the tobacco industry in these parts," Harvey took over, "and those two industries just kept growing. A & A Tobacco owns all the land for miles around, and today Updike is one of the largest, if not the largest, manufacturers of fishing gear and tackle in the world. So, even though their experiments in communal living failed, the descendants of the original Perfectionists are extremely rich people."

"Do any of them live in town?" asked Esther.

I nodded but gave no further answer.

Harvey poured coffee into huge mugs.

"Farrr out!" said Esther. "So, like, what kind of research are you doing?" she asked me. "Everybody seems to know all about them already."

"There are some ..." I cast about in my mind for the right word. "There are some problematic areas."

"Like for instance?" demanded Harvey.

Esther got down on her hands and knees in order to sift through the books on the floor. She touched them lovingly, especially the antique volumes, her long fingers lightly tracing the gilded words on the spines. Esther came to the biggest book, an enormous thing covered in night-black leather. She sucked in her breath; a hand went to her throat. "Oh, wow," Esther said, opening the tome gingerly. The title page announced, in

ornate, curlicued print, *Magick in Theory and Practice*.
Benson looked at the title page and then cocked his granny-
glassed eyeballs at me. "What the hell is that for?"

"Just, um, a theory I'm working on."

"Namely?"

"Well, the theory is in its formative stages right now."

"Come on, Paulie."

"Are you into this stuff?" asked Esther, slowly turning the
pages. "This is heavy-duty."

"I'm just doing some reading about witchcraft, that's all." I
smiled at Esther and Benson broadly. "Hey, boy, we can have
some big fun. Drinking and fishing, my favorites!"

"What is with this shit, Paul?" asked Harvey.

I waved the bottle of whiskey around in the air as I said, "It's
just a theory that some of the original Perfectionists are still
alive, and they're still alive because they performed some magical rite involving cutting off some piece of Joseph Hope's
anatomy, namely his penis, and obviously they don't want anyone to know about it, because they're 200-year-old witches and
warlocks who kill people, like Hope and Deedee and, anyway,
it's just a theory, there's no harm in having theories, is there?
Everybody has theories!"

"Paulie," said Harvey Benson, "you are a sick puppy."

"I was a witch for a while," Esther said. "The black side can
be very powerful."

"Aw, for fuck's sake," muttered Harvey angrily. "For one thing,
we know how J. B. Hope died. He was chopped to pieces with
an axe. We know who did it and where it happened."

"Where did it happen?" asked Esther.

"Here," I said.

"Here in Hope, you mean?"

"Here. Right outside, up near the barn."

"Oh, wow! That's why I kept feeling all these strange vibes.
And if you're right, Paul — if these black magic people killed
Hope so that they wouldn't die, then his must be a very restless
spirit. That's why his presence is so strong."

"Esther," said Harvey, "I'd appreciate it if you wouldn't act
like this."

"There are more things in heaven and earth, Harvey," in-

toned Esther, "than are dreamt of in your philosophy."
For a while we all drank in silence, they their coffee, me the
Irish whiskey. Then Esther said, "Do you know who they are?"
"What 'they'?" demanded Harvey testily.
"I'll show you what 'they'." I almost shouted. I went and
grabbed *The History of the Community at Hope, Ontario*, and
pulled it open, turning the pages quickly to locate page 217,
where there was a daguerreotype of Mr. Opdycke. He was a
mean and haughty-looking individual, with a bald pate and enormous mutton-chop sideburns. "Okay?" Then I grabbed *Hook,
Line and Sinker: The Updike Empire* and pulled it open to eight
pages of photos in the centre. The final photograph showed
the current president of the corporation, Bernard B. Updike.
He was dressed in a three-piece suit and smiling at the camera.
    "What," said Harvey, "they're supposed to look the same or
something?"
    "Just imagine Opdycke with those tinted glasses and a wig
like the other guy's."
    "Oh, wow . . ." whispered Esther.
    "Oh, wow, *shit*," scowled Benson. "Look, I'll admit there's a
resemblance. A family resemblance."
    "I've seen this guy," I pointed to the photo of Bernard B.
Updike, "without his toupee and glasses on. And, believe you
me, there's more than a family resemblance."
    "But *this* guy," Harvey said of Mr. Opdycke's image, "looks
like a prick, and *this* guy," (Bernard B. Updike) "looks like a
jerk."
    "That's part of his devious disguise." I flipped through some
more pages of *The History of the Community at Hope, Ontario*,
before Harvey could make any further objections. On page 341
was a reproduction of a painting, done by Mary Carter De-la-
Noy. "Lookee there," I instructed Harvey.
    Harvey did, then demanded, "So?"
    "So, don't you recognize her?"
    "If I ever saw her before," said Harvey, "I'd remember."
    "You have seen her before, except not with long blond hair.
Imagine her with short hair — short black hair."
    Harvey imagined this and admitted, "Okay, okay. It looks a
little like that bimbo Mona."

"It is that bimbo Mona!"

"It can't be, you maroon. This Polyphilia died almost eighty years ago."

"Not," said Esther, "necessarily."

"Esther, I really wish you wouldn't encourage him."

"And how's about Jonathon Whitecrow?" I said. "You can find references to him in all of these books, in Cairine Mc-Diarmid's book, in McDougall's book, and it sounds like the same guy who sits there every day in The Willing Mind having his goddam Visions."

"I thought I explained once before about how some people have fathers and grandfathers and great-grandfathers and stuff like that."

"But he's gay, for Christ's sake!"

"The current edition may be gay ..."

"And they got a monster."

"Who's got a monster?"

"Hope has a monster. A town monster."

"Paulie, you really are quite seriously ill."

"It must have been some magic gone wrong," I theorized, "and that's why they keep him a secret, all hidden away."

Esther asked, "What sort of monster?"

"A huge, hairless, immensely obese creature."

"Are you talking about Louis Hope?" asked Harvey.

"Aha! You even know its name!"

"He's not a monster, Paul."

"What is he then, pray tell?"

"He's a ... huge, hairless, immensely obese creature."

"Right on."

"Wow," said Esther, "a monster. Far fucking out."

I stumbled over to the fridge, remembering suddenly that in a drunken stupor I'd hidden a bottle of beer in the vegetable crisper. Who I was hiding it from, I'll never know. The beer was still there, nestled in among the carrots.

Harvey said, disgustedly, "I'm going to the can," and Esther turned to the section headed "Disembodied Spirits" in *Magick in Theory and Practice*. I drank my beer and stared out one of the windows.

"Oh, wow," said Esther. "It says here that sometimes a restless spirit will take over the body of an animal."

I had glanced down when Esther spoke, surprised by her voice. I had forgotten that I wasn't alone. Moreover, I was disappointed that I wasn't. I sullenly looked back to my window. The hawk sat on the windowsill and stared at me.

God's Natural World

Ontario, 1873

Regarding the followers of Hope, we know the following: some fared better than others. Indeed, their several fortunes figure concordantly with the set wagering ratio of four to one.

The land surrounding Hope, Ontario, is excellently suited to tobacco farming, a fact that Abram Skinner tried to impress upon Joseph Benton Hope. The fact was originally pointed out to Abram by Jonathon Whitecrow. The Indian had come by one day, while Abram labored in his oversized garden, puffing on a cigarette, but this was not one of his foul-smelling self-constructed ones, this was a slightly yellow and perfectly cylindrical tube with the word "CAPORAL" printed at one end. Jonathon had offered one to Abram. The Indian had many of them, all uniform, lying side by side in a tiny cardboard packet that likewise announced "CAPORAL;" Skinner was astounded, having never seen such a thing, and he had accepted.

Abram was, of course, an inveterate pipe smoker, for sucking on a pipestem suited his brooding, philosophical bent. The actual pipe-smoke Abram had always found a little distasteful. This cigarette, though, seemed to produce a cleaner taste; Abram pulled the puff all the way into his lungs and instantly felt giddy. Exhaling, Skinner discovered that he could produce a controlled and continuous stream of smoke, and for some reason this was more satisfying than the loose, ethereal clouds that leaked out of his pipe. Abram Skinner was through his first cigarette in no time. Jonathon Whitecrow opened the cardboard box and offered him another.

"Don't mind if I do," had been Abram's response. Whitecrow had then begun to speak in his cultured and refined way. For years, Whitecrow had said, cigarette smoking had been very popular in European High Society. (Jonathan Whitecrow seemed to have first-hand experience of European High Society, although Abram knew that to be impossible.) Now, Jonathon proceeded, it was beginning to gain popularity in North America. This land, Whitecrow had nodded vaguely at the gentle hills that surrounded him, would be very good for growing tobacco. Abram Skinner had nodded and accepted his third cigarette. "By jim," Skinner said, "I think you're right!"

Two days later, Abram had had to go into Trenton in order to pick up some wire needed for the production of the Opdycke Angling Spoon, Pat. 1863. Next to the foundry was a barbershop, and Abram was surprised to see a sign in the window that announced "CIGARETTOS FOR SALE." Abram felt an inexplicably urgent need for one of the dainty white smokes. He'd entered the barber's somewhat bashfully and waited for the man to finish a tooth extraction before mentioning that he was interested only in purchasing cigarettes.

"What brand?" asked the barber.

Abram was confused. He tried to recall the name printed on Whitecrow's box and, although it sounded foolish, he said that he believed he wanted something called "corporals."

"Caporals?" asked the barber.

Abram Skinner nodded.

Things became further confused. Not only was there a brand of cigarette called "CAPORAL," there was another, "SPORTSMAN'S CAPORAL," and yet another, "SWEET CAPORAL."

"What is the difference?" asked Abram.

The barber shrugged and said that the "SWEET CAPORAL" were favored by women, while men tended to be partial to the "SPORTSMAN'S." In his opinion, the barber went on, the two tasted identical. Not only that, Abram soon discovered, his choice was in no wise limited to cigarettos bearing the "CAPORAL" brand name. He could choose from all sorts, including "BOHEMIANS," "DUKE OF DURHAM," "CYCLONE" and

"TOWNTALK." Abram began to knead the skin on his forehead, finding all of this troubling. He finally elected to purchase a packet of the "SPORTSMAN'S CAPORAL." All the way back to the Phalanstery, Abram Skinner puffed on his smokes, holding the reins in his left hand, with his right trying out different ways of holding the cigarette.

J. B. Hope didn't pay any particular attention to Abram and his tobacco-farming suggestions. Lately their Spiritual Leader had become distracted—all of the Perfectionists connected this change in mood with the death of Cairine McDiarmid.

George Quinton had discovered her. He'd been sent out early one morning to chop firewood for the Phalanstery. Later, toward noon, he'd returned a bloody mess, holding Cairine's tiny body in his arms. "Sowwy!" George bawled over and over again, the only word he seemed capable of giving voice to, taking upon himself all of God's injustice.

Cairine was mauled almost beyond recognition, her black clothes and flesh dangling from her in indeterminate tatters. "Sowwy!" screamed George, and it would be many hours before he was inwardly settled enough to tell them what had happened.

Returning home, George claimed, he'd stepped into a clearing to discover a huge black bear muzzling at something. George assumed that the beast had hunted an animal, until he recognized the heavy shade of Cairine McDiarmid's mourning clothes. Even then he did not realize what had gone on, but George unleashed a terrible bellow and charged at the bear. The animal had looked up from its meal, curious and innocent; then, a little alarmed, the bear turned and lumbered into the neighboring forest.

The Perfectionists were shocked beyond speech. This was horrendously discordant with their whole way of thinking, and it seemed especially cruel that the bear's victim should have been Cairine, a woman who loved God's natural world with her whole heart. Joseph Hope told them that Cairine had gone to Heaven where all is unsullied, free of Earth's grim forces — and such was his only pronouncement on the event.

The following day, Polyphilia Drinkwater Davies held a seance—the Spirit Rappings were loud and violent. Invisible forces tore the room apart, smashing dishes, upsetting the furniture, lighting and dowsing candles at a furious clip.

So Abram Skinner didn't press Hope on the point — in the final analysis Joseph was uninterested in such pedestrian matters, and justifiably so — he just went ahead and started planting tobacco.

The Stone Boner Was Even More Apparent in the Daylight

Hope, Ontario, 1983
Wherein our Biographer, and his Friends,
attempt to Drum Up a little Good Fortune.

Esther realized that she needed something called "Durkee Frank's Louisiana Hot Sauce" (Esther was doing the cooking, making a huge pot of something that looked revoltingly like food) at the same time as Harvey decided he needed a Hoper so that on the morrow he could join me in my Mossback quest. There was nothing for it, then, but to go into town. I put on my disguise, a caterpillar cap with SCOUT stitched over its brim and a pair of mirrored sunglasses. Harvey regarded me somewhat disdainfully. "Ready?" he asked.

We three climbed into the Fiat and headed off for Hope.

"Hey, Esther!" Harvey remembered. "There's a statue of Joseph Benton Hope in the Square. And ..." Harvey giggled his horrible giggle. "There's something really special about the statue. Isn't there, Paulie? Eh, isn't there, Paulie?"

"What's special about it?" asked Esther.

"You tell us!" Harvey pulled up beside the Square and cranked up the parking brake.

The Square had more people in it that day than I'd ever seen there before: two boys tossing a hardball back and forth; three old gentlemen of a scholarly bent, studying the feeding habits of squirrels with great interest; a young mother walking her children, one in a perambulator, one strapped to the back papoose-style, another still nestled peacefully in her tummy;

some teenagers, the boys barechested, the girls halter- and tank-topped, playing with a Frisbee, throwing the day-glo disk at lethal speeds; and one old fart done up in gold-braided regimentals, ribboned and hung with medals, who marched around rather aimlessly and appeared to be Hope's version of a parade. In the midst of all this stood the stern representation of J. B. Hope, the Good Book in the crook of one arm, the other raised piously toward the sky. I had decided, based on my research, that I actually had a good deal of respect for this man. It seemed to me that he'd started his career with the most pure-hearted intentions and followed them through with a dog-like loyalty. Somewhere along the line he was branded the worst libertine since de Sade, and at the end of that line he got chopped up into morsels. I studied the statue's face. I knew now why there was such a disparity in eye size, that the larger one was in life a huge, pale blue marble. Even for a statue, the face appeared chiselled; many of the writers I'd read had commented upon the sharpness of Hope's features, describing them as "angular," "aquiline" and, many times, "hawklike."

Benson fanned his arms at the statue. "Well, Esther? Do we detect anything untoward?"

Esther looked at the statue briefly and said, "Oh, wow!"

The stone boner was even more apparent in the daylight, highlighted by the sun and shadow.

"If you rub it," Harvey went on, "it's good luck."

Esther was a good sport. She marched forward and massaged the stone boner enthusiastically, closing her eyes and mouthing wishes. Then she stepped back and looked at us. "Come on, you guys!" she said. "It's good luck!"

"I rubbed it already," I answered.

"Me, too," said Benson.

"Well, it's not like you can have too much good luck!" countered Esther, and to prove the point she gave Hope's stone boner an additional thrumming. "Come on!"

Harvey will do almost anything for someone who is in the position of denying or granting him amorous congress. He went up to the statue and laid his little fingers on it briefly, moving them a few centimeters so that the action qualified technically as a rub.

"Come on, Paulie," said Harvey.

"Why not?" I wondered aloud. In a world full of nuclear weaponry, murder and mayhem, there is no percentage in refusing to rub stone boners. I stepped forward and tried to make myself a little good luck.

And I think it probable that at that same moment, the phone started to ring back at my little homestead.

Edgar the axe-murderer seemed delighted to see me. "Hey, Big Guy!" he barked, an unusual salutation, seeing as it came from a fellow who was built like a brick shit-house (the cliche is inadequate; let's say a brick shit-house that could bench-press its own weight). "How's it hangin', Big Guy?" Edgar continued. "You haven't been around for a while."

"I've been busy."

"Yeah, I bet." Edgar trained his black eyes on my companions. "Hiya, guys!" he yelped enthusiastically. "What can I do you for?"

Harvey answered, "I need a Hoper."

"Yep, I bet you do. If you're goin' after Ol' Mossback, you sure do need you a Hoper." Edgar reached below his counter and came up with a lure. "And here's one of the little beauties right here!"

"Ah!" went Harvey, with the air of a connoisseur. "The Hoper!"

"Hey!" said I. "That's not a Hoper!" This lure was an old-fashioned fishing plug, carved and painted to resemble a small perch.

"Of course it's a Hoper," said Harvey Benson. "I've been fishing long enough to know what a Hoper looks like."

"Yeah," agreed Edgar. "It's a Hoper."

"Well, what was that thing that you sold me?" I asked. "The thing that looks like a finger or, more to the point, a penis?"

"Watch your language, Big Guy!" snapped Edgar. "There's a lady present!"

Esther smiled gently.

"A finger, then," said I. "It looks like a finger."

Edgar aimed one of his own foot-long digits at the lure in Harvey's hand. "That there is a Hoper."

"That is not a Hoper," I mumbled. I looked at Esther furtively. "Further weirdness," I whispered.

"It's a real shame about Deedee and the lib'ary, eh?" said Edgar. "That really depressed me. I almost started drinking again."

"Yeah," I nodded. "Me, too."

"She was smoking in bed," continued Edgar. "That's what they say. You'd think she'd know better, wouldn't ya? One-hundred-and-four years old and still smoking in bed." Edgar moved his shoulders in what was meant to be a philosophical shrug but looked more like a visual aid for a lecture on plate techtonics. "That's the way she goes, eh, Big Guy?"

"I suppose."

"Yeah," repeated Edgar, "that's the way she goes, all right."

"How much for the Hoper?" asked Benson.

Edgar pursed his lips and decided, "Three forty-two."

Harvey produced the money.

"Is the Hoper an Updike product?" I blurted out, almost before I'd formed the question in my mind.

Edgar's eyes darkened. "Nope," he replied. "I don't carry the Updike products. 'S how come business is so shitty," he snarled, adding, to Esther, "excuse my French."

"But isn't Bernie Updike a friend of yours?"

"Yeah, sure. Big Bernie and Little Bernie, too. But I still don't carry the line."

"Why not?" I asked, astounded at my courage.

Edgar leaned across the counter menacingly. "Ever watch that show, 'Mutual of Omaha's Wild Kingdom?' "

I nodded.

"So you know what the odds are," Edgar said quietly.

"Four to one."

"And what do you think of those odds?" Edgar's voice dropped suddenly in volume and was almost a whisper.

"Pretty fair," I whispered back.

Edgar slapped his immense hand on to the countertop with final and irrevocable judgment. "*That's* why I don't carry the Updike line."

Then the three of us left Edgar's place. We went back into the wild kingdom.

Among the Wildflowers

Hope, Ontario, 1983
Wherein our Boy Hooks into Something!

The next morning the three of us went fishing.

Of the night before, there's little I can say. Most of it has vanished into an alcoholic blackout, although little pieces of memory are seared to my brain by the cocaine. I can tell you that I wept a good deal, nonspecifically, and recounted to Esther and Harvey the entire history of my relationship with Elspeth. Actually, I made most of this up. Moreover, I refused to grant freedom to the few truths that I kept locked up somewhere within me like tiny war criminals.

The three of us drove out to Lookout Lake, stopping here and there along the way so that Esther could examine the roadside vegetation. Esther was, like Harvey, employed at Chiliast U., her field being whatever field likes to examine roadside vegetation. It took us fully an hour to drive the two-plus miles, not that I cared particularly. I was groggy and muzzy-minded because, despite all my time spent bedside, I wasn't getting any sleep. I was zooming right past sleep into that nether state that's about as restful as running a marathon.

Once, we stopped and Esther ran out among the wildflowers. Esther was wearing a T-shirt that pictured and identified Darwin, although Darwin was looking grotesquely bug-eyed and hydrocephalic. Esther's lower part was crammed into cut-off blue jeans. Harvey stared after her for a long moment and then craned his head toward me in the back seat. "I'm in love, Paulie," Harvey said.

I scowled.

Harvey reached a clenched fist toward me. I slipped an opened palm beneath it. Harvey gentled his grip, and two white pills fell into my hand.

"What are those?" I asked.

Benson shrugged, expressive of pharmaceutical fine points beyond my comprehension. "Uppers," he answered simply.

This was a little like throwing a stepladder to someone stuck at the bottom of a well, but I eagerly chewed them up.

Esther came back and presented both of us with wildflowers. As we drove she wove some blossoms into what was left of Harvey's head of hair.

It was a beautiful day. God seemed to be taking a vindictive delight in making each day more beautiful than the last. Even Lookout Lake seemed magical that day, not like it usually seemed, which was like Nature's version of a motel room. The greens were deep, the face of the water jeweled, the rocks all buffed and polished. The three of us jumped out of the car and we each took a deep breath.

"This is great!" Esther said, dancing to the lake's edge. "Mossback!" she called. "Where are you?"

I pretended that I didn't hear a little voice exclaim, Oh, boy! Company. After all, I probably didn't.

Harvey and I assembled our gear. I did this with reasonable deftness, even gave the illusion of expertise. Harvey watched me with open interest. "Where did you learn all that stuff?"

I shrugged.

Esther was dabbling her toes in the water, her long arms held out sideways for balance.

"Don't do that!" I bellowed.

Esther spun around, a hurt expression clouding her lovely face.

I patted the thin air desperately, asking my companions for quiet and stealth. "We are hunting the mighty Mossback," I whispered loudly. "The mighty Mossback gets alarmed when he sees toes in the water."

Hey, come on, take it easy on her.

I spun around, ready to bawl out Benson for defending his sweetie-pie, but when I saw Harvey working on his gear I realized he had not spoken.

"I'm sorry," I told Esther.

"That's cool," she said, sitting down on a nearby rock.

Harvey got up and presented Esther with a light-weight spin-cast outfit. He and I were using heavier gear, our Hopers linked to high-test line with wire leaders.

Harvey then proceeded to give Esther a few pointers on the working of her equipment. She listened politely, nodding oc-

casionally, and then Esther stood up, assumed a fencing stance,
and lightly tossed her lure into the middle of the lake.

Harvey nodded. "Something like that."

Esther caught a fish on this first cast, a middle-sized bass
that gave us a wonderful display of tail-dancing. Esther laughed
gleefully. "Come on, baaay-beee!" she cackled. "Do that thing!"

Harvey and I were both standing beside her, ready to give
pointers on how to land such a troublesome catch. Of course,
Esther needed no such help. She gave the fish slack when his
antics demanded it, otherwise she kept her line nice and tight.
The bass was netted some minutes later. Esther pulled it up,
her thumb and forefinger gripping its lower lip. "Three pounds,"
she judged. Esther worked out the lure, tossed the fish back
into Lookout and then slapped her hands together.

Harvey and I moved away quietly and began to fish.

After a while I muttered, "Boy, oh boy. My body temperature is something. I am talking really, really high."

"Mine likewise," agreed Harvey. He dug into his magic satchel
and produced a bottle of Scotch.

Here we go again!

"Shut up," I snarled at the water.

My buddy Jonathon drinks that stuff, too.

"Yeah, yeah, yeah. Tell it to the marines."

"Paulie, who the fuck are you talking to?" Harvey was working his lure with concentration, so this question was shot out of
the side of his mouth.

Fortunately, I was spared answering because Esther gave
out with a spirited, "Hey-oh!" and began battling another fish.
Harv and I went to stand beside her.

"This one's bigger," Esther informed us. "Feels like a pike."

Esther let the fish play itself out, and then she cranked it in.
It was indeed a pike, a rather smallish one, and when landed
seemed lifeless. Esther plucked out the lure and then gingerly
lowered the fish back into the water, her hands supporting its
underbelly. "Poor thing's all tuckered out," she told us. Esther
began to move the creature back and forth, forcing water
through the gills. The fish remained stunned for six or seven of
these passes. Suddenly life sparked. The pike slapped the water with its tail, wetting all three of us, a defiant gesture that

meant "Fuck youse" in no uncertain terms, and then the fish was gone.

"You guys having any luck?" Esther asked ingenuously.

Harvey and I went back to our spot, drinking heavily along the way.

I don't get it, I don't get it. It's not like the human brain is a precision piece of equipment or anything to begin with and, boy, does that stuff ever throw it out of joint!

"Okay, Mossback!" I shouted. "Pipe down! You just better decide whether you want wild rice or tomato stuffing, because you are going to be our dinner!"

Get this guy.

"So, Paul," said Harv — we both cast — we let our dissimilar Hopers drop deeply, then began the retrieval, "so, are you getting any work done on your second novel?"

"No, because I'm doing all this research."

"Research about Hope and his followers and such like?"

"Exactly. Research about that."

"You don't think that's maybe a waste of time?"

"No."

"Paul, maybe you should come back to T.O."

"Toronto?"

"Yeah. It occurs to me that maybe you want to come back to T.O. and move in with me. You could work in my study. I've got a word processor and everything. Then at night we could have fun and shit."

"What I want to do, Harvard," I said solemnly, "what I want to do for all my life is to hunt this fish. What I want to do with all my heart is to catch him."

I stumbled forward as a furious force attached itself to the end of my line. Bracing myself, I jerked the rod tip backward, setting the hook. For a moment there was calm. The only sound in the air was that of my breathing, already quick and labored. Then the fish on the other end of the line began to move. I let him, trying to judge his size. "He's big," I whispered. "Sweet Jesus, he's big."

"I'll get the net," said Benson.

I cautiously brought up my rod tip, seeing what kind of battle I would provoke. The fish made an effort to get away, peeling off a foot or two of line, and then it stopped dead. I cranked my reel, and the fish resisted briefly and seemed to throw in the towel.

Ugly, ugly, ugly!

What's ugly?

That thing you've got on the end of your line.

It's not you?

Well, thank you very much. As if I would behave like that wussy. If—and, mind you, this is extremely unlikely—if I ever chomp down on that whatever-it-is, you are in for the fight of your life.

I was reeling in freely, the only hindrance being the creature's weight.

Both Harvey and Esther were standing beside me. "What is it?" whispered Esther.

"It's ugly, that's all I know."

They exchanged glances.

Harved waded into the water with the net. He lowered his head and searched the water for the fish, and when he saw it he said, "Is it ever." Benson slipped the net beneath the thing and raised it into our sight.

"Is it ever!" said Esther.

It was a ling, a prehistoric fish that hasn't evolved one iota for the past few thousands of years. A ling looks like a single IQ point made flesh. This one was big, somewhere near ten pounds, and stupid, even for a ling. It had managed to gulp down the Hoper, and the lure's barbs were imbedded in the thing's throat. Blood leaked out of its gullet. This ling was a goner, not that the earth would ever notice its passing. I took out my fishing knife and dispassionately sank it into the ling's brain. As a child, as a boy, perhaps as a younger man, I would not have been able to do such a thing. I hunkered down and watched as the ling, and something else, slowly died.

Stellar Constellations and Petty Emotions

Hope, Ontario, 1983
Wherein our Young Biographer (has he become our Hero? Perhaps not.) puts on a bravura Performance and makes the Acquaintance of Master Hope.

It was midnight at the homestead, and here's what was happening. Harvey and Esther were upstairs in their bedroom, causing all of the furniture to rattle and move about. I was full of tequila and cocaine. I was deteriorating. The word had lost its sting. I was deteriorating, and I was even slightly proud of the fact. I considered having a T-shirt made up, the back of which would read DETERIORATING. Maybe I could even have DETERIORATING tattooed somewhere on my being. And on my tombstone, of course, it would be chiseled, STILL DETERIORATING.

Meanwhile my spirit was packing together its meager belongings. "Fuggit," my spirit was muttering. "I've tried and I've tried, but there's just no living with this asshole!" I climbed to my feet and stumbled over to the huge picture window. The night was there, looking like a page torn out of a cheap, black-and-white porno magazine. I was holding my bottle of tequila, my spirit was moving out (muttering all the while: "Nope, nope, I can't hack it, I've tried and I've tried ..."), the stars reminded me of Elspeth, and I only needed one thing to make me completely, and beautifully, miserable. I fired up the record player and put on the "Vocalise."

It was hootenanny time. I tilted my head and howled the melody at the moon, back where it came from, and with my hands I conducted, orchestrating the movements of constellations and petty emotions. It was a bravura performance I put on, better than Leonard Bernstein could have done, because Lenny didn't know or even care about Elspeth and Helmut.

At the end of the song, my spirit was long gone. ("And on top of everything else, there's too much goddam *noise*.") I turned away from the picture window, away from the night, and then I started to scream.

When I say I "started to scream" I mean only that I initiated the physical process of screaming, opening my mouth and sucking in buckets of air, but the scream itself got tangled up in my tear-choked throat.

All I actually produced was an odd bird-like sound, sort of a cheep. Still, it was enough to alarm Louis Hope. He took three baby-steps backward, but they were too quick, not properly engineered, and Louis fell down. He fell down slowly, crumpling like a dynamited building, and it seemed like many moments later that Louis was finally a mountain of obscenely pale flesh covering my floor.

I was holding the tequila bottle high in the air, because I'd been using it as a baton, and that's where it ended up at the end of Rachmaninoff's "Vocalise." Louis Hope's good eye was fixed on the bottle, and the look in that eye was pitiful and terrified.

"Don't hit," whimpered Louis.

It took me many moments to realize what had taken place. First of all, Louis's voice was a strange one, and sounded as if it came out through a mouthful of lopsided marbles. Secondly, I have never considered a booze bottle to be an offensive weapon (although God knows I've had just cause), but finally I connected the naked giant's fearful quivering with the tequila in my hand. I lowered it slowly, sneaking a sip from it en route.

I said, "Hello, Louis."

Louis Hope moaned something, very quietly — "Sowwy" — and then he covered his face with grief and shame.

"You like this music, don't you, Louis? I do, too. It's beautiful."

Louis parted the fingers of one hand to reveal that his milky wall-eye was aimed at me. "Boo'ful," he agreed.

"Don't be frightened," I tried to calm him. Then I had a good idea, as unlikely as that sounds, and I asked, "Do you want something to eat?"

Louis Hope parted the fingers of his other hand so that both eyes were pointed at me, albeit from two very different vantage points. "Eat?" he repeated.

The way to a 700-pound giant freak's heart is through his

stomach, remember that. I dashed into the kitchen, and when I returned I had most of the refrigerator's contents cradled in my arms.

Louis had maneuvered himself into a sitting position, his legs splayed out awkwardly. I deposited the food in this crook, and Louis began to eat.

Louis was quite naked, and every so often (if he had a free hand) Louis would reach down into his crotch and toy idly with his tiny dink. Louis Hope also kept one or the other of his eyes trained on me, ever wary. I needn't go into detail about Louis's eating habits, except to say that he got one point out of several thousand for table manners, and that one point was looking vaguely sheepish after producing a belch that registered on the Richter scale.

While Louis ate, I reset the needle of the phonograph, for the music seemed to tie things together, connect it all in some convoluted sense. Louis started to rock, slowly and almost in tempo with the "Vocalise"; he also produced quiet moaning noises that sounded as if animals were being butchered many miles away — this was meant to be singing.

After two or three repetitions of the piece, Louis was done eating. Most of his huge and off-putting body gleamed with chicken fat.

"Now what do we do?" I wondered aloud.

Louis considered the question. He cocked his head slightly to the left, then to the right, back and forth a couple of times, and then he threw his crooked shoulders heavenward. "Eat?" Louis suggested.

"No more food," I told him.

Louis Hope was saddened. He pulled a smear of grease from his belly with his forefinger and sucked on it petulantly.

"How old are you, Louis?" I asked him.

"Twenty-two," Louis answered succinctly — but then he kept going, and over the course of the next few moments claimed to be "3," "107," "54" and "406."

"I'm thirty," I told Louis Hope. He didn't appear to care. The two of us simply stared at each other.

There is, in *The History of the Community at Hope, Ontario*, a daguerreotype that pictures most of the original Perfection-ists all posed together on some lawn. It is an unremarkable photograph — many of the subjects had become fidgety, and their images are slightly blurred — except for the fact that in the background, ducking down so that his massive head manages to get crammed within the frame, is George Quinton. This is the only known representation of George. Martha, on the other hand, managed to bully herself into all sorts of pictures, even into a posed painted portrait of Adam and Mary De-la-Noy. Of course, Louis bore an uncanny resemblance to George, you probably aren't surprised to find out, as if someone had taken George's face and simply rearranged the features a bit. But even I, demented and looking for black holes in the universe, didn't conjecture that Louis was in any way the same person. This was because George Quinton's death was the most thoroughly documented of any of the Perfectionists', written up in countless newspapers, lavishly described in Rev. Dr. McDougall's book *The Lecher* (wherein George Quinton is portrayed as a martyr in the name of all that is decent) and medically confirmed and validated by a court-appointed physician. I may not have known much, back in my early Hope days, but I sure knew that George Quinton was dead; he'd been hanged for the murder of Joseph Benton Hope.

Stirpiculture

Ontario, 1879
Regarding the theories and practices of Hope,
we know the following: that in 1879 he
embarked on systematic experimentations in
stirpiculture. The result of these experiments is
known to the modern scholar — they
produced, in time, one hell of a women's
softball team.

From THE HISTORY OF THE COMMUNITY AT HOPE,
ONTARIO

By 1879, the community was inhabited by approximately one hundred sexually active adults. In the Free Love system at Hope, a man wishing to have sex with a woman would first submit a written application to Joseph Benton Hope. Hope would in turn consult the woman (who ostensibly had the right of refusal) and, more often than not, sanction the act. Strict records were kept (Daisy Cumbridge was the self-appointed secretary) which show that the average woman had two to four lovers a week, whilst some of the younger girls had as many as seven.

With the continued financial success of both the fishing-gear manufacturing and the tobacco plantations, Hope realized that it was economically feasible to abandon the practice of "wilful countenance" and to propagate. It was J. B. Hope's vision that from the small community at Hope should arise a "Glorious People." Hope asked for female volunteers who would lend their bodies to the procreative program, and made it clear that he would influence the choice of each sire.

Hope received some forty-five applications; he rejected eleven due to the person's physical condition (they were, one assumes, too old). The thirty-four left had an average age of nineteen, and were mostly virgins.

The man most favored by Hope to impregnate these women was Hope himself.

Thus began the experiments in stirpiculture.

Joseph Benton Hope was fifty-five years old. His fingers, for all his life fine and delicate, as white as ivory, had, over the last year, twisted and gnarled like tree roots. The knuckles had exploded and were as big as walnuts; the skin that covered them was red and flaky. Joseph Hope himself found the hand ugly, even as he laid it on Rachel's breast.

Rachel shivered.

Rachel's nipples were a shade of golden brown that Joseph Hope had never seen before. He was intrigued by this, after having seen so many nipples. Hope flipped his thumb across it two or three times, wondering if excitement to the amative mammary site might alter the pigmentation. It didn't seem to; the nipple merely stiffened, tiny and resolute.

Rachel was seventeen, a small girl with auburn hair. Rachel's nose was slightly crooked, which Joseph Hope found very attractive. Hope had lately found such small imperfections to be sexually stimulating.

Rachel had been one of the first volunteers to the stirpiculture program, and there had been many applicants for sire — among them Mr. Opdycke, Erastus Hamilton, both Samuel and Lemuel McDiarmid, and Isaiah Hope.

Isaiah Hope, twenty-one years of age but still as small as a teenager (as Joseph himself had been at that age) had submitted an application (his first and only) in his beautiful, flowery handwriting. Under the heading "Reason I Should Be Elected as Mate," Isaiah had written a long, finely wrought statement, which included such phrases as "mutual affection," "common areas of interest" and "intense reciprocal corporeal attraction." Having read all that, J. B. Hope had laughed his queer, birdlike laugh. Isaiah was in love with this little bit of fluff. Joseph had crumpled the application savagely, and later he publicly berated Isaiah for these "special feelings" and "exclusive attachments." Then, in a whisper, he'd told him something else. Isaiah realized that he would never be allowed to procreate. Isaiah Hope had, of course, begun to weep.

Rachel had looked away, during this humiliation of Isaiah, folding her hands into her lap and studying them with great interest. Joseph Hope gazed at her for a while, and noticed that her nose curved almost imperceptibly to the right. "I shall father the stirpicult!" Hope announced.

And now Rachel was naked, or almost so. She was wearing a pair of sheer stockings, and Hope would insist that she wear them throughout their amorous congress. Hope pulled his horny hand over her tanned body, still slightly more interested in his own paw than Rachel's youthful nakedness. Where had he seen a hand like that before? Joseph Hope watched as it traveled over Rachel's small belly, and it struck him that his hand somehow resembled a hawk's claw.

Rachel shivered again, was in fact shivering constantly.

"Are you cold?" J. B. Hope demanded. His voice was worse the older he got, and sometimes sounded like a chorus of bullfrogs at the bottom of a dried-out well.

Rachel shook her head.

Rachel's hands were timidly covering her thistle — Joseph Hope pulled them away. The coloring of her fleece was the same golden brown as her nipples, the shade that Hope had never seen before.

Joseph Hope felt the Holy Spirit enter his body, and the front of his nightdress pushed out toward the young girl. Hope pushed her backward on to the bed and hiked up the hem of his gown.

And as Joseph Hope drove the Holy Spirit from his own body and into Rachel's, Isaiah Hope sat by the edge of Lake Look Out, apparently talking to himself.

Mona Left the Sentence in the Air

Hope, Ontario, 1983
Wherein our Hero (let Us give him the Benefit of the Doubt) is given some Distressing News and Frolics Adamatically.

I suppose I fell asleep there in the living room, lullabyed by the music and finally overtaken by the drugs and alcohol in my system. When I awoke, I was knotted up on the hardwood floor. Someone, presumably Louis Hope, had covered me with whatever could serve as blankets; dishtowels, rugs, even the filthy WELCOME doormat from the flagstone patio. Still, I was goose-pimpled and shivering. My teeth chattered so hard that I could feel my brain bouncing around in my skull.

The sun was coming up hesitantly, peeking over the edge of the world to make sure the coast was clear.

I lay on the floor for a long while — despite an awesome exhaustion I knew I didn't stand a chance of falling back to sleep. I wished that Elspeth was lying there beside me (Elspeth, who clocked eight hours of slumber time nightly, regardless of the circumstances) so that I could look at her body. Elspeth wore a full-length flannel nightgown to bed, but through guile and sneaky material tugging I could usually expose enough of her nakedness to satisfy my voyeuristic tendencies.

I twisted my body to a position in which my head hurt fractionally less for a quarter of a second. A piece of paper tumbled off my chest. I picked it up and read:

WHAT THE HELL DID *YOU* GET UP TO LAST NIGHT? WE HAVE TO GO BACK TO THE CITY. SOME PEOPLE HAVE TO WORK FOR A LIVING! REMEMBER WHAT I SUGGESTED. ESTHER THINKS YOU'RE A NICE GUY! NYUK, NYUK!   H.

From outside came a horrible sound, which I recognized after a moment as the horn from Esmerelda, Mona's pickup truck. The sound was still distant — Mona had yet to turn up the laneway. When the turn was made, it was accompanied by a tire-screeching and further horn-blaring. I climbed to my feet, vacant and nauseous, wondering what the hell was going on. Then came a brake-screaming, a metallic door-slamming, and finally a heartrending "Paul!!"

I made haste to get outside.

Mona stood beside the black pickup truck and shook. She was trying to light a smoke, but her enormous hands trembled so that the match waved back and forth underneath the cigarette and wouldn't even set it smouldering. Mona's eyes were an odd mixture of red and black, red from tears, black from sleeplessness and the gravity of being.

"So, um," said Mona — she drew her forearm underneath her nose, pulling off a string of mucus — "like, Jonathon's in hospital."

"He is?"

" 'Cause he got beaten up," Mona explained. "Bad."

I began to suspect that my theories of witchcraft were misguided. I opened my arms and Mona came to me. She leaked all over my body for a good long while, leaked and trembled and whispered curses.

Finally Mona was collected enough to demand, "What's with you, anyways?"

"Huh?"

"Where have you been? What have you been doing?"

"Research," I admitted.

"Dumbfuck research," Mona muttered, burying her face into my chest. "Like about Joseph Hope and what happened and all that shit."

"Correct."

"Ever'one knows what happened." Mona broke from me, turned away and wandered down toward my pond. It was breakfast time at the water, and Mona and I stood side by side and watched the activity. We slipped our arms around each others' waists.

Mona said, "Go figure, eh? Jonathon, he's the nicest guy in the world, and ever'one aroun' here knows it. So who would beat him up so bad? He may not ..." Mona left the sentence in the air. It was astoundingly awkward up there, like a hippopotamus trying to walk a tightwire.

A kingfisher swept across the sky, and both Mona and I lifted our eyes to watch him. The bird cruised over the water, and then in an instant buckled and plummeted. The kingfisher barely made a splash as it entered the water, and it seemed like the same moment that it ripped back through the surface, going the other way. The bird now held a chubby little trout in its beak.

Mona wiped her nose again. "I called the hospital," she told me, turning and walking back up the gentle hill. "They said that visitin' hours weren't 'til like two in the affernoon. You wanna go visit Jonathon?"

"Yes. I want to go visit Jonathon."

" 'Kay. But ..." Mona tossed her shoulders up and down. "What are we gonna do 'til then?"

"Technically speaking," I answered, "I haven't been to bed yet."

"Yeah, but ..." Mona eyed the little homestead darkly. "That's the old Quinton place."

"You don't like that?"

"It makes me feel weird," she admitted. "This is where J. B. Hope got wasted."

"A long time ago."

"You know what they say? Eh? You know what?" Mona said

this rather eagerly, as if it was after midnight, and the moon was out, and she and I were five years old and trying to scare each other silly. "Louis — you know Louis, right? — he's like a ghost, or a spirit or sumpin', right, who can't find any peace! And he has to walk the earth ..."

"Waddle the earth," I amended.

"... until someone finds out the secret! And then he can find peace."

"What secret?"

"I dunno! There's gotta be a secret somewheres!"

"Maybe about the, you know, penile amputation."

"You know, for a smart guy, a writer and a researcher, you're a stupit shit. You read one book — by Isaiah Hope, no less, who ever'one knows was loony-tunes from the word go — and you get all worked up about it."

"You mean ...?"

"That's right, peabrain, J. B. Hope never got his dick chopped off."

"I have to admit, it didn't seem like the kind of thing George would do."

"George? What's any of this got to do with George?"

"He killed Hope!"

"Yeah, sure, but ..." Mona stared at me with exasperation. "You really been reading and shit?"

"Yeah!"

" 'Cause you know, like, mice-turds! For fuck's sake, if you're gonna research, research!"

She had a point there. I had gotten rather sidetracked somewhere along the line.

"Let's drive out to Lookout Lake," I decided suddenly, "and go skinny-dipping!"

"I dunno. Maybe." I guessed that Mona felt it was indecorous to go skinny-dipping while Jonathon Whitecrow lay in the hospital near death. But I knew that Jonathon would have thought it a wonderful idea, and what's more, something deep within me was monomaniacal about driving out to Lookout. I took Mona by the hand and dragged her toward Esmerelda. "You don't have to go skinny-dipping," I told her. "You can keep your bra and panties on."

"Oh, yeah, right, sure," Mona mumbled. "As if I wear that shit."

I pushed Mona into the passenger's side of the cab and then climbed in behind the wheel. I was struck by a thought as I fired up the ignition. "Hey, Mona. You call your dog Joe."

"Right."

"I thought you named him after Joseph Hope."

"Nope." Mona lit up another cigarette as I backed down the laneway. "Named him after my husband. Not really my husband. My common-law husband. Joe. Joe Gom."

"Oh, and that's why . . ."

"That's why what?"

I changed the subject, not wanting to mention the fact that Mona had whispered "Joseph" in the throes of orgasm. "So where's Joseph?"

"Joseph is *el morto*," Mona replied. "He had a little air bubble in his brain or sumpin', and one day it 'sploded. He never even knew he had the bubble. Least it was quick," Mona continued. "We were watchin' TV — "The Waltons" — and Joseph says will I get him a sandwich? Get your own effin' sandwich, I say, and he says, okay, and stands up. Ka-boom." Mona was quiet for some long moments. "Guess I should have got him the sandwich, huh?"

After a silence, Mona said, "Let's go skinny-dipping."

Soon Lookout Lake came into view.

Mona pulled down her bluejeans slowly and, true to her word, was wearing no underwear. I stood behind her and watched with wonder as she revealed her bottom. Mona turned around, caught me ogling, and smiled. Then she unbuttoned her shirt and pulled it off. Mona, majestically naked, nodded toward the water. "Strip, boy. We's goin' skinny-dippin'."

"Right." I awkwardly divested myself of apparel.

Lookout Lake was icy cold. As soon as we were kneedeep Mona's nipples puckered and my privates shriveled. This was worth a giggle or two. Then, hand in hand, we raced forward.

We made love in the water, Mona and I, which was something I'd seen in movies, always in slow motion, but never suspected was possible in "Mutual of Omaha's Wild Kingdom."

Then we climbed back on to the bank, enveloped each other in the other's body, and Mona and I went swiftly to sleep.

Well, that was highly educational.

Huh?

I've heard a lot about it, but I've never actually seen sex performed before.

Ol' Mossback?

Whom else?

Oh, right. Another of those silly dreams I have.

Whatever you say. Anyway, that human sexual intercourse is some hard work. We fishies have an easier time of it. The female lays the eggs, I cruise over, slow and easy-like, and zap 'em with the milt. Easy. Mind you, it's not an awful lot of fun, but it is easy!

How's come all you ever want to talk about is sex?

I'll talk about other things. Like, for instance, perhaps it would interest you to know that the water dropped about 6 degrees Centigrade overnight.

It doesn't.

Oh. Well, what do you suggest we talk about?

Let me ask you about something. There's a book called *The Fish* ...

I read it.

What the hell do you mean, you read it?

I didn't actually *read* it. Isaiah read it to me.

The whole book?

While he was writing it. I was kind of his technical adviser. You know that scene where the Fish dies? I had a lot of input there. The way Isaiah had it, the Fish just ate the poison and plotzed. But it wouldn't have happened that way. We fishies, boy, we put up a struggle.

It was a pretty good scene.

I take that as a compliment, coming as it does from a published writer.

Who says I'm a writer?

Whitecrow.

Oh. So, in Isaiah's book, the Fish devours a number of penises.

Right.

Any truth to that?

Ah, I think you're missing the symbolism.

Don't give this symbolism shit.

You are asking if it is a literal truth that I have in my time devoured a human penis?

Right.

The answer to that question would be in the negative.

You're being evasive here, Mossback.

Hey, know what? I'm beginning to understand this tit business. Your girlfriend, boy, she's got great tits!

Don't change the subject.

I didn't.

Have you ever eaten any portion of the human anatomy?

Eaten as in ingested, no. I chewed on something once, then spat it out.

What was it?

"Paulie?"

Your girlfriend wants for you to wake up.

What did you chew on?

"Paulie, it's time to go to the hospital."

We'll be talking to you, chum.

"Let's see if maybe *this* will wake you up."

This too is educational. We fishies don't do that.

Mona pumped life back into my body.

Suddenly It Became Clear That a Main Street Existed

Ontario, 1881
Regarding the settlers that followed Hope into Canada, we know the following: not all of them put credence in the Philosophy of Perfectionism.

The year of our Lord, 1881, was the year the Dutch came, not to join Hope and the Perfectionists, rather to farm the land. Abram Skinner had advertised in many European newspapers, a large box with "FARMERS WANTED" printed under the banner of "A & A Tobacco," the two letters joined together by a leaf of the plant, but it only seemed to create interest in Holland. The Dekeysers came first, a huge clan, twenty adults and scores of children, all of them large, chunky people, blond and looking somehow addled, smiling at everything and communicating with little grunts and hand motions.

The patriarch, Karl, was the exception. He was large and chunky, true, larger and chunkier than any of them, but Karl was a grim man, frowning at the family's clownishness, occasionally looking up toward the sky with an arrogant sneer, silently cursing the Lord and His Creation. Karl claimed most of the land around the Phalanstery, and over the next couple of years he built toward it, eventually engulfing all of the Perfectionist buildings with a number of ramshackle residences. Having done that, Karl wrote home, and soon other Dutchmen arrived, cousins and friends of the Dekeyser brood, Van Hoosens, Bontjes and Hoöckers. They worked the tobacco fields with enthusiasm, as if oblivious of the fact that most of the fruit of their labor was going into Abram's, and therefore the Perfectionists', pockets; for whom they had little affection, not to mention even less understanding.

Having surrounded the community, the Dutch began to infiltrate it. Mr. Opdycke was instrumental in this, hiring most of the immigrant girls and women to work for the fishing-gear company. Next Karl Dekeyser, despite being obviously as hardy and strong as an ox, claimed that he was too old to farm, and installed himself as the local butcher. He made his shop on Joseph Avenue — that is, he opened his butcher's shop, and suddenly it became clear that a main street existed. George Quinton constructed a sign reading "JOSEPH AVE" and pounded it into the ground.

Cigarettes, Whiskey and Dreams

Hope, Ontario, 1983
Wherein our Hero visits a Sick Friend, and is given a Clue.

On television, people in hospitals are always hooked up to I.V. bottles and such-like things, tubes running into their noses and through their veins in a manner that would have made Dr. Frankenstein proud. What was most alarming about Jonathon was that there wasn't a life-support system in sight, the closest pouch of liquid food being hooked up to some old fart three beds away. I resisted the temptation to rip it out and plug it into Whitecrow so that his eyes would open, moonlike and wise.

Mona and I stood hand in hand by his bedside. For a long time, maybe even several minutes, we simply gazed down upon him. Whitecrow was, I noticed, a wasted and ancient geezer. He looked no more substantial than a feather. But what could one expect from a man who subsisted on a diet of cigarettes, whiskey and dreams? If I had been a detective, investigating the obviously aggravated assault, I would have been dismayed, because Whitecrow's physical scrawniness didn't eliminate much of the general population from the suspect list, not even midgets, Girl Guides and pussycats. Of course, whoever beat up Jonathon was a vicious and brutal creature, but at that moment, as pissed off as I was at the world, I still wouldn't have eliminated midgets, Girl Guides or pussycats.

"Jon-Jon?" whispered Mona.

The other thing you see on television is people covered head to toe in bandages. Jonathon didn't have any of that shit either, I guess because his outside wasn't that badly damaged. It was ripped in a few places and discolored in some others, but otherwise Jonathon was externally normal. Inside Whitecrow was another story. All of Whitecrow's inner stuff was busted and dysfunctional. The doctors would have felt silly putting on bandages, so they didn't. They left Whitecrow as he was, naked except for his cotton hospital gown.

"Hey, Jonathon," whispered Mona.

Mona had said to me (as we entered through the front door —there were words carved into the stonework above the portal; they were in Latin, which made me suspicious — maybe they translated as "Hey, buddy, don't expect too much, okay?"), "I hate hospitals." People always say, "I hate hospitals," and I think it must be one of those misguided reflex phrases, like saying, "Pardon me," when a fat lady mows you down on the sidewalk. *I* don't hate hospitals. God is there, invisible in surgical greens, making the rounds, flustered and always behind schedule.

"Come on, Whitecrow, ya big faker!" Mona badgered desperately. "Wake up."

Slowly Jonathon's eyes opened. They were hollow.

"How you doing, guy?" I asked.

"Not great," Whitecrow admitted.

"This hospital ain't so bad," Mona said, pointing at the various walls and light fixtures with great animation. "Hey, Jonathon, you could get a TV in here! That'd be okay, eh? Just lie aroun' an' watch the boob tube all day, the life of Riley, ya know what I mean? I'll talk to the guy. The television guy." Mona went abruptly quiet and stared down at her feet.

"A television," said Whitecrow with some effort, "would be nice."

"The life of Riley," Mona agreed.

"Paul," said Jonathon, "how are you?"

"Fine. Good."

"Talked to Ol' Mossback lately?"

"Mmmm, yeah."

"Really? When?"

"Just today."

Mona shot me an odd look.

"How is he?" asked Whitecrow.

"Oh," I shrugged, "you know Ol' Mossback."

Jonathon nodded laboriously. "Yes. I know Ol' Mossback."

"I'm missing sumpin'," Mona said. "Why the fuck are we talking about a fish?"

"Whether we live by the seaside, or by the lakes and rivers, or on the prairie, it concerns us to attend to the nature of fishes," Whitecrow quoted.

That sounded familiar. "Who said that?" I asked.

Whitecrow moved his head and shoulders microscopically, the tiniest hint of his once grand and aristocratic shrug. "Oh," he answered, "just some asshole."

"Jon-Jon," asked Mona, "who the fuck done this to you?"

"Could have been anybody," said Jonathon. "I never saw it coming."

"Why the fuck did they done this to you?" persisted Mona.

Jonathon shrugged more forcefully, which was a painful mistake. All of the broken junk inside him shifted, settling differently. "How should I know?" he gasped.

"Like, whoever did it is dogfood," announced Mona. "An' I'm gonna find out, too, I swear I am, and when I do, so help me ..." Mona was at a loss for words, which is to the credit of the English language.

"Mona," said Jonathon, "it hurts when I shrug philosophically, so please don't make me do it."

"I'm just sayin'." Mona rammed her enormous hands into her back pockets defiantly.

"Paul," said Whitecrow, "how goes the research?"

"Pretty good."

"Who killed J. B. Hope?"

It sounded like a nursery rhyme or riddle. Surely Jonathon knew as much as I did, so for a while I just chewed on my lip, wondering what he was up to, and then I said, none too declaratorily, "George Quinton?"

Jonathon smiled.

"Am I missing something?" I asked.

Jonathon nodded, just once, up and down.

"What?"

"It's simple. Look at your notes. Look at the experiments in complex marriage."

I tried to recall them as best I could. The first experiment had been Hope with Polyphilia. Then, Hope-Abigal Skinner, Abram with Polly. Next, Hope-Mary C. De-la-Noy, Adam-Polly, Mr. O. and Abigal. Then Hope and Cairine McDiarmid . . .

It was all too complex. I massaged my brow. "There's something there that's important?"

Jonathon Whitecrow shook his head. "It's like you said before: there's something missing."

Then I saw.

From THE LECHER

by Rev. Dr. I. J. R. McDougall,
Barr. & Sol., Esq.

Karl Dekeyser was by nature an impertubious man, owing to his turgid Christian upbringing. But when Gretel came home, the very offspring of his loins, and recounted the licentiality with which she had been treated by Hope (an occurrence of concupiscent obscenity not fit for the eyes of the casually interested; readers of a more scientific and/or scholastic bent should see[1].), Karl was consumated with furor.

[1]How She Suffered At The Hands Of The Sybarite

"And he shewed me a pure river of water of life, clear as crystal, proceeding out of the throne of God and of the Lamb."

Rev. 22:1

Perhaps these very words sprang into Gretel Dekeyser's young and putrile mind on that hot summer's day. Perhaps she was searching for communion with Her Maker. Slowly, with eminent pudicity, she removed her garments, naked only to the Eyes of the Almighty, and entered the lapling river. Little did she suspect that THE LECHER lurked nearby, his evil eye transfixed by her.

To illustrate the utter lascivousity of the Libertine's mind, allow me to list the following scientific datum, taken by Mineself with kindest permission of Dekeyser the elder.

1) Gretel's breast, at sixteen years of age, measured a mere 33 inches.

2) Gretel's nipple & aureole was 5/8 of an inch on the left, differing on the right by an additional 1/16 of an inch.

3) her waist measured 24 inches.
4) her hip/buttock measurement was 34 inches.

Even a cursorous glance should inform that Miss Dekeyser, even one full year after the attack, was possessed of a decidedly boyish figure, and, to a man of moral rectitudity, would scarcely have become an object of potential defilement. But HOPE, being of impurile gluttonousness, proceeded to take her. It has been suggested that Gretel Dekeyser did not combat her Abuser with utmost vigor. I believe this is because her immersion in the chilly water (not to mention the trancendant communion with Our Heavenly Father) left her somewhat light-headed. Moresomeover, J.B. Hope, for all his physical "smallness" (small in every sense save one) was ever a man of great strength.

(A scientific note of interest: could it be that rampagent Bacchanalian bawdrage somehow promotes the production of muscle enzyme?

And allow me to add a further small appendianium in my capacity as Witness: I did determine, during my scientific investigation of Miss Dekeyser's corpus, that prior to the optative spoliation at the hands of the quenchless LECHER, her state of virginal pudicity was clearly irredemptive.)

Karl Dekeyser went to his neighbors and lit within them the flame that burns eternal in the heart of Man, the flame disdowsed by proximation to Hope and his debauchious minions, the flame kindled by most precious sabbatarianistic communion with Our Father Who Art, Etc. Indeed, was not the flame of righteousity and indignability fanned within the breasts of some (so-called) Perfectionists?

Such is the Power of the Lord!!

For among those who escorted Hope toward his punishment — Hope, animalistic purveyor of all that is sullied, for instance, FORNICATION with the distaff mounted uppermost — was Hope's son, made of his own flesh and blood, young, handsome, noble, dashing, fair Isaiah!

What transpired by the side of Lake Look Out is not shrouded in obfucious limnings, although many spurious mistellings have arisen due to bibacity and/or ghoulashness. The truth was freely recounted to mineself by Karl Dekeyser, who said thusly, "I fed him to the fishes." Yea, the justice he meted was brute yet aptful: for Karl VIVI-SECTED from Joseph Hope (his butcher's knife swift & merciful) the third finger of his left hand. Here we see the symbology of the moralousness; this digit, traditionally bounded by the golden band, represents Holy Matrimony, and this was the precious institute that

Hope had ceaselessly salubated. So Karl Dekeyser seperated Hope from this finger, and with disdainity tossed the finger toward the water — the very self-same water from which his daughter Gretel had emerged only to be deflorated!

(Scientific interuptum: The veraciousness of the transpirality need not be reproached, for what profits it thirty-eight men that they be mendacious to an individuality? Therefore, let it be publicly scriven that a FISH of prodigious proportion rose from the lake and took the disembodied digit into its mouth. Many reportages have it that Hope was more alarmed by the sight of this creature than by his own mutiliation; at any rate . . .

End of scientific interuptum.)

Hope turned and fled. Hope fled to the one place he thought would offer sancuarity; the home of George and Martha Quinton (who eschewed the married name "HOPE", as well she should!)

George Quinton was cut from differentiated cloth than were the other "Perfectionists". He was a man of thoughtful eloquance, and he had seen the EVILNESS of Hope's impurious thought; therefore he had seperated himself (and his sister Martha, a fair dainty wisp of a woman) from the others, moving out of the so-called "Phalanx" and living in solitudiousness. It was to this place that THE LECHER ran, though it was fully two miles away; and his fearfulness gave him extrahuman strength, for he ever widened the ullage 'twixt him and those in pursuit.

George Quinton was occupied at that moment with the slaughtering of a pig; for this reason he was outside and possessed of an axe when Hope appeared before him.

As is public knowledge, George Quinton would not speak in his own defense when tried for Hope's murder, leaving us only the availableness of conjested thought. Many have it that what inspired George was the blessed instinct of mercifulness, that he wished to end Hope's horrible suffering. Others (mineself included) have it that only through LETHAL CHOPPING could Hope's OBSCENOUS DISSIPATORY EVIL be FINALLY and IRREVOCABLY brought to an end and BANISHED from the FACE OF THE EARTH!

Those in pursuit saw it, albeit from a distance of many hundreds of feet. George Quinton chopped Joseph Hope with the axe, then calmly stood by the morselatic corpus. When the men reached him, George spoke to the witnesses, saying, "I really am terribly sorry."

Weird Futuristic Devices

Hope, Ontario, 1883
Regarding the downfall of Hope, we know the
following: that it was precipitous.

Hope became an official "village" in 1883. The charter was applied for by a diverse group, J. B. Hope conspicuous by his
absence. Mr. Opdycke and Karl Dekeyser seem to be the chief
instigators. Mr. Opdycke had recently conceived the idea of
selling his fishing gear through catalog mail order, and "Hope"
had to be a village in order to get a Post Office. Gregory Opdycke, twenty-seven years of age and an avid angler (if nothing else) was installed as the first Postmaster. Karl Dekeyser's
motives are less straightforward, but seem to stem from a desire for even a small amount of power. The "village" needed a
mayor, and since Perfectionism was disdainful of such sullied,
earthbound conventions, Karl had little competition. (The Office of the Mayor in the town of Hope has since been traditionally filled by a member of the Dekeyser family — the current
mayor, Edgar Dekeyser, is a direct descendant.) And so survey-
ors came (Joseph Hope noticed them, burly men with weird
futuristic devices, metal and glass, standing off in the distance
and waving frantically) and in that year the name HOPE first
appeared above a small dot in the southeast of a huge block
marked ONTARIO.

I suppose that for a moment I can drop the "voice," the om-
niscient, dispassionate voice that has been recounting the Life
of Hope. This is good, not only for narrative purposes, but because I've grown to not care much for omniscience or emo-
tionless impartiality.

Scholars of Hope and his Perfectionist followers (and you
have to understand that there are no more than twelve of these
creatures the world over, thirteen if you count me) have pointed
to J. B. Hope's alleged rape of Gretel Dekeyser as the single
crisis that precipitated his downfall. I differ. Certainly whatever
took place with the young girl was crucial, but I choose to
examine the other forces at work against him.

Joseph Hope had allowed Mr. Opdycke to lay the foundation to a huge manufacturing conglomerate. Gregory Opdycke would continue the growth, marketing in 1897 a lure called the Kitty designed to hook huge fish, a great big furry thing that became immensely popular despite, or maybe because of, its looking like a little pussycat. Gregory's son Geoffrey, who altered the spelling of the family name to "Updike," was inspired by his grandfather's trick of injuring bait-minnows to design a lure that wobbled and twisted like a fish in distress. Gregory's son James opened the huge factory near my homestead, and later one in Japan that produced inferior lures, reels and rods — but millions of them — and Jimmy's son Bernard does nothing but sit in The Willing Mind, drink martoonies and argue with his own stomach all day long. Still, Big Bernie is worth millions. Open any fishing magazine and you'll see several pages of advertisements spread throughout, ads that tell you, "If It Ain't a Updike, It Ain't About to Work!"

Hope had allowed mysticism and occultism to pervade Perfectionism. Polyphilia's exhibitions of Spirit Rapping could no longer attract huge crowds, but the occasional moony-eyed couple from Dakota or wherever would straggle in and watch. In 1904 Polyphilia died, a victim of no illness whatsoever as far as the doctors could tell. Her child Ephraim Drinkwater Davies, son of Buford Scrope Davies, grew up to be a ridiculously fat and alarmingly weird young man. He combined his mother's occultism with the philosophies of the growing cult of "Daviesianism" (see page 178) and came up with something so twisted that he was immediately given chase to. Ephraim D. Davies was chased to the edge of the continent, and that's where he finally settled, finding the climate suitable in sunny Los Angeles, California. One historical significance of this is that he took his friend and half-brother Jameson De-la-Noy with him. Jameson happened to be in a bar one evening when he found himself drinking with David Wark Griffith. Jameson hastily improvised the name Jim Delaney, which he thought sounded mechanically inclined and competent, and he served for many years as D.W.'s technical assistant. Jim Delaney is chiefly responsible for the scene in "Intolerance," a classic in cinematic history, in which Babylon is razed to the ground. For some reason Delaney threw his heart and soul into that great destruction.

Hope had allowed the twentieth century to march unhindered into his Utopia and cover the ground for miles around with a carcinogenic weed. (The Skinners, like the Updikes, are a very rich family, although no longer represented in Hope, Ontario, except by Sophie, ace pitcher for the Hope Hawks, who I've since found out *owns* both Moe's and Duffy's, and the Ball Club. Following J. B. Hope's death, Abram and Abigal, and Anne and Alice, moved to France, where Abram could brood contentedly over great works of art. Abram was deeply stung by rumors that tobacco could be injurious to one's health, but he died with his trust in Mother Nature intact. During his eighty-fourth year, his last among the living, Abram Skinner finally became un-tongue-tied, or whatever the stylographic equivalent of that state is, and produced an essay with the following title:

SHOUTING: Genuine & Spurious, in All Ages of the Church, from the Birth of Creation, when the Son of God shouted for Joy, until the shout of the Archangel: with numerous extracts from the Old & New Testaments, and from the works of Wesley, Evans, Edwards, Abbott, Cartwright and HOPE; and giving Testimony of the Outward Demonstrations of the Spirit, such as Laughing, Screaming, Shouting, Leaping, Jerking and Falling Under Its Power.

And finally (here's where I part company with those twelve other scholars, uniformly old and wrinkled men who I'm sure wank every time they think about Hope and his followers) Hope allowed, even forced, his two most loyal disciples away. George Quinton built the house that I now live in, and he lived there with Martha until his death, by hanging, in 1889.

Jonathon Whitecrow instructed me to think on the first experiments in complex marriage, and I did so. What became clear is that no mention of George and Martha is made. It is easy to assume, and those other twelve geezers do so, that George was by nature celibate and Martha for some reason faithful only to J. B. Hope. But a clue is to be found in *The Theocratic Watchman*, vol. xx, no. ix, in which Joseph Hope writes:

Therefore, all of the so-called "perversions" of mankind are, indeed, just that, perversions of *mankind*, not of our Maker. In Genesis 4, Chapter 17, we are told "And Cain knew his wife." From whence came this wife? There is no mention of a further supranatural Creation. Elementary logic dictates that Cain's wife was fully his blood sister, but the Union is patently sanctioned by the Almighty. The notion of incest is, therefore, but man-made. It should little concern us; the matter of sanguineous relationship is irrelevant. We are all of us brother and sister.

In fairness to the twelve geezer-scholars, I must add that they did not have the benefit of an antique cedar chest in their bedroom (conveniently picked open by sad Sara) where this particular issue was to be found, opened to the page in question, nestled in among a woman's dress and a blood-soaked workshirt.

The issue is dated some ten months before the birth of Isaiah Hope.

PART FIVE

Alive With Peeps and Flutters

Hope, Ontario, 1983
Wherein our Hero Fulfills his Function as Gazetteer.

"But why," I demanded into the telephone, "are you telling me?"

"It is you that he wished for us to contact." The woman spoke as if she were snipping her words out of the *National Enquirer*.

"Look, let me give you another number ..."

"No."

"It's the number of a bar. Ask for Mona Drinkwater."

"Absolutely not. I suggest that personally you contact Mizz Drinkwater. That, after all, is why you were selected as the contactee."

"My name is the only name he gave you?"

"That is the case."

"Look in the telephone book! How many people could there be with that last name?"

"Again, sir, my suggestion to you would be as follows ..."

"That I do it myself."

"Precisely such."

"You know what, lady? You are heartless and cruel!"

She stopped snipping her words. "And you know what, bubba? You are gutless! And just as cruel."

"What, do I know you or something?"

"He put down your name, Mister Contactee. Get hopping."

I cradled the phone, and went to stare out the picture window in my homestead's living room. It was too beautiful a day. I was pissed off at God, and staring at His creation, the gentle hills that had become my world, I felt like saying, "Enough, already. Enough."

I went out to the barn, where the moped was kept. Barn swallows had set up condos in there, and the ancient rotting structure was alive with peeps and flutters. Enough, already, enough. I strapped on my protective helmet, and the noise was blocked out. I climbed aboard my bike, rolled down the laneway, and then threw the lever that connected the tiny motor. Now my world was mechanical and fueled by gas.

It took me quite a while to get into Hope, mostly because I navigated a route designed to take me quite a while. I should have used the time to rehearse a little speech, but my brain seemed devoid of words. I adopted the same mental stance as the high-flying hawk, whereby the universe was mysterious, distant and of no real concern to me. It works, if you happen to be a hawk.

The Willing Mind was held in a shaft of sunlight, caught in some spacecraft's transporter beam. The tavern looked preternatural. It looked like a paint-by-numbers that God had done one gloomy afternoon.

I took a deep breath and pushed through the front door.

I couldn't believe it. The place was crowded.

Not sardine style, of course, or even elbow-to-elbow, just crowded enough to fill up the tavern, somewhere between thirty and forty people. Four young guys were playing darts, three women were seated at a table, laughing and drinking tall drinks; twelve or thirteen guys, obviously just finished their shift at Updike International, had pulled four of the tables into a long row and were currently playing Colonel Puff, a drinking game.

I pushed through these people to the bar.

"Yo! Whaddya wanna drink?"

The owner of this voice was not Mona, a fact that filled me simultaneously with relief and regret. The owner of this voice was a tiny man with a huge beard, extending in a scraggly way all the way down to his belly-button.

"Beer," I said, a stunned reflex reaction.

"Beer." The bartender winked at me. All of his features were grotesquely oversized, fashioned for a man twice as big. "Draft or bottled or what?"

"Draft. Where's, um, Mona?"

"Day orf." The man picked up a mug and tossed it into the air. It turned about seven times, and he caught it behind his back. "I'm Teddy," he informed me.

"Do you know where Mona is?"

"If I know Mona," Teddy replied, moving off toward the antique draft pump, "she's out getting her ashes hauled."

I surveyed my fellow patrons at the long bar. The fellow immediately to my left was one of those sorts that life has slapped around and left permanently groggy and punch-drunk. He sipped strong drink and tried to think of ways of starting fights. Beside him was a woman, probably his lover. She downed tall glasses of fruity liqueurs. Beside her was Big Bernie.

I rushed down and filled in the gap between them.

"Hi, Big Bernie," I said. "Hi, Little Bernie."

Big Bernie nodded bleakly. "Hi."

I bent down until I was closer to the stomach. "What's the matter, Little Bernie? You mad at me or something?"

"Just don't feel much like talking," the potbelly mumbled.

"Oh."

"Me neither," admitted Big Bernie.

I realized, with a certain amount of disbelief, that the Bernies were asking me to leave. I turned away, but knew that it wasn't that easy. "Bernie," I said, "Jonathon died."

"That was a stupit thing for him to do, wasn't it?"

Little Bernie added a snicker and a sardonic, "Shit."

"Well, you know, I was the Contactee, that's all. See you around."

Bernie seemed to soften. "It's rough being a Contactee," he said. "I'm not looking forward to it at all."

"Me neither," put in his potbelly.

"I'll buy you a drink," Big Bernie decided. "We'll drink a drink to Jonathon. He was a good guy. Owed me about ten thousand bucks. Hey, Ted." Big Bernie waved his pudgy index finger in the air. "More martoonis and shit."

"Is it your wife?" I asked quietly.

"Is what my wife?"

"Is your wife ill?"

"Not as far as I know. My wife lives in Bolivia with a guy named, get this, Chichi."

I nodded knowingly. "Mine's taken up with someone named Helmut."

When the drinks came Bernie threw a few bills in Teddy's direction. "Keep it."

Teddy bowed subserviently. "Thank you, Mr. Updike."

Little Bernie muttered, "Grovel, dog" and was hushed by Big Bernie.

"How's business?" I asked.

"Business is business," said Bernie, sticking his fingers into his drink to retrieve the olive. "As long as there's fish, people will try to catch 'em. So, okay, here's to Jonathon. He was a good guy. He used to say a poem about when he was gonna be dead. It went, um ...

> When I am dead, my dearest,
> Sing no sad songs for me.
> Plant thou no roses at my head,
> Or ..."

Big Bernie furrowed his brow.

"Or tulips at my knee."

" 'Nor shady cyprus tree,' twat-face," corrected Little Bernie. "Right," agreed Big Bernie, and then he proceeded. "Um ...

> Be the green grass above me,
> With showers and dewdrops wet.
> And ..."

His stomach finished it for him. " 'If thou wilt, remember. And if thou wilt, forget.' "

"I know the poem," I said. "I didn't realize it was such a big hit in barrooms."

"Jon-Jon used to talk about dying sometimes," said Big Bernie, "on account of ..." He fell abruptly silent, biting his lip. After a few seconds Bernie pointed at his stomach and whispered to me, "Little Bernie has cancer."

"I don't have cancer!" countered the belly. "*You* got it! How many times do I have to tell you?"

Big Bernie humored his stomach gently. "Whatever you say, Little Bernie." He winked at me through his sunglasses.

"That's why you're bald," I realized.

"I take the Little Bern to get his radiation treatments," said Bernie, taking off his four-dollar toupee to demonstrate his gleaming bald pate, "and what happens? All my hair falls out." Big Bernie giggled glumly. "It's not fair, but hey, who said anything was fair?"

"True," agreed his stomach.

"Let's get pissed," I suggested urgently.

"Now there," said Little Bernie, "is a novel idea."

Alchemistical Formulae

Hope, Ontario, 1889

Regarding the life of Hope, we don't know the following: that he brutally raped the fair & virginal Gretel Dekeyser; that she was but 15 years of age; that Hope was 65, untoothsome and gnarly.

Gretel Dekeyser stood on some rocks, her head tilted backward so that her face could be slapped by the sun. Gretel was naked. Joseph Benton Hope, standing across the water and angling for pickerel, studied her body with some slight interest. Gretel's body was teenaged; swelling breasts and hips hung on ribcages, elbows and slightly bowed legs. Joseph felt a tug on the end of his line, so he took his eyes off the young woman and fastened them to his rod-tip. The fish, apparently, was gone away; Joseph sighed and raised his eyes again to the rocks across the way. Gretel had turned around so that J. B. Hope could see her backside. Joseph loved the geometry of buttocks, he loved their fleshy simplicity. Gretel's other end was small, the cheeks hung rather low. Joseph wondered if his bait had been stolen. He raised his pole, flipped some line about the end, and saw his minnow wriggling. He sat it back in the water.

Now Gretel decided to go for a swim. She held her nose and jumped from the rock, her body twisted awkwardly and shattering the surface of the water. Gretel and Hope were separated by some fifty yards of lake, but Joseph was still irritated, sure that the little girl would put the fishes off their feed. Remarkably, Hope felt a nibble at the same moment, so he pulled skyward, setting the hook, and flipped a little fish onto the ground behind him.

He heard Gretel's voice, "Too schmull."

"You're too small," Hope croaked. Joseph took the hook out of the fish's mouth and looked at his catch. Joseph pretended he was judging its size, but secretly he was simply admiring the fish, the coolness of its skin, the mystery of the seemingly blind eyes. Hope returned the fish to the water.

Gretel climbed out of the lake and fluffed water out of her hair. Gretel's hair was a dull but healthy blond, the color of wheat. Joseph watched her breasts bounce. Gretel's nipples were extraordinarily small, and very dark given her fair Dutch coloring. Hope was reminded of something, but he knew not what.

Gretel lay down, on her stomach, her little rump presented to the sun for bronzing. Hope wandered over to his bait-bucket and grabbed a minnow. The fish writhed desperately, trapped by Hope's bent fingers. Joseph ran his hook through the minnow's back and then tossed it into the water. He looked down and saw Gretel roll over, her legs unfolding, revealing all. Gretel's genitalia were large and frightening. Hope concentrated on his fishing.

This was the first time Gretel had come so close, but she was invariably near the water when Hope went fishing. She never wore any clothes. When Hope saw Gretel he often recalled days from years ago, when the Perfectionists would go about naked. In those days, Hope recalled, they were indeed Perfect. He conjured mental images of Mary Carter De-La-Noy, Cairine Mc-Diarmid, Abigal Skinner and Polyphilia Drinkwater. Young and perfect. Now, Polyphilia was wasted and shriveled, ghostly rattling bones; Abigal was fat, her breasts hanging down almost to her waist. Mary De-la-Noy was still pretty, but in a hard, chiseled way; and Cairine was dead, mauled by a bear, and Joseph often wondered whether she was worse or better served by nature than the others. Hope looked at Gretel Dekeyser. She was touching her own breasts.

"The left," said J. B. Hope, even though he knew that Gretel, like the other Dutch, spoke only a few words of English and understood less, "is the site of the propagative spirit, while the right houses the amative soul." Joseph felt suddenly giddy. He stumbled a couple of feet, dropping his fishing pole, and sat down beside Gretel. The world was suddenly made up of old sea charts and alchemistical formulae. Joseph Hope laughed. "What could be simpler?"

"Hmm," Gretel purred, agreeing. Gretel took Hope's hand and pulled it on to her chest. Her nipple was erect, hard as a pebble. The sea charts disappeared, eaten away by emptiness.

"The amative soul," Hope continued, "is, in my opinion, almost universally undernutritioned."

Gretel moved Hope's hand to her other tit. Joseph remarked to himself that this breast was slightly smaller. Gretel took one of her own hands and placed it over her mound.

Hope wanted to tell her about phrenological sites, how they connected hematically with her intromittent organ. He opened his mouth and began to weep.

The tears alarmed Gretel, and she made a motion to sit up. Hope pushed her back roughly, and Gretel was still. Hope worked at his trouser stays, and soon his root was free, standing out of his heavy, black pants. Gretel touched her fingers to it, and Joseph brushed them away. Tears spilled from Hope's eyes onto the head of his penis.

Joseph Benton Hope turned Gretel Dekeyser over and pulled her up onto elbows and knees. Hope noticed that her little breasts, tugged earthward by gravity, long and thin like a bitch's, were off-putting. Hope drove himself into Gretel's boyish haunches and was done not many minutes later. Then he lay on his back and gazed into the sky, which was empty. It was empty of clouds and alchemistical formulae.

The Mysteries of Hope

Hope, Ontario, 1983
Wherein our Young Hero Finally Gets Down to It.

I managed to get very drunk. Note I say, "I managed" as if getting drunk was somehow irk- or ugglesome. It was, of course, rather facile. In two hours I toppled from my barstool in The Willing Mind, thereby setting up Little Bernie, who delivered this old zinger: "Well, at least he knows when he's had enough!"

I flipped about like a fish in the bottom of a canoe, and it may have been this piscatorial activity that gave me the following idea. "Hey! I think I'll go buy me a Hoper — a real Hoper, mind you, not one of the tourist variety — and then go fishing for — bum*bum*bum*bum* . . ."

"Ol' Mossback?" guessed Big Bernie.

"Right first pop out of the box! Ol' Mossback, he of the silvery eyes and tongue!"

Teddy, the dwarf bartender, was eyeing me with suspicion. "Aren't you a little drunk for fishing?"

"Hey!" I shrieked. "You sounded just like Elschpett!" When one is intoxicated, "Elspeth" is quite a mouthful. I contrived to climb to my feet. "Fare thee well!" I saluted them. I was for some reason under the impression that a war was being fought outside the door. My leave-taking was courageous and beautiful; it brought a lump to my throat. I charged, full tilt and wobbly, into the streets of Hope.

I allowed myself the following hallucination. (Some portion of my mind had gone into the Hallucination Production biz, and was constantly pitching one or another of the products to the rest of my sensibilities. We went for this one.) It was a hundred-odd years ago, and The Willing Mind was a Fourieristic phalanstery, and the road was dirt and rocks, and women floated about, naked and beautiful. Polyphilia Drinkwater drifted near, and I saw how foolish I'd been to think that she and Mona looked alike. Polly was more delicate and much fairer. Cairine McDiarmid marched by, her freckled breasts pumping like a red fire engine. Mary Carter De-la-Noy stood off to one side, and her bosom was pitching. It was awesome, Mary's bosom-pitching was. And finally I saw Abigal Skinner, a heavy, splay-footed woman who none the less possessed certain charms, not the least of which was a rear end that was a magnificent globe, a world of flesh.

I ran into one of the Elmer Fudd-hatted geezers that seemed to make up half of Hope's population. He shook a gnarled, liver-spotted fist, advising me, "Keep your mind on your business."

Sound and sage advice, I thought. I went to Edgar's Bait, Tackle and Taxidermy.

"Big Guy!" said Edgar, and then he trained his evil black eyes on me. "Big Guy," he said, "you been drinking."

Edgar, I recalled, was AA and therefore skilled at detecting drunkards. That, and the fact that I'd fallen on my face as soon as I entered his shop, trip-wired by invisible hobgoblins.

"I feel lucky, Edgar! Real lucky!" My nose, I noticed, was bleeding profusely. "So I am going to purchase one HOPER, and note that I do not want one of those whatever it was you fobbed off on Benson. Furthermore, Edgar, if that's really your name, I am willing to pay up to six dollars and eighty-three cents for the Real McCoy."

Edgar reached below the counter and produced a Hoper. A beauty.

"Wow!" I exclaimed, leaping to my feet.

"That is not *a* Hoper," said Edgar, gingerly touching the gleaming treble-hook. "This is *the* Hoper."

I took it into my hands. The Hoper was lovingly carved from fine wood. It was a yellow that put the sun to shame. This Hoper didn't remind me of either a finger or a penis; instead, it looked like something that a huge, monstrous fish would love to eat.

"Who made this?" I demanded in a whisper.

"Isaiah. While he was in prison."

"Isaiah? Why? He loved Ol' Mossback."

"He thought it might come in handy someday." Edgar stared at me intently. "I guess you could have it."

"Six dollars and eighty-three cents?" I offered, trying ineffectually to jam my fingers into my jeans pockets.

Edgar waved his huge hand in my face. "It's on the house," he said, and then he laughed. " 'Least, it's on the Fourieristic Phalanstery."

I turned to leave, but ended up spinning a complete 360 degree circle because a) I lost control and b) I had my responsibilities as Contactee. "By the way, Jonathon Whitecrow ..."

"Who?"

"Jonathon Whitecrow."

"Don't know the name, Big Guy."

"Come on! The old, gay Indian? 'Visions' and such like?"
Edgar moved his mountainous shoulders in bafflement.

"Anyway, he died."

"Friend of yours?"

"Yeppers," I nodded. "He was a very good friend of mine.
He was approximately 174 years old. The good die young." I
left Edgar's Bait, Tackle and Taxidermy.

I had another hallucination. George Quinton materialized in
front of me on the sidewalk. I walked squarely into him, squash-
ing my face against his lower stomach. George Quinton said,
"Sowwy!" and then vanished, leaving behind a huge hole in
the fabric of the universe.

"Am I ever gunned!" I bellowed at God.

In retrospect, I'm glad I did this. I sincerely believe that my
bellow attracted God's attention; He looked down from the
clouds just in time to see me jump on a little blue moped. "Oy,"
muttered God, and His mighty hand guided me safely home.

As soon as I got back to the homestead, I realized that I was
sobering up, or at least parts of me were — my great toes for
example. To catch Ol' Mossback it was necessary that I be as
drunk as possible (to lower my body temperature) so I raided
the liquor cabinet, discovering a bottle of tequila, my personal
favorite. And then I noticed that my poor heart had become
disattached from the cosmos, so I decided to listen to the
"Vocalise." I started the turntable running, bounced the needle
off the opening bars, and soon the night was magical.

"Ah, Louis," I said, as the naked monster materialized in the
picture window, "I've been expecting you." I opened the door
for him. He hid in the shadows of some trees, but his obscene
flesh glowed. "Come on in!" I shrieked. Louis had to cling to
one of the tree's lower branches so that he wouldn't topple
over. "Louis," I said patiently, "get on in here. It is of paramount
importance that you and I discuss the mysteries of Hope."

"Hope?" Louis gurgled. It sounded like an air bubble, one
that had escaped from the bowels of the earth. "Dat's me!"

"Hope," I repeated evenly. Then it occurred to me that God
hadn't heard, that all of the lesser deities had misunderstood.
"HOPE!" I screamed, silencing even the bullfrogs.

Louis let go of the branches, and his eight-foot body pitched forward. I got out of the way just in time. Louis Hope collapsed in front of me, a white mountain of quivering fat. I was reminded of my childhood; Crayola had forever failed to include a flesh-colored crayon, even in the huge 64-pack, leaving me with three alternatives; to color people an overhealthy brown, to make them a glaring yellow, or to leave them alone, as white as the paper they existed on. Looking at Louis, I thought that God had run out of flesh (and brown and yellow) crayons.

"First things first," I told Louis. "Food."

The monster began joyously to push himself up into a sitting position. I went to the kitchen and made a chicken sandwich, putting most of a boiled chicken between two slices of bread. How the chicken came to be there is another enigma; perhaps some altruistic bird, concerned for my welfare, plucked itself, leapt into some cooking pot and subsequently into the Frigidaire. Well, the fowl didn't die for naught; Louis Hope devoured her with much gusto.

Meanwhile, the "Vocalise" filled my homestead. As Louis ate, I talked over the music, fitting my words into the haunting holes opened by the melody. "My wife, Louis," I said, "that is, my wife Elspeth, Louis, is convinced that the Russians are going to blow us up. They have nuclear weaponry, Louis. We have nuclear weaponry. Everyone has fucking nuclear weaponry!! The four-year-old girl living down the road has a Cruise missile in her sandbox, Louis. But the thing of it is, is ..."

Louis crossed his eyes suddenly, indicating an interest in what the thing of it was, was.

"Listen to this music! This beautiful goddam music! This is the USSR State Orchestra, for fuck's sake! My old buddy Rachmaninoff is a Russian! How can we — you and me, Louis baby — how can we listen to this music and believe in our heart of hearts that the Russians would do that to us?" I had a drink of tequila, one that nailed me squarely between the eyes. "Ours is an unpopular position, Louis. But we've heard the music."

I climbed to my feet (I hadn't noticed, but somewhere along the line I'd fallen over) so that I could address a larger audience. "Take away the nuclear weaponry. The Russkies aren't gonna attack. They've got their own problems. Olga is fucking some

Slav on the side, Louis. Ivan is drinking too much. Everyone
has enough fucking problems of their own without worrying
about nuclear weaponry. So just fucking take it away. I trust
you agree."

Louis seemed to consider it. He stared at me and came to
some resolve. "Give it to Louis," he said slowly, awkward and
warped words.

"Give what?"

"Nookyer whapponwy."

"Nuclear weaponry?"

Louis Hope nodded. "Take it 'way." Louis gesticulated vaguely
in his own direction. "Louis is big. Louis knows how to hide."

"Good of you to offer, Louis. But it ain't that simple."

The monster was crestfallen. I thought I'd change the subject.

"All right, Watson," I said, "let's put on the old ratiocination
helmets and get down to brass tacks. Let us try to reconstruct
the night that J. B. Hope was murdered."

Lunar Muscle

Hope, Ontario, 1889
*Regarding the death of Hope we know the
following: that it was brutal.*

On the back of Karl Dekeyser's neck (which was thick, red and
wrinkled) was a mole, about the size of a nickel, from which
sprouted a tuft of wiry hair. Joseph Benton Hope was fasci-
nated by this excrescence. Hope thought to construct new
theory. Stupidity causes carbuncles. Joseph Hope laughed aloud,
the callow burst of used air alarming all of the men.

Karl Dekeyser turned around and said something in Dutch.
Hope nodded vaguely, getting the gist. Dekeyser pointed the
way then, even though everyone, including Hope, seemed to
know where they were going.

Hope recognized none of the men that served as his escort,
and found it hard to believe that so many strangers could have

intruded into his life. He'd considered telling them of Perfectionism, explaining how he'd simply filled Gretel's naked corporeal being with the Holy Spirit. But in his heart, or whatever
twisted organ now served in that capacity, Joseph knew it wasn't
so. He'd filled her with buckets of stuff, tiny wriggling minutiae
that swam hell-bent, driven by the extremely remote possibility that yet another petty human existence could be forged.
Hope didn't begrudge the men their anger, as little as he understood it.

Neither was Hope concerned for his own safety. If they chose
to kill him (Hope assumed it was some vengeance they sought,
and killing him would seem a logical one) he would simply ele-
vate on the Planes of Experience. He would become one of
Polyphilia's spiritual hooligans. Hope almost chuckled. He would
give an exhibition of Spirit Rapping, he would indeed; he would
destroy the entire town of Hope, Ontario.

They neared Look Out, too suddenly. It occurred to Joseph
that the lake itself was an accomplice and had moved to meet
them halfway. The moon was full that night, which meant
something. Hope had complicated theories about lunar cycles,
although at that moment he would have been hard pressed to
say what they were. The moon's being full simply meant something, good or ill it didn't matter, and with that Hope decided
that the moon's being full meant nothing.

Hope saw two men standing by the water's edge, and he felt
an emotion resembling surprise. One was the gaunt aboriginal,
Whitecrow. Whitecrow was smoking a cigarette and seemed
to be both impatient and at ease, like a man waiting for a train.
Beside Whitecrow (and this is what had almost startled Hope,
except that even base emotions were oddly mutated inside his
being) was Isaiah. Isaiah, lanky and gawkish, stood in the
moonlight, bathed in its light, drowning in that orb's maudlin
poetry.

"Hello, Father," said Isaiah, and there was something snide
in his voicing of the address.

"Isaiah," croaked Hope, merely acknowledging the fact that
the young man was present.

"These men," said Isaiah, "have a quarrel with you." Isaiah
laughed by sucking air through his too-long nose. Joseph wanted

to slap him.

"I take it that you do as well," said Hope. The writing of adolescent verse and silly stories had apparently not served its purpose.

Isaiah shrugged, his bony shoulders thrown up together but out of kilter. "I have just come to spectate."

"And you?" Joseph cocked an eyebrow at the Indian.

"You know me," said Jonathon Whitecrow, exhaling a thin stream of smoke. "I find this all very interesting."

"Oh, do you?" Hope half expected the dwarfish Theophilius Drinkwater to pop out from behind the trees, eager to unsettle whatever muck was about. But that man had died, at the extremely advanced age of 107, as if God had delayed as long as possible before admitting the little imp to the Holy Kingdom.

"Say you are sorry," said Karl Dekeyser, and Joseph Hope laughed his birdlike laugh.

"No," Hope said, for a variety of reasons, only one of them being the fact that he wasn't sorry at all. He watched Dekeyser's face. All of the Germanic features hardened, set by fury. Hope wondered at this. Surely it must be uncomfortable to feel anything so strongly.

In the middle of this rumination, Joseph Benton Hope noticed that his left ring finger had been neatly removed from its hand.

Joseph's reaction was outrage. Dekeyser was holding Hope's finger in the air, partly brandishing it as a prize, partly removing it in disgust. This was precisely the sort of apelike, antediluvian behavior that Hope had sought to remove from the face of the earth. "Say you are sorry," Dekeyser had said, to which Hope had answered, perhaps a tad hastily, "No."

Joseph had expected at least one more exchange; he wanted an opportunity to open his chest (an old sea chest), to haul out the Holy Books and charts, to *explain*. But no. Dekeyser, simple and simian, had taken a knife (Mr. Opdycke's knife, Joseph noticed, although the fact had little import) and hacked off the anulus from the propagative hand. This didn't hurt (blood pumped out at a sickening rate; Hope tore a piece of material from his shirttail and tied a tourniquet without thinking) but it enraged him. Hope called the men several terrible names, training his hawklike eye on the collective, and then he saw something that caused him to produce his queer laugh. Isaiah, white as the moon, had fainted, and was lying on the ground in a ragged heap. Joseph studied the man for a moment and then dismissed him.

"Well," said Hope, "that's that, is it? Unless you care for another finger, or perhaps a toe?"

Dekeyser was still marveling at the brutal sense he had caused the world to make. Hope's prattle disturbed him. Dekeyser had to do something dramatic, and he was inspired. "This is shit!" he said of the finger. Karl walked over to the lake and held the finger above the water. "Food for fish!" he said.

Some of the men, unable to look at Hope's disembodied finger, turned their eyes to the water's edge. The moon was reflected there; some of the more observant of the men noted that two moons were reflected there, round and full and side by side. And then these twin moons pushed out of the lake.

The Fish rose up almost slowly, dancing on deliberate motions of the fluke, to a height of five feet, five feet of silver, lunar muscle. Karl Dekeyser dropped the finger, and it almost floated into the fish's mouth, a mouth all needle and bone. Then, in a rapturous state, the Fish acrobatically presented his tail to the stars, spraying the night, and went back into Lake Look Out.

Isaiah had come around just in time to witness this; he promptly fainted again.

Karl Dekeyser's world ceased to make sense.

The Indian, unflappable, lit another cigarette.

Joseph Benton Hope, after a long, stunned moment, let loose with a terrible howl of anguish, and then he turned and ran away from the men. He ran, his elderly elbows and knees flapping awkwardly, toward the home of George and Martha.

At Lake Look Out, Jonathon Whitecrow took a handful of silver water and gingerly splashed it across Isaiah's brow. The young man woke up dreamily, aware only of the fact that his penis was inappropriately but enormously enlarged. "Where's my father?" he asked conversationally, merely curious.

"With your mother," answered Whitecrow.

Martha Quinton Hope had no truck with such niceties as suns and moons, day and night. If there was work to be done, Martha's thinking was do it, regardless of whether there was light enough. The world was a bully, but in many ways Martha was a bigger one. So she instructed George that it was time to slaughter some animals.

It was not, in fact, a time to slaughter animals. It was an idea she'd gotten from the moon. Martha didn't know why she'd been gazing at the moon like some foolish, apple-cheeked schoolgirl, but she had. She'd been struck with the realization that her woman's body was a horrible thing, designed by God to do horrible things, to bleed and to swell as if with disease. Of course, that was all behind Martha now, a thought that brought a tear to her eye. The tear, though, knew better than to try to sneak out through the dust-dry duct; it retreated sheepishly. Martha was suddenly filled with rage, which she covered by bellowing out a whimsical "La-dee-dah." Once she'd sighed "La-dee-dah" in the chicken coop, and one of the hens had keeled over, stone dead.

"Time to slaughter animals, George!"

They climbed into their workclothes. They did this in each other's company, both indifferent to the gross and muscular nudity. George wondered what they were going to kill. They owned a cow, and George hoped it wouldn't be this old bossy, whom George secretly named "Emily."

"Pigs," said Martha.

This happened all the time, the answering of unspoken questions. It had long ago ceased to alarm George. "Pigs," he agreed. Pigs were ham, George reminded himself. Even Martha could cook ham.

Both wore cotton workshirts and dungarees. The shirts, big even on the monstrous twins, obscured both George's massive chest and Martha's rocky bubs. Martha, looking at George, felt as if she were looking into a mirror.

George looked at Martha and felt no such thing. George was always amazed at how dissimilar they were. Martha knew things. She knew, for instance, why they had removed them-selves from the Fourieristic Phalanstery. This was the great puzzle in George's existence. Some years ago (around the time of the first experiments in stirpiculture) Martha had instructed George to make them a house. George had done so, and he'd finished building the thing (and laid the foundations for a barn) before he'd stopped and wondered why. George was happy with the others, in the town; why should he and his sister isolate themselves? George had asked Martha; she'd punched him in the stomach, a hard blow but ineffectual against his muscle. Then, alarmingly, Martha had almost cried. Her eyes became full of water; Martha screwed them shut, blinked a few times, and then seemed better.

Martha was remembering the same moment. It was the first time that she'd allowed the anger to consume her. The anger tickled her belly and throat, it slapped her in the face until she was dizzy.

Martha had talked, George remembered; at least, she'd babbled, words galloping out of her mouth. The words confused and enraged Quinton, so he disregarded them and continued constructing the barn. George never asked again.

The twins walked out to the barn and picked up their axes. These had been presents from Jonathon Whitecrow, fine tools with sturdy handles and blades that seldom needed honing. George admired his briefly as he held it in his hands; George admired simple and beautiful things.

Martha sliced the air with hers, warming up her muscles, loosening her joints.

"Go to the pen," instructed Martha, "and get a pig. Get a nice fat one. Get the old sow!" The old sow was a grotesque creature that George called "Grace." Pigs are ham, he reminded himself. George went around to the back of the barn where the pigs were kept. The old sow was asleep. George stepped into the pen, treading lightly to avoid stepping on the piglets (he did tread on a couple; they produced horrible shrieking noises, but Grace snoozed on) and crossed over to the sow. George tapped her on the back. "Time to get up, Gwace," he whispered. "You aw *ham!*"

The sow woke up, alarmed and panicking. George gingerly gathered the creature into his arms. "Even Martha can cook ham." The pigpen was cacophonous now; animals seem to sense when one of their number is destined for the butcher's block. George never heard the commotion from the other side of the barn.

Martha watched the figure stumble down and laughed a series of odd laughs, mostly a kind of harumph that she employed when amused by the brutality of the earth. She crossed her arms and looked like a schoolmarm about to deliver a stinger to a truant's ear. "Well, well, well," she said aloud. "La-dee-dah."

Hope looked up from the ground. He held out his hand, crudely tourniqueted. "Look," he said.

"Who's done that?"

"Dekeyser."

Martha nodded, chewing on her bottom lip. "It's not all that serious," she told Joseph. "Do you know, once we found a man in the harbor with gangrene in his leg. I chopped it off."

Joseph Hope wasn't sure what Martha was talking about, and then he remembered the Harbor Light Mission, the room full of unfortunates.

"I took a poker from the fire and cleaned the wound," Martha reminisced. She shrugged. "Get up and go into the house. George can look after you."

"Help me," said Joseph.

Martha harumphed, bull-like. "I helped you once before. I pulled you out of the water and made you live. I don't think I'll help you again."

"Get George, then."

"George will be back soon enough. Just keep quiet."

"I am your husband," stated Joseph Benton Hope.

Martha picked up her axe. "Joseph," she said, taking a step toward him, "you are an arsehole."

When George returned, and saw what had happened, he dropped the pig. The sow fled into the night. George saw men coming, still distant. He took the axe out of Martha's hands and said, "Go to yoh womb. Take off those clothes."

"What are you going to do?" asked Martha.

George merely repeated, "Go to yoh womb. Take off those clothes."

Martha ran for the homestead.

George took his own axe and wearily let it fall two or three times, for it was imperative that his own clothes become as bloodsoaked as his twin's.

George had died inside, and no tears came.

Blood & Semen

Hope, Ontario, 1983
Wherein our Hero is Enlightened and,
enjoying the Novelty of the Sensation, sets off
in search of Further Enlightenment.

I ran up to my room (Martha's room; George had slept in the other) and returned with the workshirt from the antique wooden chest. I laid it out in front of Louis Hope and indicated all of the rust-brown patches. "Exhibit One, Your Honor," I said to Louis. Louis picked up the garment and perused it in a sage and judicious manner. Then, inexplicably, Louis placed the shirt on his head, trying to fashion it into some kind of turban. I grabbed it away.

"What say you, Watson?" I demanded. "Have I not solved the mystery?" Deep down, I knew that I hadn't. It seemed certain enough that George had not killed J. B. Hope, his twin sister had; the question remained, though, why? Hope had condoned, even coerced, the Quinton siblings' incest, but in the final analysis could not be held responsible—the twins had to climb into bed together of their own volition (finally to produce the doomed Isaiah) and Joseph Benton Hope held no puppet strings on their human bodies — blood and semen cannot be mixed at a distance.

I needed outside help on this case. "Watson," I addressed Louis Hope, "it is time to go fishing!"

I gathered together my gear (which included not only my rod and reel but the entire contents of Benson's liquor cabinet, twelve or so bottles with a gulp left at the bottom) and then stopped, drunkenly wondering how both myself and a 700-pound monster could balance on the little blue moped.

Louis had the solution. He laboriously raised himself to his feet, teetering and tottering almost as much as I was, and then he scooped me up into his arms. Getting through the front door was a bit iffy, but once outside Louis could pick up some speed, and the speed lent him some equilibration, and Louis ran, holding me, all the way to Lookout Lake.

He Seemed to Be Missing a Piece

Kingston, Ontario, 1889
*Regarding the life of Hope, we know the
following: that this scholar is sick and tired of
it. I am going for a drink. Many thanks and
Fare Thee Well.*

George Quinton refused to speak in his own defence at the trial, so that task was taken up by the Reverend Doctor Ian John Robert McDougall, Barrister and Solicitor. He presented the case that Hope, the worst libertine since the Marquis de Sade, had it coming in spades. Several of the Perfectionists took the stand, De-la-Noy and Skinner and even Mr. Opdycke, all of them saying that George was a good-hearted man and must have had overwhelming provocation; they mourned their dead leader, they said, but George was their friend. Finally it came out at the trial what Dekeyser had done at Lake Look Out (the Coroner had pieced together Joseph Hope like a jigsaw puzzle, and mentioned in his testimony that he seemed to be missing a piece) and the general belief was born that George Quinton had dispatched Hope in order to end his suffering. Still, most people survive the loss of a finger, and hacking a man to death because he suffered this injury seemed imprudent. Besides, Canada was a young country, and had only sent a handful of men to the gallows. George Quinton was sentenced to death.

The Hangman did not calculate George's body weight well, and on the first dropping the noose snapped. George Quinton fell onto this butt and then looked around sheepishly. "Sowwy," said George Quinton.

Naked in Mutual of Omaha's Wild Kingdom

Hope, Ontario 1983
Wherein our Hero battles Mighty Mossback, a Tale of much Interest and Excitement!

Sometimes life, and the living of it, gets a hold of you, bounces you up and down — and ain't that fun? That's what happened when Louis Hope and I arrived at Lookout. My insides turned queasy, and a smile stumbled across my face. I did imitations of animals; coyotes, owls and fish — yes, I did an imitation of a fish — and the only way I could settle myself down was to pretend I was the host of a television program, sort of a cross between "The Red Fisher Show" and "Mutual of Omaha's Wild Kingdom." I whistled the theme song (Rachmaninoff's "Vocalise") while I assembled my gear. Louis wandered down to the water's edge and paddled around. Louis pulled out a crayfish and lifted it up to his good eye. After a moment's examination, Louis Hope popped it into his mouth.

I stripped, explaining why to the cosmic television audience, telling of Ol' Mossback's hypersensitivity. "I know that Red Fisher doesn't usually get naked when he fishes," I admitted, "but Red's not usually fucked up, over and sideways, either."

Louis turned his attention to the rocks along the shoreline, pulling them up and playing with all the creepy crawlers and hoppity toads.

I showed the viewers my Hoper. "If anyone knows how to catch Mossback, it's Isaiah Hope, because he and Mossback were good buddies." I tied the lure using the improved double clinch knot, taught to me by my friend Edgar the axe-murderer.

There was mist dancing on top of the water, and here and there the mist formed into columns that rose to a height of twenty feet and shimmered. I understood why some tribes once thought these formations to be gods and spirits. They would have been fools if they hadn't thought that.

The moon was still up, sharing the morning with the sun. The moon was big and silver and gorgeous.

Just before the actual fishing portion of the show got under way, I had a solemn duty to perform. "Friends," I told them out there, "Jonathon Whitecrow has passed away. He didn't beat the odds." I shrugged in imitation of Whitecrow, as if to say, "That's okay, God. You keep throwing shit and we'll keep picking through for the good bits."

Then I stood up, raised my rod, and cast. I've only done one thing in my life with grace, and that was it. I'm sorry everyone had to miss it. Even little Louis Hope was turned away, busily ingesting the wild kingdom.

The magnificence of the scene smacked me on top of the head and punched me in the belly. "God, this is beautiful!" I told the viewers. "My sweet Jesus, it is beautiful." My cast was subtle but purposeful, like a fish. The reel hummed as the Hoper flew. "Friends, there's a phrase, a Latin phrase, *nil admirari.*" The Hoper hit gently. I let it sink. "It means not finding anything wonderful or beautiful. I guess it's some kind of disease." I began the retrieval, not a smooth one, rather a jerky, spasmodic tugging that was therefore more imitative of life. "I just wish some of you could join Louis and me, naked in Mutual of Omaha's Wild Kingdom. It is very wonderful. It is very beautiful."

My retrieval stopped abruptly. "Say now, friends, I seem to have tied into a rock or fallen tree or something. It happens to the best of us. Ugh! Son of a gun, it's not going anywhere. Come on, now. I can't get stuck, I've got serious fishing to do. Oh-oh."

Slowly, almost imperceptibly, line started stripping off my reel. "That tree or rock looks like it's rolling or something . . ." There was a short but violent burst, and for a split second the air was full of noise. Then silence again, a moment of it, during which I said to my viewers, "Tell you what, friends. I don't think this is a rock or a tree. I think . . ."

The line exploded off the reel, and I was pulled toward the water. I managed to get both hands on to my rod, and I was hanging on for dear life. The line screamed away at a dizzying clip. I went to adjust the drag. Another short burst of irrefutable energy hauled me even closer to the lake. I caught my heels on the rocks and pulled backward, the tension so strong that I was soon leaning almost perpendicularly with my back to the earth.

I had to thumb the line. I placed my pudgy digit on to the whirling reel, slowly applying pressure. My thumb immediately became burned and blistered, but I had no real choice in the matter. And then a force pulled me upright, and then further, and I realized that in a second I was going to be pulled into Lookout Lake. There was a sensation of weightlessness, and I prepared for the ice-cold slap of the water.

It never happened. I remained suspended in the air. Louis Hope had caught me. He had his huge baby-fatted arms wrapped around my waist.

"Attago, Louis!" I bellowed. "You hang on to me while I play this sucker!" I could feel Louis brace, solidifying like a mountain.

My thumb was carved to ratshit, bleeding profusely, but I had managed to slow the creature's progress. I had almost run out of line, and I judged that the fish had almost run out of lake.

Then, abruptly, my line went slack. "FUCK!" I hollered, assuming that he'd broken free. But some strange power still smouldered in my gear — I tried to feel the energy of the lake. "Yikes." I realized. "That motherfucker's coming back at us!" I cranked at my reel for all I was worth, my wrist aching and sore. Just as I got the line taut, the fish broke the surface of the water, rising into the air and writhing like a demon in death, trying to throw the hook. I eased up on the rod, still holding tight to all of the fury, and finally the fish dropped back into Lookout.

And it was Ol' Mossback.

"Round One to me," I whispered, all of my body gloriously atremble, "but that baby's got a few more tricks up his sleeve."

Slowly and methodically Mossback started stripping line from the reel. I looked in the direction it was headed, wondering what the Fish had in mind, and finally I detected the distant dark shape under the surface of the water. "He's taking us into a log," I said aloud. I couldn't stop him. Both my drag and my bloody thumb would prove ineffectual against Mossback's singleminded determination. Louis's breathing, high above me, was loud and rapid. "Louis!" I screamed. "Run!"

Louis took a couple of awkward steps forward.

"No! That way! Away! Away from the log! Away from the fish!"

Louis stopped himself, wobbly, and then started off in the direction I'd steered him. His first few strides were splay-footed and clumsy, but soon he had some speed up. Louis ran, unmindful of the rocks and shrubberies, and after some moments I felt the tension ease up in my gear. "It's working!" I told Louis. "Keep going!"

Louis was actually running with something resembling agility, his fat toes pushing lightly off the earth. "Come on, Louis baby ..." I whispered, and I began to pump. "Pull up, reel down," I reminded myself. The first pull upward was excruciatingly painful, my arms seizing up with lactic acid and spasms. I refused to let myself realize that this action, which brought as much physical hurt as anything I'd ever done before, would have to be repeated countless times if I wanted to land Ol' Mossback. I pulled up again, my arm muscles screaming. There was momentary relief in the reeling down, but then it was up again, a pull that brought a muffled scream into my throat. In some moments I was completely exhausted, my energy depleted, but I fired the nerves and synapses and contracted the muscles. I pulled up, I reeled down, as Louis Hope carried me across the world.

Louis's breathing was huffy and puffy, my body longed for death, but Ol' Mossback was slowing. Something was going to give out eventually.

Toward the end, I remember watching Ol' Mossback as he allowed himself to be pulled to the surface (the moment's respite would grant him strength enough for another flight toward liberty). His eyes were huge and silver, and had nothing to do with humanness.

I can't give any accurate record of how long we battled—at any rate, it was long enough for the moon to disappear and the sun to take full and radiant reign of the world, long enough for Louis to make two complete circuits of the lake.

And then Louis could take no more, and he slowed, and began to teeter, and stumbled, and then Louis Hope collapsed gently to the ground.

And I pulled once more, a final, desperate pull as my body gave up the ghost.

When I came to—or did I come to?—Ol' Mossback was lying

beside me, exhausted, breathing as hard as I was.

Ol' Mossback said, "Fuck. I can't believe it."

I lay on my back and looked at the sky. I was too tired for conversation, but I asked, more out of politeness than anything else, "Can't believe what?"

"I can't believe I really went for that silly-looking thing — which, incidentally, is still stuck in my mouth, do you mind?"

I rolled over and looked at Mossback's maw. "Nicely lip-hooked," I said. The Hoper dangled down, seeming to gleam brighter for victory.

" 'Nicely lip-hooked,' " mimicked Mossback.

I reached over — "No biting now" — and pulled out the lure. "The Hoper!"

"Dumb name," muttered Ol' Mossback.

"The *Hope*-er."

"So you said."

"Name doesn't ring a bell?"

"Oh! I get it."

"As in Joseph Benton Hope. It might interest you to know that right over there is a direct descendant, kind of." I gesticulated toward the slumbering naked giant.

"Who? Louis?"

"How the hell do you know Louis?"

"Everyone knows Louis," said Mossback. He flipped a bit, moving a few inches closer to the lake. "It's been a slice, pally. Now, if you don't mind, I can only breathe this air for so long." Mossback began to flip more quickly. I more-or-less tackled him, and we lay together on the rocks.

"Not so fast," I whispered. "I caught you."

"Ha. I let myself get caught, just for a change of pace."

"A likely story, fish-face. I caught you, fair and square."

"So? You can't eat me or anything. I'm chock-a-block full of mercury and other assorted industrial pollutants."

"I'm going to have Edgar stuff you."

"Oh, please. How undignified."

"Then I'm going to hang you up on my wall."

"You can't stuff me. I don't — " Mossback coughed, or the fishy equivalent. His gill-plates shook convulsively. "I don't want to turn mystical on you, but what would Jonathon Whitecrow say? His spirit is in the lake, etcetera, etcetera."

"I will not be dissuaded. Catching you is the best thing I've ever done."

"But ... but ... I don't deserve to die."

"So what? No one deserves to die. Did Joseph Benton Hope deserve to die?"

Mossback flipped for no good reason, like an epileptic. His breathing was becoming extremely labored. "Sure he did," Ol' Mossback gasped.

"Why? What was his big crime? I mean, all that fornicating and stuff doesn't really amount to diddley-squat, does it?"

"His crime was ..." Ol' Mossback stopped talking abruptly. His operculum began to fan at a dizzying clip, and for an instant the fish's body went stiff as wood. "His crime was indifference," Mossback managed to say. "It's the only real crime there is. Hope did not give a ..."

"Hope did not give a what?"

"Fuck." Mossback's eyes went empty. He no longer seemed like a mythical, silver-tongued fish. He seemed like a cumbersome beast, hardened with pain, robbed of the water that was his subsistence.

Louis Hope woke up at that moment and crawled over to us. He gazed sadly at the monster.

"I done it, Louis-baby," I said proudly. "I caught Ol' Mossback."

Louis reached forward an enormous index finger and prodded the fish. The silver body jerked briefly.

"That's the best thing I've ever done," I told Louis.

Louis prodded Ol' Mossback again, with no effect. The air smelled of death. Louis Hope cocked his head and stared at me.

"You're quite right," I said. "It's the *second* best thing I've ever done."

I got on to my knees and slid my arms under Mossback. Somehow I managed to climb to my feet, the creature's enormous weight straining at my exhausted muscles. Mossback's tailfin quivered almost imperceptibly. "Gangway." Louis Hope obediently stepped out of my way, and I rushed into Lookout Lake. The water was enormously cold, the bottom slippy and coated with green slime. "Wake up, Mossback!" I screamed. I twisted my trunk sideways and then swung around, moving the huge fish in a semicircle, hoping to force water through the gills. Mossback remained inert. "Come on, Big Guy," I said to him. I made another pass. "Please." I lifted my eyes heavenward and said a simpler, more heartfelt, "Please." Holding Mossback out and away from my body, I ran ten or twelve feet forward. The bottom fell away. There was a frantic moment as I sought to regain my footing, and then I ran back the other way. Ol' Mossback was seeming to weigh more and more, and I wasn't sure how much longer I could carry him.

On the shoreline Louis Hope was excitedly turning himself around in lopsided circles. Louis was always doing that, spinning circles, so I paid scant attention. Then it occurred to me that there was a unique sense of urgency, and I stopped briefly to watch.

"Do!" Louis bellowed at me.

"Aha! Gotcha, Louis-baby!" I held Mossback and began turning circles. I could feel the water flow around us. I turned faster, so fast that I was soon dizzy. "Mossback," I said aloud, "you'd better revive pretty soon, because I'm going to ..."

Ol' Mossback came alive in a glorious instant. He slapped the water with his tailfin, noble and insolent. Ol' Mossback disappeared.

"... pass out," I said, and I did.

From *O, But the Days Were Sweet*

by Cairine McDiarmid.

On a day hot as tea we elected to go through the hills to the lake. All of us went, and we had no need of clothing there, and we went into the water, all of us young men and women, naked as we were made. As a child I'd lived by the sea, and it was a terrible one, full of whitecaps and waves, forever swallowing men and ships, throwing death upon the shore. The world was a cruel thing then. But in our lake there was Grace, and we drank of it, and covered ourselves in it, and splashed each others' bodies with it. And soon the night fell, though we'd had no notion of its coming, and even the night was gentle. The night was splashed with stars, the sky more light than blackness. We lay on the grass and touched hands. I knew then that it was right, that the world was not cruel. We rolled into each others' arms and I heard Our Lord whisper, "Yes."

Epilogue
The Dogstar Baby With My Toes

Hope, Ontario, 1984
*Wherein our Hero and Biographer Ties up a
Loose End.*

This child has my toes. There are no other resemblances to me (mind you, the child doesn't resemble the mother either, except for the manner in which it squidges together all of its facial features and looks supremely pissed off at Creation; for that matter, the child doesn't really resemble a member of the human species, and I often suspect my wife of infidelity with an inhabitant of the Dogstar Sirius), but it has my toes. Poor thing. Friends have pointed out that my feet set a new standard of pediatric ugliness, the main factor being my toes. God apparently ran out of complete sets when he was making me, and had to make do with ten leftover odds and ends, even though some were designed for dwarves, others for giants. One would think my feet would therefore be unique in the universe, but this here child has an identical pair.

Presently, and momentarily, the child is asleep, entrusted to my care. I am at the homestead. In the fridge are two bottles of expressed milk, and in the child's diaper is a lot of green shit. While the child slumbers, I thought I'd just finish this book, *The Life of Hope*. But first, I have to make sure that the Dogstar baby with my toes is still breathing.

All is well and good.

Today, by the way, is my thirty-first birthday. This evening we're having a small party — the Bernies, Edgar the axe-murderer (only now I know him as Eddie Dekeyser, mayor of Hope) and Edgar's wife, Myrt, who does indeed say that things are "a little dear." She also says that food is "scrumpdeli-itious" and a host of other cutisms, but when you ask for Myrt's support on an issue, if it is forthcoming at all (she can be very contrary) it usually comes forth as "Fuckin' A." I've had a word with her about watching the language when around the child.

I won't get drunk on my birthday. I haven't had a drink since Louis Hope fished me out of Lookout. I was delirious and babbling incoherently, or so they tell me. Edgar introduced me to his fellowship, AA, and whenever I feel the urge to become intoxicated I turn to him for guidance. Edgar usually raises a huge fist and gestures menacingly. Whatever works, I say.

The child is squirming now, emitting a strange series of beeps, which I think are a transmission back to the dogstar. I'm going to plug in the pacifier. This is not perfect parenting, I know, (and if any of you tell on me, you're dogfood) but this book needs finishing.

In rereading these pages I was bothered by a little loose end — no doubt you the reader will be bothered by any number of them, but this is the only one that got to me. Jonathon White-crow, while on his death-bed, quoted something to me. It sounded familiar then, and now I know why — it was used by poor, doomed Isaiah Hope to stand at the head of his novel *The Fish*. The passage states:

> Whether we live by the seaside, or by the lakes and rivers, or on the prairie, it concerns us to attend to the nature of fishes, since they are not phenomena confined to certain localities only, but forms and phases of the life in nature universally dispersed.

When asked to whom this statement was attributed, Jonathon answered, "Just some asshole." Now, it would be easy to simply dismiss this as flippancy on Whitecrow's part (it would be just like him to be flippant on his death-bed), but having given it some thought, I've decided that Jonathon meant for me to realize that the author was just that, an *asshole*. Was, indeed, by way of being the high muck-a-muck asshole, for sure the state and/or regional champion. And that region was, coincidentally, synchronistically, Joe Hope's old stomping grounds, Massachusetts, home of the dark Merrimack.

Let me tell you about this asshole, and let it stand as my tribute to Jonathon Whitecrow.

Like most assholes, this one was funny-looking. His nose was long and bulbous, his eyes darkly hooded, so that he resembled a doleful bloodhound. He was a little asshole, and he dressed funny. He dressed like a mortician, except that he was such a consummate asshole that he could never keep buttons, collar-stays, etc., organized, and his clothes were always too large, so that the effect was far more clownish than somber. Like a lot of assholes, this one had a name that was hard to say — most people tried to render it with a French pronunciation, others anglicized it, but few did it correctly.

This asshole behaved weirdly, naturally, and was much interested in things like literature, poetry and philosophy. He hung around with an older, faggy writer named Ralph, which didn't enhance his standing in the community. But above and beyond all this superficiality, what branded him forever a champion asshole was this particular stunt: he burned down a forest.

The forest-burning was, of course, purely accidental. He and a friend had been practising the Art of the Angle and caught some fish, and they decided to cook them right then and there, so they built a fire, roasted their shorelunch, had their fill and then wandered away without properly extinguishing the flames. It could have happened to anybody. No one was killed in the fire, but one has to understand how dependent the townspeople would have been on the forest; it provided shelter, fuel and the raw material for everything else. Their's was a wood-oriented society, that's for sure, so you can see why burning down one entire forest was viewed as monumental, supreme assholishness. As he walked through the streets of Concord I'm sure he was pointed at continually, and the whisper would be everywhere in the air — "There's the asshole who burned down the forest."

Our asshole was sorry but unrepentant, and his subsequent

behavior showed no evidence of improvement. Not long afterward he moved away from the town and lived beside a pond for two years. Had he been anyone else, people might have granted him a kind of aesthetic nobility and applauded this action, but what with him being an asshole people just shrugged and thought that it was a dumb thing to do. And all the time he was there, he wrote and wrote and wrote, and the book was published years later and a few people read it and liked it, and the asshole died at a fairly young age, forty-five, and there you have it.

I guess it's fairly obvious that I've employed a Sunday school story-telling technique, as in, "He was an itinerant preacher, dressed in cheap rags and dusty from his journey" so I'll just out and tell you that the asshole was Henry David Thoreau (who, when last spotted between these covers, had the misfortune to be stuck on a train with the Reverend Doctor Ian John Robert McDougall, Barrister and Solicitor). If this seems somehow an anticlimax (if you said, "Oh, *him*," or worse, "Who?") then let me indulge in a small bit of didacticism. Thoreau (accented on the first syllable) wrote an essay *On Civil Disobedience*, which influenced Gandhi, who in turn influenced Martin Luther King, etc., etc., and if in your opinion these guys did nothing, so be it, but me, I say that thanks to such men we at least have a fighting chance, and H. D. Thoreau started the whole ball rolling.

And he was an asshole.

So, and I believe that this is what Jonathon Whitecrow was getting at, never be cowed by your own assholishness. Never think, hell, I'm just an asshole, what does it matter? I'm going to tell the wife this, because she often feels small and insignificant and, logically, she has every reason to. I'm going to tell her, be proud, we're assholes! We have a long and illustrious history. Our child shall be raised as an Asshole, and the heritage shall not die!

Furthermore, I suspect that St. Matthew edited and expurgated the Beatitudes. That is, Christ probably said, "Blessed are the Assholes, for they shall inherit the earth."

The child is awake.

Hope, Ontario, 1984